A Song for Kitty

ANGELA CAIRNS

Interior typesetting by Platform House Publishing
www.platformhousepublishing.com

Cover Design by Brittany Wilson | Brittwilsonart.com

To my beautiful and talented grandmother –
Gladys Perkins (nee Hallett)
1896 - 2002

A songbird, gifted with perfect pitch and the ability
to play for hours without music.

"Books are a uniquely
portable magic."

Stephen King

Happy reading!.

Angela Cairns

ACKNOWLEDGEMENTS

To my Friday Friends from the Writers Company at Wivenhoe — thank you for beta reading.
www.thewriterscompany.co.uk

To Soulla Christoloudou my kind-but-firm editor — thank you for your constant support.
www.soulla-author.com

To Becky Wright at Platform House Publishing for her stunning interior artwork, and formatting — I would be lost without you.
www.platformhousepublishing.co.uk

To Kay Kipling at Fullproof Editing for copy editing — thank you for being patient with my speech punctuation.
www.fullproofediting.co

To Ian Hooper at Leschenault Press — for his vision for independent authors.
www.leschenaultpress.com

To my social media writing family, it would be hard to find a more supportive group anywhere. There are more, but this is my reading team — Do check out their amazing books and recommendations.
@juliablakeauthor, @julieembletonauthor,
@lilus_library, @beckywrightauthor,
@helenstarbuck_author, @ianhornett.

Chapter 1

L ily shrugged against the cold wind whipping in from the sea and pulled her woollen shawl more tightly about her neck. She steadied her hat with one hand and dug the hatpin deeper into her long brown hair with the other. Swept up for the first time in a chignon, her new hairstyle felt precarious in the wind, the hat even more so. Lily hoped the rain would hold off until she reached the workroom.

Under the coat, her lightly starched skirt rustled as she walked, and her leather boots clicked on the pavement. She hurried down Eastfield Road; she couldn't afford to be late. Mrs Winchett, who owned the workroom and the small modiste's shop, 'Gowns by Anastasia' on Commercial Road, was a stickler for punctuality and would dock wages for as little as five minutes.

Now seventeen, her big moment had come. After spending the last three years of her dressmaking apprenticeship running errands, today was her first day at the table. Although she would start by sewing on endless buttons, she was eager to begin.

A year older than Lily, Grace Kirby was already sewing and setting sleeves and had recently moved to bodices and earned eight shillings. Currently paid five shillings, Lily only dreamt of what she would do with the extra money.

Now she was at the table, Lily could use some of her wages to buy materials from Mrs Winchett at cost and begin to design clothes. Passionate about fabrics, Lily ran soft silks and fine wools through her hands, imagining the draped material falling into garments.

As she stepped along the road, she felt the weight of her new skirt and wool coat against her legs. She had designed both to last and be practical, but Lily dreamed of the swish and sway of more refined fabrics.

Music was her second love. She could buy more sheet music from Aiden Donnelly, her neighbour, with her extra wages as well.

Portsmouth was fine in its way. Lily loved the long promenade and the sea, even when, like today, the breeze was trying to snatch her hat. Since childhood, Lily had watched boats in the Solent and visited the amusements on the two piers, but she longed to see London. Lily didn't know what a visit to the metropolis could accomplish but felt sure if she could get there, something would change her life. She could work in theatre costume design or for one of the exclusive dressmakers.

One day, she would make evening gowns, dripping with lace bows and tightly ruffled flounces like the one in the photo of Camille Clifford Aiden had given her. Ladies would parade around the showroom of her modish establishment in her designs.

Lost in her daydream, Lily ignored the tiny, terraced brick houses she passed each morning. Each boasted a tiled apron frontage, setting the doors one step up from the road and a small back garden.

Many of them housed the Royal Marine families from the new Eastney Barracks. She passed several tall, broad-shouldered men in their uniforms. They disappeared on commissions for months on end. With a dismissive sniff, Lily's mother said, "They may look glamorous, but it's no life for their families. Don't you get tangled up with a soldier."

Her parents, Maggie, and Edward Matthews, with the help of her grandfather, had bought one of the new two-up, two-down houses. The long terraces and grid patterned streets marked the city's expansion into green fields.

Maggie and Edward paid a guinea a week back to Grandpa, and Lily knew her parent's dream was to own their house outright. Lily had no desire for such stability. Stability was a commodity she was too familiar with to value, and she felt their dreams lacked imagination.

A shout from behind broke into Lily's thoughts. She turned to see Aiden running to catch up with her. Slender as a reed with pale skin, dark hair, and deep blue eyes, he was two years older and had been her friend and confidant forever. Neither had siblings, and he had been the brother she never had. They had hung over their back garden wall and chatted since they were tall enough to balance on crates.

Aiden was shy, and the lads at school had teased him for being musical, not sporty. However, music had served him well. Aiden was working his way up at Conrad and Sons, a piano and musical warehouse, and now played for customers in the showroom to help them select their music.

If Mr Conrad was in a good mood, he gave Aiden spare copies of sheet music, and he and Lily learnt some of the popular stage songs together. Like Lily, he travelled daily to Commercial Road in the city centre. She suspected he discreetly watched for her so they could travel together.

"Wait for me, Lily." He was slightly out of breath when he reached her, his blue eyes twinkling under his smartly combed-back hair. "You look fine as fivepence," he said, giving a low whistle.

She pulled back one corner of her coat to show him the plain navy skirt beneath. It had three small kick pleats on one side, held in place by a buttoned tab. She had seen a picture of one like it in the showroom and had worked hard to copy the design.

"I've got you something to celebrate." He pulled a twist of white paper from his dark suit pocket. "Aniseed balls."

Since starting work, Aiden had saved her a few sweets from his visits to Gilbert's, the sweet shop on Milton Market. From amongst the tall jars full of rainbow-coloured boilings, he knew aniseed balls and pear drops were her favourites.

Lily accepted the packet, then frowned. "That worn cuff needs turning, Aiden."

He blushed and pulled his jacket sleeve down. "Ma hasn't had time; she's been teaching more. Pa, well, there was no work last week."

Seeing Aiden's embarrassment, Lily said, "Give it to me over the wall tonight, and I'll do it for you." She pushed an aniseed ball into her cheek and continued, "I bet I can make this last all the way to work."

Aiden's embarrassed flush subsided with the change of topic, and he matched Lily's brisk pace to the tram stop.

They paid their halfpennies, and Lily tucked her ticket into her glove.

Their tram moved at an alarming speed and swayed when it clacked over joints in the rails. The tram coming the other way showered sparks from the overhead wires as the connector rubbed along the network of cables. The bell scattered pedestrians and horses as the carriage swept through the roads. Lily liked to sit on the upper floor, peer into the passing houses, or spot unusual people in the street.

"You look different with your hair up, Lily, more grown-up."

"Still the same old Lily."

"Do you think now you're seventeen, your pa would let us go to the pier to a tea dance or to hear one of the orchestras play?"

She looked doubtful. "Pa might. You know what he's like, though. But I'd like to go."

"I'd like to take you, so I'll ask him."

She took a satisfied suck on her sweet and changed it to the other side, showing the tip to Aiden as she swapped it. "I can't feel my cheek with the aniseed, but I still have it."

He grinned. "Be careful you don't drop that sweet on your new skirt."

As the houses changed to the taller commercial buildings of the city, they made their way down the steep stairs of the tram, ready to get off. Aiden swung off the back platform around the pole and handed Lily down at their destination. "Good luck today."

Lily gave him an excited, slightly nervous smile. "See you tonight."

Aiden turned right, Lily turned left, and the crowd quickly swallowed them. Workers milled like ants as they headed for shops, offices, and banks in the city's centre. Lily thought *something is always happening here.* She deftly sidestepped a pile of horse dung in the road, then watched its perpetrator trot smartly away, drawing the bank's strongbox behind it. London must be even more exciting.

The entrance to the workroom was at the side of the shop. Narrow, stone stairs with a metal handrail led down to the half-floor below the showroom. Lily took her calico pinafore from the hook and replaced it with her hat and coat. She smoothed the apron over her skirt and patted her hair to ensure the chignon was in place. Mrs Winchett liked her girls neat and tidy.

"Good morning, Miss Matthews."

Hearing her full name, Lily felt a momentary glow. Mrs Winchett had promoted her from plain 'Lily', now she had her place at the table. The feeling faded fast. Mrs Winchett's sharp eyes had taken in her new skirt. "You haven't set those pleats correctly," she tutted. "Trying to run before you can walk."

"Yes, Mrs Winchett." Lily dropped her gaze and took her place at the table beside Grace.

"Old cat," Grace whispered. Lily gave her a startled look. She had never dared say anything derogatory about her boss.

No one spoke as Mrs Winchett gave out the order of work for the day. Lily had hundreds of tiny pearl buttons to add to dresses and blouses. She was also assigned a tailor's dummy and her supervisor, Miss Laidlaw, who would begin to teach her how to set a sleeve.

6

Miss Laidlaw had been Grace's supervisor too. Known to be strict, she made Grace unpick and unpick until her stitches and the set were as perfect as her excellent work. Lily wouldn't mind that; she wanted to be the best dressmaker in the workroom.

At lunchtime, she and Grace, arm in arm, took their packets of sandwiches wrapped in greaseproof paper to the new Guildhall Square. Grace giggled as a young bank clerk tipped his hat to them. "I'm going to marry someone with a good job and lots of money, so I never have to sew a stitch again. Maybe go to America even."

Lily looked at her. "Not me; I'll have a modiste's shop in London and be a dressmaker to the theatre stars."

Grace laughed. "You want to come to America with me then. My rich husband can introduce you." She extended her hand elegantly as if smoothing a long glove along her arm.

Lily shook her head, putting on a serious face. "You won't like America. You can't cope with mice in the storeroom, and there are mice the size of cats over there and rats on the boat."

Grace shuddered. "I can bear anything if someone else does the sewing."

The Guildhall clock struck the half-hour, and Lily jumped up. She didn't understand Grace. Lately, she had no interest in her work and mainly wanted to talk about boys. "Come on, we'd better get back, or we'll be in trouble."

Lily knew America was not for her; London was far enough. Boats sank, and people drowned. Awful it was, her Pa had told her. He'd read a story to her the other night from his paper. He and Ma had been to the new Electric

Theatre to see the newsreel, and Ma said she hadn't slept a wink that night thinking about those poor souls. If that was ships, Lily didn't want to be any closer than watching them sail past The Hard and waving at the sailors on deck.

When Lily left work that evening, her eyes felt strained from focusing on the tiny buttons.

Miss Laidlaw had given her a sample blouse, almost like a doll's outfit, to practise setting a sleeve into. Lily had to show a leg of mutton sleeve on one side with its gathered top. On the other, one of the new-fashion straight sleeves. Lily's first attempt ended in failure and was unpicked and folded in her workbasket for tomorrow. Miss Laidlaw had pointed out Lily's preparation, and the foundation tacking stitches were not accurate enough.

When Lily finished the sample blouse to Miss Laidlaw's satisfaction, her next job would be to make a work blouse for herself. If that passed muster, she would begin to work on clothes for paying clients.

After work, Aiden was waiting at the tram stop for her with a brown bag tucked under one arm. Poking out, the pink and green cover with a white bandstand on the front proclaimed, "Alexander's Ragtime Band."

"You got it!" squealed Lily as he removed the sheet music to show her. Lily's blue eyes sparkled with excitement, then clouded with concern as she looked at him. "Did you spend your own money?"

He grinned. "No, young Mr Conrad said I could take it because the back corner is torn. I made a good sale today, so he was happy."

"Can you play it already?" She started to hum a snatch of the syncopated tune quietly. Aiden glanced around the other passengers and shushed, laughing.

He shrugged. "I think I can. I've been practising in case I have to play it for customers. If you ask your ma, will she let you come in when we get home, so you can sing?"

Aching shoulders from stooping over her sewing were forgotten as Lily dragged Aiden home. Gone was the grown-up young lady of this morning, and back was the girl.

Pa had taken the family to the new bandstand last summer, and the band had played this number. They said it had been a smash hit in America, and ragtime was taking England by storm. Granny hadn't approved, she thought it new-fangled and fast, but Lily loved it.

Ma answered Lily's frantic raps at the door, neat and composed as ever, her brown hair, now tinged with grey, in a tight bun at the nape of her neck. Her blouse and skirt were unwrinkled despite all the work of the day.

Before she married Pa, Ma had been the cook and housekeeper to an elderly gentleman who owned the estate and farm at Milton. Lily was amazed at how she always appeared unruffled and moved with a calm gliding movement as she went about her jobs.

"Despite my advancing years, I can still hear the door knocker the first time, Lily."

Lily interrupted, "Ma, Aiden has the music to Alexander's Ragtime Band. He wants me to go in and sing it for practise. May I? Please?"

Ma frowned. "Lily Matthews, will you draw breath? Take off your hat and coat, then come in before you bombard me with questions."

It was no good trying to rush Ma once she had that look, and Lily did as she was asked, bursting with impatience.

"Ma, please, can I go for a while? Mrs Donnelly says it's alright."

Maggie relented, seeing her daughter's eagerness. "For a while. We'll be eating as soon as your father's home. Tidy your hair and wash the smuts off your face first."

Lily hugged her mother and ran upstairs. Eager to go next door, Lily barely noticed the faded roses on her bedroom wallpaper or the smell of lavender beeswax from her freshly polished dressing table. She poured water from the pitcher on the washstand, rubbed the wet flannel impatiently across her face, and then patted it dry. She'd empty the bowl later.

She hurried back down the stairs, steep and dark with a slightly worn carpet runner. Lily almost lost her footing, which earned a tut from her mother.

"Take these in for Mary." Ma held out a plate of jam tarts. "I baked them this morning. Be careful not to drop any, and Lily?" She glanced at her daughter, "Will you walk like a lady, please."

Lily knocked eagerly at the Donnelly's house, then glanced back at her mother to wave. She couldn't read her expression but wondered if she may be worried. Lily couldn't think why.

Chapter 2

Mrs Donnelly opened the door. A pale, patient lady, Lily thought her large brown eyes were too big for her face. Mary Donnelly played the piano beautifully, which enabled her to give piano lessons. Aiden's parents lived a more precarious existence than Lily's, who were older.

On a Sunday, the Donnellys didn't attend St Pats or the Devonshire Road Methodist Chapel with the rest of the street. Instead, Mary wore a black veil to their church, St John's, the catholic cathedral. It was why Aiden's father, Sean, didn't always have work, Pa said, shaking his head.

Lily stepped into their front room and offered the plate of tarts.

"How thoughtful. Please thank your mother for me." Mrs Donnelly's voice was quiet and musical. She looked genuinely pleased with the gift.

"Can we taste them?" Aiden eyed the plate hungrily and reached out a hand.

Mary tapped it gently. "Not until you've finished playing. I don't want sticky fingers on my keyboard." She turned and put the plate on the dark sideboard.

Like most houses on the street, the Donnelly's front room was only used occasionally, on high days and holidays. Unless, like today, Aiden and Lily were practising or Mary was giving a lesson.

On top of the sideboard, two matched vases stood on lace circles with framed family photos between them. In the leaded glass cupboards at either end, the best glasses waited patiently for Christmas, along with several china ornaments.

More photos and a carriage clock which chimed the hour graced the fireplace. Someone had neatly laid the grate, but today, no fire was alight, so the room was chilly. A large rug covered the varnished floorboards, and visitors were welcome to sit on either a horsehair sofa or one of two captain chairs. The suite had wooden spindle backs, topped by a padded cushion that made you sit bolt upright. All the chair legs boasted Bakelite cups under the feet to stop them from marking the rug.

Lily didn't mind the chill or the uncomfortable chairs. She was there for Mary's piano, a beautiful upright instrument in golden yew. It boasted ornate, hinged brass candle sconces and an inlaid pattern in ebony and mother of pearl that glowed when the candles were lit.

"Come on, Lily. I'll play, you can sing. Listen, Ma."

"I'm listening." Mary laughed and settled on the sofa, hands neatly placed in her lap, gently restrained as they were not required to play.

The neighbourhood women talked about the Donnellys, but conversations stopped if Lily listened. Rumour on the street had it that Mary Donnelly had married beneath her and had had to leave Ireland.

"Let him without sin cast the first stone," her mother always said, frowning if Lily asked why the women didn't take to Mary. Maggie didn't have much truck with gossip and was apt to find a job to keep Lily busy when she asked too many questions.

Aiden sat on the piano stool and twiddled the large wooden knob on the side to adjust the height, then, satisfied, opened the music sheet. Lily stood behind him, looking over his shoulder at the tiny, printed lyrics under the music, and began to sing after the foot-tapping introduction.

Her voice was rich and true, unexpectedly deep for a young girl. She wasn't entirely sure of all the phrasing and fumbled some of the lyrics, picking them up as Aiden continued to play. Lily strained to reach the notes at the top of her range, hand to chest and chin lifted.

"Aiden, transpose it down for Lily. This isn't her key."

He nodded, played a few descending chords, and began again in a lower register while Lily stared in awe at his skill.

They laughed at their mistakes and gradually got the hang of the song, which was trickier than it sounded. Mrs Donnelly left her seat and stood to Aiden's right, leaning to turn the thin sheet music which had a habit of falling if he tried to do it himself. Lily lost her place if she sang and turned for him.

The group, so absorbed, didn't hear Mr Donnelly until he said, "Have I stumbled on a party?"

"My goodness is that the time?" said Mary, moving across the room. She accepted a light kiss on her cheek but looked guilty.

"Don't stop because I'm here. Play it again."

Mr Donnelly had a soft Irish brogue and a merry laugh which Lily often heard through the wall. He wasn't a big man, not much taller than Mary, but he was powerfully built. He worked in the dockyard, which could be precarious as there were no contracts, and he didn't always get hired. Her father, a stonemason with his small firm, always had work.

Lily felt embarrassed. She knew everything stopped in her house when her father came home, and they ate dinner together. "I'm sorry. Perhaps I should go now."

"Then who would sing for me? And my wife may see me steal a jam tart if you don't distract her." He winked at Lily. "I love a song."

Mr Donnelly clapped as they ran through the song again and said, "Mary, it's your turn. Sing Danny Boy for me."

It must have been a favourite because Mary played without music. As she sat at the piano and spread her hands on the keys, it was like hearing a different instrument. Aiden's touch was strong and confident, hers lyrical and soft. Her sweet soprano voice brought up goosebumps on Lily's arm. Out of the corner of her eye, she saw Mr Donnelly dab a tear. She had never seen her father cry.

As the song finished, a suspended silence hung over the room, everyone captivated by the emotion in the stillness beyond the last note.

Lily broke it, "Mrs Donnelly, how beautiful."

"Songs from home." Mary made a barely perceptible shake of her head. "And now I must attend to supper. Lovely to see you, Lily; you're welcome anytime to practise. You should both perform at the community concert. Don't forget to thank your mother. I'll return the plate."

Aiden showed Lily out, and she whispered, "After you've eaten, pass me your shirt over the back wall."

As her mother answered the door, Lily said, "Did you hear Ma? Isn't Mrs Donnelly's voice beautiful?"

"What I heard from the kitchen was lovely. Now your father's home, wash your hands. Supper is ready."

Lily brought serving dishes through from the kitchen. Maggie's table was always impeccable from her days in service, and she did not serve even the simplest dinner plated. In response to her mother's questions, her father described his work on renovations to a house in Festing Grove.

Lily, who had only been listening with half an ear, said, "Ma, Mrs Donnelly thanked you for the tarts."

Her father pricked his ears. "Tarts, Maggie? Where are you hiding ours then?"

"Don't fret. There are plenty for us." She collected the dinner plates, and Lily carried them into the kitchen. Small tea plates from the dresser replaced them while Maggie served the tarts on a fluted glass dish.

Lily watched as her father selected one. He sank his teeth into the tiny tart, a delicacy of mouth-watering, crumbly pastry and sweet, sharp-tang curd.

Now was a good moment. "Pa, Mrs Donnelly suggested Aiden and I could sing at the community concert before Christmas. Now I'm seventeen, may I please?"

"Pass me another tart. I'll think about it."

He drifted into a reverie as he slowly munched a raspberry jam tart. Lily could barely contain herself. "Pa?"

"He's teasing you, child. Let him be. Pestering will only make him worse."

"If I hadn't fallen in love with you, Maggie, I'd have married you for your pastry alone."

Lily could bear it no longer. "Pa, please?"

He winked at her. "I see no objection, but you'd better ask your ma."

"As long as it's at the church hall, I don't see any harm."

Eyes like stars, Lily asked to be excused from the table and headed for the back garden. "If Aiden's outside, I can tell him."

Her mother frowned. "Don't stay out there for long, Lily. We have dishes, and I want you to mend your father's best shirt."

As Lily pulled the door closed, she hugged herself. If she was going to make costumes for the stars, she needed to know what performing was like. There was a cash prize for the best act. If she and Aiden won, it could go to their London fund.

Lily gave a low owl hoot by blowing into her hands. It was their signal, and Aiden appeared.

"They said 'yes' to the concert, Aiden. Imagine if we win the prize."

"We will."

She looked back at the house. "I can't stay long. Have you got your shirt?"

He pulled the folded garment from under his jumper and passed it to her. Lily ran back into the house with his shirt tucked into her apron.

After dinner, Maggie always took the chair on the other side of the fireplace to her husband. Sitting slightly set back, Lily began to mend her father's shirt. Her mother was distracted, attention focused on the hem of a sheet she was decorating by drawing threads from the cotton to make a

16

delicate pattern of holes which she then over-stitched. Lily discreetly swapped to Aiden's cuffs, deftly unpicking the seams, and turning the worn edges.

As she held the garment, she noticed it smelled like Aiden and Pear's soap, which made her blush. She checked the neat stitches, folded the shirt into her pinafore and took up her father's torn shirt setting tiny stitches to draw the edges together as her mother had taught her.

When Lily announced she was going into the garden for air, Ma looked up and said, "Please put the kettle on the stove as you go past. I think we'll have our tea."

Before they observed her too closely, Lily fled into the kitchen and through the back door. Ma hadn't caught her, and her heart thudded with relief.

Aiden must have been watching because she heard the Donnelly's backdoor open. Lily threw the shirt over, not waiting to see or speak to him. She had meant it kindly when she offered to turn his cuffs, but she knew Ma would disapprove as soon as the shirt was in her hands. Holding something of Aiden's that was so personal felt bold.

Lily warmed the teapot and counted in two spoonful's of tea from the wooden caddy, which allowed her heart rate to return to normal. The small wooden chest had a tiny lock with a silver key. Ma had always locked the tea caddy in the house where she worked when she was younger. As a housekeeper, she kept the key on her chain, as tea was expensive. The downstairs staff made their tea from the second brewing.

Pa had found their caddy in an auction. He often bought Ma bits from auctions for the table or the kitchen because he knew she liked nice things.

Arranging cups on the tray, Lily carried the tea in with shaky hands.

Pa pinched her cheek gently and said, "You're a good girl, Lily."

At that moment, she felt nothing short of wicked.

Chapter 3

The community concert brought together two churches in Eastney. Concert rehearsals took place in the Methodist Hall, under the watchful eye of the curate from St Pat's and the Devonshire Road Methodist Chapel minister.

Many years ago, the hall was decorated dark green under the wooden dado rail and shiny cream above. The cream paint had since yellowed with age. Drab green curtains framed the small stage at one end, and a piano that miss-hit several notes but was otherwise in tune stood to one side.

A tea urn with a burner underneath sat on the corner table, making the room smell of paraffin. The minister's wife, a spare unsmiling woman, presided over the refreshments and dampened any over-exuberant spirits. Preparations for the concert, however, were always jolly, and the performance took place on the Saturday after Christmas.

Rehearsal was every Tuesday and Thursday, and Aiden offered to knock after dinner and walk Lily there. Each week he ran the gauntlet of Ma and Pa, fussing and making him promise that she would be delivered home no later than nine o'clock. Pa watched them down the street and was always on the front before nine to see them back down the road, his pocket watch in hand.

Although quiet, Aiden was always in demand at rehearsals because he was a good accompanist. Lily didn't see much of him during the evening but sometimes caught him watching her as she waited her turn to sing with the others.

Someone else who paid her particular attention was Harry. One of the Brodys, Harry was a big beefy lad, handsome square-jawed, and obviously loved himself. All the girls hung on his every word.

He had joined the Royal Marines as a recruit and had developed a habit of singling Lily out during rehearsals. He sang in a confident baritone voice, and the minister, who knew nothing about music in Aiden's opinion, had paired him with Lily to sing a duet.

Harry managed to bring Lily her tea and biscuit before Aiden had the chance, which she noticed made Aiden cross.

"If Harry Brody is making a nuisance of himself, bothering you in the tea break, you let me know," said Aiden on their walk home.

"Harry Brody?" She looked at him in amazement, pulling her hand away from his arm. "I barely know him, but he seems nice enough and has a lovely voice." She sensed this was not what Aiden wanted to hear. "Although it's much nicer when you get my tea because I feel comfortable with you."

With her face turned towards him, Lily saw a new expression on Aiden's face and, for a moment, wondered if he would try to kiss her. But they were about to turn the corner when they would be under Pa's eye again, and she was relieved he didn't.

The following Sunday after church, when lunch was over, and Pa had removed his stiff shirt collar and rolled up his sleeves, Lily heard a knock at the door. She heard Aiden's voice. Curious to know why he was calling, she made a show of wiping the table mats in the back room to get closer to the front door.

Her mother's voice from the kitchen made her jump. "Lily Matthews, you'll wear that dishcloth out, not to mention my table mats. Come away from the door. Listeners hear no good of themselves."

Flushing red, Lily reluctantly returned to the kitchen. She sometimes felt her mother could see through walls.

"Was that Aiden, Pa?" she asked when her pa returned.

Pa nodded and settled in his chair by the fire for a comfortable doze, replete with Maggie's steak and kidney pudding. Lily watched the familiar signs with misgiving. Surely, he wouldn't sleep without telling her what Aiden wanted.

She cleared her throat, and Pa's eyelids re-opened. "I wondered if Aiden was looking for me."

"No, no, he came to ask me something." Pa allowed his eyes to close again, and Maggie came in from the kitchen, wiping her hands on a small towel.

"Don't tease the girl, Edward."

He opened his eyes, and now Lily could see they were laughing. "He asked me if he could take you to the pier to go roller skating this afternoon."

Lily took a deep breath, crossing her fingers behind her back.

His face was serious again. "I said 'no' because I knew you wouldn't like it."

Lily gasped. "But I would very much like to go, Pa. Grace from the workroom has been and says gliding on the skates is wonderful. Please, may I go?"

Unable to keep a straight face as he looked at Lily's dismayed expression, Pa relented. "I said he could collect you at half-past two, and you must be home by five o'clock."

Lily threw her arms around his neck and kissed him. "Thank you, Pa. Grace said there are fairy lights when it gets dark, and when you get confident, you can glide really fast."

He laughed. "You're a daredevil, Lily. You wouldn't catch me on those things risking my neck."

Ma shook her head. "You be sensible, my girl. You don't want to be giving Aiden ideas, and you can't afford to hurt yourself."

Pa winked at Lily behind Ma's back.

Running upstairs to find her coat, she was puzzled at what Ma meant. *What ideas?* She set the comment aside. *Just Ma fussing,* she thought. Lily's eyes shone, she knew Aiden could skate, and he would teach her.

At two-thirty precisely, Aiden knocked. "Five o'clock and no later," Pa said sternly. "I'll be watching for you." He reached his index finger and thumb into the top pocket of his open waistcoat and bestowed a penny on Lily. "Treat yourself to some chestnuts."

The skates were uncomfortable as they tied on over Lily's boots, and she struggled to keep her feet. The tiny wheels threw her weight backwards, but she managed better when Aiden was beside her.

"Push out with the right, then the left, do it with me; one-two, one-two."

Lily wobbled, and Aiden tightened his arm around her waist, holding her up as she tried to get her rhythm. They reached the end of the pier, and her face flushed with the effort, the cold wind, and the unaccustomed feeling of Aiden's arm around her.

After two more pier lengths skating together, her balance improved. Apart from an occasional glitch, it felt like dancing. Aiden hummed the skater's waltz, and their pace matched the tune. Thrilled by the speed, Lily turned sparkling eyes to him. They laughed as they acknowledged her new skill, adrenaline making her heart pump faster.

As Aiden caught his breath, he looked at Lily with unusual intensity. Confused, Lily looked away momentarily, affected by the sudden mood change between them, then returned his gaze. It was just Aiden, her Aiden, after all.

"You looked like a painting then, Lily, when we finished skating."

She raised her eyebrows. "That's a funny thing to say. I hope you meant a beautiful portrait with a perfect complexion and rosy cheeks."

He laughed. "That would be telling."

Walking without the weight of the skates on her feet felt strange, and she had to stop herself from bobbing beside Aiden.

With his brasier on a cart, the chestnut seller called his wares on the corner by the pier. Lily was glad to warm her hands as he scooped a flat skillet of blackened, roasted chestnuts into a paper cornet. Aiden tossed each between his hands like a hot coal, splitting the charred skin with deft movements to avoid burning his fingers. Lily noticed his long, slender fingers as he handed her fragments of the sweet, nutty treats. Aiden had musicians' hands, not rough or calloused like their fathers, who worked in the trades.

She laughed at his antics while they nibbled the hot chestnuts and strolled along the seafront, chatting, accompanied by the easy roll of waves on the pebble beach. An almost full moon sat low in the sky, casting fractured moonlight glints on the water. They strolled to the end of the promenade, past the barracks and towards home, absorbed in each other's company.

Pa waited on the front apron sitting on an old chair and enjoying his pipe. Lily could see occasional puffs of smoke he huffed from one corner of his mouth while clamping the stem. The smoke made him squint, and his generous moustache was tinged with orange from the tobacco. He nodded to Aiden. "Just in time, Son. Lily, your mother's in the kitchen."

Lily hesitated but knew the treat was over. There would be no more time with Aiden today. "Thank you for teaching me. I had a marvellous time, Aiden."

Under Pa's gaze, Aiden became formal. "My pleasure Lily. I'm glad you enjoyed it." He took no time disappearing into his house, briefly turning to wave.

Ma called out, "Lily? Hang up your coat and come to help me."

Lily did as Ma bid and danced into the kitchen, where she was presented with a butter knife and thin-cut bread from yesterday's loaf. She buttered out of habit, her thoughts still at the pier. "Skating was wonderful, gliding so fast. I wasn't graceful, but I could do it."

Her mother took in her air of suppressed excitement. "It was thoughtful of Aiden to ask you, being so much older. Kind of him to treat you. When he starts to walk out with someone, I don't expect you will see as much of him."

Her words, as intended, felt like a shower of cold water on Lily's excitement. Aiden walk out with someone. They had always done things together, and Lily had never considered a time beyond that. A tight fist balled inside. Lily thought *I wouldn't like her, whoever she was*, mentally passing girls they knew under review and discarding each one with certainty.

"It won't do for you to get too close and get your hopes up, Lily. I don't doubt Aiden will choose someone from their church." She tutted as she watched Lily, miles away still. "Watch what you're doing. That's too much butter. There'll be none left for the rest of the week. Pop some jam in a glass dish and put it on the table. Your father may want some cheese as well."

Lily obediently scraped some of the butter onto the next slice and thought, *why is she saying that?*

Pa wanted to hear all about the skating. However, although she enjoyed telling him everything that had happened, what Ma said continued to bother her.

"I think you and I should go and try this dancing on skates," Pa said with a wink to Lily.

Maggie shuddered. "You won't catch me on those nasty contraptions. If God had intended us to skate, he'd have given us wheels instead of feet. I can see you youngsters have enjoyed it, but you can leave wheels for carts and charabancs as far as I'm concerned."

"When you were Lily's age, you'd have been the first person skating. Your Ma was a lovely dancer, Lily. You should have seen her when they had the servants' party at the big house. It took me all evening to get up the courage to ask for a dance, her being indoors staff."

Maggie blushed, and Lily looked from one to the other. She couldn't imagine her mother young and giddy.

"She was seventeen when I asked her to marry me, but she kept saying no because she wanted to be the head cook. She was properly on the shelf, twenty-seven before she said yes to me after the old man died."

"Pa, you waited all that time. I'm seventeen, and ten years seems forever."

He smiled at his wife. "Weren't no one else for me but your ma, Lily. I knew I'd get her in the end."

Ma laughed. "He married me for my cooking, Lily, don't believe a word of his flummery."

Lily saw the glance that passed between them. Even though they were old, Lily could see they still loved one another.

That evening, Lily brushed her hair in front of the speckled mirror in her bedroom, made a plait and secured the end. Hugging a pillow, she glided around the room as if skating. Lily's thoughts strayed to Aiden at the pier and the feel of his arm around her waist. She wondered what Aiden was doing now.

If she'd been able to see through the wall, she would have seen Aiden lying on his back on a narrow bed, looking up at the painted glass lampshade in his room, a small smile playing around his lips and the memory of Lily laughing up at him, occupying all his thoughts.

Chapter 4

The following day Lily woke with her nose outside the blankets and eiderdown. Her face felt cold. From behind the dark curtains, tendrils of light crept across the floor, and she knew there would be that one hard step on the freezing floorboards before she could hop onto the rag rug in front of the washstand. The thought of leaving her bed did not appeal.

She heard her mother's footsteps on the stairs and the familiar tap before she came in with a hot water jug.

"Time to get up, or you'll be late. Your father's already left." Ma moved to the window and swung the heavy curtains back. The panes of glass in the sash window were misted with condensation and let in a draft of cold air.

"Come on, Lily. You won't be cold once you move. The kitchen's nice and warm."

Lily extended a cautious foot from under the covers and retracted it immediately. "Five more minutes," she bargained. The eiderdown was cosy and gloriously new. It sat on top of her scratchy woollen blankets. The underside was pale turquoise, covered with a pattern of pink roses, the top quilted with patches of turquoise and pink, and had a frill in the same colours around the outside seam. Ma and Granny had made it for her seventeenth birthday, and Lily loved its cosy comfort.

Ma's response was to briskly whip back all the covers and fold them back to air the sheets.

"Ma! I only wanted five minutes." Lily shivered in her white cotton nightgown and grabbed her shawl from the chair.

"I'll five minutes you. Breakfast is ready, and your tea is getting stewed."

Lily made a face behind Ma's back and set about washing and dressing. She wasted no time pulling on layers of underwear: Knickers, and a camisole, followed by a petticoat, then her work blouse and skirt.

Lily frowned as she noticed a mark on her skirt and rubbed at it with her washcloth. She couldn't keep her hair in place and called downstairs, "Ma, can you help me, please?"

Ma returned and took the brush, tugging briskly through Lily's brown hair. Finally, with a deft twist, she secured it in a ponytail, then wound the thick skane into a bun, pinning it neatly as she went.

"Ow!" Lily squeaked as a pin stabbed her.

"Hold still. Pride bears a pinch," Ma said through the hairpins in her mouth. She looked at Lily's reflection in the mirror and nodded. "You'll do." The ghost of a smile crossed her face.

"Walk, Lily," came her mother's voice as Lily flew down the stairs. She spooned thick porridge into a bowl and added a sprinkle of sugar. The coarse, sweet grains gritty in her mouth complemented the creamy porridge, and she felt its warmth begin to spread. Lily lifted the heavy brown everyday teapot from its stand, poured herself a cup of amber tea, splashed milk in from the jug and sipped with both hands around the cup. She was singing her concert number with Aiden in her head, and her left foot tapped as she leaned against the range.

Ma came through the door carrying an armful of washing. "Lily Matthews, sit down to drink your tea and hold the cup by the handle."

Lily smiled at her mother and shook her head. "No one's looking, Ma, and I'm in a rush."

Ma raised her eyebrows and looked pointedly at the chair. "Good manners cost nothing, and you can take them anywhere."

Lily slurped her tea loudly before saying, "Yes, Ma." And then burst out laughing.

"Get on with you. That's your father in you." Ma chuckled.

Lily finished her tea, put her lunch in a small netting bag and took a halfpenny from her pot on the sideboard for the tram. She kissed her ma on the cheek and said, "I'll see you after work. It's my rehearsal in the hall this evening."

Ma nodded. "You'll miss these rehearsals when you've done the show."

Lily's eyes sparkled, and she did a little two-step dance, swishing her skirt from side to side. "I can't wait! I want to tell them about my idea for a costume. There's a trunk full of old clothes under the stage, I had a rummage through, and I think I can alter one of the dresses to fit me. I want to look like my picture of Camille Clifford for my duet with Harry. I'll need something simpler for the ragtime song with Aiden."

Ma raised her eyebrows. "Very fancy. Just remember you're only seventeen, so nothing too fast. We can look for material at a jumble sale. Some net curtains would cut up nicely to look like lace for a stage dress, and we may find some old ribbons."

Lily had half expected her ma to veto the costume idea altogether, so she danced out of the door. Ideas jostled in her brain for converting the lavender dress she'd seen.

When Lily met Aiden on the walk to the tram, he was less enthusiastic than she had expected while she laid out her plans. Suddenly he blurted out, "Lily, I hope our song is your priority because we said we wanted to win the prize. For our London fund."

"Whatever do you mean, Aiden Donnelly? Of course, our number's important."

Aiden's face took on the blank look he got when upset about something. "Only, you seem more interested in your duet with Harry."

Stung by the unfairness of his remark, she said, "What a mean thing to say. I want both costumes to look good because if they do, I hope to earn extra money, making dresses for people in my spare time. I need to practise if I'm going to make stage costumes."

Aiden shrugged and looked away. "I suppose he'll show off, strutting about in his uniform."

As Harry had already said he would be wearing his uniform, Lily was at a loss for what to say. "Aiden, don't be cross, you'll be the one playing the piano, and you're wonderful. Everyone will be listening to you play."

"A good accompanist is invisible," he said, sounding more despondent than ever.

"Not to me," she said, squeezing his arm. "I tell you what, you'd look ever so handsome with a fancy waistcoat and matching cravat. I can make you both for the show if we find some fabric. Perhaps we could look tonight."

His face brightened. "Thank you, Lily, I'd like that."

The orders at work for Christmas dresses and New Year gala ballgowns meant the workroom was humming, and Mrs Winchett's temper was short. Everyone had their head down working. Lily's sampler had passed muster, as had the work blouse she had made. Now under Miss Laidlaw's supervision, she was working on her first order, a simple blouse with leg of mutton sleeves and a high neck in delicate blue cotton. It needed all Lily's concentration to set the sleeves and conceal her tiny stitches.

The morning passed quickly, and she was surprised when the bell rang for lunchtime. Lily stood up and stretched, then wandered across the workroom to examine the details of a beautiful evening gown on a tailor's dummy. It was a design Miss Laidlaw was making. As she took in the details, she heard hurried steps on the backstairs.

Grace, more slender and taller than Lily, had been called upstairs to model gowns for a client viewing that morning. Apart from a quick 'hello', lunch break was their first chance to speak all day.

Grace took Lily's arm and propelled her up the steps to the street with barely time to button her coat. Lily grumbled as the cold winter air hit her face, and she noted the heavy grey clouds overhead. "What are you so giddy about?"

Grace grinned with a 'cat who's got the cream' expression. "George Dent has asked my father's permission to walk out with me."

Lily said, "Goodness, that's exciting." Then ruined the effect by adding, "Who's George Dent?"

"Dent's the corset factory in Fratton! George is the youngest son of Mr Dent. I met him several weeks ago at the band concert on the common. He and his friend gave up their chairs so my sister and I could sit. By coincidence, he was there again with his friend the next week, and so were we."

Lily rolled her eyes. She imagined Grace had more of a hand in that coincidence than the fates but said nothing.

Grace carried on, slightly breathless, "He isn't exactly handsome, but he has poise and knows such a lot. He's older than me, of course."

Only nods and the occasional 'yes', 'really', or 'no' were required from Lily, so she munched her sandwiches and kept her counsel. As she listened, Lily formed the impression that George was plain as a pikestaff and the sort of know-it-all she disliked. She chided herself for being uncharitable. They had never met, after all.

Grace looked at Lily earnestly. "You would never know his family are well-to-do. His father believes in hard work, and all his brothers had to start at the bottom as apprentices and work up."

Lily raised her eyebrows. "How many brothers has George got?"

"He's the youngest of six boys."

"Goodness, his poor mother. Imagine all that washing and cleaning." Further down the street where she lived, Mrs Ray had four boys and looked permanently exhausted.

Grace laughed. "I think she has a staff, Lily, imagine that! But she has raised all the boys on liberal principles," she added hastily. "His mother goes to the women's suffragist meetings and campaigns for them. George says she'll take me if I like."

Lily looked at her friend in amazement. She didn't think Grace would know women's suffrage if she fell over it. She was more likely to read a penny dreadful than the newspaper. Lily only knew about it because Pa read aloud from the papers, and Aiden's ma mentioned attending meetings. "Goodness," Lily said, to add variety to her other monosyllabic answers.

"If she asks me to go, will you come? I might say the wrong thing."

Lily swallowed. She wasn't sure what her ma would think and said uncertainly, "I could ask. Do you honestly like George? You aren't walking out with him because his family has money, are you?"

Grace blushed. "I do like him, and I didn't know his family had money when we met. Anyway, he intends to make his own way." She paused, then words tumbled out in a rush, "He wants to go to America to set up a branch of the firm. He thinks corsets will be outdated. He wants to make gloves."

Lily shrewdly imagined that even being the sixth son of a factory owner meant he still might start with more money than most children could hope for. She thought of her two shillings at home and Aiden's struggle to save anything.

"America! Now I know why you like him."

But Grace wasn't laughing. "No, George is not like anyone I've met. I'm sure you'd like him because he's ambitious. He has plans. Maybe we could meet up at one of the band concerts, then you could see for yourself."

Lily abandoned her teasing expression and smiled warmly. "Why not? Or you could invite him to our community concert."

Lily linked arms with Grace as they returned to the workroom. "I can make your wedding dress and travelling clothes for America." She had been joking, but she could see Grace was already thinking about her future. She hoped all would be well and George wouldn't let Grace down.

Lily had a strange, unsettled feeling all afternoon. With the earlier tiff with Aiden and now Grace's news, the world around her was shifting. She'd felt like this when the old King had died earlier in the year. Change you made yourself was one thing, but change that buffeted you around like a leaf in a storm was something different.

Aiden wasn't at the tram stop after work. Lily waited, but there was no sign of him, so she boarded the next tram alone. She wondered what had kept Aiden and if he would be at rehearsals later.

All day, the heavy clouds had produced a fine drizzle which brought down the smoky, mineral smell of chimneys. As she watched, the raindrops smudged and were blown back across the tram windows as it rattled forwards. She cast her mind back to their disagreement this morning and hoped Aiden wasn't avoiding her. Perhaps she was overthinking things, and he had simply finished late.

Lily put her anxiety aside, preferring to let her body sway to the rhythmic clicking of the wheels over joints in the rails. The click-clack made her imagine a short dance routine she could do as she sang at the show.

Two men in the seat in front of her were talking about work. She wasn't deliberately listening; however, Lily couldn't help but overhear them discussing the dock workers handing out leaflets about pay and working conditions with threatened strikes.

They both tutted gravely and agreed it was tantamount to a rabble uprising.

Lily's mind flew towards Aiden's father. Would he be involved? She knew he was a union man, but Mr Donnelly wasn't a troublemaker, and she knew other men who worked in the dockyard. They weren't rabble. She felt confused and indignant. Why would the men think that? She would ask Pa about it tonight.

Lily jumped off the tram, the drizzle cold against her neck and walked briskly, lost in her thoughts. She turned into Eastfield Road and walked down the grey street, its small, tiled frontages shining slick with rain. For the first time, she wondered how many families would have a good meal this evening.

Lily had often seen her ma pass dishes of food over walls, and she knew money was tight for some families. Even the military wives struggled when their men were away on commission. She had never equated it with poverty, though. In her mind, poverty meant families in the workhouse.

Ma opened the door and peeled Lily's coat off, shaking the raindrops off it under the small porch roof which sheltered the entrance. "Go and hang it by the range. Give me your hat." Ma smoothed the hat's brim, stuffed the crown with newspaper and hung it on a peg by the door. "There's tea in the pot."

Lily was sitting near the range when her mother came in. "Some men on the tram were saying the dockers may come out on strike, and they are troublemakers."

Maggie looked at her daughter. "Lily, it's easy to judge when you don't live hand to mouth. There are a lot of men who work as hard as your pa and yet can barely feed their families. Hard workers should earn a living wage. I'm not for lawless behaviour, but I can see why they're complaining, and the government should act."

Lily stared. She had never heard her mother voice a political opinion before. "So, do you think they are right to go on strike?"

Her mother sighed. "The unions are trying to join forces to pressure their employers and the government. They hope a larger group will be successful and the politicians will listen. I'm not for a strike if they can get change without it. But there is no denying something must be done soon. People are desperate."

Lily wanted to ask more, but her mother continued, "Anyway, enough of that. It will be time enough to worry when it happens. Go and change your clothes and mind you hang them up neatly. Your father will be here soon, and supper is ready early so you can get to rehearsal."

Sometimes Ma and Pa surprised her, and she wondered how much they shielded her from hardship. At least one thing seemed apparent if her mother had political views, perhaps she wouldn't be against her going to a suffragist meeting with Grace.

Chapter 5

A iden looked tired when he knocked for Lily later but didn't seem cross anymore. Pa took out his pocket watch as usual and pointedly tapped the face. "Nine o'clock, no later, you two. I'll be watching down the street."

Aiden offered his arm, and Lily placed her hand on his forearm as they set off.

"Are you alright?" Lily looked at him anxiously. "I missed you on the way home."

He looked down at her with a gleam of excitement. "Yes, we were busy today. Kitty Marion is coming to Portsmouth."

Lily looked puzzled, and he continued, "She's a music hall star, Lily, and I've been learning to play some of her songs. People are bound to want them."

"That's so exciting!" Lily skipped a couple of paces.

"That's not all. I'm writing a new song for her. I may have a chance to play for her, and I was up late finishing the melody."

"Imagine if you could play for her, and she sang your song. Do you think she will come into the shop? How does the tune to your song go?"

He laughed but looked proud. "One question at a time. You'll have to wait for the song because I haven't got it perfect yet. There's a chance I may meet her, but I'm not allowed to talk about it."

Lily pouted and frowned. It wasn't like Aiden to be secretive, especially with her. They shared their secrets. "You know I wouldn't say anything. You can tell me."

He shook his head. "Honestly, I will as soon as I can. When I finish the song, I want you to sing it with me, so I know it's right."

Lily lifted her chin and fixed him with what she hoped was a cold stare. "I'll try to find the time."

He pinched her arm. "Don't be like that. It's not my secret to share."

"Ow!" Lily looked back at him crossly, but he tilted his head and looked at her with his soft smile. Eventually, she had to smile in response. "Alright, keep your secret. See if I care."

They walked on, and to break the silence, Lily said, "Grace from work is seeing George Dent. His pa owns the corset factory, and his ma is a suffragist. She's going to invite Grace and me to one of her meetings." Lily couldn't keep a note of excitement from her voice.

Lily wondered if she had imagined it, but his eyes widened in surprise momentarily, and then he looked disappointed. "Ma goes to those meetings. A lady in Cosham, Mrs O'Shea, runs them at her house. You could go with Ma if you like."

Lily wondered what his first reaction had been about. She felt sure he approved of the meetings. So, what made him look like that?

"I've got to ask Ma and Pa first, and I think Grace wants me to go with her. She's worried she'll feel out of place with George's mother."

He shrugged, but there was no time for any more discussion. The excited hubbub inside enveloped them as they arrived at the church hall.

While waiting for her turn to rehearse, Lily took one of the small oil lamps, turned up the wick and lit it using a spill. Leaving the warm yellow glow of the gas lamps in the main hall, she stepped into the darkness behind the stage to the costume box with only the lamp's small circle of light around her. She swallowed her dislike of spiders and tried to ignore the shadows beyond the lamplight as she pulled the box from underneath the stage.

On top was the old-fashioned silk gown she had seen before. The bodice was all wrong, it looked dated and was made for a much bigger woman, but it had a voluminous, gathered skirt. Lily held the dress upside down and roughly measured the width, nose to hand. If she unpicked the skirt, she could make a more fashionable, narrower style with a bustle and imitate the gown in her photo by adding a fancy blouse.

Avoiding the Minister's po-faced wife, whom she was sure would disapprove, Lily darted across to the vicar and asked if she could use the dress to make costumes. Busy organising chairs and distracted by an indignant, red-faced mother trying to attract his attention, the vicar absent-mindedly agreed to Lily's request. Before he changed his mind, she bundled the dress out of sight to be retrieved later.

She noticed that the woman, whom she thought was Lizzie Banham's mother, was now gesturing vigorously and kept looking at Aiden as she spoke to the vicar. He placated her with a calm stillness broken by nods of his inclined head and quiet responses that Lizzie's mother had to lean in to listen to. Lily caught the words 'Catholic' and 'unsuitable' from the woman. 'Christian values', and 'extraordinary accompanist' from the vicar.

Lily felt a wave of simmering anger and a surge of protectiveness towards Aiden. What a meanspirited lady. Anyone would think being Catholic gave Aiden two heads. She couldn't linger longer without seeming to eavesdrop and hoped the woman wouldn't cause trouble for him.

Aiden was pushing the piano across the hall towards the stage, and she dashed over to help. Lily was optimistic Aiden hadn't overheard the conversation, but his first remark was, "Mrs Banham is trying to get me sacked."

Lily looked to where the vicar was still with the lady in question, who fortunately appeared mollified.

Lily, in dismay, said, "Why would she do that?"

Aiden shrugged, pretending not to care, but Lily could see the hurt in his eyes. "Because she doesn't want her daughter contaminated by my heretic beliefs."

"But we're all Christians, and this isn't about the church. It's a community concert."

He snorted. "Right, Lily, Christians! You're so naïve. People have been slaughtering each other over less for centuries. Talk to my Pa about it."

Lily couldn't bear to see the raw wound under the surface. She cast around for something to say, to take away his haunted look. She thought about the dress, and in her urgency to tell him some good news, she forgot about their conversation this morning and how touchy he'd been. "I've got the dress to make our costumes."

"What dress?" he said, more concerned about not bumping the piano as they manoeuvred it.

She sighed. "The silk one; I can make a dress for me and a waistcoat for you for our number."

He shrugged, turning away. "I thought the dress was for your song with Harry."

"I'll do a costume for both. Aiden, don't be like that."

"Like what?" he snapped and turned away, busying himself with sorting music.

Lily felt a chill she'd never felt with him and hoped her number with Harry wasn't always an issue. It would spoil their pleasure at the concert.

When rehearsing their ragtime number, Lily took her courage in both hands and added her dance steps to the performance. She marched on singing and in step to the music as if she were the conductor of a marching band. Then turned to the audience tracing squares right and left with a four-step routine, beckoning with her fingers as the lyrics invited them to hear the ragtime band. She finished, breathless and looked toward Aiden.

His previous mood had lifted, and to her relief, he half stood up from the piano stool, grinning. His hands were raised in mimed applause matching the ripple from the hall.

Lily ran down the steps at the side of the stage to the piano. "Did you like it?"

Aidan laughed. "I'll be writing songs for your music hall act soon. You'd be wasted making costumes."

After rehearsal, they returned home and parted at Lily's front door on good terms.

The next day Lily took the lilac dress to work wrapped in a sheet and folded over her arm. She had carefully pressed the skirt. At her mother's suggestion, Lily would ask Miss Laidlaw's advice about redesigning it. She hung the dress behind her coat, feeling shy about asking. When everyone was seated at the table, and Mrs Winchett had given out the work for the day, she cleared her throat. "Miss Laidlaw, I hope you don't mind my asking, but I wondered if you could help me."

"What is it, Miss Matthews?"

Her words came out in a rush, "I'm in a community show and have an old costume with lots of silk in the skirt. I want to make a skirt like this." She pulled out the postcard of Camille Clifford from her apron pocket. "Would you look to see how I could best do it?"

She smiled, not unkindly. "Put the postcard away for now, I will try to find time at lunchtime, but we need to get on with our jobs."

"Yes, Miss Laidlaw." Lily breathed out, not aware she'd been holding her breath. "Thank you." She looked down and continued to stitch.

At lunchtime, Miss Laidlaw asked Lily to lay out the dress so she could see how the seamstress had made it. She showed Lily how to unpick the gathers without tearing the silk. She pointed out the bound seam where the skirt joined the bodice and made several deft snips with a tiny pair of stitch scissors freeing part of the gathered skirt.

"May I see your postcard again? What are you going to sing?"

Lily explained the two songs, and Miss Laidlaw looked again at the photograph, a slight frown between her brows.

"If you made a separate bustle detachable from the skirt for the formal gown and made the skirt reversible, you could have both your costumes in one. No one would see from the audience. I believe they use tricks like this on stage all the time."

Lily and Grace stared at her in amazement. "That's a wonderful idea, Miss Laidlaw."

"It may make the skirt heavy." She paused to think. "It won't matter too much what the fabric on the other side is like because it's only a costume." She tapped her lip thoughtfully. "A pale muslin would be pretty or a voile. Then the lilac silk could show through."

Grace said, "You talked about using net curtains as fake lace. You could find some for the skirt."

Miss Laidlaw quickly took Lily's measurements. "I'll make you a template this evening to help you cut the panels. We can talk about the faux bustle another day. Now you girls run and eat your lunch. Don't be late back."

Grace and Lily decided to eat at the small table at the back of the workroom. As they unwrapped their sandwiches, Grace said, "George's mother has invited me to a meeting in Cosham. Next week on Wednesday, please say you'll come."

Lily frowned. "I still have to ask. Ma and Pa may say no. I think that's the meeting Aiden's ma goes to, and they might let me go if they know I'm with her."

Grace turned imploringly towards Lily. "Will you ask today? Every time I think about it, I get butterflies in my stomach, but George wants me to get on with his ma. I'll help you sew your costume if you do; I promise."

Lily laughed. "Goodness, you are desperate."

Grace nodded, grinning. "Ma and Pa have said I can go with Mrs Dent but are worried about me getting involved because some ladies in London have done some bold things." Her voice sank to a whisper. "You don't suppose they will want us to do anything dreadful, do you? I don't think I could."

Lily thought about Aiden's gentle mother and said, "I think it's talking and writing letters to get the vote for women. Aiden's ma wouldn't hurt a fly. Anyway, we don't have to go back if we don't like it. I think women should be able to vote. Mrs Donnelly says we are as clever and can form opinions the same as men, and she's right."

Grace looked worried. "I don't know if I'm that clever, and I'm not interested in the news. Pa says women are better at looking after the home and raising a family, so I don't need to bother my head."

Lily gave her friend a gentle push. "But you're the one who wants to go to America, that's brave, and you want the freedom to do that."

"That's travel Lily, it's exciting, but it isn't politics. You don't need to be clever to have adventures."

There was no time for any more discussion. It was time to get back to work. Lily thought about what Grace had said as she stitched. Why did Grace feel that way about herself? She thought her friend was selling herself short.

Although strict, Lily realised her parents had always supported her in believing in herself. Ma looked after their home now, but she had followed her ambition before she married Pa. He had never suggested they were less than equal to him in intelligence. They often read the paper together and talked about events. *No man would ever tell her what to think,* she thought firmly.

On the tram home, Lily asked if Aiden had ever been to the meetings in Cosham.

"Sometimes. I go when Ma is speaking or needs help folding leaflets. Some of the speakers are interesting. Ma lets me play the piano for their song at the end, and sometimes the ladies put on a short entertainment." He shrugged. "My passport to everywhere. I'm a good accompanist."

There was a note of self-deprecation that made Lily feel indignant. "If people only appreciate you for your playing, they miss out on all your kindness and what a good friend you are." She narrowed her eyes. "They're plain stupid!"

He laughed. "My goodness, you're fierce this afternoon, Lily, but thank you."

His eyes rested on her with an expression she couldn't explain, which made her pulse race. She looked away, embarrassed.

"I'm going to ask if I can go to listen next week."

Aiden grinned. "Ma would like that. She believes all grown-ups should have the vote, regardless of how much property they own or what they do for a living, especially women."

Over supper that evening, Lily raised the subject of the meeting with her parents and watched anxiously for their reaction. "I want to support Grace because she's nervous, and I'd like to hear what they say."

Pa leaned back in his chair and rubbed a thoughtful hand up and down his braces. Ma pursed her lips and spoke first. "I don't know, Lily, you have to work the next day, and you're already going to rehearsals. You'll get overtired."

"Mrs Donnelly says we'll be home just after nine o'clock, and it's just this once. I think I should be informed about the Votes for Women campaign."

Ma raised her eyebrows. "If I know anything about meetings and committees, if they see you're keen, you'll have a job before the end of the evening. Then you'll be there every spare minute."

Pa laughed. "Now then, Maggie, no need to take on because you fell afoul of the church fete committee."

Maggie scowled. "Two hundred scones and never so much as a thank you."

He laughed again and turned to Lily. "Your mother has never forgiven them."

She smiled, hoping they weren't heading off the subject. "What do you think, Pa?"

"They should at least have thanked your ma. They were good scones too. Made a fortune on the teas that afternoon!"

He looked at Lily with a deadpan face, and she squealed in irritation. "About my meeting Pa."

He burst out laughing and drew his handkerchief from his pocket to wipe away tears of mirth. "No one rises to a fly as quickly as you, Lily. I'm surprised you're interested at your age, but it doesn't hurt anyone to understand what's happening in the country. If Ma has no other objections."

Ma pinched her lips into a thin line. "I'll have a word with Mary Donnelly tomorrow to check it's suitable and make sure she is happy to keep an eye on you. I'm not promising."

Lily knew better than to say anything more and instead explained Miss Laidlaw's ideas for her costume to her parents.

"It's a pity I'm not still at the house. There were trunks of old curtains and linens stowed in the attics there. We'll walk up to Granny tomorrow; she has all sorts stashed away, and she asked after you on Sunday when you were skating."

Lily nodded.

"Show me the dress again. If you light an extra lamp, I'll help you unpick."

Chapter 6

When she returned from work the next day, Ma said, "Mary says it's your future, so better you go into it prepared to take up the responsibility. I can see there's something in that. The world is changing at such a pace."

Lily looked excited as her ma continued, "I'm not too worried about you going. Mary says it will be interesting to hear what someone like Nora O'Shea says. She's not too radical and involved with the good of the whole community. She recently became a Parish Councillor, apparently."

"Thank you, Ma. I'm sure Mrs Donnelly will take good care of me."

Ma wiped her hands briskly on a tea towel. "She's a nice lady and had some sensible things to say about not thwarting teenagers prone to think themselves martyrs and sulk."

"Ma! I do not sulk."

"It won't do for you to be getting sweet on Aiden, and I wonder if I should let you two mix so much."

Judging it to be time to escape before Ma changed her mind, Lily said, "There's time for me to visit Granny before supper to ask about voiles."

Her ma snorted. "Changing the subject, Miss?" But she nodded, and Lily grabbed her coat quickly and fled up the road.

Granny welcomed her in and made tea.

"So, what brings you along, Lily? We don't see as much of you now that you're working."

Lily sighed, feeling guilty. "I know, Granny, the weeks fly by."

"Still, we're happy to see you getting on, aren't we, Grampa?"

She looked at Grampa, who nodded sagely with his pipe tucked into his mouth. Sitting like that, he looked remarkably like an older version of Pa.

"Come and have supper with us one evening if your ma can spare you."

Lily nodded. "I will, Granny. That would be nice. Can you make your liver cake? Ma never makes it."

Granny laughed and clapped. "Bless you. You used to love that when you were a little girl. Let me know when you're coming, and I'll do my best."

Taking a deep breath, Lily got to the reason for her visit. "Granny, I'm in the community concert after Christmas and need some voiles to cut up for my costume. Do you have any old ones?"

Granny narrowed her eyes, making the fine lines into deep creases. "Voiles." She shook her head. "I don't think so, Lily. Sorry. What about the jumble sale?"

Lily nodded. "Don't worry, Granny. It was just a thought. Ma and I can look at the sale."

Lily finished her tea and kissed her grandparents goodbye, smiling as Gramps pressed a cough candy twist into her hand from his pocket. She dashed home, eager not to be late for the meeting.

Having eaten her supper, Lily was putting on her coat and hat to meet Aiden and his mother for the bus ride to Cosham.

Maggie fussed around her daughter, lifting her coat lapels to set the shoulders straight. "Do not agree to do anything outside the meeting, Lily. You have enough on with work and the concert." She tapped the barometer in an absent-minded way. The needle pointed to 'wet', and she huffed in annoyance and tapped it again as if that would make a difference.

It had indeed been raining all day, and it gave small comfort for tomorrow that the needle wasn't moving.

Lily took the clothes brush from her mother's hand and said, "Ma, stop fretting. I'm only going to listen." She felt excited and nervous about going to a grown-up event alone. Her mother's reluctance made her impatient. *What's the worst that can happen? The biscuits may be soft!* She thought of church meetings but said, "Mrs Donnelly will be there, and I'll meet Grace."

Maggie sniffed. "Whatever is said, and I don't doubt there will be a lot of enthusiastic talk. Remember, taking stock and making up your own mind is always best. There are different opinions in any argument."

Lily looked at her mother, exasperation giving way to fondness as she saw the tension in her upright posture and pinched lips. She recognised the concern and love behind the worry. "You're making me nervous, Ma." She brushed her mother's cheek with a kiss and smelt the familiar faint scent of lavender water Maggie made.

Mrs O'Shea, a petite lady with flaming red hair and a warm smile, answered the door to the large house on Havant Road. She greeted Mary and Aiden with familiar ease and welcomed Lily, who felt shy under the woman's appraising stare.

The hallway was startlingly bright. Lily realised it must be lit by the new electric lights. She noticed no soot above the glass shades, and the warm, drowsy smell of gas lights was missing.

A brass umbrella stand stood inside the front door, already full of droplet-covered brollies, at least fifteen. Lily added the umbrella her mother had given her to the number. As she handed her coat to a waiting maid, Lily noticed dark splashes along the hem and a smell of wet wool.

She followed Aiden and his mother, who were familiar with the layout, taking in her surroundings. The hall ceiling was high, with ornate plasterwork. Smooth black and white chequered tiles covered the floor. Tall wooden plant stands with trailing ferns flanked the wood-panelled walls and softened the stark contrast on the floor. They headed towards open double doors on the left. A vast mirror along the hall reflected the people gathered in the room that would house the meeting.

Mrs O'Shea's was the fanciest house Lily had ever visited, and her mouth felt dry as she followed Mrs Donnelly. As they entered the meeting, Lily was surprised to see a handful of men beside Aiden. She had only expected women present. Chairs were arranged in the beautiful sitting room, but everyone was still standing, and a hum of conversation filled the room.

Lily immediately saw Grace through the gathering, looking as shy as she felt. Grace stood beside a fashionably dressed lady, presumably George Dent's mother. Mrs Dent appeared youthful but must have been close to her ma's age as she had six boys. On the other hand, Lily guessed that she and Grace were the youngest women in the room. Some of the other ladies were well dressed, but there were ordinary-looking women too, and the atmosphere was friendly judging from the nods and smiles they received.

Aiden excused himself and moved to where most men were gathered. Mrs Donnelly worked through the crowd towards Mrs Dent, who looked glossy as a freshly opened conker. Mary Donnelly seemed drab in comparison, but Lily felt the quality of her quiet grace as the two women exchanged greetings.

"Miss Matthews, how lovely to meet you. I hear you, young ladies, work together." Mrs Dent's voice did not have the musicality of Mrs Donnelly's, but she twinkled and seemed genuinely pleased to meet Lily.

Lily glanced reassuringly at her friend. "We're both interested to hear the speaker this evening, Mrs Dent."

Mrs Dent whispered conspiratorially, "The cake is usually delicious too! It is a real treat to have your company this evening." She looked from Lily to Grace. "I hope this is the first of many meetings. We need young ladies like you."

Mrs O'Shea called the meeting to order, and Mrs Dent shepherded the girls to chairs while Mrs Donnelly took her place at the piano. An opening prayer was read, and they sang a hymn. Lily glanced around for Aiden, sitting at the back of the room, and he gave a brief wave.

Nora O'Shea introduced both girls to the room and welcomed them. Lily couldn't help glancing back at Aiden, whose smiling eyes crinkled back. Lily was glad he was there; he seemed relaxed here, which gave her confidence.

Mrs O'Shea introduced the speaker for the evening, a tall, gaunt lady called Mrs Merritt, who ran a branch of the NUWSS in Southampton. When she spoke, it was with intensity, and Lily found herself glued to Mrs Merritt's words.

Equality of opportunity and votes for all adults suddenly seemed obvious necessities. Who could disagree? Lily wondered why there was any difficulty with these issues at all.

In answer to a question from the floor about political support, Mrs Merritt replied, "We have no difficulty obtaining signatures to launch our ideas. However, the Liberals with Asquith will not support us currently. They are too afraid our members will vote conservative if we gain the vote."

A murmur of assent rippled around the room. Mrs Merritt continued, "The Labour Party is interested in votes for working men in the unions, and the Irish Parliamentary Party want home rule as their priority."

She laughed with a mirthless sound. "I never thought I would say this, but Ladies, our best hope to gain women's suffrage is the Conservatives. Sadly, they are conservative with a small c! How often have we had enough support for a private member's bill and seen it set aside for 'more important issues?' We must redouble our efforts and demand the vote until the politicians give it."

There was a cheer from the room. "Demand the vote until politicians give it." Everyone stood to applaud the rallying call.

Mrs O'Shea gave a vote of thanks. "Ladies and Gentlemen, we must never tire in our aim. With that in mind, I urge you all to stay to help the working parties before we serve the tea. As always, I have prepared letters and leaflets."

Lily got the sense of hidden force in this efficient, persuasive woman. "Also, I need volunteers to speak to other ladies' groups. I have a list of invitations." Hands went up, and she nodded approvingly before finishing, "Our message is being heard all over the country, and we must continue the fight until we achieve our goals."

Nora O'Shea paused, and Lily saw her look around at the eager faces in front of her. "After tea, I have exciting news for everyone regarding next week's meeting, so please stay."

Members pushed the chairs back, and maids appeared with several folding tables. Mrs Dent settled the girls at a table with two other young ladies and gave them a large pile of leaflets, a box of envelopes and a list of addresses. "I have a committee meeting next door, but I'll be back shortly."

"Aiden, Dear, favour us with some music while we work," called one of the ladies from across the room.

As he began to play, one of the young ladies with Lily and Grace said, "He's handsome, isn't he?" with a dreamy look.

The other, Jane, clicked her tongue in annoyance. "Rose! We're here to work for the cause, not make sheep's eyes at young men." Then addressing Grace and Lily said, "Please excuse my sister."

Lily narrowed her eyes at Rose. It was none of her business how handsome Aiden was.

Grace stared at both sisters and Lily, torn between annoyance at Rose's forward remark about Aiden and surprise at Jane's outburst, she did not know what to say. Fortunately, as Rose had dropped her head and flushed beetroot red, no remark was needed.

Jane continued to speak. "Next month, on the nineteenth of November, there will be a protest march in London. Hundreds of us from the NUWSS and our sisters from the WSPU will march on parliament. The Pankhursts will be there, and Princess Duleep Singh." Her eyes had a worrying fervour as she continued, "You should come. It's better than stuffing leaflets in envelopes." She folded one with vehemence, then gasped and sucked her finger as the treacherous page sliced a narrow paper cut from which a bead of blood welled.

Lily whispered to Grace, "Let's hope that isn't an omen."

Grace's eyes were round as saucers until she realised Lily was joking, and she gave an uncertain giggle. "Jane's a bit frightening," she whispered back.

Lily remembering her mother's advice, wasn't sure she warmed to Jane.

After an hour's work, during which some of the ladies sang along to Aiden's playing, Mrs O'Shea clapped, announcing tea was served in the hall. Mrs Donnelly, who had worked at another table, re-joined the girls. Mrs Dent reappeared from her committee meeting and swept Grace away to meet some of her friends. Aiden tapped Lily on the shoulder. "Can I get your tea, Lily, Ma?"

"Thank you, Aiden, that's kind of you. I enjoyed your playing. You make me proud." Mary Donnelly squeezed his arm lightly, and a warm, loving look passed between them, mother to son. More than that, Lily realised, they had a mutual understanding due to their shared love of music. Seeing it warmed Lily's heart. She felt proud of Aiden too.

They sat together at the table where she and Grace had stuffed leaflets. As they sipped tea and enjoyed the rich, crumbly ginger cake, Mrs O'Shea called for their attention again.

"Ladies and Gentlemen, before the meeting closes, it is my great honour to announce our speaker at next week's meeting. One of our sisters from the Women's Social and Political Union and renowned music hall singer, Miss Kitty Marion. She will speak to us about her work with the WSPU and her career on the stage."

There was an audible gasp and a sudden buzz of chatter. Once again, Nora continued calling for order, "She is a great champion of women's rights. We hope to prevail upon her to sing a song for us before her appearances on stage in Portsmouth, and I am sure she will take questions from the floor."

Lily whipped around to cast Aiden an indignant look, and he grinned broadly. "I can't believe you kept this a secret from me," she hissed.

"I wanted it to be a surprise. I was going to invite you as a treat, but when you said you'd be here tonight, I knew you'd find out anyway."

Her indignation forgotten, she said, "Is your song for next week? Are you going to ask her to sing it?"

He looked from her to his mother. "I wouldn't dare ask Miss Marion outright, but if I can play the melody or perform it for her as part of the evening, this may be a break for me. It's nearly finished. Will you come and try it?"

"It's a beautiful melody and will suit your voice Lily, but don't get your hopes up too much. There may not be time for music, and Miss Marion may not notice the song either," said Mary Donnelly.

Aiden looked downcast, then countered, "You know what Pa says. There is no harm in seizing the day."

She laughed. "No, indeed."

On the train home, the talk was about Kitty Marion's impending visit. Lily bubbled over with excitement as she talked about it with Ma and Pa when she arrived home.

"It would be no bad thing if young Aiden got the chance to go to London. Providing you don't get any ideas, Lily."

Lily blushed, knowing her parents would disapprove of her dreams.

As she undressed for bed, the serious political considerations that had swayed her earlier became eclipsed. Lily had stars in her eyes as she imagined Aiden writing songs for the London stage and her fitting costumes for the famous Miss Marion.

Chapter 7

L ily woke with a bubble of excitement inside her. Miss Laidlaw said the pattern for her costume would be ready today. After work, she would sing Aiden's new song and hopefully perform it in front of Kitty Marion next week.

Last night at the meeting, she was treated like a person in her own right, entitled to hold opinions. Her world seemed to have expanded overnight, and her heart raced at the prospect.

She jumped out of bed, refusing to let the steady drip of rain outside or the cold floor underfoot dampen her spirits. She pulled on her robe and ran barefoot downstairs to get a jug of hot water. She skidded on a heap of laundry as she burst into the kitchen.

"Lily! Be careful. You'll dirty my washing even more. Come in now you're here. Shut the door. Why don't you wash in the kitchen today? It's nice and warm because the copper is heating. I'll leave you in peace for a few minutes."

"Thanks, Ma." Lily hesitated, sensing her mother's uncertain mood. In contrast, her joy bubbled over. She caught her mother up and whisked her round in a polka step to place herself by the sink and her Ma facing the door.

"Lily Matthews, you're a giddy goat, calm down," said Maggie.

"Are you alright, Ma?"

"I'm worried about that meeting, Lily. I want you to be happy, finish your apprenticeship, and eventually meet a nice young man to marry. Music hall stars, friends heading for America, and suffragists seem like distractions you could do without. I won't deny that it's playing on my mind."

Lily looked at her mother. "It was a meeting, Ma, and I'm not planning to go to America, don't worry so much." She didn't add a certain blue-eyed boy from next door was fast becoming the man she wanted to marry.

Adding an umbrella to her usual work attire, Lily left the house, ducking under the drips from the porch roof, which pattered harmlessly onto her umbrella. She noticed the nets in Mrs Donnelly's front window twitch and smirked. She felt sure Aiden was watching for her.

Aiden confirmed her suspicion when his front door banged immediately. He called after her, his steps splashing through the water on the pavement as he caught up.

"Hey, wait, Lily, I finished it last night, the song for Kitty Marion."

"Finished? That's wonderful, Aiden."

"We can try it out tonight if you like."

She chattered on about the meeting until he laughed. "Lily, it was just a meeting."

"It was exhilarating, though, so many ideas. Didn't you feel it? Jane said she is going to London to protest in November, fancy that."

He frowned. "She needs to be careful. Ma says the police are none too gentle with the protesters. She could end up in prison. It isn't a silly game, Lily."

She wasn't exactly sure what he meant but replied, chin in the air. "I know. I'm not a child, Aiden. I'll keep saving because I want to go to London to work, then I can protest too."

Aiden rolled his eyes.

"If Miss Marion likes your song, she may offer you a job in London with her. There may be one for me too."

"Would you miss me if I went to London?"

Raindrops balanced on his hair and upturned collar. As Lily looked at him, she swallowed hard and blinked. His face was as familiar as her own. Aiden had always been there, and she couldn't imagine life without him.

"I would. You know I would."

"We'll both manage to go somehow. Even if I have to go first."

In all her dreams, they had been in London together. For the first time, she realised he might go to London without her.

Lily was quiet on the tram ride to work, and for once, Aiden didn't seem to notice. She let him enthuse about the meeting next week while her mood plummeted. Of course, Lily wanted to meet Kitty Marion and hoped Aiden's song was a success, but as he chatted, there was a look of elsewhere in his expression Lily had never seen before, which made her shiver.

Grace lay in wait for her outside the workroom, impatiently fidgeting as Lily approached. "What did you think of George's ma last night? Do you think she liked me?"

"Why ever wouldn't she like you, you goose? I thought she was friendly to both of us. She acted as if we were grown-ups, not like someone's mother at all."

"I thought she might think George should be with someone whose family has money. But George said his ma and pa aren't like that. She's beautiful, don't you think?"

Lily thought about George's mother; she was more handsome with a strong face. Mrs Dent certainly had a stylish air and a friendly smile, sometimes making people appear pretty despite their features. Grace was waiting for an answer with a starstruck expression. "Very," Lily said promptly, murdering her previous thoughts.

Grace continued, "George says if we go to America, his parents are more concerned we make a good team and are prepared to work hard."

Lily noted that 'George says' was creeping into Grace's conversation more often. She hoped Grace wouldn't get lost and become a shadow of George's ambitions. Surely walking out with someone didn't mean you had to lose yourself entirely.

Miss Laidlaw was already in the workroom and handed Lily a paper bag to put with her things. The promised tissue paper pattern was inside by the rustle as she took it. Lily stuttered her thanks. Miss Laidlaw inclined her head. "We'll talk about the bustle to go with the skirt in your lunch break. Be careful when you're ready to cut the skirt that you have double-checked your pattern placement, Lily. I have marked the pattern with arrows, so you cut into the grain of the fabric. It would be a sin to waste the silk."

The morning's excitement resurfaced as she thought about how she would look in her costume. "Yes, Miss, I will. My ma will help."

"You may like to use my sewing machine for the main seams, Lily. It would save you time. I would happily show you how to use it one weekend."

Lily flushed red. Miss Laidlaw must have her own sewing machine at home. "Thank you, Miss, if it would be no trouble." Lily had seen the treadle machines in the workshop and how quickly and evenly they joined long seams, but she had never used one. Mrs Winchett insisted on handsewn sleeves, hems, and cuffs and all the apprentices were required to sew by hand, but the machines made straight work faster.

Grace winked at her as they sat down at the table. "Teacher's pet," she whispered, nudging Lily.

Lily frowned. So *what?* she thought.

Lily worked hard all day. She didn't want to let him down. Aiden had asked her to try to finish on time so they could practise his song before rehearsals.

She wished Grace a hurried goodbye and half-ran, half-walked to the tram stop. She saw Aiden running from the other direction and a tram waiting to leave as she approached. They both ran the last twenty yards and jumped on board as the tram pulled away, then collapsed into one of the double seats laughing and out of breath. Lily patted her hat and replaced a loose hat pin. "Ma would tell me off for being a hoyden," she gasped, catching her breath.

Aiden paused, then shook his head. "You look lovely, Lily, flushed and breathless."

Lily gasped at the unexpected compliment. She held Aiden's gaze momentarily, then looked away, feeling unaccountably shy.

Mary Donnelly, pleased to see Lily, offered her and Aiden some tea and a slice of bread and butter before they began. Tempted to refuse because she was impatient to hear Aiden's song, hunger won the day. Mrs Donnelly served sweet tea in sturdy mugs, and as Lily bit into the thickly sliced, grey bread, she chatted to Mary about her and Aiden's costumes.

They moved to the chilly front room to practise, and Mary wrapped a thick woollen shawl around Lily's shoulders. Lily knew better than to refuse its tufted warmth.

Aiden's song was hand-written on cream manuscript paper, the tiny black notes with their sharp flags above flying neatly between the fine staves. The lyrics beneath were written in Aiden's cramped, angular handwriting, so different from her rounded copperplate.

"I'll play it through first, and then we can take it phrase by phrase." Aiden spread the sheets across the piano's music stand and twisted the small catches to hold them in place.

Mary lit the candles in the bracketed sconces and brought an extra lamp. The circle of light illuminated the keyboard and the music. The rest of the room had a faint glow from the street's gas lamps.

Lily watched, enchanted, as Aiden's hands floated across the keys, producing a rounded tone from the piano. He concentrated on the music, a slight frown between his brows, while his head and body swayed with the melody. Lily had expected something upbeat, but Aiden played her a poignant ballad in waltz time, sweet and tender.

As he finished the playthrough, he looked at her, half shy, half expectant. "Well? What do you think?"

"It's beautiful. Kitty Marion would be a fool not to sing it."

His face lit up. "You'd better sing it first, Lily."

"It would be my pleasure." Lily looked at the hand-written lyrics and raised her eyebrows. "Can you read the words through, Aiden? Your writing isn't as beautiful as your playing. You'd better get me to scribe a copy for Miss Marion."

He grinned sheepishly and began to sing the first verse.

"When love songs start, they fill my heart with tender memories of you.

Your hand in mine, your eyes that shine, with laughter and love so true.

Tell me you'll love me forever, my dear,

This romance will always be new.

Our lives will be forever entwined the day I say I'll marry you."

Lily swayed a waltz step on the spot as he sang and said, "Aiden, how romantic. I can hear girls humming this and hoping their beaus will be asking for their hand."

He blushed a deeper shade of red. "If it's too soppy, you would say, wouldn't you?"

"Don't change a word. It's perfect."

Suddenly he was all business. "So, if I play the introduction, you'll come in as I nod. Let's run through the first verse."

Lily spent the next hour singing and stopping to achieve the precise tone Aiden wanted from her voice. Eventually, she held up her hands. "Aiden, I won't have any voice left for tonight, and I need to go for my tea, or Ma will be banging on the door. Will you knock for me later to walk to rehearsal?"

"I will. I'm sorry, I didn't realise how long you'd been singing, Lily. This song is so important to me."

Her heart sank as that elsewhere look came back, but she said, "Of course it is. I don't mind you being a perfect beast about my singing."

"Lily! That's not true." Aiden looked horrified.

"A brute! 'Lily, you're sharp on the top D'; 'Lily, slow down through that phrase'; 'Lily, more light and shade!' You will be well-served if I refuse to sing it at the meeting next week."

Lily laughed as she turned to collect her coat and go. Aiden took her hand. "I can't think of anyone I'd rather have sing it."

And there it was, a tug of something powerful between them she couldn't identify, and she looked away, confused. "Except Kitty Marion." She laughed shakily.

He looked confused and laughed at himself. "Maybe except her."

That evening, the rehearsal for the community concert fizzed with anticipation of the performance creeping ever closer. All the performers were present, some with parents, so the hall was full. As the bodies in the room heated the air, and excited chatter rose and fell between the acts, the black windows where the night pressed in clouded over with condensation. Dust motes rose from the green stage curtains as they practised opening and closing them between numbers. They would need to be taken down and beaten outside, Lily thought. Otherwise, half the songs would be disturbed by sneezing.

It was a joy-filled evening until Lily's duet with Harry finished. As Lily and he began to descend the stage steps, she lost her footing. Harry steadied her by the waist and lifted her as if weightless. He swung her around and placed her safely on the floor. He then tipped an imaginary hat and, with his face brim-full of laughter, said, "I need to take better care of my partner." Then offered his arm to walk her back into the room.

Aiden, who saw Harry lift Lily, abruptly pushed back the piano stool, his face like thunder. It tipped, then fell with a resounding crash, music spilling from under the lid. Everyone turned to stare, and Lily, red to the roots of her hair, withdrew her arm from Harry's. For a suspended moment, she wondered what Aiden would do. He turned away. Fortunately, the noise of the stool falling, and the staring faces stopped him. The vicar rushed over, putting himself between Aiden and Harry. He placed a hand on Aiden's shoulder, saying, "Goodness me, careful old lad, let's collect this music. Are you alright?"

Harry looked amused and sauntered past the piano, grinning. Lily went to help Aiden, who muttered, "You should tell him to keep his hands off you."

Lily looked at him in amazement. "Whatever has got into you? He was helping me."

Aiden gave her an angry look. "It looked like more than that from here."

"Well, it wasn't anything until you made a scene."

"Have it your way but watch out for him. He overstepped the mark."

The vicar's wife interrupted them, calling Lily away to help serve the teas.

By home time, Aiden had calmed down, and Lily decided to avoid the subject of Harry. She tried to keep up a flow of chatter as they walked home, aware Aiden's replies seemed forced.

Angered by his monosyllabic answers when she was trying so hard, she said, "Aiden, are you still sulking about Harry?"

He spun to look at her and glared. "I'm not sulking. I'm angry with him for being so forward. You need to be careful Harry doesn't get over-familiar."

She put her hands on her hips and said, "He's a friend, Aiden. I see him at rehearsals. He saved me from falling. I don't think you're being fair. Why are you acting like this?"

Aiden ran his hand through his hair. "You don't understand, Lily."

In a gentler tone, she said, "Explain then, Aiden, because I don't."

Before they turned the corner into Eastfield Road and in sight of Edward Matthews, Aiden drew Lily into the shadows of a front garden rowan tree.

He seized both her hands and looked at her. His words tumbled out, "Lily, if I get the chance to go away, I want to ask your pa if we can walk out officially. Then we can plan to be together, and nobody will bother you anymore. I'm in love with you. I think I always have been."

The visceral tug Lily had felt earlier was back. Aiden stepped in close to her, as close as when they had been skating. Lily's heart pounded as his arm circled her waist, and he leaned forwards to kiss her.

She knew she should be shocked, but being in the circle of his arms felt so right. She felt light and almost as if she might float away if he didn't continue to hold her.

His arm tightened, and he whispered, "Can I, Lily Matthews? Can I speak to your pa?"

Lily nodded against his cheek and said quietly, "Yes." This was not sudden. Aiden had always been there for her, and these new, powerful feelings she had been having must mean she loved him too.

As Lily imagined the conversation with Pa, she pulled away, sudden worry cascading through her as she thought of him waiting on the porch for them. He still thought she was a little girl.

"Not tonight. Promise you won't ask tonight. Ma and Pa will say I'm too young unless there's a good reason like you going away." She didn't mention Ma's views on Aiden being Catholic.

"Not tonight, but we'll find a way whether I go or not. They must understand we want to be together, and they can't stop us."

Lily nodded but felt puzzled. Why would he say that? Ma and Pa may say she was too young, but in the end, she didn't think they would stop them from being together. They liked Aiden. She touched his arm. "Aiden, we have to go. Pa will walk me to rehearsal himself if we're late."

They emerged from the shadows holding a new secret between them.

Chapter 8

Aiden nodded to Lily's pa and said goodnight to him. Lily was sure that Aiden's kiss and their secret promise were written across her face for all to see. Her heart was still pounding, and she had a cloud of butterflies flapping and tumbling in her stomach.

Ma called from the kitchen, "Is that you, Lily?"

"Running upstairs, Ma, be down in a minute." Lily closed her bedroom door and lent against it, her hands on her cheeks. She felt her world had tilted, and she was still off-balance.

"Everything alright?" Ma called up.

Lily smoothed her skirt, took a deep breath, and re-emerged. "Fine, Ma, I needed a clean hanky."

She heard the tut from downstairs. "I hope you're not coming down with a cold after all that gadding about in the rain last night."

In the kitchen, Ma gave her an appraising glance. "You certainly look feverish, my girl. Either you're ill, or you're over-excited." She raised her eyebrows expectantly, and Lily felt a pang of remorse as she replied with half the truth. "I feel fine. You're right. Rehearsal was exciting, Ma. The songs are beginning to sound wonderful, and everything is coming together. I have the pattern for my costume, and I didn't tell you, but Miss Laidlaw has a sewing machine at home I can use for the long seams."

Ma was thrown off the scent and said, "How thoughtful of her, Lily. You must think of a small thank-you gift. A card with the flowers we pressed in the Summer, or you could embroider a handkerchief."

Encouraging her mother away from her previous scrutiny, Lily said, "What about some of your lavender water, Ma? It makes everything smell so fresh."

Her mother shrugged away the compliment as she was wont to do. "I'm sure Miss Laidlaw would rather see something you have made yourself, but lavender water with a handkerchief would be acceptable." As Pa entered the kitchen, rubbing his hands and warming them on the range, she continued, "I imagine your father is more interested in when you'll be making his tea, Lily, if you would be kind enough to warm the pot."

Pa made a mock stern face. "You and Aiden were nearly late tonight, Miss. My hands got cold waiting. I was about to walk up to find you."

Lily nearly dropped the teapot. "We came straight back after rehearsal, Pa." Imagine if Pa had caught them kissing. She was horrified at the idea and swallowed hard.

His face softened, and he relented. "No need to look so worried, Puss. I was teasing. Your ma says young Aiden has written a song for some London singer. Is that right?"

Glad to change the subject, Lily said, "It's for Kitty Marion. I sang it with him after work. It's beautiful, Pa, romantic. She'll be at next week's meeting."

Lily handed him his tea and poured a cup for her ma.

"Be prepared to walk to rehearsals with your old pa next week, then Lily. Aiden's head will be full of Miss Marion. He'll fall in love with her and be off to London. You mark my words. You know what these young lads are."

Looking sharply at her husband, Ma said, "There is no need to make insensitive remarks, Edward. Aiden's a talented boy. If, through Miss Marion, he got a chance for advancement, it would be an excellent thing."

Lily's elated mood plummeted, and her shoulders sagged. Aiden said he loved her, and she was sure he meant it, but he hadn't met Miss Marion yet.

"Just a bit of fun, m'Dear," Pa muttered.

Lily pushed her tea away. "Do you mind if I head for bed, Ma? I am rather tired."

As she began to walk upstairs, Lily overheard her mother's voice. "What on earth were you thinking, Edward, nothing more designed to make the girl fancy herself in love with Aiden than telling her he'll fall for someone else."

Her father sounded irritable. "I thought you wanted him to go to London. I can't keep up with all this."

She heard her mother sigh. "I do, but Mary Donnelly was right. The worst thing we can do is make Lily feel she's a martyr."

"Stop fretting, Maggie. Lily wasn't upset; she was excited about his song and the concert, no thoughts of anything else in her head, I'll wager."

Her father's chair scraped, and for fear of being caught eavesdropping, Lily scampered up the stairs and into her room, closing the door quietly.

They thought she was still a child and wanted to keep her and Aiden from falling in love. It was too late, she already loved him, and he loved her.

Lily pulled off her clothes and shrugged into her night dress, shivering against the cool cotton. She removed the stone hot water bottle from the bed and set it aside. She manoeuvred her feet onto the warm spot where the bottle had been and tried to ignore the contrast with the still cold sheets around it. As Lily snuggled under the covers, the weight of the wool blankets and eiderdown felt comforting.

Although her body was still, her mind raced on. Memories of the day flashed through her mind: Aiden laughing on the tram, playing the piano with a frown as he concentrated, all so familiar. She had seen every expression a hundred times before. Then Aiden, with anger etched on his face, protective and furious with Harry. So different from the Aiden holding her close, in the shadows, someone new and intense. She barely recognised him. Her heart began to pound as she remembered the visceral pull of his closeness. The memory made her restless and confused, but she knew she wanted him to hold and kiss her again.

Thoughts chased across her mind like leaves on a windy day. She imagined herself in a white gown on a sunny Spring day, with cherry blossoms floating down. Aiden's face as Pa placed her hand in his at the altar of St Pat's Church. Ma would dab her eyes, and Mr and Mrs Donnelly would look proud. After the wedding, she would board a train with Aiden in smart travelling clothes for their honeymoon. Their parents would wave fondly at the station as the steam billowed and the train drew out. Lily hugged her knees. She and Aiden would return to their house or maybe a flat in London, close to a theatre.

Pa didn't know she and Aiden were in love, but what if he were right? Lily opened her eyes in the darkness. Kitty Marion was undoubtedly sophisticated and elegant. Aiden had written a song for her to sing. What if she was a siren? Maybe once Aiden and Miss Marion had met, he'd change his mind about loving the girl next door.

Lily imagined having to wave Aiden goodbye as he set off for London alone. A tear pooled in the corner of her eye and trickled down her face until she brushed it away. She would not cry. Instead, she balled her hands fiercely until the nails dug into her palms and thought, *not if I can help it. Wait until Aiden sees me in my costume for the show. That will take his breath away.* She decided to ask Miss Laidlaw to help her at the weekend.

Anyway, she consoled herself. Miss Marion was bound to have a wealthy London beau who showered expensive gifts on her.

She couldn't wait to ask Grace's advice tomorrow. A year older and already walking out with George, her friend had more experience with men.

Lily's imaginings left her heavy-eyed and tired when she woke.

"I think you need a few quiet days, Miss," Ma said as Lily entered the kitchen. "All this racketing around is wearing you out."

Lily looked alarmed. She fully intended to be busy on her costume over the weekend. "I'm fine, Ma, honestly. I'll go to bed early tonight."

Ma compressed her lips and studied her daughter. "Well, see you do, and don't make arrangements to go out anywhere."

Fleeting images of an outing with Aiden this weekend and, more pressing, the visit to Miss Laidlaw to get her costume stitched flashed through her mind. She knew better than to argue now, though. "Yes, Ma. I would like to sing through Aiden's song with him some time, so we're ready for next week's meeting."

"Not tonight, Lily. I want you home quiet before you wear yourself to a fiddle string." Ma turned away, muttering, "Suffragists and concerts, they'll be the death of both of us. I shouldn't wonder." She sniffed. "In alt one minute and subdued the next. I could have sworn you were on the edge of tears as you ran away to bed early. It's not like you."

Lily left for work on time, and as usual, Aiden ran to meet her, eyes softening on seeing her. "You look tired, Lily. Were you awake thinking too? I was. I couldn't sleep for excitement."

Lily cast him a glance and looked down. "Were you thinking about the song or us? Because, if you've changed your mind, Aiden, if you said more than you meant to because you were angry, it's alright."

He looked affronted. "Changed my mind, Lily? No! Whatever do you take me for? Have you changed yours?"

Lily felt her heart lift and shook her head. "No."

She tried not to mind when most of the conversation on the tram was about Miss Marion. However, he said, "Of course, she may not like the song, Lily. Pa says I mustn't pin my hopes on it too much, and he's right. But Ma thinks my song is good and wouldn't encourage me if she didn't think it."

"It is a beautiful song. I hope something comes of this. It would be wonderful if your song were published. Even if Miss Marion doesn't sing it, you could send it to some music publishers."

"It would be better if it had her backing."

Lily agreed and hoped it wouldn't be too much of a blow next week if the song wasn't successful or Miss Marion ignored them. She was worried the community concert prize might seem a let-down after setting his hopes high. They had been excited about the concert before. A small part of her wished so much hadn't happened this week.

Grace was nearly late, so Lily barely had time to greet her before Mrs Winchett was in the workroom, allotting the work for the day. She whispered to her friend, "I need to talk to you at lunchtime." Before a frown from Miss Laidlaw made her drop her head to her work.

The bell sounded for the end of the morning, and Grace dragged Lily away. "What's happened? I'm nearly bursting my stays."

About to answer, Lily was stopped by Miss Laidlaw's calm voice. "Miss Matthews, before you go."

"Yes, Miss Laidlaw."

She handed Lily what looked like an apron-shaped cushion attached to a belt. "I thought about the line of the skirt for your costume, and you could wear this under it to accentuate the hip line at the back. Remember to taper the hem of the skirt so it is longer at the back when you cut to take account of the shaping. When you reverse the skirt, your silhouette will be different on stage if you remove the padding, which should solve the problem."

"Thank you, Miss Laidlaw," Lily stammered, "I will be cutting the pattern this evening, and I wondered if it is still convenient for me to use your machine for the seams?"

"If you would like to join me at two o'clock this Sunday, I hope we can do all the machine sewing in one afternoon. Here is my address." She handed over a note. "Now do go and put Miss Johnson out of her misery. She is all agog to hear what you must tell her."

Lily blushed red to the roots of her hair. "Yes, Miss, thank you." She hurried to the coat rack, stored the bustle pad on her peg and shrugged into her coat.

"Well, whatever has happened?" Grace looked round-eyed with excitement in the bright winter sunshine.

"It's Aiden. Last night, he got annoyed at rehearsals because Harry lifted me down the steps off stage, but then Aiden kissed me and asked if we could walk out together on the way home."

"Lily Matthews! I knew it; Aiden's been secretly sweet on you forever. He's a dark horse, seems so quiet, then goes and takes liberties." She put a hand to her heart in a dramatic way. "I'm shocked, but it's so romantic; Was it nice?"

Lily blushed again, nodded, then said thoughtfully, "Aiden seems quiet if you don't know him well, but when you talk to him properly, he's intense about serious things like politics and hates any kind of injustice."

"Did him good to realise you weren't just the girl next door." She grinned. "Certainly intense about that Harry flirting with his girl," Grace added with a giggle. "For all he's high-minded, he was still jealous last night." She unwrapped her sandwiches and gestured to Lily to do the same, pointing at the time on the Guildhall clock.

As Grace bit into her sandwich and chewed, it was Lily's turn to look surprised. "Do you think so?"

"Of course! Why do you think he kissed you? When's he going to ask your pa?" She wiped a crumb off her coat lapel and looked at Lily.

"I told him not yet, so Ma and Pa know nothing about this. If Aiden gets the chance to go to London, if Miss Marion likes his song and can help him, he could ask them then. Only Pa said last night that when Aiden sees Miss Marion, he will fall for her and forget me. Just funning, of course, but do you think he might? Aiden does talk about her a lot." Lily twisted the greaseproof paper from her sandwich into a tight knot.

Grace popped the last crust of her sandwich in her mouth and chewed thoughtfully for a moment. "I don't think so, Lily. I think if you love someone, you do. Look at George. He could be walking out with anyone, but he isn't. He's walking out with me. Anyway, Miss Marion must be at least thirty, if not more. She's ancient."

Lily tugged at her lower lip. She hoped her friend was right and young men didn't fall for older women. After all, girls marry older men all the time.

"Come on, Lily, stop looking so worried, we'd better go, or the old dragon will be onto us. When George and I get married, it will be wonderful. I won't have to take orders from anyone."

Lily caught Grace's arm. "Oh, Grace, has he asked you already?"

"Not exactly, but we've been planning to go to America, so I know he will when we're ready. Imagine, you and I could have a double wedding. George makes my knees feel weak when he kisses me. Did you feel like that?"

Lily glanced behind. "Grace! Shhh, people will hear you."

"You're so sweet, Lily Matthews, still a baby. Bet you laid awake all night thinking about your beau." Lily scowled at her, and Grace laughed. "I knew it."

Chapter 9

True to her word, Ma refused Lily's request to rehearse with Aiden.

"Oh, Ma, please, we're singing in front of Miss Marion next week."

"It will do you good to have an evening off. You don't want Miss Marion to see you with that whey face, now do you? Come into the kitchen. I've got a treat for you."

Lily dragged behind her, unable to imagine anything that would replace rehearsing with Aiden.

However, Ma had been baking, so there was fresh cake from the oven with her tea to soften the blow. The kitchen was cosy compared to the Donnelly's front room, and Lily grudgingly admitted to herself she was tired. She still had to broach the question of going to Miss Laidlaw's on Sunday, so she decided to give in about the visit to Aiden without a fight.

Ma said she had been sorting donations for the church jumble sale that afternoon with Granny. "We found some heavy lace curtains that might make an overskirt for your costume. They are currently drying over the range on the pulley. They smelt musty, so I've washed them."

Lily hugged her mother. "Thank you, Ma, they look perfect." Ma was so kind; Lily felt any disappointment about not seeing Aiden would be disloyal.

Ma smiled. "We could pin the pattern on the silk tonight if you like and cut it out when the light is better tomorrow."

"I like it when we do things together."

Lily jumped up and ran out to the hall. She came back with the bag Miss Laidlaw had given. She pulled out the fake bustle. "I forgot to say, Miss Laidlaw lent me this to accentuate the backline of the skirt."

She held up the back pad, and her mother laughed. "I haven't seen one of those for a while."

Lily hitched up her work skirt and shimmied the padding underneath it, tightening the belt around her waist. She preened in front of the dark kitchen window, looking at her new shape. The pad made her waist look narrower and exaggerated the curve of her hips. "I should wear a corset to pull in my waist. That's what the ladies in the shop do for their evening gowns."

"Over my dead body Lily Matthews, you have a lovely trim waist. How would you sing, trussed up like a chicken? And why would you torture yourself?"

Lily thought *to look as sophisticated as Kitty Marion* but knew better than to say so. Ma wasn't a believer in vanity. "Perhaps if I make a high waistband to accentuate my waistline, it will do."

"We need to cut the skirt panels longer at the back so the back hem doesn't poke up like it is now," Ma said, pointing at the back of Lily's skirt.

Lily danced a little jig, then paraded across the floor with a queenly expression, pretending to fan herself and nodding at her reflection in the window.

Lily and Ma were both laughing when the door opened, and Pa walked in. "What are you two gigglers up to in here?" He took in Lily's hitched-up skirt and the padding, which had slipped a bit and laughed. He slapped his thigh as Lily squealed. "That girl's a card, Maggie. Whatever does she look like."

"Shh, we're trying out the effect of a bustle for her costume, don't laugh. You'll upset her." Maggie sighed. "For a minute there before the padding slipped. You looked so grown up, Lily."

After dinner Lily and Ma laid out the pattern pieces on the kitchen table and pinned them on the lilac silk, ready to cut in the morning. As the evening passed away peacefully, Lily looked at Pa, smoking his pipe in the armchair by the fire with Ma opposite. Ma always frowned as she tried to read in the gaslight, and Lily thought, *it's nice to be at home sometimes.*

It wasn't until she lay in bed that evening that she thought about Aiden again and remembered their kiss and his words – *I love you, Lily.* She hugged the covers around her tightly, feeling a bubble of excitement inside. She loved home, but she could feel the call of adventure. She wondered what being Mrs Aiden Donnelly would be like.

Lily's hands shook slightly the following morning after breakfast as she held the scissors poised above the first pattern piece. "I'll check I have this right," she said to her Ma, withdrawing the scissors again and fussing with the pattern.

Ma said, "Although you've checked it twice, and so have I. Would you like me to do the cutting? Would it make you happier?"

Lily set her face in a determined line and took a breath. "No, I'll do it. I've got to take the plunge sometime."

She bit her lip with concentration, and the blades of Ma's dressmaking shears sliced through the silk taffeta with a scrape. She folded the cut panels neatly and put them aside until they were all done. Removing each pattern piece carefully, she pinned the sections of the skirt together.

With Lily standing in her chemise and petticoat, the back pad around her waist, Ma lifted the pinned garment and slid it over her head. It felt too loose as it settled around her, and Ma adjusted the pins.

Lily lifted the skirt off over her head. She quickly put on her clothes, for all the fire was lit, there was still a nasty draught coming through the sash window.

Ma put the skirt on the table. "If you sit there in the light, you can tack those panels together, ready to stitch. Did you set a time with Miss Laidlaw?"

Lily looked up hopefully. "She invited me at two o'clock tomorrow. I'll show you her note. Please may I go? I know you're worried I'm tired and said no outings this weekend, but I don't want to seem rude."

Ma looked at her closely. "I'm bound to say you look better for a good night between the sheets, so I don't see any harm. Pa can walk you there."

Lily hoped Aiden might accompany her, but she didn't dare suggest it. Ma might well change her mind. She still had to broach the question of another practise session with Aiden but decided to get on with her sewing and ask later.

As it happened, Aiden resolved that dilemma. He called over the wall for Lily, and as Ma responded, he asked her himself. She reluctantly agreed that Lily could go for an hour when she'd finished her sewing.

Mary Donnelly had been correct, the song suited Lily's voice, and she glowed as she sang the romantic lyrics. Even Aiden, her harshest critic, jumped off the piano stool and said, "Well done," when she finished singing. His mother had stepped out of the room momentarily, so Aiden took the opportunity to hug Lily, and the hug turned into another stolen kiss.

"When we're married, we won't have to ask anyone's permission to be together, Lily."

Lily nodded, everything seemed so simple when he had his arms around her, but something told her Ma and Pa would not be overjoyed at their plans. She concentrated instead on the tingle she felt when Aiden kissed her.

"This must be some song," her ma said when Lily returned home, "your eyes are shining like stars."

"I'm excited for Aiden," Lily replied, covering the half-truth by singing the first verse. "Imagine waltzing to this with someone handsome at the bandstand Ma; it's romantic."

"Not with your pa stepping on my toes; it wouldn't be. Pa was enthusiastic but better at the country dances. That said, he's a good man, and that's worth all the romantic nonsense in the world."

Lily's romantic vision withered on the spot. Was this what being married was like?

Chapter 10

The Sunday routine in the Matthews household was well-established. Lily slept in for an extra half an hour and woke to the mouth-watering smell of bacon frying. Ma always cooked it for breakfast on a Sunday. It came from the pan, served with crispy fried bread slices soaked with bacon fat. The Yorkshire pudding batter was already made and resting, and Ma put the joint in the oven after breakfast before they walked to church for the morning service.

After breakfast, Pa said, "Maggie, help me with this dratted collar, will you."

Lily watched as Ma helped him attach a stiff white collar to the shirt with brass collar studs. Pa contorted his face and said, "Careful, love, you're choking me." As she tied his tie and folded the collar down.

"You always make a fuss." She retorted and passed him his waistcoat from the chair.

With the waistcoat fastened and his fob watch attached, Pa shrugged on the long suit jacket and looked at his watch. "Come on, you two, look lively, or we'll be late." He slid his thumbs, hooked under the adjustable braces, up and down as he spoke.

Lily shook her head. As if it hadn't been him holding everyone up, she thought. Still, as he angled his hat in the mirror by the front door, she thought how smart he looked and different to when he wore his baggy corduroy work trousers and leather waistcoat.

They got to church on time and squeezed into the pew beside Granny and Gramps, who were saying their prayers.

Advent was Lily's least favourite time in the church year. The church felt cold, and as Lily followed the morning service in her prayer book, the smell of old, damp paper rose from the pages. The hymns were drab compared to the Christmas carols to come. After singing O come, O come, Immanuel, they sat down, and she shivered.

The vicar expended some effort in his sermon, taking Luke 1, 78-79 as his text and convincing the congregation solemnly they were living in darkness, under a cloud of death, all in need of God's light and compassion.

Pa maintained a saintly expression throughout the sermon, which Lily suspected covered a wandering mind. Ma, however, listened to every word, nodding at appropriate places. Lily knew she should be concentrating too but felt fidgety. She wondered if God knew she had kissed Aiden and couldn't help wanting the time to pass, to walk to Miss Laidlaw's house.

After the church service, the congregation filed into the church hall for coffee and chat. Unaffected by the gloomy service, there was much laughter and loud conversation.

Lily was waiting for the right moment to slip away and say hello to her friends when Harry appeared in his regimentals and embarrassed Lily by coming straight to speak to her. Lily felt obliged to introduce him to Ma and Pa, glad Granny and Gramps had already left to go home. Lily thought the Marines were on church parade at the barracks. What was he doing here?

"I ran down here after church parade to see how you are after you tripped at rehearsal," he said, apparently all solicitude but with a barely concealed twinkle of devilment in his eye.

"I'm perfectly alright, thank you," Lily replied and made as if to turn away, not wanting to encourage him.

"What's all this?" Pa said. "You didn't mention a tumble, Lily."

Lily shrugged. "It was nothing, Pa. I tripped."

As Harry took his leave, Pa said, "He seems a nice young lad, Lily, not like some other young recruits, wild to a fault. And you're singing a duet together; that's nice."

"Don't be taken in, Pa. He may have a lovely voice and good manners, but he's as full of himself as the others." She hunched a shoulder and shook her head.

Lily caught Pa as he winked at Ma, who frowned him down.

Ma turned the conversation to the need for early lunch if Lily was to be on time for Miss Laidlaw. Pa was hurried away from the church hall, protesting he hadn't had time to enjoy a cake or drink his tea.

The smell of beef roasting met them as they opened the front door.

They hung their coats, and Ma hustled Lily into the kitchen to help prepare vegetables. Ma put the beef in the warming oven and dropped potatoes into sizzling dripping from last week's joint. She set aside the meat juices from today's joint to make gravy. Lily loved watching her mother work in the kitchen, precise and orderly.

"When you are running your kitchen, Lily, you'll need to remember this," she said, customarily talking Lily through every step of the meal and encouraging her to be involved. "As well as knowing how to haggle with the butcher about the price of beef and liver."

That time had always felt many years away, but she realised she needed to pay more attention after Aiden's proposal. The prospect of finding a dinner to make every day seemed dull though she already had a neatly recorded journal with family recipes and tips on household management that Ma had made her write down.

After lunch, Pa escorted Lily to Miss Laidlaw's rooms in the semi-basement under a large house in Southsea.

"Do come in, Miss Matthews. I'm excited to see what we can achieve with this costume." She extended her hand to take Lily's carpet bag. "You can hang your coat there." She pointed to a neat row of coat hooks behind the door.

Miss Laidlaw pulled a thick velvet curtain across the door as she closed it to keep out draughts.

As Lily entered the small sitting room, she saw that the plots must slope as the back of the house opened via French doors onto a small garden. Miss Laidlaw had sited her sewing table and treadle machine in front of the back window in the best natural light.

"Now, what have we here?" She looked at the skirt that Lily presented with a practised eye. "Step behind the screen and pop it on, and I can check the fit before we sew the final seams." She unfolded a painted screen to make a small dressing area. "I design for some private clients," she explained.

Lily hurried to put on the skirt, remembering to put it on inside out and stepped out.

With a pin cushion over her wrist, Miss Laidlaw circled Lily, lifted the skirt slightly and made several deft adjustments. "You've managed this nicely. Well done, Miss Matthews." Seeming eager to start, she added, "Take the skirt off, and I'll show you the sewing machine."

Lily flushed with pleasure. Miss Laidlaw at home seemed much softer than Miss Laidlaw in the workroom.

The sewing machine, shiny black enamel with embossed gold patterns on the cast iron body and sewing plate, seemed intricate as Lily tried to follow instructions to pass the cotton through various levers and around bobbins. She felt she had three thumbs as she attempted to thread the fixed needle at such an awkward angle. Miss Laidlaw showed her on a piece of scrap material how to adjust the tension to make the stitches even, and then she pronounced them ready to begin.

Miss Laidlaw sat at the machine and snapped the first seam under the sewing foot. She placed her feet on the treadle and worked it in a steady rhythm as she threaded the material through under the foot. The needle flew in and out of the seam at a dizzying pace.

"You don't need to go quite that fast," Miss Laidlaw said. "Come, sit here and have a go. It takes some practise to manage the treadle."

Lily sat nervously in front of the handsome machine. Miss Laidlaw released a small handle inside the big wheel to the side.

"You can practise the treadle without the needle moving now. One foot on top of the footplate, one on the bottom, with your heel on the floor. Now gently rock between your two feet, don't let the plate hit the floor."

There were several jerks before Lily got a smooth rhythm, allowing the balance wheel to whir evenly. Lily decided that you had to feel the resistance in the pedal plate and dance with it.

Miss Laidlaw leant over Lily's shoulder. "Well done. I'll re-engage the needle now, and we'll try a sampler."

Lily clamped the square of fabric under the foot, rocked the balance wheel and began to treadle. She squealed as the needle darted in and out, but her line of stitches veered off madly. Panicked, she lifted her foot. The machine freewheeled to a stop in a tangle of threads to the side of the cloth.

Lily blushed and stammered an apology. "Oh, no! I hope I haven't broken anything."

Miss Laidlaw laughed and clapped. "Don't worry, it runs away with you, to begin with." She cut the material free, and Lily began again. This time she stayed on the fabric, but the line of stitches wove drunkenly across the sampler.

"Why don't I leave you to practise while I make us tea?" Miss Laidlaw suggested kindly.

Lily nodded gratefully. "Thank you, that would be nice." It was nerve-wracking to have Miss Laidlaw watching over her shoulder. *I'm going to get this if it kills me,* she thought. It had looked so simple when Miss Laidlaw had demonstrated.

Each try gave a better result until Lily finally had a straight line. She gave a triumphant whoop and showed the sampler to Miss Laidlaw as she came in with a tea tray.

The chairs in the sitting room were old. Lily noticed that the upholstery was worn and shiny under the neatly embroidered antimacassars. Delicate tambour tables stood beside each chair. Miss Laidlaw poured from the tray, balanced on her table, and handed Lily a china cup and saucer. Silence descended, and the clock's ticking on the mantlepiece sounded abnormally loud. Lily couldn't think of anything to say, but Miss Laidlaw saved the day.

"I want to commend you. You seem to have a natural talent for dressmaking, and you work hard." She looked away over Lily's head, voicing private thoughts. "Fabrics and colours come alive, and with artistry beyond good technique, it's possible to create beautiful objects with them." She looked at Lily again. "If you continue to perfect your skills, I sense you have it in you to excel."

Lily stared at the unexpected compliment, her cup halfway to her mouth, surprised beyond measure at the passion she heard from her ordinarily calm, restrained mentor. She realised that someone else understood how she felt.

"Sometimes fabrics flow through my fingers, and I imagine I can see a garment taking shape. It's hard to explain." She stopped, embarrassed. "I'm sorry, that makes me seem fanciful. I still have to learn, but I want to design, not just sew."

Miss Laidlaw paused, considering, then said, "I design too. Would you like to see them?"

Lily nodded and watched as Miss Laidlaw pulled a large cloth-bound drawing book with leather corners and a tasselled cord page marker from behind her chair, its pages stiff and overlaid with thin tissue protectors.

Inside the book, sweeping ink lines shaded with watercolours depicted beautiful gowns, full of movement, unlike the stiff fashion plates she had seen before.

Some were daring, heavily patterned with beading and fringes which would show a lady's leg to the knee as she moved. Cut simply on the cross without a rigid structure and weighted by the beads, Lily could imagine the gowns flowing around the wearer like liquid.

"They're beautiful." Lily gasped in awe. "Do you think anyone would dare to wear them?"

Miss Laidlaw laughed. "On the stage or for a Parisian show. High fashion often starts there and trickles down to the public." She closed the book, smoothing the transparent paper over her artwork lovingly. "I have almost finished the beading on one of my designs. I'll show you when I've finished. Now though, shall we finish your skirt?"

Lily sat back at the machine, and Miss Laidlaw helped her place the skirt.

Tongue pushed against her upper lip, and with a frown of concentration, Lily guided the long seam under the sewing foot, watching the darting needle catch the two sides of the fabric together with even stitches. She breathed out and grinned at Miss Laidlaw as she arrived at the hemline without disaster.

"Bravo! You've mastered it." Miss Laidlaw mimed applause as Lily sat back, her first seam complete. "Now, move over. Let me finish the last seams. I'll be quicker."

After finishing, Lily was amazed to see Miss Laidlaw unthread the cotton, unclip bolts on the table's side, and rotate the top, lowering the machine upside down and leaving a smooth worktable.

"I'll leave you to set the waistband, and you must hang the skirt and let the fabric drop for several days before you sew the hem.

Lily nodded and rushed to say, "I can't thank you enough, Miss Laidlaw, for all your kindness."

"Nonsense, I've enjoyed myself. Now about the lace overskirt, we don't need to complicate things by reversing the skirt, as I first suggested. Making a lace overskirt that attaches to the waistband with concealed buttons will be simpler. You can remove it for the second number or add it, whichever song comes first."

She unfolded one of the curtains. First, roughly pinning darts to shape the top, she wrapped it around Lily's waist and pinned it to her skirt on either side. At the front, she folded back both bottom corners and tucked them into the waistband. The drape of the lace folds formed a half skirt that scalloped over Lily's slim hips and transformed the costume into something more stylish.

"You could use it over the lilac skirt or disguise a simple day skirt. I know your photograph had bows and ruffles, but I think the swagged lace looks less fussy and how top fashion houses are designing these days. What do you think?"

Won over by Miss Laidlaw's elegant draping and love of more simple lines, Lily wondered how she could have hankered after frills and bows.

All the way home, Pa listened, and Lily talked, barely drawing breath. "It's good to hear you're wrapped up in your fashion ideas but don't get too distracted from your work, Lily."

Little did he know that part of Lily's joy was the sure knowledge that Aiden was about to see a modish version of herself, guaranteed to rid his mind of London music hall stars.

Chapter 11

On the evening of the next suffragist meeting, Lily dressed in her Sunday skirt and blouse with particular care. Ma lent Lily her cameo brooch, which looked well against the high neck of her blouse, and a paisley scarf, a gift from her late employer. In front of the mirror in her room, Ma brushed Lily's long hair until it shone in the candlelight, then pinned it up in a simple bun, with tendrils waving around her face.

"You look nice, Lily. The scarf brings out your complexion. You're pale, but I expect you're nervous about singing." Maggie scrutinised her daughter, then, with both hands, pinched lightly along Lily's cheekbones to bring up her colour. "Enjoy yourself. It won't help to fret."

"I don't want to let Aiden down. He's set his heart on this."

"That's as may be, and if wishes were horses, beggars would ride, my girl. You can only do your best; you can't make Miss Marion like Aiden's song. Don't forget you are there to hear Miss Marion speak, and the biggest compliment you can pay is to give her your full attention."

A mixture of fear and excitement warred inside Lily as she met Mrs Donnelly and Aiden. However, Mary Donnelly, her usual poised self, enquired after Lily and her parents in her quiet voice.

Aiden seemed distant, his eyes gleamed, and he had poise in his bearing that made him look confident and purposeful. Lily tried to engage him in conversation, but it was as if he had an invisible bubble around him. Was he cross with her?

The electric lights in Mary O'Shea's house blazed a glow that extended beyond the windows and cast a graduated shading across the lawn. A maid greeted them and took their coats. Mrs O'Shea was nowhere to be seen. Lily was astonished to see the press of people in the hall. They had to move slowly through the crowd, weaving around groups who chatted animatedly. Kitty Marion had drawn a crowd.

Mary took Lily's arm and guided her to seats at the front of the room. "These have been reserved for us."

Lily turned to Aiden. "Aren't we luck…" but Aiden had already approached the piano and was wholly absorbed in arranging sheet music on the stand.

"Don't mind, Aiden, Lily. He's shutting out the world to focus on his playing. Performers can be self-absorbed, you know. How are you feeling?"

Relieved that it was nothing she had done, Lily smiled hesitantly. "I'm nervous, Mrs Donnelly. There are so many people here."

"Our sister group in Southampton has joined us. Everyone is eager to hear Miss Marion speak." She raised her eyebrows. "And I suspect, sing. Although I doubt they would admit to anything less than serious political interest."

Lily recognised Mrs Donnelly's gentle cynicism; her ma had similar views on people's attendance at church. She was learning that under the polite face of the adult world lay a complex web of ulterior motives.

Mary leaned into her again. "Aiden will play some music while we wait for Miss Marion to speak, and then you will have a chance to sing during the tea break. Afterwards, we believe Miss Marion will favour us with a song."

Mary handed Lily a small phial. "Pop some on your wrists, and breathe the scent deeply if you feel jittery."

The oil inside smelt like the inside of churches, a rich woody smell. "What is it?"

"Frankincense — it's calming and good for the voice." Mary glanced at Lily. "Being nervous before you perform is natural and good, provided it doesn't overcome you."

Lily glanced back to see if she could see Grace. She and Mrs Dent were about halfway back. Grace waved and mouthed, "Good luck."

The chatter in the room died, and an expectant hush replaced it as Mrs O'Shea led a lady of medium height into the room. She wore an ankle-length skirt in deep plum, with a jacket of severe cut and a high-collared shirt with a tie. The sheen on the fine wool fabric and the perfect tailoring took Lily's eye immediately.

A fox fur was draped negligently over one shoulder. Her lustrous chestnut hair was swept up in a complicated style framing her face, and dark eyebrows arched perfectly over pale, ice-grey eyes, which swept the room, seeming to draw the attention of everyone in it. Heavy embroidery on the front of the jacket softened the severity of the cut and was picked up again around the skirt's hem, under which peeped patent leather boots.

Not classically beautiful, Kitty Marion acknowledged the audience confidently as a smattering of applause broke out.

Lily tried but couldn't decide how old she was, perhaps thirty, given her assured manner, although she still had smooth skin and a delicate complexion. She was compelling, and Lily barely heard Mrs O'Shea's introduction as she stared at Miss Marion, wishing she could exude the same magnetism.

Lily was surprised to hear a European accent when Kitty spoke. "I believe Miss Marion was born in Germany," Mary Donnelly whispered.

After thanking Mrs O'Shea, Kitty Marion caused a gasp in the audience as she began her talk by announcing boldly, "I am delighted to be out of prison and free to speak with you this evening. The police will undoubtedly arrest me again as I fight the cause of women's suffrage. I am proud to stand with my sisters in the fight for women's rights, many of whom suffer the indignity of assault and force-feeding as they struggle to draw attention to our cause."

She described the work of the WSPU and explained that even when selling WSPU newspapers in the street, passers-by spat at and jostled the suffragettes. The police, sanctioned by politicians, often assaulted even peaceful demonstrators too.

Miss Marion justified the more direct acts of vandalism as 'necessary' to shake politicians from their complacency. Still, she acknowledged that such activity was not possible for everyone.

She praised the efforts of the NUWSS in continuing to petition those in power steadfastly.

"Make no mistake, Ladies and Gentlemen, this is a war. We must be prepared to fight with any weapons for justice and equality to prevail. I believe in deeds, not words."

The effect on the room was electric. Some of the audience were uncomfortable. Others were open in their admiration of her courage and commitment. Aiden appeared transfixed. He sat upright at the piano, his eyes never wavering from her face. Lily was unsure what she thought. Miss Marion was magnificent in her suppressed fury. She seemed dangerous somehow, and Lily could not imagine being so rebellious. Questions poured in, all answered with the same evident dedication to the suffragist cause.

Mrs O'Shea declared a break for tea, and Miss Marion remained in her seat to take any further questions.

Lily felt a gentle nudge from Mrs Donnelly beside her. "I think you should go to the piano, Lily."

Aiden whispered, "While Miss Marion is right here, let's do my song first in case she moves off."

Lily took a deep breath and straightened her shoulders. She stood beside Aiden, her hand resting lightly on the casing of the grand piano. He nodded and began to play the now-familiar introduction. As she sang, people paused their conversation and turned to the piano. Lily's confidence grew as she felt the warmth of the reception from the audience, and she finished in her best voice.

There was a silence as the last note faded then enthusiastic applause rang out in the room. A call of "Brava" came from a dark-haired young gentleman standing behind Grace and was followed by several more.

Miss Marion paused in her conversation to applaud with an encouraging smile, and Lily remembered to curtsey, bursting with pride. Aiden beamed at her and continued to play an improvisation on the melody of the song. To Lily's astonishment, Miss Marion excused herself from the group, gathered around her chair and came to the piano.

"Well done indeed. I'm not familiar with that song, Miss?"

"Miss Matthews. It's an original song, Miss Marion, composed by Mr Donnelly in honour of your visit this evening." She introduced Aiden to Miss Marion and stepped back slightly as Kitty followed him to look at the music.

"Would you play the melody again for me?" She smiled directly at Aiden as if he were the only other person in the room.

Aiden flushed and began to play as Miss Marion hummed the tune. "Lovely," she said, "something out of the ordinary. My accompanist is indisposed, and I am requested to sing after tea. I wonder if perhaps you might accompany me instead, Mr Donnelly? Mrs O'Shea mentioned that you or your mother might do me the honour."

"Miss Marion, the honour is all mine." Aiden stood and made a tiny half-bow. To Lily, he looked bewitched.

"That is all settled." Miss Marion whispered, "I must first try not to shock these good people any further." She threw a laughing glance over her shoulder and returned to her chair, leaving behind a trace of lilies, roses, and musk.

"Aiden, how wonderful," Lily said loyally.

He nodded, looking stunned. "I'll offer Miss Marion the neat copy you made when she finishes singing. She's friendly, not at all aloof and beautiful."

Lily nodded mutely. She agreed with him but had hoped Aiden hadn't noticed.

Lily stepped away from the piano as Aiden sat down to play again. He rapidly became surrounded by other audience members. She heard several people ask where they might procure a copy of the song and felt a flush of pride. From their enthusiastic reaction, Aiden would probably achieve his dream of having his music published.

As she avoided the crush around the piano, she received compliments about her voice from people she didn't know. Lily was pleased to bump into Grace eventually.

"Hello Lily, your singing was lovely. I'd never have dared, not in front of Miss Marion. What did she say to you?"

"She liked Aiden's song, and guess what? He's going to play for her to sing in a minute."

Grace looked dreamy. "Her outfit is to die for, and she's, well, I don't know, fiery and brave, a bit scary too." Grace lowered her voice. "Did you hear her? She's been in prison!"

"Fire and ice." A man's voice behind them made Lily jump. "Miss Marion is all cool eyes and conservative dress, but she smoulders underneath. Intriguing."

Lily turned to see the tall, handsome, dark-haired man who had called out 'Brava'. He was dressed in an expensively tailored suit and a spotless white shirt. However, underneath his polished veneer, he had a world-weary expression.

Grace stammered slightly as she introduced him, "Lily, um, Miss Matthews rather, this is Mr Stephen Dent, George's eldest brother."

"I shall call you Lily. It suits you, and you must call me Stephen. Let's not stand on ceremony. After all, I gather Grace will be family soon, and you are good friends."

He took Lily's hand and placed a light, well-practised kiss on the back. His breath felt hot against her lace glove, and his lips lingered a fraction too long, making her want to pull her hand away. As she blushed, he smiled charmingly, holding eye contact that she found hard to break.

Something in his manner made Lily uncomfortable, and she felt as if she was being toyed with, like a mouse by a sleek cat. She shook herself for being fanciful as he offered to fetch refreshments for both Lily and Grace in a gentlemanly manner.

Grace watched him weave through the crowd and turned to Lily. "He's handsome, don't you think? He looks like Aiden, only more elegant and older."

Lily looked at her friend. "Yes, he does a bit." Both men were tall and slim with dark hair. "But Aiden has blue eyes, and I don't know… a kinder face. Mr Dent seems much older than George."

"I don't know exactly. Stephen's maybe twenty-eight or thirty, he said he came to escort his ma, but I think it was mainly to see Miss Marion. I don't think George likes him much, but my brothers are constantly fighting too, so I don't set much store by that. I'd like to get on with all his brothers."

When he returned with tea and cake, Stephen was agreeable, complimenting Lily on her singing, teasing her that Miss Marion must now be nervous. Lily noticed that while no longer playing, Aiden had not joined them. Instead, he was going through music with Miss Marion. Lily told herself that Aiden needed to before she sang. Still, she hoped he noticed she, too, had an elegant companion.

Her voice was deeper than Lily's and more mature, filling every corner of the room. Miss Marion sang three songs. One was a funny number called Come Josephine (in my flying machine.) Everyone tapped their toes and laughed at her exaggerated faces as she pretended to be Josephine and her beau. Then two sweet romantic ballads followed, 'When Irish eyes are smiling' and 'Let me call you sweetheart'.

Miss Marion knew how to catch the light on her face as she sang and presented an enchanting picture. Her voice had an emotional, haunting quality that brought a tear to many. She finished to rapturous applause and generously acknowledged Aiden after taking a bow.

As the meeting closed and people drifted away, Mrs Donnelly sighed. "She certainly has charisma and a beautiful voice. It's hard to imagine her breaking windows and fighting the police, isn't it?"

Lily was thoughtful. "Do you suppose all the passion in her voice is inside her and comes out in her life too?"

An arrested expression came over Mrs Donnelly's face. "Do you know, Lily, that is a wise thought, and you are probably quite right. I sometimes think that's why Aiden's creativity and playing have such quality. He has a strong sense of injustice which fires him."

Lily didn't know how to respond. It was as if she had heard an inner thought spoken aloud but not entirely meant for her. To Lily's relief, Mrs Donnelly continued, "Shall we go to Aiden, my dear? I am sure he's on cloud nine."

As they approached the piano, Miss Marion excused herself from the committee group she was speaking to with

Mrs O'Shea and smiled at Lily. "Mr Donnelly tells me you would like to make theatrical costumes and are training to be a dressmaker?"

"Yes, Miss, that's correct. It's been my dream. I'm making some of the costumes for our local community concert."

"As you sang so beautifully earlier, and I understand you copied out this song so I can read the lyrics…." She paused and tapped Aiden playfully on the arm with the roll of sheet music tied with a ribbon. "I would like to invite you both to join me backstage at the theatre for the Saturday matinee. You can meet my dresser and see what theatre life is like. Mr Donnelly can meet the musicians."

Lily was speechless and looked from Miss Marion to Aiden, then stammered, "Thank you, Miss Marion, I would like that. You are very kind indeed."

Mrs Donnelly looked on proudly. "What a wonderful opportunity for you both. Miss Marion, I'm sure neither will sleep a wink tonight with excitement."

"Your son is talented, you must be proud, and I'm glad to see him supporting women's rights. I would like to encourage both. And now I see Mrs O'Shea beckoning to me. I must go. Until Saturday, Miss Matthews."

Mrs Donnelly kissed Aiden on the cheek. "Well done indeed for your playing tonight, all from sight too. And you, Lily, for presenting the song beautifully to Miss Marion. Exciting you both have the chance to visit Miss Marion at the theatre."

She looked at the two glowing faces beside her. "If you're both ready, we should collect our coats. It wouldn't do to miss the last bus."

As Lily waited for a maid to bring her coat, Mrs Dent approached with Grace. "Congratulations, my dear, and to you too, Aiden, quite the star of the evening. You've met my eldest, Stephen, already…."

He nodded to Aiden. "Donnelly." He immediately turned to Lily and pressed a kiss on her hand. "Your obedient servant, Miss Matthews, thank you again for entertaining us. I do hope we meet again soon. Grace must bring you to the house one day."

Lily nodded as enthusiastically as she could. Miss Marion had indeed given an outstanding performance. As Aiden's eulogising continued, however, she began to let his voice wash over her. Her mind wandered to Miss Marion's sophisticated dress and, she suspected, carefully embellished complexion.

"Don't you agree, Lily?"

His question brought her back into the moment. "I'm sorry, I'm tired. What did you ask?"

"I said, our visit on Saturday will be wonderful. You will love seeing Miss Marion's costumes, I'm sure."

"Yes, indeed." Lily's head was beginning to ache, and for some reason, her enthusiasm for the theatre trip felt dimmed.

As they alighted the bus, Aiden offered Lily his arm. "I hope you're not too done up, Lily. You were amazing this evening, and we did it."

As her spirits lifted with his praise, they sank again as he added, "Miss Marion has such presence, pitch and depth to her voice. I can't wait to see how it sounds when she sings my song. She promised to try it out at Conrad and Sons tomorrow."

"I'm sure Miss Marion will sing it professionally, but her voice won't have Lily's sweetness." Mrs Donnelly continued, "Aiden should be grateful to you."

He flushed. "Indeed I am." He placed his hand over hers as it rested on his arm. "You were fearless this evening."

Fearless! Lily didn't want to be brave. She'd prefer to be charismatic and confident, trailing wafts of expensive perfume behind her.

Chapter 12

At home, Ma and Pa, both in warm dressing gowns, were ready for bed. Ma's hair fell over her shoulder in a thick plait, and Pa looked more vulnerable somehow.

Ma pressed a cup of tea into Lily's hand and offered her a slice of bread and butter. Her parent's eyes were trained on her expectantly, and Lily felt their pride from across the table. Lily felt a catch in her throat as she realised how much they loved her and she them.

Pa said, the light showing his stubble flecked with grey, "Tell us all about it then. Your Ma is bursting to hear, but she won't say so. Parties were part of her world when she worked at the big house."

Ma frowned and rapped him on the arm with the cloth she held. "Don't exaggerate, Edward. I'm not saying we didn't have some wonderful occasions. We did, but it was my working world. I wasn't a guest like Lily."

Lily hurriedly began, "It was much busier and way fancier than last week because of Miss Marion. I felt quite overcome, to begin with, but Mrs Donnelly put some oil on my wrists, which calmed me down."

"I hope Mary Donnelly isn't brainwashing you with Papist ideas, Miss. I never knew a situation where some deep breaths and sensible thinking didn't suffice."

"Ma, that's not true; you've waved smelling salts under my nose before. It was a medicinal oil, not a religious one."

Ma sniffed, and Pa said, "Let the girl speak, Maggie."

Lily pulled a face. "I waited to sing most of the evening until after Miss Marion's speech. My legs were shaking under my skirt, but I sang without any mistakes. Miss Marion came to the piano and asked about Aiden's song. She liked it enough to go to his work tomorrow and try it out."

Pa clapped, then leaned forward to pinch Lily's chin gently. "That's marvellous, Lily. Well done you. You must be a born performer. I'm sure Aiden's thrilled."

Ma nodded. "Goodness, Lily, an honour indeed. What was Miss Marion like?"

Lily wondered how much to say about Miss Marion without shocking her parents. "She was sophisticated, Ma, in a beautiful, tailored suit with her hair wrapped and piled on top. She spoke with a foreign accent; otherwise, you wouldn't know she wasn't English."

Ma nodded and said, "Fancy!"

"She was passionate about what the suffragettes are doing in London. Some of them have been to prison even. I can't imagine that."

Ma snorted. "Nor should you. I've nothing against change, and heaven knows it's time women had more say in their lives, but there are ways of doing things. Throwing bricks and setting houses on fire doesn't seem necessary to me. Causing a commotion will like as not turn people against them."

Pa nodded. "You stick to writing letters and handing out leaflets, Lily. There is many a revolution that has happened quietly with persuasion."

Lily shifted anxiously in her seat. She didn't want to jeopardise her visit to the theatre by telling them anything more.

"Miss Marion has invited me to meet her dresser at the theatre on Saturday and see what happens backstage. Aiden is going to talk to the musicians too. Aiden told her I'm interested in costumes."

Ma frowned. "It's a kind invitation, but we don't know this woman for all. She's a London star. And we don't know who else you might meet either, being theatre people. What do you think, Edward?"

Pa looked from Lily's anxious face to Ma's uncertain expression, and as if inspiration had suddenly struck, his mouth slowly stretched into a broad grin. "I think it's a long time since you and I had a treat, Maggie. I shall go to the theatre tomorrow and buy tickets for the matinee. We can take my mother and father too if they'd like to come. That way, we can walk Lily there and bring her home. Who knows, if Lily can peek out from behind the curtains, we may get a glimpse of her with her big London star."

Lily flew out of her chair and flung her arms around Pa's neck. "That would be wonderful, Pa. Thank you."

Pa blushed pink to the roots of his hair, and Lily turned to her mother. "Please say yes, Ma, Pa's right. You both deserve a treat."

Ma's face gave nothing away, but Lily sensed she was tempted. "I won't deny that I'd be happier to know we will be there. If Lily's uncomfortable with any of the 'goings on' backstage, she can always come to find us." Having made this dark pronouncement, she added, "I enjoy a show, and I can't remember when we last went. It's thoughtful of you, Edward."

Lily felt more confident about the visit now her parents would be in the theatre.

"It means that Aiden won't have to escort me home afterwards either, if..." she gulped slightly then over-brightly said, "if Aiden gets caught up with Miss Marion over his song."

Ma glanced at Pa, who raised his eyebrows. "I'm sure we'll all have a wonderful time, and we don't need to trespass on Aiden's good nature, kind as he is. Now, I think it's time you headed for bed. You have work tomorrow."

Lily sighed. "I am tired now. You're right, Ma." She folded her mother's shawl, unpinned the cameo, and passed them to her mother. "Thank you for lending me these, they are lovely, and I felt special in them. I'll see you in the morning." She kissed them both on the cheek and left. The hall struck cold after the warm kitchen, and as she climbed the stairs, she allowed her shoulders to droop for the first time that evening. Miss Marion had been all she had hoped for and more. Pleased for Aiden, Lily still wished Miss Marion hadn't been as intriguing as she was. All she could see were Aiden's eyes which had not left Miss Marion's face.

As Lily undressed, she guiltily realised she was hiding things from Ma and Pa for the first time, making everything seem complicated. They were kind to her, and she wanted to be truthful about the engagement, London, and Miss Marion too, but suspected they would not understand and worry.

Lily swallowed hard. *I will tell them later when things are more straightforward.*

The following day, Lily dressed quickly and styled her hair. She wasn't hungry but knew Ma would make a fuss if she didn't eat, so she forced down a small bowl of porridge. Ma wisely left the subject of Miss Marion's visit to Conrad and sons out of the conversation, choosing instead to tell Lily that she would walk to the haberdashery today.

"I thought I could buy a plain handkerchief for you to embroider for Miss Laidlaw. We mustn't forget how kind she has been."

"Yes indeed, thank you, Ma."

"I could also look for some ribbon in the right shade of lilac to decorate the neck of your best blouse. Small touches like that will make the skirt more of an outfit for the concert."

Ma had to be satisfied with a brief smile and a second thank you. Lily's mind was elsewhere.

In truth, Lily felt confused. She was as drawn to Miss Marion's charismatic charm as Aiden, excited to visit the theatre too, but in the pit of her stomach had a sense of dread that she couldn't shake off.

She was nearly at the tram when Aiden caught her up. He had a thin leather pouch that Lily recognised as his mother's music carrier.

"Thought I'd try to make a good impression," he said, indicating the folder. Lily recognised his best shirt with the high collar and a smart burgundy tie carefully tied and tucked into his dark waistcoat. His boots were clean and polished to a high shine which disguised the scuffed toes and worn leather.

"Very smart," she said. He looked anxious and more like the Aiden she knew.

"Lily, about the other day, you said not to speak to your pa…."

Lily's head shot up, and she lifted her chin. "Aiden, I understand if you think we should wait. I won't tell anyone you asked me to marry you, especially as Miss Marion may be able to help you. I would understand because so much has happened in the last few days."

He looked aghast. "That's a terrible thing to say. I haven't changed my mind at all. It's a big day today. If something comes of this chance, it'll show your pa I've got prospects. I meant that he may say 'yes' to us getting engaged."

Lily flushed scarlet.

After a night of worrying that pa's prediction had come true, she blurted out, "How was I supposed to know? It wasn't me making sheep's eyes and fawning over Miss Marion last night. You never stopped talking about her, Miss Marion this, Miss Marion that, what was I supposed to think?"

His ordinarily soft blue eyes hardened. "And it wasn't me having my hand kissed by Stephen Dent." Aiden mimicked Stephen's drawl perfectly. *"'Your obedient servant, Miss Matthews, do come to my house la-di-da.'* At least Miss Marion wants to help us. I don't trust George's brother at all."

Lily gasped. She stopped walking and spun to look at Aiden. "I didn't ask to have my hand kissed. He just did it."

"Like Harry just happened to lift you off the stage, I suppose?"

She couldn't believe he'd said that. His eyes blazed, she'd only ever seen him this angry after being bullied at school, and it was not pleasant. However, she held his gaze without wavering.

As angry as Aiden now, Lily said, "Aiden Donnelly, you take that back. That's plain mean and spiteful. Whatever has got into you?"

"Or what?" His chin jutted forward belligerently, his knuckles white as they gripped the music pouch.

"Or nothing." Lily ventured a rueful smile. "Sorry, I shouldn't have said those things, but neither should you."

Aiden relaxed and grinned sheepishly. "Alright, I'm sorry too, but I can't bear other fellows making up to you because they don't know we're engaged."

Lily sighed. "Pa says in a partnership, you've got to trust each other, Aiden. Otherwise, there's no point."

The argument made them miss their tram, and both needed to hurry to avoid being late for work.

When Lily entered the workroom, Grace was in full flight, telling everyone about last night, extolling the virtues of Lily's singing and Miss Marion. Overhearing this exciting description, as she entered the workroom unseen, Mrs Winchett cleared her throat, and silence fell. "Much as I do not encourage idle gossip in the workroom, Miss Matthews, you may describe Miss Marion's outfit for us, as I'm sure it came from a London modiste."

Lily dropped a slight curtsey. "Her outfit was simple, Ma'am, but beautifully tailored and in fine cloth with a subtle sheen. It was raised above the ordinary with cream embroidery over the plum jacket and skirt. The skirt was slim cut, and the jacket close-fitting. She wore a tie too."

"Well observed, Miss Matthews."

Mrs Winchett turned to the other girls. "We must always observe what is around us and take inspiration because fashions change. As modistes, we must be ahead of the game." As Miss Laidlaw nodded in agreement, she continued, "Fabric ladies, the fabric is everything, that and cut. Now Miss Laidlaw, if Miss Matthews and Miss Kirby can recall the outfit's details, you may sketch it. Miss Marion will sing in Portsmouth for a week, so a small line inspired by her outfits may interest our clients."

Lily raised her hand. "Mrs Winchett, I have been invited to meet Miss Marion's dresser and see some of her wardrobe before the matinee on Saturday."

Mrs Winchett's eyes gleamed. "Excellent, Miss Matthews. We shall be most interested to hear about that. Follow me for a moment."

In Mrs Winchett's office, Lily stood nervously in front of the desk. "What will you be wearing on Saturday?"

Lily hesitated. "I hadn't thought, but I expect my Sunday skirt and best blouse."

"Well, Dear, attractive as I'm sure they are, you will be representing our establishment in some way on Saturday, and there is no better advert than seeing an outfit on a pretty girl. I propose that we lend you one of our sample tea dresses. Nothing too ostentatious but elegant."

Mrs Winchett motioned for Lily to turn around and narrowed her eyes. "Yes, it's a pity you aren't taller, but we can adjust a showroom gown and add a heeled shoe." She motioned to Lily to approach her chair, then added, "I'm sure you will be happy to mention us to Miss Marion when the opportunity arises or if anyone comments about the dress."

Lily stammered her thanks and assured her that she would indeed mention the showroom.

"Now, run along and begin your work. I will call you up for a fitting when I have chosen an outfit."

Lily floated back to the workroom. When she took her place at the table, she told Grace, "I can borrow one of the sample outfits to wear to the theatre on Saturday."

Grace looked at her with an envious expression. "Oooh, we shall have to curtsey when you go by Lily Matthews."

Miss Laidlaw hid a half-smile. To Lily, she said, "Well, that is kind of Mrs Winchett, although I'm sure she feels this may be an excellent business opportunity."

The remainder of the morning passed in a haze of pleasure as she and Grace described Kitty Marion's outfit. Miss Laidlaw sketched an elegant lady, somewhat taller and more slender than Kitty Marion, in an excellent copy of the suit Lily had so admired.

"Many of the suffragettes wear ties now for day wear. It adds gravitas to their appearance." Miss Laidlaw leant back from her sketch and looked at it critically. "The severe tailored cut is flattering, I think. Better to let the design and the fabric do the talking."

Lily, who had until recently hankered after frills and bows, did not hesitate to agree with her tutor. Grace, a romantic soul, looked more doubtful. "It looks rather mannish, don't you think?"

"Perhaps; it resembles a riding habit. It's convenient and hard-wearing because the hemline doesn't brush the floor, but the tailoring shows the female figure. I look forward to hearing you describe Miss Marion's evening dresses, Miss Matthews. They will be more to Miss Kirby's taste."

Lily felt she needed to pinch herself when she saw Mrs Winchett's selected dress. Simply shaped with a round neck and long sleeves, the white cotton lawn material was heavily embroidered with an ochre thread. A sleeveless three-quarter overdress in plain ochre cotton met edge to edge at the front to sinch the waist but was severely cut away with a circular hem to frame the skirt of the underdress. The hemline stopped at the ankle, and a pair of silk shoes embroidered in ochre with a long tongue and two-inch heel completed the ensemble.

She turned this way and that while Miss Laidlaw made tiny adjustments. Lily could hardly believe the fashionable girl in the mirror was herself.

Mrs Winchett suggested a hat was not required, but perhaps a delicate confection of silk flowers might set the outfit off to advantage.

Eager to meet Aiden after work, Lily hurried to the tram stop, glad she had some exciting news to share. Not that Aiden would necessarily be interested in her dress, but even he couldn't fail to see how elegant she looked when he saw her at the weekend.

Aiden appeared to be in shock. "Lily, you won't believe this. Miss Marion came to the shop and requested me to play for her. She stayed over an hour trying out songs and bought four pieces of music."

Lily's heart sank as she visualised their heads together over the music and the subtle touches between them as Miss Marion stood close to him singing, her perfume weaving its sweet threads around them.

Unaware of Lily's thoughts, Aiden continued, "She was clever and asked Mr Conrad to listen to my song. She said she would sing it on Saturday if he could get copies printed in time, as she was sure people would wish to buy it."

Lily knew this patronage was invaluable to Aiden and felt a lift of excitement beyond her personal feelings. "That's wonderful. What did he say?"

"Mr Conrad said he would pay for a limited run, provided Conrad and Son could be on the front sheet as sponsors under my name. And listen to this, Lily. Miss Marion will send a copy to Francis, Day, and Hunter in London with a recommendation."

Lily adjusted her features into an expression of appreciation to match his, then had to ask, "Who are Francis, Day, and Hunter?"

"They're famous music publishers up in London. They must receive thousands of manuscripts daily, but I will likely get a contract if mine is printed and has Miss Marion's approval."

Aiden paused, looking both proud and disbelieving simultaneously. "Miss Marion says if I join the Musical Copyright Association, no one can steal my song and pretend it's theirs. I'll get paid royalties every time it's sung or sold."

"Aiden, that's amazing. Oh, imagine if you get your song in print."

Lily felt she could just about put up with hearing Kitty Marion's name every other sentence if she helped Aiden. However, he immediately put her good intentions to the test.

"Miss Marion says I must keep my feet on the ground because nothing is easy or fair in the music business, but I can't help dreaming. They might even put a picture of her on the front."

114

Lily sighed inwardly and decided to keep the news about her dress for another time, maybe even keep it a secret until he saw her on Saturday. Aiden was too excited to listen today, so she would have to tell Ma and Pa instead.

He had endured so much teasing and a thousand indignities at school because the other boys saw him as an outsider, catholic, with an Irish father, not one of the gang who played football and supported Portsmouth FC. Lily thought that those boys would have to eat their words if he made it up to London. She looked at his glowing face and felt this would be payback indeed. She hoped there would be a place with him for her.

Chapter 13

L ily said goodbye to Aiden at the Milton Market shops as he had some errands to run for his mother. Usually, Lily would have accompanied him, but today, she declined.

"I have some sewing I want to finish. I'll walk on." She blushed slightly as she told the white lie. She did want to work on the handkerchief for Miss Laidlaw. Truthfully, however much she respected Miss Marion and was pleased for Aiden, she felt she had heard enough about the singer for one day.

"I'll knock for you before rehearsal then, shall I?" he called after her, surprised.

"If you like," she said over her shoulder.

As she turned into Eastfield Road, Lily noticed a commotion near her house. A gang of kids clustered around a vehicle parked in the street, and one or two men were there too.

Lily quickened her step and realised as she got closer a gleaming car was parked outside her home. Her first thought was for Ma and Pa. Her heart lurched. Was it the doctor's car? Had Pa had an accident at work?

116

Forgetting her long skirts and her dignity, Lily began to run. She arrived at the house out of breath and hammered the door.

Lily was relieved to see Ma. "Has something happened to Pa?" she blurted out.

"Pa? No, whatever makes you say that?"

Out of breath, Lily pressed against her ribs with her hands to ward off a stitch. "The car outside; I thought it was the doctor."

Ma patted her arm. "You have a visitor waiting in the front room."

Lily looked wide-eyed at her mother, a visitor for her? Ma peeled off Lily's coat and unpinned her hat, then licked a handkerchief and dabbed away a couple of smuts on her face. She nodded her approval and led Lily into the front parlour. Standing in front of the fire warming his hands was Stephen Dent.

"Lily, I believe you know Mr Dent through the meetings at Mrs O'Shea's house. He tells me that Grace and his youngest brother are engaged."

Stephen surged forwards, his face wreathed in smiles. "Your mama has been kind enough to entertain me, Miss Matthews. I wanted to see that you weren't unduly fatigued by the evening yesterday, but I see you are equal to anything and looking radiant."

Taken aback by this flow of eloquence, Lily blushed and stammered, "You are most kind, Mr Dent, but I am quite well, thank you."

He took her hand and said, "Come and sit by the fire. You must be chilled." He settled opposite her, easing his check trousers with a neat tweak which exposed immaculate brown ankle boots with a snow-white, button-down cuff. He relaxed back in the chair as if perfectly at home.

After a short silence, he produced a small, tightly tied posy of lilies from beside his chair. "For you, as a small token of thanks for your singing yesterday." He half stood to offer them, and she caught an unfamiliar smell of cologne. None of the men she knew wore perfume.

"Thank you." Unable to think of anything further to say, she glanced at her mother in disarray. This kind of afternoon visit was the sort of thing which happened in books.

"How thoughtful, Mr Dent. I am sure it was Lily's pleasure to sing yesterday, and I understand Miss Marion was also persuaded to sing."

A flash of irritation surged in Lily, Miss Marion again!

"I believe someone else did sing." He flashed Ma a twinkling glance and asked Lily, "Do you remember another singer?"

For all his cheek, Lily had to laugh. "You are teasing me, Mr Dent."

Stephen put a manicured hand to his heart over a brown waistcoat that matched the check of his trousers and wool jacket. "No, indeed not."

Relaxing under the influence of his easy charm, she added, "Miss Marion has invited me to attend her matinee performance this weekend, which I am looking forward to."

"What a coincidence. I am hoping to be there myself. Perhaps we shall meet?" His bland look belied the blatant fib, and Lily had to smile again.

Stephen stayed another ten minutes, chatting easily, then glanced at the clock on the mantelpiece and took his leave of both ladies. He shrugged on an ankle-length overcoat and smoothed leather driving gloves over his strong hands. "I mustn't detain you any longer but will look forward to seeing you at the theatre. Your obedient, Miss Matthews, Mrs Matthews."

Suppressing an instinct to peep out of the window, Lily heard a choked mechanical cough, followed by an engine spluttering into life. She imagined Mr Dent cranking the car and whipping away the starting handle as she'd seen at the fair. Her head was in a whirl. Why was he visiting her?

Ma appeared at the parlour door and looked at her bemused daughter. "Best put those flowers in a vase, Lily, or they'll wilt. What a dashing young man, to be sure." Ma accompanied her statement by raised eyebrows, so Lily felt that she had been less impressed than Mr Dent might have imagined.

"Grace introduced us, but I don't know why he came here. I only met him briefly yesterday. He's attentive but quite grand."

Ma nodded. "Mr Frazer at the big house had a young nephew like him, fancied himself a charming man about town. Mr Dent seems rather older than that, but he was proper, staying a short while. Young men, you know, playing off their tricks to impress. Lily, the flowers are a pretty gesture, but don't let them go to your head. We may never see Mr Dent again."

Lily nodded. She wasn't sure if that would be a good thing or not. "No, Ma, I won't. I know he's being gallant. It's nice to meet someone who isn't obsessed with Kitty Marion, though."

Ma looked surprised. "I suppose you are aiming that remark at Aiden. It's no wonder Miss Marion has turned his head a little, Lily. Still, I'm sure having an admirer makes you feel special too."

She turned away from Lily and started to look for something on the side. "I bought a handkerchief for Miss Laidlaw today. You could draw a design for the embroidery before you go to rehearsal."

The subject of Stephen Dent's visit was closed.

No one had ever given her flowers before, and she felt flattered. She thought she might copy them onto Miss Laidlaw's handkerchief. They would look different to the usual violets or roses.

When Pa arrived home, he closed the door and said, "It's a fine thing when a man can't get into his own home after a hard day's work for dratted questions about automobiles and flash young men." He pinched Lily's chin. "I imagine you know something about this?"

Lily rushed to take Pa's coat as Ma poured hot water into a jug for him and took it into the scullery. "It was a friend of Grace's, Pa, her fiancée's brother. He wanted to congratulate me on my singing last night."

Stone dust on his face gave Pa a chalky pallor. He scooped water in both hands onto his face and rubbed hard to remove it. Then rolled the bar of soap between his hands and methodically washed, scrubbing his nails with a bristle brush. Lily hovered uncertainly until his ritual was complete. Pa said mournfully, "I suppose the house will be overrun with your admirers now, Lily, and you'll be too grand for your old pa."

Lily's face relaxed into a smile, and she said, "Never."

He winked at her. "As long as they don't make my dinner late and treat my girl respectfully, let them come." He looked at the posy on the table. "Don't let that turn your head, my girl. Any scoundrel can buy flowers. It takes an honest man to stand by you through thick and thin."

Lily had barely swallowed her dinner when Aiden knocked at the door. Pa greeted him, watch in hand and said, "No later than nine o'clock, young Donnelly, I shall be watching."

As they walked away, Aiden said, "Your Pa is fierce. I'm not looking forward to asking him about our engagement. He's like a bulldog or a mastiff standing guard."

Lily's heart jumped when Aiden mentioned their engagement. She thought of their stolen kisses and blushed as she glanced at his familiar profile. His lips had been soft against hers, and she'd been surprised at how strong his arms were as they'd circled her.

Lily's mood plummeted again as he added, "Still, if Miss Marion can recommend me for a job in London, he surely won't say no. I am looking forward to our visit on Saturday."

Stiffening slightly at the mention of Kitty Marion's name again, Lily said airily, "Stephen Dent says he may come to the theatre on Saturday as well. He visited today with a posy. He was in his motor car."

Aiden scowled. "Well, Lily, you'd better tell that, that *rake*, you don't want his posy. I don't trust him, trying to buy his way into your favour."

Forgetting that she wasn't entirely sure about Stephen Dent herself, Lily said, "I'm sure I don't know what you mean, Aiden, he's gentlemanly, and the posy was thoughtful. It's beautiful."

Rather pleased to see him looking cross but ashamed she had boasted about things Aiden couldn't afford, Lily's hurt pride won. She thought, *serves you right, Aiden Donnelly, it's all very well for you to talk about Kitty Marion non-stop, but it's different if I even smile at someone else. You can't have it all ways.*

Lily detached herself from Aiden as they entered the church hall, making sure he saw her offer Harry a beaming smile.

Rehearsal was torture. Aiden played his accompaniment well but with no merry looks or his usual tricks. He didn't stand to play while dancing the ragtime rhythm with his feet or look up from the music to smile at Lily. He didn't come over at tea break either.

Suddenly the room seemed overly busy and bright, the sound of the girls singing shrill and loud. Her performance felt forced, her mouth stretched in a fake smile, feet and hands going through the motions of her routines.

Lily realised she was dreading the walk home, worried that she and Aiden would argue. They seldom quarrelled. One of the things she loved about him was how comfortable they were together. When their dreams seemed to be materialising, they argued nearly daily. Lily felt tears pricking behind her eyelids. It was unfair.

As the room swam out of focus behind unshed tears, she saw with relief that Pa had slipped into the back of the hall, and she hurried across the room and hugged him.

Pa patted her back and brushed away a solitary tear. "What's all this then?"

His calloused hand felt rough, yet its familiarity was comforting. "I came to hear my girl sing as you are rousing all the young men in the area to admiration with your nightingale voice."

He handed her his pocket handkerchief. "It's nothing, Pa, Aiden, and I quarrelled about Stephen Dent calling, and

I'm sick of hearing Kitty Marion this and Kitty Marion that."

Pa nodded slowly. "Ah, I see. I must have a word with that young man."

"No, Pa, please don't. There's no need."

He kept a straight face. "Oh, but I must. He's made a serious mistake." Lily bit her lip anxiously as he shook his head gravely. "Never praise one woman to another."

Lily looked at Pa's twinkling eyes, full of mischief but also a warm understanding, and eventually had to laugh. "Pa! You think I'm jealous, but I'm not, and anyway, you're supposed to be on my side."

"There's my girl. I am on your side. There's plenty of time for you to break young men's hearts before settling down. And Aiden is no doubt excited. Miss Marion may be able to further his career, and it helps to have a sponsor. Now run along. I'm looking forward to hearing that song, Puss."

Rehearsal ended with a collective prayer and a reminder from the vicar that they should reflect on the season's true meaning as Christmas approached.

Lily saw Aiden collect his music promptly and noticed his eyes search the room, stopping as he saw her and warming to a hesitant smile.

Aiden managed monosyllabic answers to her Pa's heartless and cheerful conversation throughout the walk back. As they arrived home, he tried one last gambit. "Mr Donnelly, could I have a word with Lily about Saturday?"

"Not tonight, Aiden. Lily is tired, and you'll have plenty of time to chat on the tram tomorrow. Goodnight, Lad."

He shepherded Lily inside and closed the door, leaving Aiden on the pavement. Lily knew how sensitive Aiden was

123

to slights and that he would have hated being dismissed as a child, especially as she knew he wanted to impress Pa.

I've been cowardly, she thought, *hiding behind Pa; rather than talking to Aiden in rehearsal, I'll make it up to him tomorrow.*

Inside the house, Pa sighed. "It's a good job I went up there tonight, Maggie. Young Aiden was like a bear with a sore heel over something, and Lily was on the verge of tears over him praising Miss Marion to the skies."

Lily looked daggers at Pa. She wished he hadn't told Ma.

"I shall be glad when Saturday is over. Kitty Marion has set everyone at sixes and sevens." She stood up, smoothed the neatly folded towels by the range, and sat back down. "I don't want you distracted from your apprenticeship by a pack of young men hanging around. Stephen Dent is a good deal older than you, Lily. Goodness knows what he wants, coming around here with flowers."

Lily blushed. If only Ma knew about her plans to go to London with Aiden.

"Don't you start getting worried now, Maggie. You were never distracted from your work by admirers. I had to wait years for you." He patted her hand and looked at Lily. "Lily will likely be the same. As for Stephen Dent, he's probably being kind because she's Grace's friend, or maybe his brother put him up to it to win favour with his girl."

Lily gasped, outraged. "Pa! That's not nice."

"I don't know. I wouldn't describe Stephen Dent as kind. I can't put my finger on it. He had excellent manners and said everything proper, but I couldn't quite warm to him." Ma shivered. "Let's hope everything returns to normal when Kitty Marion leaves."

Chapter 14

When she woke the following day, Lily lay watching the fingers of winter light creep under her curtains. The familiar lift and drop as they caught the draft that whispered into every small space between the sash window frames. It was rare to have a day with no wind blowing in Portsmouth.

Hurrying to get dressed, she ran downstairs to find her ma in the kitchen. "Ma, I forgot to tell you with all the excitement yesterday."

Ma looked up from the sink and rubbed her wet hands on a tea towel. "Slow down, Lily, take a breath. I can hardly believe yesterday had anything else packed into it." She passed her daughter a cup of steaming tea and a bowl of porridge with a blob of homemade jam in the centre.

Lily spoke thickly through her first mouthful of the creamy breakfast. "Mrs Winchett is lending me one of the sample gowns to wear to the theatre on Saturday to represent the shop. Isn't that kind? It's heavenly, Ma, white with yellow embroidery, an over-jacket, and matching shoes."

"Very kind indeed, not but what I suspect she has an eye to business, hoping for an order from Miss Marion or one of the other ladies."

"She's having it altered and everything, Ma. The fabric is so fine it floats over you when you put the dress on. I felt like a princess in it."

Ma raised her eyebrows as a blob of porridge narrowly missed Lily's blouse and landed on the table. "Princess, is it? You'd better practise your princess manners and stop talking with your mouth full, Lily, is all I can say." She swooped in with a cloth and wiped the offending blob as they both laughed.

"I can't wait to wear it."

"I'm sure you'll have a lovely time. Don't let all this go to your head, my girl. Let's keep our feet on the ground."

"I know it's a treat." Lily ran to put her coat on. She wondered how Aiden would be this morning.

It seemed Aiden had also thought better of his bad mood yesterday, and it was a shamefaced pair that met in the street, eager to make amends. Listening for Aiden's feet behind her, Lily turned to give him a welcoming smile. "Aiden, I'm…."

He held up a conciliatory hand. "No, Lily, don't apologise. It was my fault, and I'm sorry. I shouldn't have said what I did. I wish we could tell the world we're engaged, and then those fellows would stop bothering you."

Desperate not to rekindle their quarrel, the conversation continued in a stilted way. Both were at such pains to be polite and interested. In the end, Aiden said, "This is worse than quarrelling, Lily. Stop being formal. I'm truly sorry I was cross yesterday. It was that Dent fellow; he got my back up."

"Aiden, don't be silly, I didn't ask him to call, and I couldn't tell him to leave; he was waiting in the sitting room. He's George's brother, after all."

Lily saw Aiden grit his teeth, then he swallowed resolutely and appeared to remember he wasn't going to argue with her this morning. "No, no, quite. Lily, be careful. I don't like him."

Lily raised her eyebrows. He hardly needed to state the obvious. "Well, I won't talk about him if you stop talking about Miss Marion all the time."

"But that's different, Lily. Miss Marion will help us both, and you'll see her too. We both need to talk about her."

Biting back a sharp reply, Lily sighed. "We'd hardly heard of her a week ago, and she'll be gone next week. Let's not argue about this."

"What shall we talk about then?"

Unable to think of a single safe topic of conversation, she said, "You think of something, for goodness sake. Why does it always have to be me?"

Glancing behind him and seeing they had no one close to them, he took Lily's hand and said, "When can I speak to your father about us, Lily?"

Worried someone would see them, she squeezed lightly and withdrew her hand despite the heady feel of touching him. Her heart raced, and she answered breathlessly, "I don't know when would be best, Aiden. Perhaps after Christmas, but not before the community show." Lily twisted her hands anxiously. "After we visit the theatre at the weekend, everything may change. If Mrs Winchett gets lots of orders from me modelling her dress, I might get a pay rise, and I'm sure you will sell hundreds of copies of your song."

Thrown off stride, Aiden said, "Dress, what dress, Lily?"

"I meant to tell you yesterday but forgot because you had important news. Mrs Winchett is lending me one of the sample dresses from the showroom to wear."

Aiden gave a low whistle. "Miss Lily Matthews, you'll be the belle of the ball!" He added hastily, "Not that you don't look beautiful always, in my eyes anyway. You could be dressed in rags, not that you are, of course, ever…."

"Aiden, stop digging a hole. I know what you mean." He coughed and ran a finger around his collar as if it were suddenly too tight. Lily continued in a respectful voice, "You should see the dress. It is beautiful. I can't wait to wear it."

Aiden smiled, and Lily, the image of herself in the gown still fresh in her thoughts, didn't notice she hadn't wholly held his attention.

The last working day dragged by as Lily willed the hands of the clock to turn. She then passed a restless night. Frantic thoughts about her day at the theatre jumbled with dreams of how Aiden would look at her when he saw the dress. Bizarre scenes chased each other through the night as she tossed and turned.

When Saturday finally came, Lily could barely eat her breakfast. She ran out into the garden to see if Aiden was looking out his window. He saw her and waved, then ran out to say hello.

A small cloud drifted over the sun of her exciting day when she asked Aiden if his parents were excited to see the show. He shook his head, mouth tight. "They won't be there. The dockyard laid Pa off again, and it's too expensive. I hate this bigoted town with its small-minded people. Pa's a hard worker; laying him off is unfair. It's because we're Catholic and Irish."

She had to kick her heels in the workroom, anxiously pacing before Mrs Winchett arrived and called her upstairs. Finally, Lily was standing on the dais in the showroom, for all the world, as if she were a client, having last-minute touches added to her outfit by Miss Laidlaw.

In the tiny drawstring reticule, the bag Lily was to carry, nestled a small stack of engraved cards bearing the name 'Gowns by Anastasia' in flowing script. As she handed the cards to Lily, Mrs Winchett said, "Be sure to offer a card to anyone who asks for details of your outfit."

Lily's head was buzzing with Mrs Winchett's instructions – stand tall, move with poise, don't rush, don't eat anything until you take off the dress, accept compliments and smile.

Miss Laidlaw whispered with a conspiratorial smile, "Don't forget to enjoy yourself."

Lily met everyone near the Guildhall, a short walk from the Theatre Royal. While Lily joined Miss Marion backstage, Pa intended to treat Ma and his parents to lunch in the theatre café. He had also bought Ma a small gold box of fondants and jelly sweets for the performance. Lily looked enviously at the sweets, and Ma promised to save her one of each.

Lily clutched the stage door pass Miss Marion had left with Aiden in her lace-gloved hand. The alley which led backstage was less grand than the ornate ironwork and glass porch and the beautiful marble and mosaic foyer at the front of the building. It was narrow and dark, with dank moss crawling across the path.

Lifting her skirts instinctively, Lily prayed there wouldn't be a rat lurking anywhere and tiptoed carefully to save her silk shoes. A large man with a shaved head overflowed around the edges of a small wooden chair inside the door, and she handed him her pass.

He studied it carefully and then held it up to the light. His face broke into a lopsided grin showing several missing teeth, and he winked. "Just teasin' Miss; Kitty's dressing room is upstairs, fourth door on the right, her name's on the door – make sure you knock."

Lily swallowed and nodded.

She took off her coat, folded it neatly over her arm and smoothed her dress before mounting the stairs, bare except for painted edges which had flanked a carpet runner at some time, she supposed.

The world that greeted her at the top of the stairs was curious and wonderful, with people everywhere. Men in rolled-up sleeves and braces with pencils behind their ears moved swiftly about. They placed ladders here and props there, weaving with practised ease amongst the performers.

A mix of people of all sizes, costumes and nationalities swarmed the wide corridor and spilt out of dressing rooms spreading a kaleidoscope of colours against the dark walls. Everywhere was movement and chatter. The dancers warmed up with their legs stretched onto bars and chairs, and singers breathed in exaggerated exercises and sang repetitive consonants, the sounds humming through their chests. Here was all of life, and Lily could feel its pulse beating in time with her heart.

A few people turned to glance curiously at Lily, their features distorted by heavily etched makeup like living masks. Girls clad in corsets and stockings with robes wantonly sliding from bare shoulders laughed among themselves. Lily was shocked to see one of them smoking a cigarette in a long holder.

Two muscular men brushed past, speaking in a guttural foreign language. They wore knitted all-in-ones tightly belted around the hips with broad leather supports. Further on, a slender lady dressed in a shepherdess outfit with a small white dog was rehearsing tricks. Everywhere smelt of grease-paint, sweat and excited apprehension.

She knocked timidly at the dressing room door and heard Kitty's voice, "Come.".

Miss Marion was seated in what appeared to be a bower of floral displays, swathed in a Chinese silk robe, her hair wrapped in a towelling turban. In front of her was a large, mirrored dressing table with bright electric bulbs casting a harsh light on her face.

"Lily, welcome. I'm glad you could come, and you look most elegant." Her bright eyes crinkled. She grimaced and indicated her robe and the towel. "As you see, I am preparing to do my 'maquillage' and for Greta to style my hair."

A lean lady of some fifty years old emerged from behind a rail of dresses and a large trunk propped open on its end to form a makeshift cupboard. "Greta! We have a visitor. Lily is an apprentice dressmaker, hoping to work in the theatre one day, and she's a friend of Aiden's, the new accompanist. I promised you would show her my costumes."

All Lily could think about was what Kitty Marion had said. *Aiden, her new accompanist, whatever did she mean?*

Miss Marion had turned to the case of grease-paint and pencils on her dressing table, and Greta cleared her throat discreetly, indicating that Lily should follow her.

Lily did as she was bid, despite her mind racing and a sinking feeling in her stomach.

Greta threw off the dust covers to show an array of gowns and costumes, from elegant evening dresses to a romantic Pierrette. Lily's worry temporarily eclipsed as she stared in awe at the collection. Here was the embodiment of her dreams.

"We have a small number of her costumes on tour with us," Greta explained, "We store many more in London."

"What is Miss Marion wearing today?" Lily allowed the layers of tulle in the Pierrette costume to brush over her fingers, its scratchy texture rough against her skin.

Greta unhooked an apricot taffeta evening gown, its low cut off the shoulders disguised by a chiffon swag at the neckline. Holding the hanger high, she allowed the skirt to flow over her other arm. "Romantic ballads today, romantic costume." She sniffed, feigning indifference, but Lily knew differently. The loving way she presented the gown, and the immaculate condition of each costume belied her words.

"Did you make these gowns?" Lily asked the taciturn dresser.

"Most, some came from Paris." Greta raised her chin, jutting it towards Lily. "You make your dress?"

"Not this one. My tutor, Miss Laidlaw, designed and made it." Remembering the cards in her reticule, she passed one to Greta. "I'm training at Gowns by Anastasia, but I would love to make dresses like these for a singer or an actress."

"Be prepared to give up your life then, always travelling, always working in the shadows. People only notice you when something goes wrong. I've been with Kitty since she was a teenager."

Lily blurted out, unsure what to reply, "Miss Laidlaw makes designs like I've never seen before, wonderful daring dresses that would be fabulous on stage. I want to develop new ideas the way she does."

"You and she both got the sickness then."

Kitty joined them, her makeup complete. "Don't let Greta scare you off with her stories, Lily. She wouldn't be anywhere else; she's as much an artist as I am."

Kitty scooped Greta into a hug. "I couldn't do without her. But Greta's right, if you want to succeed as a costumier, finish your training, don't get distracted. If you're with a man, he'll follow his career come what may. There aren't many who want their wife to be as successful as them."

Greta interrupted, "Miss Kitty, it's time to do your hair, let me show Lily how to see the show from the wings, and I'll be straight back."

As Lily followed Greta, she asked, "What did Miss Marion mean when she said Aiden was her new accompanist?"

"That fool Miss Kitty brought with her can't leave the drink or the ladies alone. He's got a broken hand from brawling with an irate husband. Aiden's agreed to play for her."

Initially, with a surge of delight for Aiden's luck, Lily's heart thudded. "Poor Miss Marion. I'm sure Aiden will do a wonderful job today, but what will she do on tour?"

"What do you think? She'll bring Aiden with her. He's a find, and the show must go on."

"Oh, but he won't be able to. He and I are hoping to win a prize. We have a show of our own after Christmas in a few days. We're saving to go to London together."

Greta shrugged. "It's you who may need another accompanist."

Chapter 15

Still unable to process what she'd heard, Lily barely registered that the half-time curtain had fallen. The noise and chatter backstage had risen in volume, and the cast milled about talking and laughing again. Through the noise and chatter, Lily saw Aiden striding towards Miss Marion's dressing room with the orchestra conductor beside him.

She raised her hand in greeting and called out, "Aiden, Aiden, over here."

Excusing himself to the older man, he joined her. "Isn't this fabulous, Lily? Do you love it?"

She saw his flushed cheeks and the glitter of excitement in his eyes. "Yes, yes indeed. And Miss Marion says you are to accompany her this afternoon."

"Better than that, Lily, wait until I tell you. But not now. I must go and find her." Aiden turned to go, then frowned and looked concerned. "I saw your family in the audience from the orchestra pit. Why don't you meet them in the foyer during the break rather than being here alone? You could cut through from the stage. There's time."

And with that, he was gone, without mentioning her dress or how beautiful she looked. Lily could have sworn he barely saw her.

With a heavy heart, Lily neared where she'd seen Aiden emerge and joined the auditorium via the orchestra pit stairs. She registered mild surprise that her legs still moved and that she could answer all her parent's delighted questions. *Yes, indeed, she had seen the show; the contortionist had been unbelievable and the comedian hilarious;* on and on, the questions came, but behind the polite answers, a mantra repeated in her brain, *he's going away, he's going away.*

Granny was shocked by some of the bawdy humour and was about to hold forth about the theatre being ungodly, but Gramps distracted her with a suggestion of ice cream, to which she was partial.

Just as Lily felt sure she would scream or pass out; she felt a firm grasp under her elbow and looked around. Stephen Dent smiled at her, a quizzical gleam in his eye. "Miss Matthews, what a pleasant surprise to see you here and looking radiant too."

"But you knew I would be here…."

Stephen laughingly put a finger to his lips and turned to a woman and a young girl behind him. "You know my mother, and this is my cousin Amelia." He indicated a rather mousy girl older than Lily, who did not look pleased to see her and gave barely a nod.

Mrs Dent greeted Lily warmly and begged permission from her parents to introduce Lily to some friends of Stephen, thus drawing her away. Stephen took her arm. "Mother, doesn't Lily look well today?"

"Indeed. Your dress is very stylish, Lily. I like the design, something out of the ordinary. Is it one of your designs? Grace tells me you have a talent in that direction."

Lily explained that her teacher Miss Laidlaw had designed the gown, and Mrs Dent said, "Amelia, Dear, we really must visit the showroom with your mama and speak to Miss Laidlaw. I'm sure it is too late to procure anything before Christmas, but with all sorts of Spring outings to London around the corner, we must think ahead about a wardrobe."

The mousey girl acknowledged with a fake smile and looked daggers again at Lily, pointedly staring at her hand on Stephen's arm.

Lily tried to pull it away, but Stephen closed his other hand over hers and said, "We are joining friends for refreshments. May I buy you an ice cream, Miss Matthews? Lily."

"You are most kind, Mr Dent, but I should be getting back before the second half. I'm here as Miss Marion's guest."

"Stephen, please, call me Stephen. I thought we had agreed. I had forgotten you are Miss Marion's guest. The second half of the show will be all the more delightful now I know you are just out of sight in the wings."

Unsure how to respond to Stephen's charm, she felt rising rancour towards Aiden, who professed to love her and said he wanted them to be married but had barely given her the time of day. Lily said, "It was a pleasure to meet you again, Stephen."

"The first of many meetings, I hope," he replied smoothly.

Bestowing a smile on Stephen, to which he responded with a half bow, Lily slipped back through the auditorium, where the audience drifted back to their seats.

The theatre renovated a few years before, was magnificent. She paused to admire the act drop with its painted scene of HMS Victory. Luxurious cream and gold stage curtains swagged and looped to frame the painted screen.

If she had felt less miserable, she would have marvelled at the gilded boxes and the ceiling painted as a summer sky full of birds, but her anxiety allowed her only to notice them in passing as she took up her place at the side of the stage.

Thoughts of Aiden's brief greeting and his possible betrayal of their plans raced through her mind. She pictured Stephen's charming manner in contrast. *At least someone appreciated her.* However, it was cold comfort when it seemed that the man you had agreed to marry had forgotten your existence.

As Miss Marion was top of the bill today, she closed the show with four songs, but not Aiden's. From her vantage point, she could see the top half of Aiden's head as he accompanied Miss Marion, and she wondered how he felt about her leaving out his song after all the trouble he'd gone to.

Lily watched the glances that passed between Aiden and the singer. She recognised the complicity that up until now had been between him and her when they sang together. She fumed silently.

After rapturous applause and two curtain calls, Miss Marion raised her hand to address the audience in her low-pitched, accented voice. "As an encore, I would like to sing a new song written by local songwriter Aiden Donnelley. He has stepped in as my accompanist this afternoon at short notice, for which we must thank him and his employer Mr Conrad of Conrad and Sons." A spotlight swung onto Aiden, and he stepped beside the piano to bow to his first round of professional applause.

Lily felt a swell of pride despite herself as she heard the introduction to Aiden's song, and Miss Marion began to sing the familiar words. There was complete silence as the audience watched the singer, seemingly enthralled. When the song ended, a suspended moment ensued as if everyone in the auditorium held their breath, followed by a storm of applause and shouts of 'encore'. Miss Marion took another curtain call, invited Aiden to join her, and as she swept a curtsey, Aiden executed a stiff bow before the stage curtains swung together for the final time.

Greta greeted Miss Marion at the side of the stage and placed a wrap around her shoulders. She then hurried her towards her dressing room like a mother hen.

Lily supposed Aiden had gone the other way, towards the musicians, because she couldn't see him.

A hum of voices rose from the audience, accompanied by the click of seats folding and the rustle of coats. She mustn't keep her parents waiting, but it would be impolite to flee without thanking Miss Marion, much as she longed to run away quietly to think.

Her heart sank further as Lily dodged and sidestepped the cast and crew. She had nothing to offer Aiden compared to the world that had opened up before him. It was no wonder he was going away.

She knocked and waited, then entered the dressing room as bid. Miss Marion stood her back to Greta, having her gown unhooked. As it slid off her shoulders, leaving the singer in her underclothes, Lily blushed and looked away until Kitty had donned a robe.

Wishing herself anywhere but here, Lily saw the sophisticated singer so comfortable in her skin and felt young and stupid. She said, "I won't delay you, Miss Marion. I wanted to thank you and Greta for this wonderful opportunity. I have enjoyed myself beyond anything."

"Come here, Lily Matthews. I don't doubt you hate me. Greta tells me she let slip that Aiden agreed, only this morning, to come on tour with me. The news should have come from him."

She let go of Lily's chin but held her gaze with those compelling ice-grey eyes. "Take my advice and don't stand in Aiden's way, Lily. You're close, he tells me, almost engaged, and perhaps you think you'll lose him? But don't forget that this is a wonderful opportunity for him."

Lily squeezed her fingers into her palms until her nails bit into the skin. She would not cry. She stared at Miss Marion, who seemed to be reading her thoughts.

"If he loves you, Lily, he'll come back. Meanwhile, invest in yourself. You have talents and ambitions. You don't need a man to help you follow your dreams."

Kitty turned away to face the mirror, smearing cold cream on her face and beginning to remove the heavy cake makeup. She glanced at Lily in the mirror. "I'll help you however I can, but you must finish your training first. I owe you that much. You introduced me to Aiden." She smiled. "I'll contact your Miss Laidlaw before we leave, too. I'm interested in her stage designs."

Lily stammered a thank you. She should be grateful that

such an important person would show interest in her. Resentment won out, however; she hated feeling at a disadvantage and compelled by the force of Kitty's personality.

"Take my advice, work hard, and stay with Mary O'Shea's group. You'll learn a lot that's important there. Aiden will also meet some influential people in the London movement, and we need young people like you to campaign for justice and equality."

Her ice-cool eyes blazed as she warmed to her theme, and Lily felt the room seem to shrink. Miss Marion had an unnatural force about her.

A knock at the door broke the moment, and Greta opened it. Despite Miss Marion being only in her robe, she admitted Aiden. He was flushed with success and bubbling over with thanks to Miss Marion.

"Hello again, Lily; Kitty, wasn't that beyond anything great? You were wonderful. The audience was in the palm of your hand, and to hear you sing my song, well, I can't thank you enough."

Miss Marion laughed. "However many venues you play, savour today, Aiden. There will never be a feeling like your first applause. Bottle it for dark days."

Lily said quietly, "Congratulations are in order, Aiden; you are to follow Miss Marion on tour."

Looking from his feverish excitement, now tempered with guilt, to Lily's barely concealed dejection, Miss Marion said, "Why don't you walk Lily back to meet her parents, Aiden? Then, I am sorry, Lily, but he must come back, as I want to discuss arrangements with him. We have a lot to organise with Mr Conrad and my theatrical agent. I must ensure Aiden is protected and, at the same time, make all this possible. Theatrical work can be like white slavery if you aren't careful, not only for women."

Outside the theatre, in the alley, Aiden turned to Lily and took both her hands. "You haven't said anything, Lily. You do understand, don't you? Working for Kitty is the chance I've been waiting for to get away from Portsmouth and make something of myself."

Lily's mouth drooped, and she shrugged, pulling her hands away. "I can see how excited you are, and it's wonderful, of course. I thought we were going away together, Aiden."

"Don't you see, though, this will be for us. I can come to your father with my head held high before I go away and ask him to let us be engaged. Give me a year, and I promise we can marry."

Lily shook her head and looked down, pushing the dirt in the alley from side to side with one foot, he touched her arm, and she looked up. "I can't see how, Aiden. You'll have to travel with Miss Marion, and I won't have finished my apprenticeship in a year and…"

Aiden interrupted her, "But if my songs are successful, you won't need to work, Lily."

Lily shook her head. "But I want to, Aiden. We talked about our plans." Lily remembered their excited conversations over the garden wall, him playing and writing songs, and her creating beautiful gowns and costumes for the theatre. They had dreamed of conquering the music hall world together.

He ran his hands through his hair. "We'll sort something out, Lily, as long as we're together."

A flicker of hope still inside her, Lily said, "You will be here to play for the community show, won't you?"

"Look, we'll talk tonight. Come to the back garden after supper. Better still, I'll speak to your pa before I leave. Look, I must get back. Will you be alright to walk up to the road?"

Lily stared after him as he hurried away, Miss Marion's words that she should invest in herself warring unpleasantly with Aiden's suggestion she might give up her job. His continued desire to marry her made her feel special but also nervous. What would Pa say if Aiden proposed today?

The crowd in the theatre foyer had thinned; her parents were in conversation with Stephen Dent.

Stephen saw her first. "Here she is. Did you enjoy the second half, Lily? I told your parents what a fine, mature voice Miss Marion has. She has half the town at her feet. Donnelly is fortunate to have had the chance to play for her."

"He was pleased to help."

"My musical tastes are for something less produced. I told your parents how beautiful your rendition of the encore song was."

Pa responded, "Lily has a beautiful voice. I heard her rehearsing for our local Community concert last week."

Stephen leapt on the opportunity. "I hope you will permit me to hear you sing again. If you can obtain three tickets, I will bring Grace and George. We could make an enjoyable party."

Seeing Lily's stricken face, Ma intervened, "It's an amateur evening, a local entertainment, Mr Dent. I'm not sure you would find it interesting."

"Now you are being too modest, Mrs Matthews. I'm sure we shall all have a most enjoyable time." He placed his hat on at a jaunty angle, bade them a good evening and left, leaving behind a faint lingering note of his cologne.

"Well, bless my soul, Lily. I believe you are fair bidding to outshine Kitty Marion." Pa offered his arm to Ma, and Lily walked beside them.

"Pa, the community concert may not be quite what we planned." Lily hesitated, then thought, *they'll find out anyway*, "Aiden is going away. Miss Marion has offered Aiden a job as her accompanist."

Ma and Pa exchanged a quick look.

Lily omitted to add, *and Aiden might be coming to ask to marry me this evening.* Her head swam, and her stomach flipped over at the thought.

"I don't doubt that is disappointing after you've practised so hard, Lily, but a great opportunity for Aiden. We must be glad for him," said Ma.

Pa added, "I'm sure the vicar's wife or someone else will step in to play."

Not in the mood to be rational, Lily had a horrific vision of the vicar's wife at the piano, thumping out wrong notes with all the sensitivity of a bull in a china shop. She shuddered. "You don't understand; it will be dreadful. Aiden leaving has ruined everything. I'd rather not sing than have the vicar's wife play."

Ma frowned. "Now, Lily, just because you've been invited to the theatre today, there's no need to be overdramatic. I'm sure something will work out, and don't forget you have the wonderful dress Miss Laidlaw helped you with."

Lily gave her mother a withering glance. "What's the point of the dress? There won't be anyone important to see me in it."

Ma compressed her lips. "Lily Matthews, the whole community will be there, including your pa and me. Miss Laidlaw has gone to all the trouble and effort to help you feel your best and practise your skills, not to impress Aiden Donnelly! I'm surprised to hear you say such things."

These were not the words of parents expecting their daughter to be engaged to Aiden shortly. Lily looked mutinous but did not reply. Pa, looking uneasily from one to the other, said, "Now then, let's not spoil the afternoon with a quarrel. Granny and Gramps have already left. They were tired. How about I treat you both to fish and chips on the pier, and we can see the Christmas lights."

Usually, Lily would have enjoyed such a perfect treat, but she shook her head. She had to speak to Aiden before he came to the house. *What if he had to leave straight away? The company had finished their run in Portsmouth.*

"No, thank you, Pa, I'm tired, and Mrs Winchett said I mustn't eat in this dress anyway."

Ma's face cleared. "Let's get you home. I don't doubt that's why you feel out of sorts if you've had nothing to eat since this morning. You need a nice hot cup of tea and a slice of apple pie."

Pa nodded. "I don't mind admitting I'm sharp-set myself. Lunch at the theatre was a tad dainty for my appetite. We'll take a walk down to see the lights tomorrow."

"You don't have to baby me. I'm not a child," Lily grumbled. Everything seemed complicated now after all that had happened this afternoon. Being dressed like a lady with a fashionable hairdo had not brought the joy she'd imagined. She felt like a cloth that had been through the wringer, and home's safety seemed inviting.

Chapter 16

As Lily walked with her parents from the tram to home, she noticed the shop windows along Milton Market decorated for Christmas. Fir branches covered in glass baubles and bunches of holly and mistletoe tied with bright ribbons were on show. Some displays had paper chains and miniature Christmas trees surrounded by toy sacks. Others had chosen nativity scenes. More daring still, some left electric lights burning, illuminating the tableaus at night. The storekeeper's efforts were rewarded as families strolled by entranced, and children laughed and pointed at their favourites.

Christmas was out of keeping with Lily's mood, and she wanted to be back at home. Turning into Eastfield Road, Lily dreamed of her slippers and taking all the pins out of her hair. The borrowed shoes were pinching across her toes, and their heels made the balls of her feet burn.

However, before they reached home, Lily thought two familiar figures were walking towards them, Mr, and Mrs Donnelly, probably returning from Saturday evening mass.

"I am glad to see you all. Have you had a wonderful afternoon? I've been thinking about you and, of course, Aiden. Tell me, was his song well-received?"

An awkward pause ensued. Lily smiled mechanically. "Miss Marion sang Aiden's song as her encore, which sounded wonderful. There was a standing ovation, and I am sure people will flock to Conrad and Sons to buy the sheet music."

Pa, beginning to feel the cold, shuffled from foot to foot and said, "Why don't you come inside? I am sure the ladies would love a comfortable gossip about the show; Donnelly, you and I could indulge in a glass of Maggie's homebrewed wine to check it before Christmas."

Lily knew her Father meant well, but she didn't know how to face the Donnellys. Did they even know about Aiden leaving yet? However, it was too late, and they accepted the invitation. With the proviso, Mrs Donnelly left a note for Aiden to know where to find them.

Lily would have to brave it out. After changing, Lily returned to the parlour in a humbler skirt and blouse. She left her hairstyle as a vestige of today's elegant turn-out, despite knowing her hopes for the day were in tatters.

Ma and Mrs Donnelly had cups of tea and were balancing small plates with mince pies on their laps. Ma indicated a cup for Lily that she had poured and patted the chair beside her. "Come and sit down. Tell Mrs Donnelly all about your afternoon."

The conundrum of what to say about Aiden's offer was rapidly solved. "Lily, I explained to your mother that we have been to church to give thanks for Aiden's good fortune. Miss Marion visited us early this morning to ask if Aiden could play today and with an exciting offer to

147

accompany her on tour. My head has been in a whirl ever since."

Lily's smile was wan as she replied, "He was excited, and I understand he will be leaving imminently."

"Yes indeed, Miss Marion has engagements in several cities over Christmas. We will, of course, miss him most dreadfully, but we must be grateful. As you know, it has been his dream for a long time."

Ma glanced at Lily, who clasped her hands tightly in her lap, the knuckles whitening as she gripped, then added, "Well, I am sure we will all miss him, especially Lily, but we are delighted for him. 'It's an ill wind that blows no-one good,' as the saying goes."

"He was most concerned about his commitments to the Community Concert and his song with you, Lily. He felt guilty for letting you down." Lily glanced at her friend's mother, unable to mask her disappointment." He has asked if it is acceptable to you for me to take his place."

Lily wanted to scream *it won't be the same,* her thoughts inevitably turning to romantic walks home from rehearsal and stolen kisses, but she replied, "That's kind of you, Mrs Donnelly."

Pa chipped in from his place opposite Mr Donnelly, "Now then, Puss, that's good news. You dreaded having the vicar's wife. She is a good woman, but even I know she isn't blessed with musical sensitivity!"

Ma covered her amused smile rapidly by saying, "Edward! What on earth will Mr and Mrs Donnelly think of you?"

"Well, for my part," laughed Mr Donnelly, "If her playing is anything like our Priest's housekeeper, I'd think he has the right of it. She plays out of duty, not love, as Mary and Aiden do. The result is frightening."

The two wives rolled their eyes, and Ma said, "You are not to repeat that to anyone, Lily Matthews, but I'm sure you are grateful to Mrs Donnelly for her kind offer."

Lily nodded mutely. The grown-ups in the room didn't understand. They were all joking about the situation because they didn't know how much the concert meant to her. She thought the show and their plans had mattered to Aiden as well. Now she wasn't sure how he felt at all.

Mary Donnelly continued, "Mr Conrad has been most accommodating. He has offered to give Aiden a leave of absence on the understanding that I take his place." She continued in a confiding voice, "I think he perfectly sees the advantages to the shop in being able to talk about Aidan being accompanist to the famous Miss Marion. He was already talking about an announcement in the Portsmouth Evening News and hinting that Miss Marion could recommend the shop."

Lily was thoughtful for a moment. "I suppose she did, by association, during the performance when she sang Aiden's song. And I don't think Mr Conrad was accommodating. When Mrs Winchett asked me to wear that dress, I thought she was kind, but what she saw was a business opportunity. I had to pass out cards."

Pa looked up. "Now, don't take on Lily, I'm sure it was a mixture of both, and there is no shame in being business-like. It's how people like Mrs Winchett and Conrad can offer opportunities to others because they run their businesses well."

Sean Donnelly looked up sharply. "If only all employers ran their business well and offered opportunities to their employees. Too many of them get away with murder, in my view." His expression hardened. Lily had never seen him look like that; he was usually light-hearted.

Pa nodded in sympathy. "You men at the docks have had it hard. It's a bad business, what with pay cuts and layoffs. I don't deny it. It's time there were some laws to stamp out exploitation." Pa's eyes were grave. "Is there any news on the strike?"

Sean Donnelly nodded. "It's bound to happen. Some of the good men are starving; they can't support their families when they never know if the next wage is coming in — the work is always piecemeal because the bosses won't commit to contracts." Pa nodded, and Mr Donnelly continued, "Take me, it's wrong that they can discriminate because I'm Irish, and for the church I attend, how does that affect my work? The men have had enough."

Mary added in her quiet way, "It's even worse for women. Mr Conrad will pay me less than Aiden, even though I'm older and have more experience, just because I'm a woman. But we can't afford to lose the income."

"You shouldn't need to work if you don't want to. I should be paid a wage that supports my family." he punched the palm of his other hand in frustration but forced a smile on his face. "Sorry, indeed I am; this is a social occasion. We shouldn't be talking politics."

Pa squeezed Mr Donnelly's shoulder in solidarity as he poured him more homemade wine. Lily stared at the adults and saw chinks in the façade of comfortable security that she had never questioned before.

A knock at the door brought the distraction of Aiden bounding into the room. A blast of cold sea air wafted off his clothes, and a bubble of excitement surrounded him, filling the space with enthusiasm and hope for the future.

Mr Donnelly looked suitably proud, but Lily wondered if, inwardly, he felt diminished by Aiden's achievements and his wife's need to provide for the family, even if only temporarily. Pa had never been out of work, and Ma was always at home, although she had a responsible position before marriage.

Lily took their situation for granted and couldn't imagine Pa at home all day while Ma worked. Lily felt an ache in her heart, she was proud of Aiden too, but as he rode the crest of this wave, he seemed less familiar than the boy she knew and loved. Lily wondered what all this meant for her and Aiden's future hopes.

His parents showered Aiden with questions. He held up his hand to stop them; he and Miss Marion were wearing the garment even as they knitted it, he joked.

Pa offered him a glass of wine and proposed a toast that the ladies joined, clinking their teacups.

Lily's head felt like it was bursting, and the pins in her hair felt like miniature spears that evil goblins were poking into her scalp. Aiden had said he would ask Pa about their engagement, but all he was talking about was going away. *Had he changed his mind?*

As Aiden's parents left, Aiden hung back and asked for the honour of a few words alone with Pa. Pa's benevolent wine-flushed face froze momentarily before he recovered and said, "Um, yes, yes, of course, my boy. No time like the present." He shepherded Aiden towards the parlour and said over his shoulder, "Maggie, if you and Lily would care to remove to the kitchen."

Lily's heart thudded uncomfortably in her throat, and

she flushed hot, then cold. He was going to ask to marry her; what was Pa going to say?

Much as Lily longed to press her ear to the parlour door, Ma calmly asked her to clear the plates and whisked her off to the kitchen as bid.

Neither of them spoke initially.

Eventually, Ma said, "Has young Aiden already asked you to marry him?"

Lily nodded, breathless with excitement and fear, a slow flush spreading from her neck.

"This is what I was afraid of. I told your Pa the way the wind was blowing, but he didn't believe me. It was wrong of Aiden Lily. He should have spoken to Pa first. You don't understand, you are young still, and there are barriers."

She looked at her Ma, frowning. "Barriers, what barriers? You like Aiden, he has a career, especially now, and we love each other."

Ma wiped her hands roughly on the kitchen towel. "Yes, I believe you, and that is all very well, but love alone is not enough to make a good marriage, my girl. We should never have let you two get as close as you have. You've grown up too fast. This has caught us off guard." She began to untie her apron, then hesitated and retied the bow.

Lily took her mother's hands and said, "Stop fussing with your apron Ma. What on earth do you mean, 'barriers'?"

"You and Aiden; he's Catholic, Lily, and you aren't. You would have to convert or not be married in a church, and if you did that, you might be shunned in both communities. We have always been neighbourly with the Donnellys. We like them, but we don't share their beliefs. You've seen how people talk about them, how Aiden got bullied at school, and how hard it is for Aiden's Pa to get work. Is that what you want for yourself and your children? It's hard not to belong anywhere, lonely."

Lily's eyes flashed. "I don't care about those mean-spirited people and their stupid prejudice."

"Lily, you think you won't care, but you will. A marriage is made in a community as well as in a home. You can't easily live outside your community. For example, Granny and Grandpa wouldn't attend a Catholic wedding. Many things make up a happy life, and other people do matter, believe me."

Pa entered the room, unusually stern and sad. "Lily, Maggie, please step into the parlour."

All three returned along the hall, the silence deafening, and Lily rushed to Aiden's side as she entered the room. The two young people stared at Lily's parents with a mixture of defiance and despair writ large on their faces.

Pa cleared his throat. "Lily, as I think you know, Aiden has asked to marry you, and I have refused."

Aiden balled his fists, and Lily said, "Refused? Pa, why?"

Pa looked pained but resolute. "I have said no for your own good, Lily. However, I haven't said no forever. You are just seventeen. If you were to marry Aiden, you would have to convert from our family faith, and I deem you too young to understand what is entailed properly. When you attain your majority at twenty-five, I promise I won't stand in your way if you still desire to marry Aiden."

"Twenty-five, Pa! But that's eight years away." She cast a shocked glance at Aiden. "I will be positively ancient by then. And Aiden is going away. Pa, please, at least let us be engaged." She looked at him, her eyes swimming with unshed tears.

"This seems a blow, but you have your apprenticeship to finish, and Aiden will be running all over the country and even overseas, which is no life for a married man. When you are my age, you'll realise that eight years will pass in a flash. Live life a little first, both of you. It will be different if you're still of the same mind when you're older. You'll be mature adults, not a pair of children. I won't deny you correspondence and visits when you can during that time."

Aiden drew himself up without looking at Lily and said, "I'm disappointed in you, Mr Matthews. I did not expect this religious prejudice from you. My parents were momentarily guests in your home. I had no idea of your bad opinion of us."

Feeling the tension in the room crackle, Lily pulled on his arm. "Aiden, Aiden, stop. Don't say horrible things to Pa because you're angry. Let me talk to him."

But Aiden's expression was cold as he replied quietly, "Lily, I love you, and I hope you'll wait for me. I will never waiver. But I will no longer be insulted about my religion, heritage, or class. I've been made to feel second class all my life by small-minded people. I am finished with this bigoted town."

Lily breathed raggedly, shocked by the cold, angry stranger beside her. "Aiden, Pa didn't mean. Pa doesn't think…"

But Pa spoke across her and opened the door. "Aiden, those are noble sentiments, lad. I had no intention of insulting you, but you've forgotten yourself and who you're speaking to. I suggest you leave."

Aiden flushed but continued to stare at Pa pugnaciously.

"Go and cool your heels, young man, before you say anything else you regret, and I am obliged to throw you out.

154

Believe me, if you love my girl, she is worth waiting for. I waited ten years for her mother."

Aiden bowed stiffly to Lily, stalked out of the room without saying goodbye and slammed the front door with a force which shook the house.

Pa grinned ruefully. "Young hothead, with his high flights — won't be insulted, indeed!" He snorted. "Full of romantic ideals and not a feather to fly with." Warming to his theme, he continued, "He's no more ready to be a husband to you, Lily, than that other lad Harry. They must be out in the world, cut their teeth and make a few mistakes."

Ma nodded. "You're right, Edward."

Pa sighed. "I should have listened to your mother and not let you two get close." He shook his head, "The harm's done now. We'll have to get through it as best we can."

Lily stared at him, disbelieving. He didn't understand.

Brightening, Ma tried to be positive. "Lily, you have much to look forward to before you start looking after a house and a husband. There's your dressmaking and singing…."

Pa laughed. "And if I'm not mistaken, a few beaus keen to dangle after you." He began to sound more confident. "No, if you and Aiden are still intent on getting married after a few years, we'll see what we can do, but I think we've done right suggesting you wait. I'm sure the Donnellys would say the same."

Stifling a sob, Lily ran upstairs to the refuge of her room. She flung herself face down onto the bed, gulping great breaths of air as her heart broke. Her tears flowed unchecked, soaking her eiderdown.

Chapter 17

A gentle tap at her bedroom door woke Lily.

Ma tiptoed into the room. Soft light from a candle lamp cast a circle around her, and she sat on the bed beside her daughter. She unfolded a warm flannel sprinkled with lavender water that she'd brought up. Ma began gently to remove tearstains and soothe swollen eyes. She smoothed the hair strands from Lily's cheek and methodically began to draw the pins holding her bun, allowing it to tumble in heavy strands about Lily's shoulders.

"There's soup and apple pie downstairs, Love, come down. It's cold up here. Try to eat." She chafed Lily's cold hands and nodded encouragingly.

Lily shrugged. "I'm not hungry, and I don't want to see Pa this evening."

Ma hugged the rigidly upright and miserable figure beside her, pulled her in close, and kissed her head. "Oh, Lily, Pa is upset too. You know he'd never intentionally hurt you."

Lily laughed mirthlessly. "I've known Aiden all my life."

Ma reached for Lily's brush on the dressing table. She ran it rhythmically through her daughter's long hair and said, "And that's part of the problem, Lily; you haven't seen anything of life yet. There is much to see and enjoy before you settle down. Married life isn't all roses and sunlight. You need to know yourself very well before attempting to be a loving partner to someone else."

Ma gathered the top section of hair away from Lily's face and tied it with a ribbon from the dresser. "That's better! Take a couple of minutes to compose yourself, and then come down. Remember, Pa hasn't said no forever. He wants what's best for you, Lily, and Aiden too. Neither of you is ready to get married yet or make promises that would be hard to break if you changed your mind."

"I won't stop loving him." Lily raised her chin, "however much you try to keep us apart."

"We won't keep you apart; if anything, Aiden's new job will do that. Enjoy being young, have fun and finish your training; that's all we ask. Aiden will be doing the same and busy making his reputation."

In the face of Ma's calm, good sense, Lily found it difficult to remain angry without seeming childish. The wind of outrage had been taken out of her sails, and what remained was a dull feeling of inevitability, disappointment, and the pain of Aiden's imminent departure. She felt a pang of envy. At least he was going away to do something exciting while they waited to be married. She would have the same old routine every day. Even Grace was going away to America.

Lily wrapped a thick shawl around her shoulders and went downstairs, hesitating outside the sitting room door, her hand on the brass doorknob. Lily squared her shoulders.

Unfortunately, her mother foiled her grand entrance as she called from the kitchen. "I'm here, Lily; come and eat your soup. Pa has already eaten and gone to see Granny and Gramps."

She put a bowl of chicken soup in front of Lily and sat down to watch her eat. During the silence which fell, a knock at the front door made them look up. "Who on earth is that at this hour? It must be at least eight o'clock. Has your father forgotten his keys?"

Her mother patted her hair into place and went to answer the door.

Lily heard a woman's voice, then footsteps in the passage. The kitchen door opened to reveal Mrs Donnelly, usually pale and calm, looking flushed and anxious, as Ma ushered her in.

Ma said, "Sit down, let me make some tea, explain to Lily."

Mary Donnelly sat and, with a struggle, composed herself. "Aiden returned to the theatre for tonight's show in a rare temper, threatening never to come home." Her long slim fingers, typically still unless playing the piano, fidgeted, picking at the folds of her skirt. "He told us about his proposal…."

Ma placed the tea on the table and, without asking, spooned in plenty of sugar and passed it to the distressed woman.

"Lily, I am sorry for the pain this has caused." She reached forwards to touch Lily's hand, then withdrew her hand as if unsure the gesture would be welcome. "We feel as your parents do that it is not suitable for you both to be engaged or married at this time — you're young and have dreams of good careers ahead of you."

Lily interrupted, "We dreamed of developing our careers together."

"If only life were that simple. There are many difficulties facing a marriage like yours. We know, and we don't want it for either of you. Aiden has taken it hard, and I'm apprehensive he might do something silly," said Mrs Donnelly.

"Pa shouldn't have told him off like a child. Aiden hates to feel patronised or put down."

Ma sighed. "Lily, Pa was quite right. Aiden was rather outspoken; forgive me, Mrs Donnelly. He forgot where he was and who he was speaking to. Without meaning to, your father has touched a raw nerve, though, and Aiden feels slighted, I see that."

"His father has gone to the theatre to find him, but I've come to ask a favour, Lily. Will you talk to Aiden tomorrow, before he leaves, to calm him down? He'll listen to you."

Lily's head snapped up. "He's leaving tomorrow? Of course, I want to speak to him. I may not see him for months."

Ma sat opposite Lily and took her hand. "Painful as parting is, my love, if you speak to Aiden tomorrow, you must try to pour oil on troubled waters, not inflame things further. The last thing any of us want is for Aiden to go away under a black cloud."

Mrs Donnelly nodded. "I wouldn't ask Lily; only young men can be impetuous, and he's like his father was at that age. My father wouldn't countenance Mr Donnelly as a husband for me at first, and what with his pride in tatters,

Aiden's pa nearly went to the devil, drinking and fighting everyone who looked at him sideways."

Lily looked at the two older women and felt they were speaking to her as an equal, not a young girl, for the first time. Her voice faltered, "I'll try to talk to him, get him to calm down. It's strange. You think I'm mature enough to do this, but not to know my mind about being married. This is all wrong. We were happy with our plans. When is he leaving?"

Mary Donnelly sniffed and brushed away a tear. "Miss Marion has booked him a ticket on the seven o'clock train. She said she had something to do before leaving."

"Would you permit us to take a walk after church?" Lily glanced at the kitchen clock. By this time tomorrow, he'd be gone.

The two older women nodded at each other over Lily's head. Ma said, "I'm sure Pa will have no objection. If he does, I'll speak to him." Mrs Donnelly reached out in gratitude grasping Ma and Lily's hands in each of hers. Lily sensed the gesture was the formation of a pact, a circle of solidarity, unspoken but no less intense for that.

Ma showed Mrs Donnelly to the door, where they exchanged hushed sentences that Lily couldn't hear, then returned to the kitchen. "Well, I'm glad that's settled. Young Aiden isn't steady enough to think of marriage, and there's the proof, if any were needed."

Lily stood abruptly and paced across the kitchen. "It's unfair to say things like that about Aiden, and you mustn't say them to me. He is steady and hardworking. We never dreamed you would object to him being Catholic."

Ma sighed and rubbed weary hands across her face. "Oh, Lily, don't take on so. It isn't only us. The Donnellys are against it too. You heard Mrs Donnelly earlier."

She bustled around the kitchen in a show of being busy that Lily recognised as her mother feeling upset. Lily would have tried to comfort her if she had not felt bewildered and heartsore. As it was, she felt trapped in a nightmare of everyone's expectations and opinions and couldn't see a way out of the maze.

"Ma, would you mind if I went to bed?"

Ma nodded. "No, love, go and get some sleep; it's been a difficult day. Things will seem different in the morning. I'll wait up for Pa."

Although tired, Lily realised she wouldn't sleep until she knew Aiden and Mr Donnelly had arrived home safely. Instead of getting into bed, she got undressed, put on her dressing gown, wrapped herself in the eiderdown, and pulled a chair to the window.

The first person to walk along the street wrapped up against the December cold was Pa. She recognised his outline in a hat and greatcoat. His walk was distinctive, too, his muscular arms swung away from his body, and his back, stiff from years of working with stone, gave a roll to his gait. He turned into their front, his weathered face momentarily illuminated by a streetlamp as he fumbled for the front door keys. He glanced around as if sensing Lily's scrutiny but failed to look up.

She sighed. *Oh, Pa! You still think I'm a child, and I'll make the same choices you have. But it isn't my dream to make my life in Eastfield Road like you have with Granny and Gramps.* She frowned, *not yet anyway. I want to be independent, see London and be part of the theatre world I glimpsed this afternoon.*

Perhaps she should run away with Aiden. Lily spent a few moments imagining herself breaking away from her parents, jumping onto his train at the last minute and seeing her parents disappear in the puffs of steam and smoke as the train pulled out. However, her imagination ran out there. She had no idea how life would be after doing such a wicked thing.

It was thoroughly disheartening. Why hadn't Kitty included her? Was her middle name Patience? Or Virtue? Lily wondered whether she had 'home-bird' written across her forehead. Why didn't Kitty Marion see she had a passion inside her as much as Aiden?

She had to giggle. Miss Patience Virtue sounded like a pale-skinned heroine in a novel from the lending library.

The moment of wry humour was fleeting. A horrible thought crossed Lily's mind. *Aiden, attracted by Miss Marion's confidence, political mind, and evident sophistication, was smitten. Perhaps Kitty Marion wanted Aiden for herself, so she advised Lily to stay behind. Needing an accompanist and the suffragette's cause were excuses to lure him away. Perhaps she was stealing him from under Lily's nose, a woman of loose morals! Lily gasped, her back straight as a ramrod.* Indignant, half-convinced that Aiden was lost to her, still something Stephen Dent had said earlier gave her comfort; *He preferred her voice and hinted that Miss Marion was a little over-ripe.*

Fortunately, before her thoughts became entirely disordered, Lily heard men's voices and craned to see down the street. Mr Donnelly had his arm around Aiden's shoulders. He was shorter and thicker set than his son, who took more after his mother. He was chatting to his son in a placatory way. Aiden stooped slightly to hear him.

Unlike Pa, as they passed Lily's house, Aiden stared up at her window with such accuracy that Lily thought he must do the same every time he passed.

Her heart gave a leap of joy. She raised her hand in a half-wave and smiled as tenderly as possible but wished she had not bundled up in an eiderdown like an invalid. Aiden stopped dead, causing his father to lurch, and with an unusual boldness, he blew two extravagant kisses and placed his hands over his heart in a dramatic gesture before staggering back two paces.

What on earth was going on? She blushed at the open romance of the blown kisses — in front of his Pa too. It didn't seem like Aiden, but at least she knew he was safe, and he still loved her.

Chapter 18

When she woke, it was early, and Lily took great pains to dress her hair in an imitation of her style from yesterday. She lifted her thick brown mane over a soft roll to give it volume, then captured it in a bun at the back. Finally, she teased tendrils free to soften the effect and flatter her face.

Lily looked longingly at the dress and shoes Mrs Winchett had lent her, which Aiden had barely noticed yesterday. She didn't dare wear them again. If she spoiled the outfit, she would work for nothing for years to pay Mrs Winchett back.

She chose a cream blouse with a high neck and pinch pleats at the front to wear with her Sunday skirt. There was nothing for it; Lily knew she'd be cold but did not want a thick cardigan under her coat. She would rather suffer.

Lily dabbed some of her mother's rose water on her skin, wanting Aiden to link the smell of roses to her, not Miss Marion.

She had just finished her toilette when Ma called her down to breakfast.

When her mother caught sight of her, she frowned. "For goodness sake, put a shawl or a cardigan on. You'll catch your death. It's nearly Christmas, not the middle of summer, Lily."

"I'm not cold," Lily replied airily, worried the goosebumps on her arms would give her away.

Ma nodded briskly and continued to make breakfast. "You won't be any use to Aiden with pneumonia, or worse, consumption if that's who you're trying to impress. I thought you had more sense, Lily Matthews."

With a grand disregard for Miss Laidlaw's prior claims, Lily decided to give Aiden the handkerchief she had embroidered with lilies as a keepsake. She was also determined they should have one more kiss, even if he thought her fast. She had a photograph of herself taken on the pier last summer that she would write some personal words on, perhaps a few lines of poetry.

This, not the sermon, occupied most of her thoughts in church. Eventually, she decided on some lyrics from Aiden's song.

Every time Kitty Marion sang it, he'd be obliged to think of her, Lily thought triumphantly.

She recited the liturgy's familiar words by rote and mindlessly sang hymns. Her entire being focused on meeting with Aiden.

When the service ended, Lily barely suppressed her irritation at the chatter in the church hall during the social, which she usually enjoyed. Today, Lily couldn't wait to get home.

The hands of the clock moved achingly slowly around to one o'clock when Ma served lunch. As Lily spooned the last of Ma's apple pie and custard, she asked, mouth still full, "May I get ready to meet Aiden?"

Pa raised his eyebrows. "Your ma has talked me into this against my better judgement, Lily. I know Granny and Gramps would disapprove. Aiden could have come here for tea which would be more seemly."

"Pa, we are going for a walk. We've done it hundreds of times, and I want to say goodbye to him properly. I may not see him for, well, for months." The thought made her swallow hard and blink away a tear.

"I didn't like his attitude yesterday, but I'll make allowances. He's had a lot of change in a short time, so it's maybe gone to his head. I'm not one to hold a grudge."

Lily leant forward and kissed Pa on the cheek, then scurried upstairs to check her hair and collect the keepsakes for Aiden.

With her mother's eagle eye upon her, she could not leave the house without a shawl. Lily pretended to have acquiesced to the imposed warm clothing, comforted by knowing she had a plan.

As Ma gave her some money to buy tea and whispered, "Have a nice time, Lily." She felt a pang of guilt that she was being deceitful. However, an image of Miss Marion and Aiden exchanging warm glances on stage flashed into her mind, and Lily put her scruples away. She may not be going to London with Aiden, but she intended to leave a lasting impression.

She hurried up the road until she was out of sight of her home, then removed the shawl and bundled it behind old Mrs Andrew's wall. She noticed the cold wind whipping around her neck immediately.

She retraced her steps and knocked at the Donnelly's front door. Mary Donnelly answered, and Lily said, "Is Aiden ready?"

Aiden emerged from the back of the house, looking more pale than usual and with black circles under his eyes. "Hello, Lily," he muttered, looking down, embarrassed.

As soon as the door had closed, Lily took his arm and said, "Are you alright? You look dreadful."

He freed his arm, pushed his hands deep into his pockets and shrugged against the cold. "I'm fine. You wouldn't understand."

Lily looked at her now free hand and felt like he'd slapped her. "You could try me," she said.

"I was drunk last night."

Lily gasped and put a hand to her mouth. She'd never seen anyone get drunk.

"I played the show, then went out with the musicians to drown my sorrows and would have stayed out if Pa hadn't come to find me. I wanted to shake the dust of this place off my feet. I was sick as a dog when I got home and feel like hell today. Satisfied?"

"No need to take it out on me, Aiden Donnelly, because you made a fool of yourself."

He flushed red. "The worst of it is you're right, Lily. I'm an idiot. I'm sorry, I don't know which end is up since yesterday. If Kitty had seen me drunk, she would probably have sacked me. That was the problem with her last accompanist. The musicians seem to drink a lot."

"I don't care about what Miss Marion thinks or what the others suggest you do. Don't drink too much for your own sake. Pa says drinking doesn't solve anything, and the vicar says it lets the devil into your soul."

Aiden shot her a look. "If you don't want to hear about Kitty, I certainly don't want to hear about the vicar or your Pa. He had no reason to block our engagement, even if we had to wait to get married. The world is changing, Lily. We'll force it to change. Religious and class prejudice will go, and we'll see equality for everyone you see if we don't."

Aiden's face lit up with new fervour as he spoke, and Lily's heart sank. Meeting Kitty Marion had fanned the flames of his natural resentments. Lily wanted to see progress too, but her Pa said changes came slowly, hard-fought using the democratic process. Aiden wanted things now, and she could see he might be destined for more disillusionment.

"I hope you're right. When we're married, we can campaign for change together. If we're happy and successful, we can show the world their concerns are stupid."

He looked at her fondly and drew her arm through his. "You'll be a warrior here, and I shall be one there. It won't take eight years, you'll see." That was more like the Aiden she knew.

"But Aiden, you won't get caught up in anything dangerous, will you?"

"You are not to worry about me, Lily. I shall write to you regularly and tell you how I'm doing. What harm can come to me playing the piano and writing songs?"

"How can I write to you, Aiden? You'll be moving from place to place."

He handed her a slip of paper in his spikey writing. "This is my agent's address in London. All my letters can go through him until I have my address."

168

She folded it carefully and put it in her bag, which reminded her about the keepsakes inside.

They joined the Eastney end of the seafront and walked past the barracks towards the bright lights of the pier. Lily pulled his arm and ran down the slipway to duck behind the bathing huts.

"Lily! What on earth are you doing?" Aiden said as their feet hit the deep pebbles, and they scrambled to stay upright.

"Shh!" She said, finger to lips and peeked around the end of the row of huts. "I saw Grace and George ahead. I don't want them to see us."

"That's not very ni…" He encountered her incredulous look and changed to, "Oh! I see."

Hidden behind the beach huts with the light fading and only the winter sea to spy on her, Lily turned to Aiden, stretched on tiptoe, and placed both hands on his shoulders. She kissed him first on his cheek, then full on the mouth.

"Lily Matthews," he exclaimed, laughing, and pushed her back by the arms. He studied her face as if to memorise every detail, then pulled her in close again and kissed her slowly.

Her heart raced, and she could feel his beating wildly too. He was warm and solid as he wrapped his arms around her. She couldn't believe that later tonight, he'd be gone.

"I will miss you terribly," she whispered into his chest.

"I love you, Lily; I'm coming back for you, don't ever forget that."

She sighed and said, "I'll wait."

A loud voice broke in on their reverie. "Oi, you two down there, what's going on?"

Lily gasped, frozen to the spot. Aiden grabbed her wrist. "Run, Lily."

He dragged her across the pebbles and up the slipway, neatly avoiding the patrolman coming in the other direction.

They ran until Lily had a stitch, and her hat was coming loose from her hair.

Gasping for breath, Aiden looked back. "We're clear. That was close, Lily."

She grabbed her side and, for a moment, fancied she saw devils dancing in his eyes. He looked so alive.

"Come on, let's get tea, and then I'd better take you home before you get us arrested. I can't believe you had the cheek to be lecturing me."

As they sat in the small tearoom on the pier, Lily thought they could be engaged, for all the world would know. Shyly, she took the small packet she'd made from scented paper and passed it to him. "These are for you."

He slid out the photograph and the handkerchief and looked at her, sadness clouding his eyes. "I shall look at your photograph every day, Lily, and keep the handkerchief close by me for luck. I'll wish I could call over the wall and talk to you. You're my best friend as well as my girl."

Lily looked down, knowing she was close to tears. He was her best friend too, and tonight he'd be gone.

As they walked home, Lily asked about Aiden's travel arrangements. "Do you know where you are going yet?"

He shook his head. "I know sketchy details. We're going to London first to stay with some WSPU friends. Kitty will receive a medal from the WSPU for her work for the cause. Then we must rehearse for her private engagements in the

North. After that, I think it's back to London via Colchester for the Pantomime season."

"It's exciting, Aiden. I wish I were coming."

"You could run away with me," he said, half-joking.

She gasped, shocked. "We both know that's not true; Don't tease me. I'm underage, and I couldn't work. I'd be a millstone around your neck. Pa would set up a hue and cry, then what would everyone think."

He shrugged sulkily. "If only your pa…"

The corners of her mouth drooped. "Pa hasn't said no forever, Aiden; at least we can write and see each other. I'm sure they'll come around."

Satisfied she had tried to fulfil her promise to Ma and Mrs Donnelly, she changed the sensitive subject. "Are you meeting Miss Marion at the station?"

"Yes, Ma and Pa are coming to see me off. It's hard on them too. Will you pop in to see Ma sometimes?"

"I will, and I'll be seeing her at rehearsals and the meetings with Mrs O'Shea." She tried to inject brightness into her voice, but even she could hear the false note.

Their time together had flown by quickly. As they turned into Eastfield Road, her steps began to lag. She wanted to cling to him and feel his heart beating as she had on the beach, but she knew it was impossible in front of the neighbour's houses.

As they drew closer, Aiden said, "Lily, nothing will make this any easier, and we both know we have to go in, so I'm going to kiss your hand and escort you to your door. All the while, I'll remember our kisses on the beach. Every song I play, I'll play it for you, and you must do the same when you sing. Promise?"

She nodded, unable to answer, her throat constricted by unshed tears.

Aiden pressed a long kiss to her hand, rapped the doorknocker briskly and turned away before the door opened. She saw him vault over the low wall between the two front doors and heard his key scrape the lock in the Donnelly's door.

As her front door opened, spilling a crescent of light over the dark front, she half ran, half stumbled into Ma's arms. All Lily could think was, '*he's gone*', chased by the realisation that Aiden hadn't waited to see her parents. He had neither forgiven Pa nor offered him an apology.

Chapter 19

*T*he hardest thing in the world is to be the one who's left behind, Lily thought miserably as she made her lonely way towards the tram. She carried the dress of dashed hopes over her arm and nursed the pain of Aidan's departure.

The day had dawned grey, gloomy, and leaden, which reflected Lily's mood perfectly. Her tea had been too hot and scalded her tongue, she'd snapped a lace as she'd tied her boots, and Ma had questioned her about the missing shawl.

She'd forgotten to retrieve it on the way home last night and had to admit her deception. Ma had been disappointed in her, which was way worse than her being cross, and Lily had endured some lengthy quotes from the bible about practising deception.

As she passed Mrs Andrew's, she bent over the wall and picked up the shawl, damp from being outside in the Winter air all night. "You got me into trouble this morning," she grumbled. "I hate you anyway. You may be warm, but you're ugly." Lily didn't know what to do with the shawl. She did not have a free hand with the borrowed dress to carry and her bag, so she wrapped it around her. Lily grimaced as its cold, damp tufts touched her face, a far cry from Aiden's gentle hands yesterday.

At work, all the girls clustered around to ask about the theatre on Saturday. What was it like to be backstage? What were Miss Marion's gowns like? The questions went on and on until she wanted to scream.

She was pleased when Mrs Winchett clapped, and everyone hurried to their places at the table.

After distributing the work, she beckoned Lily. "Miss Matthews, a moment if you please. Miss Laidlaw, please join us."

"I have this morning received a note from Miss Marion, commending you for your interest and enthusiasm during your visit at the weekend and noting your elegant attire. For which we must give credit to Miss Laidlaw's talent."

Lily bobbed a curtsey, and Miss Laidlaw nodded, accepting the compliment elegantly.

Mrs Winchett paused for effect, then continued, "She has particularly noted your interest in costume design, Miss Matthews, and would like to support your training by commissioning a dress from us for her new song. She specifically wishes you to collaborate with Miss Laidlaw in its design."

As she processed what Mrs Winchett had said, Lily was rendered speechless. *Miss Marion had kept her word* — Lily's first rush of pleasure was followed swiftly by a surge of anger at her position — *This keeps me neatly tied in Portsmouth, and now I'm indebted to her as well. She has organised to have everything her way.*

Miss Laidlaw flushed a delicate pink and said, "Thank you for the compliment, Ma'am. I am sure Miss Matthews and I are delighted to have this exciting opportunity."

Mrs Winchett shot a look at Lily, who remained rooted to the spot, speechless. "The dress is for new shows in January, and apparently, Miss Matthews knows the song referred to. I am pleased with how you represented us on Saturday, Miss Matthews. However, I would caution you to remain modest as you apply yourself under Miss Laidlaw's tuition. You still have a lot to learn. Miss Marion's request is a great honour."

Lily struggled to look up and mumbled, "Yes indeed, thank you, Mrs Winchett."

When they were out of earshot, Miss Laidlaw said, "Whatever's the matter, Lily? It is most gracious of Miss Marion to sponsor us in this way and a wonderful opportunity. I thought you would be over the moon."

Lily looked at Miss Laidlaw. She clasped and unclasped her hands nervously. "I am — I mean, it's everything I could have wished for, dreamed about, a month ago…."

Miss Laidlaw frowned. "And now?"

Lily hesitated, then blurted out her concerns. "I don't trust Kitty Marion. She talks and talks, and then suddenly, everything changes, and you don't know where you are anymore. She's stolen Aiden and whipped him into a frenzy about social injustice. I don't know if she wants him to play for her, do dreadful things for the cause, or be her beau."

Miss Laidlaw suppressed a smile at the dramatic tirade, eyed her young protegee kindly, and said, "That sounds very bad indeed. Let's go to the silks room to be private and discuss what we can do about this."

Miss Laidlaw closed the door to the silks room. In the style of an oversized airing cupboard, it had rows of wooden shelving which carried ells of fabric of all different descriptions. Usually, a favourite place of Lily's, the smell of new material and the jewel colours spoke to her soul, but today Lily could barely be bothered to look.

"What on earth has happened, Lily? You were excited on Saturday morning. Am I to understand that Aiden has transferred his affections to Miss Marion?"

Lily looked embarrassed. "No, well, not exactly, no. He asked Pa if we could be married or at least engaged, and Pa won't allow it until I reach my majority."

Miss Laidlaw nodded sympathetically. "Did he say why?"

"He said we were too young, that I must finish my apprenticeship, and because Aiden is Catholic, I must be twenty-five before he consents."

"I see, and all this despite Aiden having prepared some accommodation for you and shown himself able to provide for a family."

Unsure what to say, Lily rubbed the corner of a bolt of satin close to her. "Aiden's sold his first song but will travel with the show. He will be successful, I'm sure. If we were together, I could make costumes, and we would have stayed in boarding houses or with friends." Her voice faltered.

Miss Laidlaw nodded slowly. "Of course, it sounds like the sort of adventure we all would like, and I'm sure that not all boarding houses are damp and smell of boiled cabbage."

Lily wrinkled her nose.

"You know, of course, that many places would turn you away for being Catholics? Of course, you do. You and Aiden will have spoken about this." She paused. "Sorry, I presume it would be you changing faith?"

Lily went to speak, but Miss Laidlaw continued in a conversational tone. "Did the company need a seamstress?"

Lily looked at Miss Laidlaw. "I don't know, I assumed…." She frowned, then lifted her chin. "Are you making fun of me?"

Miss Laidlaw shook her head. "Not at all. I wonder if your parents feel you would be more comfortable with them until Aiden establishes himself."

Lily scowled but didn't reply,

"If you finished your apprenticeship here, you would certainly command more respect and a better wage. I've always felt there could be nothing less romantic than poverty, and I understand that theatre companies are not always reliable employers." Miss Laidlaw paused, tapping her top lip with her finger. "As to your faith, only you can decide about that and whether you are strong enough to be perhaps isolated from your friends and family."

Lily sighed. "Grace is going to America with George Dent to set up a business there, and her parents have said yes."

"Indeed, but if I understand correctly, Mr Dent is secure financially, and they have the same religion. Your situation is not comparable."

Lily looked mutinous. "Money, that's all people care about, that, and what society thinks, even if it's beastly and unfair. Catholics are Christians too."

Miss Laidlaw shook her head. "Oh, Lily, it's hard to swim upstream against the tide, although I admire your determination to try." She leant into Lily. "If I may say so, you must not repeat this. Miss Kirby lacks your creativity and flair with a needle. One might even suppose she positively despises needlework. She will be much happier not being a seamstress and has the type of forthright resilience to serve her well in supporting a new business venture."

Seeing Lily relax, Miss Laidlaw continued. "Lily, you have real talent. Please don't throw it away. If your parents see that you and Aiden are sensible and work hard to have some security, I am sure they'll reconsider. It will be good for you not to rush. One cannot simply change one's beliefs as one does one's dress."

Lily looked down; everyone was saying the same.

"For now, shall we enjoy working together on this costume? Having such a prestigious name in your portfolio to offer future employers is remarkable."

Lily shrugged. None of this advice offered any chance of re-joining Aiden.

"Whatever you think of Miss Marion, there is no harm in letting her further your interests. She has offered you a wonderful opportunity here, not only to design a gown but also to keep her in your sights. Don't forget we will need to see her for the fittings."

Lily examined Miss Laidlaw's bland expression and candid eyes as she pondered this unexpected worldly wisdom. She had failed to see any possibilities in her situation until now. "I think Aiden is half bewitched by her. I can't explain, but she has such, such presence."

Miss Laidlaw relaxed her shoulders imperceptibly. "Remember, Lily, at present, you have no reason to doubt Aiden's affections. Trying to hold onto people too tightly pushes them away. Let him prove himself. After all, if he is fickle, you would hardly wish to be married to him."

Lily hung her head. "He isn't like that."

"Good. For now, you can only make the best of a difficult situation. Show your parents how serious you are. And always, always play to your strengths."

Lily nodded uncertainly; the only other option she could think of was to run away after him. Maybe she could visit at least if she could win the concert prize. After all, Aiden had left her behind with a stash of promises but had gone after his dream anyway.

Having a plan made her feel better but didn't make the pain any less.

"Now, this gown, what colour shall we think of for our creation?" Miss Laidlaw reached up and took down a bolt of silk in the most dramatic kingfisher blue. "I have always wanted to use this, but it's a bold colour, not easy to carry off for most women. What do you think?"

Lily thought Miss Marion had the force of personality to carry off anything. She thought of those ice-grey eyes and realised she had never met anyone more extraordinary. She narrowed her eyes as Miss Laidlaw draped the fabric across her body diagonally. "The song is a tender, romantic waltz. I don't think using a strong colour like that will make the design romantic."

Miss Laidlaw looked at the rich colour and the texture of the fabric. She shook her head with regret, re-rolled it, and replaced the ell. "You're right, Lily. Perhaps something with more movement, then? Several layers of silk chiffon will float as she moves. We could set in godets from the knee to enhance the effect."

Lily paused and looked at Miss Laidlaw with a tiny lift to the corners of her mouth. "I suppose it's out of the question to make her look dowdy and old?"

Miss Laidlaw laughed. "I think what is required here is dignity, Lily, not revenge. If you design wonderful dresses for her, Kitty Marion won't want to upset you."

She was tempted, despite herself, to enjoy the task of her first costume design. "Maybe something that looks quite simple when standing still but flares and moves if Miss Marion dances a little. With a soft, loose bodice caught into a waistband."

A different girl exited the silks room. Lily had grown in stature, a new glint in her eye. If she wanted to get to London and perhaps secure a job at the theatre, she knew she had to use all the weapons at her disposal.

Lily leaned into her friend as she sat down. "Can we meet for lunch, please?"

Grace sniffed. "Oh, I thought you'd be eating upstairs with Mrs Winchett now."

"Gracie, don't be cross with me. Wait until I tell you about the weekend. I promise you nothing has changed between us."

Grace looked slightly mollified, and her curiosity got the better of her. She added, "You're not the only one to have news, Lily Matthews. I've got news too."

"Ladies, too much chatter. Concentrate on your work." Miss Laidlaw's calm voice made both girls put their heads down over their sewing, each eager for lunchtime to come.

A gust of wind straight off the sea nearly knocked them sideways as they stepped outside. Lily felt the warmth from her skin evaporate. They set off to find a bench in the lea of a building, but everyone had the same idea, and the only seats exposed to the cold breeze were available.

"Quick!" said Grace, her teeth chattering. "Eat your sandwich, and we'll go into the tearoom for a hot drink." She stuffed a good quarter of her sandwich into her mouth and turned to Lily, cheeks bulging. "Cwum un!"

Lily laughed. "Grace! What would George say if he could see you now?"

She swallowed, then banged her chest as the massive ball of dry sandwich scraped painfully downwards. "He'd say, forget the sandwiches; let's get warm." She stuffed another large chunk and dragged Lily up. "My treat."

Lily closed her eyes momentarily; she could only imagine what her ma would say if she'd seen that.

The windows of the tearoom were misted with condensation behind the prim lace curtains. They had to squeeze onto the last tiny table in the corner near the counter.

The waitress kept saying, "Excuse me," as she squeezed past Lily's chair through the narrow space.

Lily cupped the china cup between both hands and sipped. "You first," she said to Grace.

Grace looked smug and said, "We've set a date for the wedding, March the thirtieth. We sail on April the second. Pa Dent's agent has found a suitable building for the factory in New Jersey. The agent is staying to interview for a works manager and a team to install the machinery and fittings." Grace squealed and drummed her feet under the table. "We're actually going, Lily."

Lily thought how different things were when your fiancée was wealthy, but she put it aside as unworthy. "Oh, my goodness, Grace, it's all happened quickly. Aren't you even a bit scared?"

"Scared? Lily, I can't wait to go. There's a flat beside the building, called an apartment, for us to live in, and we can be whoever we want to be out there. It will be a new start away from stuffy old Portsmouth."

"But what about your ma and pa? Won't you miss them?" For the first time, Lily had an insight into what it might feel like if she had to renounce her family for Aiden.

"Lily, you're a bit naïve. My house isn't like yours. We're bursting at the seams. The boys broke their bed bouncing on it the other day, and Pa lashed it together with some rope. They've got to sleep on it like that now. My sister will get our room to herself. If I can make something of myself, I can help them. They expect me to get married and move out. Going to America is a good thing for all of us."

Lily looked down. In the face of Grace's cheerful pragmatism, she felt that perhaps she had led a sheltered existence. She hoped that Grace truly loved George.

Grace looked at Lily expectantly. "Your go, Miss Teacher's Pet. Why are you so popular all of a sudden?"

Lily frowned. "Don't call me that, Grace. It's mean."

"Keep your wool on, I'm only teasing, but you'd better toughen up because others will be jealous."

Lily smiled ruefully. "They wouldn't be if they knew."

Grace's expression softened. "Lily, you were on top of the world on Friday. Whatever's happened?"

"Aiden's gone away, Grace, and Pa won't countenance our engagement." Grace gasped; Lily's weekend story came tumbling out along with Miss Marion's two offers. All the pain and self-doubt, the disillusionment and fear.

"I get it's bad that he's Catholic and all. I wouldn't want to tell my pa that. He'd probably lock me up and throw away the key. But I'd escape." Grace winked at Lily. "You'll see him, won't you? I mean, you'll go to London, not accept this."

Lily looked up from under her eyelashes. "I hope to see him when Miss Laidlaw and I do Miss Marion's dress fittings. I'm saving to visit, but otherwise, how can I? I don't even know where he's going to be, Grace. Once Pa had said no to our engagement, Aiden didn't ask me to go with him."

"Well, Lily Matthews, I know exactly what I'd do! I'd make sure I had plenty of exciting things to write to him about, when and if I chose to write." She flicked her wrist in a gesture of insouciance. "I would not be languishing at home behaving like a wallflower."

Lily opened her eyes wide at the sudden attack. "Grace, I don't know what you mean. What do you mean?"

Grace laughed. "Stephen has a tendre for you, and so does this, Harry. Well, play them along. Have some outings, only as friends, but make sure Aiden knows. Because I can guarantee that Aiden will enjoy himself, it won't do for him to take you for granted."

Lily looked shocked and said, "Grace, I intend to wait for Aiden."

"Wait, if you like, but I don't see why you shouldn't have a bit of fun in the meantime." She held up both hands, then made an impression of a wilting damsel. "Where's the interest in a girl moping at home waiting for your next letter? No incentive to make him hurry back. And another thing, it will be an excellent smokescreen for your parents.

They won't be able to say you haven't tried to do as they ask and meet someone else."

Lily shook her head. "I don't know, Grace."

Grace laughed. "Well, I do. I shall tell Stephen that you need cheering up; you watch how quickly he comes to find you, Lily."

Alarmed at the turn in the conversation, she caught Grace's hand. "No, please don't, Grace, don't!"

She looked at Lily and frowned. "Why ever not? He's charming and funny, perfect for taking your mind off things, and never serious about anything. You won't break his heart, and he won't break yours."

Lily hesitated. How to put what she was about to say without being rude? Stephen was about to become Grace's brother-in-law, even if George didn't get on with him. "Because I don't feel quite comfortable with him. He frightens me."

Grace was incredulous. "Oh fiddle, Lily Matthews frightens you indeed. I didn't have you down as such a mouse. Stephen won't hurt you. It's only for a lark."

Lily didn't reply. She couldn't fault Stephen's manners. He had always been pleasant and engaging, but there was something about him. Lily couldn't exactly say what. But then he was older and sophisticated; what did she know? Thinking about him gave her the jitters, but not the same pleasant heart flutters she felt when she was close to Aiden.

Chapter 20

After supper, Lily and her parents sat around the fire. Ma and Lily discussed the merits of adding a swag of flowers or a single flower on the dress for Miss Marion, and Pa had disappeared behind his newspaper.

Lily made a couple of rough sketches on the sketchpad that Miss Laidlaw had provided, trying, not entirely successfully, to emulate her flowing design sketches. The subject of costume design exhausted, Lily put her drawing aside, and now she and Ma were hemming. Pa regaled them with stories from the newspaper. He suddenly stopped, sat upright in the chair, and snapped the newspaper to see an article better.

"Well, upon my word, listen to this, Maggie."

'A suspicious fire at the Hampshire residence of Lord Charles Beresford MP for Portsmouth began on the afternoon of Sunday the eighteenth December. The fire failed to take hold and was extinguished due to the brave efforts of the fire brigade, summoned to the scene by household staff. The family were not in residence at the time. Investigations are currently underway to rule out the possibility of arson.'

Pa shook his head. "I don't know what the world is coming to."

Ma tutted. "There seems to be more and more unrest. It's all they put in the papers these days."

Pa nodded. "Beresford's in the House of Lords, though, and the Peers stirred up a lot of unrest, holding up the welfare reforms last year. It can't help but breed resentment when poverty is rife."

Ma looked at him over her glasses. "I know things are hard, but I don't hold with setting fire to property like that."

Pa frowned. "When all is said and done, Beresford served his country. You would think a navy man would command some respect here."

Ma nodded her agreement and said, "Mind, it makes sense for those with plenty to contribute more taxes to support welfare for the poor. When the elected government wants the change, the House of Lords looks as if it's protecting the wealthy by blocking the bill."

Lily looked up. "Aiden says there will be an uprising to force the issue."

Pa added, "He may be right. There'll be trouble if the man on the street loses faith in the democratic process. There's already trouble in Ireland."

Lily sighed. It was time she finished the hem on her costume for the community show. She thought about what she had heard during her meetings at Mrs O'Shea's. "Women are getting restless too; that's why people like Kitty Marion advocate radical action. She says it's the only way women will be heard."

Ma looked up swiftly. "I hope they aren't feeding you any of those ideas at Mrs O'Shea's. A lot of those women end up in jail for their trouble. Don't get any illusions about how romantic it all is."

"Mrs O'Shea believes in lobbying and education."

As the evening wore on, Lily began to feel poorly. She had a scratchy tickle in her throat, and her head ached.

"Ma, my throat's sore. Will you make me one of your soothers, please?"

Ma laid aside her hemming and stood up. "Come over to the light. Let me see."

Lily approached her mother. "It's nothing much; I'm worried about rehearsal."

Her mother looked at her over the top of her pince-nez. "I'll be the judge of that. Open and say 'ahh'."

Ma said, "You're lucky; I have a lemon left from making curd last week. I'll make you a lemon and honey drink, but before, you'd better gargle with salt water."

Lily pulled a face. "I think the honey and lemon will be enough. Can we not bother with the salt water?"

"You're the one who wants to sing. It's up to you." Ma gave Lily a stern look. "If you'd listened to my advice at the weekend instead of gadding about in thin clothes, you mightn't have a sore throat now."

Lily hunched a shoulder. It wouldn't matter that she probably got it from Francie, who had a cough at work. In Ma's eyes, it had to be not wearing a shawl when she went out with Aiden! "Oh, alright then, I'll gargle. But if I swallow any, it'll make me sick."

Ma headed towards the kitchen, muttering, "Fuss about nothing. I never did."

Ma measured a pint of hot water from the kettle and dissolved a teaspoon of salt. "Little sips," she said to Lily as she handed her a small metal bowl to spit into and put a towel around her neck.

The first effort was pathetic. Lily managed two or three glug-glugs, then spat the salty water out disgusted. "I can't remember how to do it," she complained.

Pa had followed them into the kitchen. He laughed. "And you're supposed to be a singer. They gargle all the time." He took a mouthful of the saltwater and emitted a cacophony of high and low-pitched gurgling noises as he sank the water deeper into his throat and back up again. He raised his eyebrows at Lily and grinned.

Ma laughed. "Edward Matthews, will you ever grow up!"

Never one to back down from a challenge, Lily tried again and managed better than before, but still not as well as Pa. Piqued, she tried with the last of the gargle, finally achieving a loud burbling sound.

Ma shook her head as Pa laughed, and Lily begged him, "Don't make me laugh. It hurts."

Ma twisted a large dollop of honey from the jar into another cup and tipped in the freshly squeezed lemon. She poured boiling water on top, saying, "Now go and get undressed while this cools, and you can drink it by the fire. Mind you wrap a scarf around your throat."

It was later in the night that Lily woke feeling hot and thirsty. She gulped down the cold honey and lemon Ma had left on the bedside table. Fretfully she pushed off the covers, then regretted it as she began to shiver and retrieved them.

"Ma", she croaked, "Ma, can you come."

She heard movement in the bedroom next door, and her

mother appeared, her hair in a plait and her thick woollen dressing gown hastily tied askew.

"What's the matter, Lily?"

"I feel terrible, Ma, I'm hot and cold, and everything aches." She started to cry. "I can't be ill, Ma, not now, with the show coming up."

"Shh, we'll worry about that in good time, don't cry now." Ma turned her pillow over and plumped it up. "I'll go down and make you a drink."

Ma returned with a cup of tea and a blue glass pot.

"Let's rub some of this in and wrap you up."

Ma wrapped a long strip of lint around Lily's throat and tucked the ends into her nightie. She then placed a cloth soaked in lavender water on her forehead. The pungent smell of the Vicks Vaporub made Lily's eyes water.

A crease furrowed Ma's forehead. "I'll sit here for a while. Try to get some sleep."

Ma settled into the chair beside Lily's bed. Lily was vaguely aware through the night of her mother changing the lavender cloth and offering her sips of water. She heard Pa's voice as well,

"Is everything alright, Maggie?"

"Lily has a fever, Edward. I'm trying to keep her cool and hoping it will break. Something is troubling her because she keeps calling out. Before you go to work, you'll have to take a note for Mrs Winchett. She won't be working today."

Lily no longer felt hot when she woke in the morning, but her throat and head still ached. She thought about getting up, but every part of her felt heavy and reluctant to move. She listlessly looked towards the window and saw fern-like ice patterns on the glass. It must still be early.

189

She heard her ma's footsteps on the stairs and called out. Her mother came in with a bowl of steaming water and a cloth, which she placed on the chair beside the bed. "I thought you'd like to freshen up."

She gently washed her daughter's face and hands, drying them with a soft towel, then rubbed more Vicks and replaced the lint. "No work for you today. There's a nice fire in the sitting room, and I've made a bed on the sofa. If I help you downstairs, would you like to be there or prefer to stay here?"

"Can I come down with you?" Lily's voice came out as a whispered rasp, and she touched her sore throat.

"I've got a nice fresh nightgown here; we'll slip that on you, and you can wear your dressing gown and slippers. No one will see you but me, so we'll just braid your hair for now."

Ma's gentle plans were comforting, and Lily gave herself over to being nursed.

"I called over to Mrs Donnelly, but she's gone to work. Mr Donnelly answered and kindly agreed to fetch some more lemons from the greengrocer. Your pa has let the workroom know, so you don't need to fret."

Lily looked at Ma eagerly, her eyes seeming over-large in her pale face. "And have the Donnellys heard from Aiden?"

"Bless me, no child. He's only been gone two days; we can't expect any news yet."

Lily slumped. "No, no, of course not."

Lily's legs felt like they didn't belong to her, and she was grateful to have Ma with her as she walked downstairs. On the sofa, feeling exhausted, she watched the flames dancing in the grate as Ma returned with a dainty dish of scrambled egg and some bread-and-butter fingers. Even the soft food felt like needles going down as she swallowed, and after two mouthfuls, she pushed her tray aside. "I can't manage anymore, Ma."

"There now, don't cry. It will all be better soon. You rest for a while and see if it isn't."

As Lily dozed on the sofa, strange, complicated dreams troubled her. She was marrying Aiden, but no one was in the church, and the vicar turned out to be Stephen Dent. Then running down a long street, Lily called to a tall, dark-haired man who stayed ahead however fast she ran. He always disappeared around the next corner before she reached him. Lily stumbled and cried out, then woke to feel her mother's hand on her head. "Drink this, Lily. You've got a fever again."

Lily felt strong arms around her and under her legs and breathed in the smoky smell of her father's pipe on his shirt. "I'm taking you back to bed, Lily-Lou."

Lily-Lou! No one had called her that for a long time.

It was dark when she woke sometime later; a candle burned on the dressing table, which shed a warm glow.

Ma stood up from the chair in the corner. Her back looked stiff as she straightened slowly. "How are you feeling? Could you manage some soup? Or I've made an egg custard."

Ma looked tired, so Lily croaked, "Let me come downstairs." She swung her legs out of bed, thinking of standing up. As she did, she felt the blood drain from her lips, saw dancing black spots, and the room began spinning.

"Silly girl. You stay where you are. I'll bring up a tray." Ma fussed, plumping cushions behind Lily. "I've got a nice surprise for you as well."

Lily's heart leapt, news of Aiden perhaps. However, when her mother returned, it was with a pretty arrangement of winter foliage laced with gold ribbon and a candle in the centre.

"Mr Dent came to leave his card and bring his mother's invitation to a small soiree on Christmas Eve. As soon as he knew you were ill, he returned with this to cheer you up. Very thoughtful. Perhaps I was hasty before when I felt he wasn't quite the thing."

Lily nodded listlessly; the thought of a soiree made her headache, and she wished Aiden had brought the flowers.

"And Pa brought this note from Miss Laidlaw," she handed Lily a folded sheet.

> *My dear Miss Matthews,*
>
> *Forgive my hasty scribble. I wish you a speedy recovery and look forward to continuing our design soon.*
>
> *With best wishes,*
>
> *Anis Laidlaw*

"How kind she is." Lily passed the note back as her mother placed a tray on her lap with a small bowl of chicken soup and a spoonful of egg custard in a glass bowl. "And how kind you are, Ma. You look exhausted. Did you sleep this afternoon?"

Ma looked surprised. "No, indeed, but I shall sleep well tonight. I've asked Pa to set up the camp bed for me here. Then you can call if you need me."

Lily reached out her hand. "No, Ma, don't. Sleep in your bed, please. You can put the small bell on my table."

Ma laughed. "That reminds me of my days in service, Lily, always listening for a bell to ring. Let's see how you are this evening; your fever may return. It would take more than a sleepless night to lay me low."

A light tap on the door signalled the arrival of Pa, who tiptoed in, looking concerned. His expression lifted as he spied the empty dishes on the tray. "Now, that's better; you've managed to eat something. I've brought you a book Mrs Donnelly thought you might like. Short stories and light reading, she says. If you have the energy, I'll sit down while Ma has a rest and read one to you."

He settled beside her on the chair. "Now then, Lily-Lou, beginning, middle or end?"

Lily smiled at the joke. He would tease her as a child and pretend to read stories back to front or in the wrong order. "As I'm all grown-up now, we should start at the beginning Pa."

He flicked to the back of the book and looked at her. "Sure? This looks like the best bit."

Ma said, "Mrs Michelson, down the road, always reads the end of the story first. She can settle down to enjoy the book once she knows how it ends."

As Pa began to read, a tear ran down Lily's cheek. Could she turn her back on all this love if she had to choose between her family and Aiden? Then she thought of her long conversations with Aiden over the wall and the thrill of kissing him and wondered if she could bear to lose that either.

In Lily's mind, she had planned to run away to Aiden, a noble heroine and the victim of cruel persecution. That was all very well in a book, but in real life, how would they manage to live? Eight years seemed an eternity to wait.

Why wasn't real life like a story, where everything came right in the end?

Chapter 21

It was five days before Lily felt well again, and even then, she was pale and tired.

She had spent the last two days in the kitchen watching Ma bake mince pies and make fondants and tiny biscuits. Today Ma set her to shape and paint marchpane fruits with the leftover paste from the Christmas cake. All were arranged in small baskets or tied in circles of material to give as gifts, and Lily knew she would find some in her stocking too. Ma's sweetmeats were renowned. When she worked at the big house, she had learned to make all manner of delicacies and liked to make them for special occasions.

Lily had missed two rehearsals and the last meeting at Mrs O'Shea's before Christmas. Her mother had not needed to forbid her to go. She had been too ill, much as she longed to be there.

Her spirits lifted when the postman arrived with one of the new postcards. It had a cheery Santa on the front. A brief message was on the back in Aiden's cramped handwriting — *Now in Manchester, busy with shows and Kitty's meetings. Happy Christmas — I will think about you on show day. Write more soon, Your Aiden.*

The message was disappointing. Lily was sure Aiden meant well, but Lily didn't want to hear he was having a wonderful time with Kitty. She wanted him to be pining for her.

Lily put the card on the table. If she won the competition prize, she didn't care what anyone said; she would get on a train and visit Aiden to see what was happening. Even if she had to go behind her parent's backs, she needed to speak to him properly.

Seeing Lily looking wan, Ma had agreed to a visit from Grace and Miss Laidlaw, who came after work.

Miss Laidlaw handed her a bag with four small oranges. "To build you up," she explained. "We're missing you in the workroom with your quick fingers. Finishing and fitting all the orders before Christmas is the usual panic."

Miss Laidlaw had made additional drawings for Kitty Marion's dress and looked with interest at Lily's sketch pad too. Miss Laidlaw's sketches were romantic and full of movement. The dresses made your mouth water.

War raged in Lily's head. The seamstress in her was excited to make a designer dress, but she wished it wasn't for the woman who'd stolen Aiden away.

Grace's interest in the dress rapidly waned. After she had told them more about her wedding plans, she was uncharacteristically quiet, staring around the room at the ornaments and pictures. "What are your plans for Christmas, Miss Kirby?" Miss Laidlaw smiled kindly, attempting to draw her back into the conversation.

Grace started. "Um, when we finish at the workroom on Christmas Eve, if we ever do finish, I am going to my fiancée's parents for a soirée. Otherwise, I shall be at home with my family. We play jolly games, but usually, it ends up in a fight when the boys get overexcited. Are you coming to the Dent's party, Lily? Stephen said his parents invited you."

Lily shook her head. "It was kind of Mrs Dent to think of me, but I'm not ready to go anywhere yet. I am trying to save my voice and build my stamina to sing in the concert. Tomorrow I will try out my songs with Mrs Donnelly to see if I can hold a tune. It's the dress rehearsal on the twenty-seventh."

Grace pouted. "It won't be the same without you. If you rested during the day, I'm sure Stephen would come and fetch you in his car."

Miss Laidlaw frowned. "Miss Kirby, if Miss Matthews isn't well, you mustn't encourage her to overtax her strength. I'm sure she's as disappointed as you are."

Lily shot Miss Laidlaw a grateful look. "I'm sorry, Grace, I really am." She turned the conversation quickly, "And you, Miss Laidlaw, what are your plans for Christmas?"

"I shall be visiting my cousin, who is older than myself. Her husband eats well and sleeps better. We shall chat comfortably in the afternoon, punctuated by his gentle snores from under a paper crown." The two girls looked aghast. For them, Christmas was about excitement, games, and surprises. Seeing their faces, she laughed out loud. "I shall do very well, and they are most kind to invite me."

Unable to contain her curiosity, Grace blurted out, "Lily, have you heard from Aiden?"

Lily blushed and reached over to the table where she'd left the card.

Lily tried to joke about the brief message. "He must have been in a hurry; look, he has stuck the stamp on crookedly."

Grace looked as if she would burst with excitement, and Lily looked at her questioningly, but she discreetly shook her head.

Ma returned to the room to offer more refreshments, but Miss Laidlaw stood and began to take her leave, thanking Ma for offering them tea and saying, "Lily is beginning to look tired; I think perhaps we should let her rest."

Grace tweaked Lily's sleeve and jerked her head as the two ladies talked, indicating to Lily to draw back. As she did, Grace whispered excitedly, "It's a secret code on your card. I read about it in a magazine. Depending on which way the stamp is, the message is different. Let me see."

Lily held out the card, and Grace grinned at her. "This means 'I love you,' – how romantic."

One of the showgirls must have told him about the code. She was sure Aiden wouldn't have known otherwise. Perhaps if the chorus girls knew he loved her, so did Kitty Marion.

The next day, Lily bundled up with a muffler to keep the cold air away from her voice and made the short walk to the Donnelly's front door. Mary Donnolley welcomed Lily in and assured Ma the fire was alight in the front room.

"Just half an hour, mind," Ma wagged a finger at Lily. "You're still not properly over this."

"I promise not to tire her out. One run-through to see if singing on the thirtieth is an option. Everyone is hoping she'll be there."

As the door closed, Lily confided, "Ma doesn't understand about performing. I so want to do this."

Mrs Donnelly looked at Lily. "Aiden told me that you were hoping to win the prize to take a trip to London."

Lily blushed. "Oh! Mrs Donnelly, please don't say that to Ma and Pa. I haven't told them about that, and the trip may never happen."

Mrs Donnelly smiled. "Your secret is safe with me." She drew Lily into a chair by the fire and said, "Let me tell you a story."

Lily sat on the edge of her seat and wondered what on earth she was about to hear.

"Back in Ireland, when I was a girl, my family owned land. Grandfather's family were bankers from Scotland, and they'd settled in Connemara. We were quite well-to-do. However, there were bad times because of religious factions and as landowners, we were resented, especially because we were protestant."

Lily thought *the rumours about Aiden's mother being upper class were true.*

"Sean, I mean Mr Donnelly, his family had a smallholding close by, and he helped me one day when I fell off my horse. I sprained my ankle, so he lifted me back and led the mare home. He was funny and charming and came back the next day to enquire after my health and bring a posy."

Mrs Donnelly looked far away as if Lily was no longer in the room.

"Father told him he was presumptuous and that while he was grateful to him for helping me, not to get ideas." She shook her head and said, "I was ashamed of my father for his rudeness."

198

"But he came around, your father, in the end? Because you're married."

Mrs Donnelly shook her head. "We carried on meeting in secret. Sean wanted to confront Pa, and when I wouldn't let him, he started to be outrageous, getting into fights and drinking too much. I told him I wouldn't see him again if he didn't stop."

Lily looked at Mrs Donnelly. "It's what Aiden did at the weekend," she whispered.

"Yes, and that's why Sean understood, Lily. Even though we disapproved."

"How did you get married in the end? What happened?"

Mrs Donnelly blushed. "Sean stayed away for six months. My father thought it was over; then Sean came to the house. His father had made him leave home because he insisted he wanted to marry me out of his faith. Sean told me he had packed his bags and was leaving for England. He asked me to go with him. I had to make a choice…."

"But how? How did you get married?"

"We ran away."

Lily gasped. Mrs Donnelly was always calm and gentle; she couldn't imagine her doing something so shocking and unconventional.

"We travelled with his sister, and Sean took me to his aunt in Liverpool. I spent a year with her, the kindest Christian woman I have ever met. I had to study with her priest and participate in the church's life to ensure that I wanted to convert to Catholicism. I was given the sacraments at Easter the following year, and we were married in the summer."

Lily didn't know what to say.

"My father was a proud man. He refused to acknowledge us and forbade my mother to speak to me. Even when Aiden was born, their only grandchild. He believed I'd forsaken my soul."

Mary Donnelly reached out her hand to Lily. "Lily, this is not to advise you what to do with Aiden. That isn't my place. You will know in your heart if you can face the consequences of your decision because there will be consequences. My faith permitted me to worship the same God but from within a different framework. But does yours? Does Aiden's?

Lily, the beliefs our parents and our communities hand us run deep within us. It's why religious wars are vehement."

Lily thought about how she and Aiden had grown up together as friends and now loved each other. She had never seen him as 'other'. And until now, faith was faith. Everyone went on a Sunday, some to different churches; she had never thought deeply about the implications of holding other Christian beliefs. What Mrs Donnelly told her was a new and harsh reality.

"People said I'd regret what I did, that our marriage wouldn't last because of the extra pressure. Things haven't always been easy, and the reality isn't as romantic as I'd imagined, being 'us against the world'. The worst thing has been seeing Aiden face the consequences of our decision. It makes me sad."

Mary Donnelly smiled at Lily. "Take your time to decide, Lily. There is much to consider." She looked at the clock on the mantelpiece. "Good gracious, I promised your mother only half an hour. We haven't started the songs; can you still manage to sing, do you think?"

Lily's voice was shaky, particularly at the top of her range, and somehow the sparkle and fun had gone from the performance of Alexander's Ragtime Band for her. After anxiously quizzing Mrs Donnelly, she decided her voice was good enough to sing in the concert and that the extra day's rest would help.

Solemnly wrapped up before taking the few steps back home, Lily was surprised by how utterly exhausted she felt. She was certainly glad not to be going to the Dent's party.

Midnight Service was one of Lily's favourites of the year. She looked forward to singing carols after Advent and loved leaving the church afterwards into the stillness of the night. She always experienced a tingle of excitement for the celebrations to come. Ma made mulled wine to have when they got home, and their house was filled with the smell of spiced oranges and cinnamon as it warmed on the range.

However, this year, after helping Ma dress the parlour with holly and ivy and eating a small portion of the fish pie for tea, Lily fell asleep on the sofa. She only stirred when Ma suggested she go to bed.

"But Ma, Midnight service, I want to attend church with you. We always go, and I feel much better from the sleep."

Ma shook her head. "I don't think that's wise, going out in the cold. Pa feels tired, too, so he's staying here with you. I'll walk up with Granny and Gramps. You want to enjoy your day tomorrow."

Lily put up only token resistance.

As she got ready for bed, Lily looked out of her window. It was a frosty night, and ice crystals sparkled like diamonds on the pavement. Stars speckled the clear night sky, and the moon lazed on its back, wrapped in a hazy white covering. She could imagine it casting a silver glow on the sea and remembered kissing Aiden on the beach. Perhaps Aiden was looking up at the sky and remembering too. It comforted her to think they could see the same stars.

Would she have to make the same choices that Mrs Donnelly had?

Ma had put a hot stone bottle in her bed and folded the pillow over it. Lily put the pillow back at the head of the bed and jumped in, savouring the warmth as she snuggled in. She looked at Aiden's postcard on her bedside table with its secret code, 'I love you', and tried to forget that he was with Kitty Marion.

When Lily woke the following day, she could feel an exciting crackle at the bottom of her bed. Pa's stocking! Ever since she was little, Pa had bought or made tiny trinkets and luxuries and filled a stocking for her and Ma. He used to say that Santa Claus had left it, but they had abandoned that pretence some years ago.

She dressed quickly and hurried downstairs with the stocking to share the unpacking with her parents. Ma was already busy in the kitchen, and steam rose from the plum pudding pan. "Happy Christmas, Lily. How are you feeling today?"

"Happy Christmas, Ma. I feel better today, no sore throat." She scrunched her stocking gently and smiled. "Go and get yours too. Where's Pa?"

Ma glanced at the kitchen clock. "He won't be long. You know he likes to take a small gift round to the men and their families, and he says the walk does him good before all the eating. You can help me peel the vegetables while we wait. I thought we'd have breakfast together."

Ma fetched the potato crock and a stalk of sprouts from the pantry. "Don't forget to put a cross in the bottom of the sprouts, Lily, and a teaspoon of soda in the water to keep them green."

"Ma, what do Roman Catholics do that is different to us? They believe in Christ as we do and go to church. I don't understand why it is such a big issue for Aiden and me."

Her ma sighed and rubbed her hands down her apron. "Lily, I don't exactly know the differences because, at one time, it was all one church. As far as I can see, Henry VIII split from Rome over money and women, although I can imagine it all got dressed up in some fancy facts. I know Catholics believe that the Pope is God represented on earth, and much as I respect men called to holy orders, I don't believe anyone is God. Well, I've yet to meet a man who is." She sniffed. "I like my faith practical and straightforward; I don't want a million saints to pray to, and if I've done wrong, I'll say I'm sorry and make amends. I don't need the vicar making me pray over beads to feel remorse."

Lily looked at her mother and felt disheartened. That hadn't helped her much.

"Maybe talk to Mrs Donnelly. She may know more than I do. For heaven's sake, please don't bring it up when Granny and Gramps are here. They already think we give you too much licence."

Lily looked up, shocked. "What licence!"

"Licence to answer back for a start." Ma chuckled at her quick retort, then added, "Every generation thinks the one after is daring, Lily. You'll think the same about your children too."

When Pa came home, Lily heard him humming 'We Wish You A Merry Christmas' as he hung his coat up. He stood with his back to the range warming his back and rubbing his hands together. "Miss Lily, has Santa been to visit?"

"He has Pa, look!" Lily held up her stocking. "Ma has one too." She laughed; his mood was infectious.

He feigned astonishment. "Well, I never. I must live with two of the best-behaved ladies in Portsmouth."

Lily got up from her seat to hug him. "Can we open them, Pa?"

"If your ma gives me some tea and a slice of that gammon I spied cooling in the larder yesterday, I shall enjoy watching you do it."

Ma had spiked the ham with cloves, and the brown sugar on the top had baked to a glossy mahogany hue. Lily's mouth watered as Ma carved generous slices and laid their plates in front of them with pieces of homemade bread.

Lily's stocking contained an orange and two sugar mice with string tails at the top, which made her exclaim with delight. Pa gave her sugar mice every year, a tradition since she was tiny. They were resting on a pair of soft wool gloves in a pretty shade of lavender. In the toe of the stocking was a small box which contained a polished tortoiseshell hair slide in the shape of a bird.

"Oh, Pa, it's beautiful." Lily showed it to Ma, and the colours glowed as she held it up to the light.

Pa beamed. "For my songbird, I'm glad you like it."

For Ma, there was a decorative box containing chocolates, each with a crystalised violet on top. Also, a lace collar that Lily had told Pa she admired and a painted brooch.

Ma gave the brooch to Pa to pin onto her blouse. It looked very well at her throat decorating the high collar.

She looked flushed and breathless as Pa kissed her, then swung her around, feet off the floor.

"Edward Matthews put me down; whatever next!" She protested, but Lily thought Ma was secretly pleased.

Lily wondered if Ma's heart still raced when Pa did that and if they'd ever stolen kisses before they were married as she and Aiden had. She couldn't imagine Ma head over heels for anyone, but she must have been.

Thinking of Aiden made her wonder if he'd received her reply to his card. She'd written a long letter and addressed it care of his agent in London. She hoped they were reliable and would faithfully forward her correspondence. She wondered if Aiden was in a fancy London house with friends of Miss Marion or in a boarding house room which smelled of boiled cabbage.

Despite missing Aiden, Lily had a jolly day. After church, they returned home with Granny and Gramps, whom Ma invited to lunch. Granny, who professed to be tee-total except for a daily tot of homemade wine, which didn't count, got tipsy on Ma's beetroot wine. She regaled them with stories about Pa as a boy, making him blush. They played charades and tested their skill with Pa's shove ha'penny board, laughing and teasing each other.

As Granny and Gramps made to leave, Granny produced from her carpetbag a white cotton tablecloth embroidered with white flowers in each corner. "You don't need this now, my dear, but you can put it in your bottom drawer. I expect you've begun to save bits for when you have a happy day."

Lily blushed and looked at the delicate white work. "Granny, it's beautiful. I shall treasure it."

"Only having boys myself, like this great lummox," she tapped her son on the shoulder affectionately. "It's been lovely to make this for your collection. It certainly beats knitting those thick socks your father likes. I shall carry on with some bits and pieces if my arthritis lets me. I look forward to seeing you happy and walking down the aisle one day."

Chapter 22

On the day after the dress rehearsal, a letter from Aiden arrived. Stephen Dent also presented himself at Lily's house on the pretext of enquiring about her health and collecting his tickets for the community show. Lily was in an agony of anticipation as politeness obliged her to talk to Stephen first. She wished he would cut short his visit so she could read her letter. However, he showed no signs of doing so. Instead, he settled back in the front room chair as if he belonged there and engaged her and her mother in conversation.

"Grace and George are looking forward to the concert, Mrs Matthews, as am I. Perhaps the four of us could spend the evening together afterwards to toast your certain success, Lily. Dinner, perhaps?"

She thought Stephen had cleverly made it sound like they were all close friends. But she barely knew him or George. Lily looked at Ma, who nodded encouragingly. Lily could not think of a reason to refuse the invitation without being rude. And if she were honest, it was flattering that he should wish to take her to dinner, so sophisticated.

After Stephen left, Ma said, "What a pleasant visit. I'm sure you'll enjoy an evening out with your friends. On further acquaintance, Mr Dent seems personable and thoughtful as well."

"Grace told me that Stephen and George didn't get on. I'm surprised he suggested it."

Lily tapped her heel nervously.

"Lily Matthews, you're like a fly in a tarpot, go and read that letter and stop fidgeting me."

"Yes, Ma, sorry. Thank you." Lily fled to the hall coat stand, where Ma had propped her letter.

After reading Aiden's letter, the proposed evening out with Stephen seemed infinitely more alluring, and Lily felt close to indulging in a fit of pique.

Aiden wrote *Leading up to Christmas; Miss Marion embarked on a series of evenings comprising political conversation and musical interludes. She is electric when she speaks on matters like the Women's Suffrage Bill. Billed as a "Music Hall Artiste and Militant Suffragette," she drew large attendances, I can tell you. After one meeting in Colchester, the local paper wrote, "The awe experienced by the audience was quickly succeeded by delight, for the lady proved a charming vocalist".*

She sings my song at almost every performance and looks forward to receiving a dress, which I understand she has asked you to help design. She is such a good-hearted person and tells me she is looking to support your advancement.

Kitty says she will continue to protest in London, but you must not worry if you hear reports of her being imprisoned. She is quite willing for that to happen. I shall be safe as I have a room at her friends' whenever I need it, but we are mainly on the road. I scarcely have time to unpack my bags.

I think of you every day and am happy to feel that though we are apart, I can work towards our independence by helping the suffragette cause.

Lily scanned the remainder of the letter impatiently, looking for some mention of missing home or the upcoming Community Concert. However, these seemed forgotten in all the political talk and praise for Miss Marion. Having spent the last half an hour being courted and flattered by Stephen, Lily found the letter an unwelcome contrast. She hunched a shoulder.

The time flew between the dress rehearsal and the concert, with her costume to finish and last-minute run-throughs with Mrs Donnelly. In quiet moments before sleeping, Lily dreamed of Aiden arriving breathless off the train as she went on stage, having come back to play for her. In her dream, they would give a storming performance to win first prize and return to London together in the teeth of all opposition.

That morning, Ma had carefully pressed Lily's costume. Lily was proud of her first stage creation, and despite her intended audience being somewhere in London, she was still looking forward to wearing it.

"Lily, you're so clever. Your costume looks like it came straight off a fashion plate in The Lady," said Maisie, whose costume was that of a street urchin. She had daubs of mud on her face and bare feet and was drooling with envy.

"Miss Laidlaw, who teaches me in the workroom, helped. I couldn't have done it without her."

"I wish my beau could see me in that, not in this." She looked down at her ragged skirt, dirtied with mud and shook her head. "We're going for fish and chips after on the pier. What about you?"

Lily was embarrassed to say she was dining at the Grand Hotel. It sounded a bit stuck up and instead said, "Oh, my family are coming to watch…."

Mrs Donnelly came backstage to tell everyone that the hall was filling fast and wished them good luck before taking her place at the piano to play a medley of the show songs. As the music floated into the makeshift changing room, someone said, "I feel sick." Lily's stomach lurched, too. Would her voice hold out after she'd been ill?

Lily's first number was her and Aiden's song, Alexander's Ragtime Band. She took up her position in the wings. The jaunty introduction started, and she faltered momentarily, her vision blurred by tears. She angrily dashed her hands across her eyes, pinned on a smile, and marched onto the stage singing.

Seeing the faces in front of her, Ma with Pa, Granny and Gramps, felt surreal. Gramps tapped his thigh, and Pa beamed encouragingly. Stephen Dent sat off to one side with George and Grace, who waved and almost put her off her words.

She was on the last verse. Just a few more dance steps to go. Harry was in the wings, and he mouthed, "Bring it home, Girl!" Lily redoubled her smile and exited the stage leaning back, her waving hand the last thing the audience saw. Applause rang out, and several hands propelled her back on stage to take a bow.

"Well done, Lil'," Harry said. "Great job. I could see you were nervous."

"Lil'? Lil'!"

No one had ever called her Lil in her life. In that instant, for all his tall, good looks, Lily knew why she loved Aiden, not Harry; he was neither insensitive nor brash.

Oblivious to the defining moment, Harry winked and said, "Our duet is coming up. Get your skates on and get ready."

One of the boys from the Methodist church sang 'Let Me Call You Sweetheart' in a light tenor voice which also delighted the crowd. Lily listened backstage and felt less confident that she had the winning song. She badly wanted to win the prize money to go towards her London fund for a visit to Aiden.

She and Harry strolled on from different sides of the stage and sang 'By the Light Of The Silvery Moon.' Despite feeling cross with him still, Lily managed to school her features into a playful smile as they sang the romantic lyrics and pretended to 'spoon', him behind her with his hands on her shoulders as they swayed.

At the end of the performance, the judges seated at the back of the hall scribbled on the judging forms and discussed their decision quietly. The panel comprised Mr Gilbert, the sweetshop owner who helped sponsor the prizes; their local councillor, a jowly man in a checked waistcoat; and Mrs Timms, the headmistress of the local school.

The vicar bustled to the front, rubbing his hands together. He asked for more applause for the cast, who all shuffled on stage for a final bow. He thanked Mrs Donnelly for stepping in to play at the last minute and presented her with a small posy of flowers. Next, he introduced the jury and thanked them for their time and Mr Gilbert for sponsoring the prizes. He reminded everyone that refreshments would be provided after the judging.

"Ah," he continued, face wreathed in smiles. "I believe we have tonight's results."

A ripple of anticipation spread through the audience and cast alike as Mrs Timms threaded her way past the rows of chairs, followed by Mr Gilbert with the much-coveted prize envelope and what looked like a box of chocolates.

The vicar slowly unfolded the sheet of paper they handed him.

Prolonging the suspense, the vicar turned to smile at the cast and said, "The judges have commended everyone for their excellent performances and the work you have put in. They wish to say what a difficult decision this has been."

Lily gripped her hands together, waiting. "Without further ado... The second prize and this delicious box of handmade chocolates go to our delightful duet, Miss Lily Matthews and Private Harry Brody."

There was a scraping of chairs as Lily and Harry's friends and family stood. Stephen and George added to the massive round of applause with whistles and cheers. Pa looked as though he would burst with pride, and Ma nodded and clapped higher as she caught Lily's eye.

Harry and Lily came forward to shake the judge's hand. Lily accepted the chocolates with a curtsey. Harry leaned in to congratulate her and said, "We'll have to divvy those up later."

"You can have them, Harry."

He was about to reply, but she shushed him. "The judges have awarded our generous first prize to... Mr David Jenks, one of our good friends from the Methodist Union."

Biting her cheek to stave off a wave of disappointment, Lily turned away to remove her costume. Harry looked after her with a perplexed frown, then shrugged and smiled endearingly at the gaggle of girls crowding about him.

In the hall, Lily accepted a cup of tea from Pa and professed delight at her second place as congratulations came in from all sides. Only Ma's shrewd eyes showed understanding. Lily knew she saw through the smile to the disappointment behind it.

A familiar voice behind her drawled quietly, "Not only blind but deaf too. I believe the judges robbed you."

Lily turned to see Stephen Dent, whose laughing eyes teased. She raised her chin. "David sang well, and I'm still a little out of voice from being ill."

"You were my favourite, and I challenge anyone to say otherwise." He momentarily feigned a pugilistic pose, and Lily was obliged to laugh. "That's better. I hate to see you downcast." He turned to her family. "Mr and Mrs Matthews, lovely to see you again, and…" he paused, waiting for an introduction.

Lily laughed. "Well, coincidentally, Mr and Mrs Matthews, my grandparents."

"Pleased to meet you." He shook hands with both, then addressed Pa again. "Forgive me, but we have an early supper booked if I may whisk Lily away." He turned to Lily, offered his crooked arm, and said jokingly, "If you're ready, Miss Matthews, your carriage awaits."

He bent into her confidingly as they walked away and wryly remarked, "I understand you turn into a pumpkin at nine o'clock."

Lily flushed scarlet. "Pa! Has he placed his usual curfew?"

Stephen laughed. "I am under strict instructions. It's refreshing."

"Anyway, surely your car, not me, will turn into the pumpkin. I shall flee the ballroom leaving one of my slippers behind."

He looked at her intently. "You are intriguing and a constant challenge Lily Matthews. Where do you inherit your spirit from?"

With pride in her voice, she looked at him and replied, "Pa, Ma, Gramps, all of them."

He nodded thoughtfully as if taking note. "Excellent."

George and Grace waited in the car. Stephen handed Lily into the back beside Grace and placed a thick rug over their knees.

Grace giggled self-consciously. "Thank you, I'm sure, Stephen." He ignored her, focusing on Lily as he tucked in the blanket beside her legs, watching as he registered the catch in her breath at the contact. The moment passed in a split second, and Lily was annoyed to feel her heart race.

The dining room at The Grand was well-appointed, with bay windows overlooking the sea. Tonight, the sea was a uniform dark mass with just the winking lights of the pier reflected in the water.

In shades of cream, pink and pale green, the atmosphere in the hotel was restful, and the hum of conversation from the other diners gentle in the background. Lily was more interested in watching the world and his wife walk past their vantage point.

Stephen insisted on Champagne to start the evening and proposed a toast, "To the beautiful Miss Matthews' singing."

Lily rarely drank alcohol, and then only the sweet wines her mother and grandmother made. The bubbles danced and pinged, hitting her face, and she wrinkled her nose as the dry wine surprised her.

"Lily's singing," responded Grace and George as they lifted their glasses. Grace took too big a mouthful and cough-snorted, clapping her napkin to her mouth.

George patted her on the back, laughing and said, "Steady on, Old Girl."

From her mother's days in service, dinners were always served formally in Lily's house with the correct cutlery so the restaurant did not intimidate her. However, she noticed Grace hesitating over which knife and fork to use when her starter arrived, and she quickly picked up hers to show Grace the protocol.

The evening was jolly, with laughter, and Stephen was attentive and good company. As she sipped her Champagne cautiously and refused a second glass, Lily noticed that Stephen drank steadily throughout dinner. The wine appeared to have little effect on him.

"He's a card; Stephen is," Grace giggled tipsily as she and Lily went to powder their noses. Grace did a twirl in the corridor. "This is the life for me." She looked at Lily. "You're mad if you don't snap Stephen up."

"Oh, do be quiet, Grace. People are staring. That Champagne has gone to your head."

"Snap him up," Grace repeated and emphasised each word with a tap on Lily's shoulder.

The men had paid the bill when they got back, and as they rose to leave the hotel, George put his arm around a giggling Grace and said, "I think we'll walk back from here."

Stephen looked regretfully at his pocket watch. "Into your carriage, Cinderella, before the clock strikes the hour."

Lily stepped into the front of the car, looking at Grace's retreating form and knew her parents would not be pleased if they realised that she was alone with Stephen.

She sat bolt upright in her seat and declined the proffered blanket.

Halfway home, Stephen laughed. "I shan't give way to uncontrollable urges and ravish you in an open car at nine o'clock at night. Relax."

"I'm not afraid of you."

"No?" He trailed the fingers of one hand down her forearm. "Good."

The flesh burned where he had touched her. His casual touch felt far more improper than any of Aiden's kisses. She was grateful when the car turned into her road, and she could see the figure of Pa waiting at the front, a red dot brightening and fading as he smoked his pipe.

Stephen jumped from the car to help Lily down, and he bid her goodnight with great decorum. As he drove away, she realised she could breathe out entirely for the first time since they left the hotel.

Chapter 23

A week after the concert, another letter arrived from Aiden, commiserating with her on not winning the money prize and hoping she wasn't terribly disappointed. He omitted to mention whether he was disappointed. After all, she thought, the prize money had been intended to fund a trip to London for them to meet.

"It's alright for him," she exclaimed loudly, poking the letter crossly.

"What's alright for who?" Ma asked.

"Aiden, he's sorry I didn't get the first prize at the show. He isn't that sorry, or he'd have been there to play."

Ma pinched her lips into a thin line. "Lily, I know you're disappointed because you've been cross as a cat ever since. It was all unfortunate, what with you being ill and Aiden getting his chance to go away. You can't blame the lad for wanting to make something of himself."

"You think I'm a bad loser, I don't think I am, but we would have won that competition with Aiden playing and my normal voice."

The truth was, she needed to talk to him. She was frightened for another reason.

A week ago, Pa read aloud that a property near Colchester had been set alight, exactly where Aiden wrote Kitty and he had been performing. His letter also said they were now at a theatre in Kingston doing pantomime.

Earlier, Pa had commented, "I see some of the suffragette ladies are taking more militant steps." He'd tutted and shaken his head. "Listen to this, 'Suffragette Arson; Near Kingston, train seriously fire damaged.' The protesters left carriages littered with suffragette leaflets doused in petrol, then lit candles under the seats. Apparently, they damaged the train badly, but no one was hurt because it was in the sidings."

Ma had replied, "Goodness gracious, whatever next. They will give a legitimate cause a bad name."

Her parents clearly disapproved.

Ma looked over her half-moon glasses at Lily. "What else does Aiden say?"

Lily was deliberately vague, hoping Ma and Pa wouldn't make the same connection. "Oh, they're travelling quite a bit and have been performing in pantomime."

Lily became gripped with a fear that Aiden had become involved with this law-breaking. She could have asked him straight if he had been here, but she didn't dare write her suspicions down in a letter.

Pa looked at Lily with a crease between his brows. "I'm glad your Mrs O'Shea and the NUWSS are more sensible. I wouldn't like to think of you involved in causing criminal damage."

Pa picked up yesterday's neatly folded paper, ready to be used as a firelighter and smoothed it out. "Yes, here it is, 'the women of the WSPU were involved in clashes with the police during a march on the House of Commons.' They are taking things a step too far."

Ma nodded. "I'm sure Mrs Donnelly wouldn't be involved with anything untoward like that. Let's hope Aiden isn't either."

Lily pretended to agree but knew they didn't see the rebel inside him as she did. They hadn't felt the force of Kitty Marion's personality either.

The rest of Aiden's letter was disappointing, he told her he missed her and still loved her, but it was mainly London talk, and Lily felt her connection with Aiden was slipping into the past. Her news of meetings at Mrs O'Shea's and what she did at work seemed mundane compared to his exciting life.

He had visited St Pauls and climbed The Monument. Did Lily know that people swam in the Serpentine every day and had to break the ice to do so sometimes? He had been to watch them on Christmas day. He had done a Jack the Ripper walk in the East End with a storyteller who had chilled him to the bone.

Since the concert, the only exciting thing she had done was to begin Kitty's new costume, but he would scarcely be interested in that.

He didn't know when he might get home but remained her loving Aiden.

She put the closely written sheets aside and sighed. Aiden wrote beautiful lyrics for Kitty Marion to sing. However, Lily didn't find much romance in Aiden's letters. Lily wished he spoke to her a bit more as Stephen did. There was no mention of how he loved her beautiful voice or how her eyes sparkled. There was nothing much of the lover at all.

Lily flushed as she remembered Stephen's touch. It wasn't anything, yet it was. It contained a promise of something unknown and compelling. She shook her head to clear her thoughts. *He's lost interest anyway. It must be at least a fortnight since I saw him.*

Lily refused to admit she felt piqued. After all, she loved Aiden, not Stephen, but it still wounded her pride to have been dropped.

When she got to bed, Lily mulled over her foiled plans to visit London. Now she hadn't won the prize; she cast about in her mind for any way forward with little success.

Finally, Lily remembered what Miss Laidlaw had said about dress fittings for Kitty Marion and that they might be in London. A small glimmer of hope burgeoned despite everything. She hugged the idea close to her as she drifted off to sleep. Indeed something had to work.

At work the next day, Miss Laidlaw had a new sketch. Her eyes gleamed with excitement belied by her usual calm exterior. "Look at this, Miss Matthews. I believe I have solved the problem." She flipped onto the last page, and Lily gasped.

What she saw before her was both stunningly beautiful and incredibly daring at the same time. "Oh, yes," she breathed and looked at Miss Laidlaw with sparkling eyes. "Will she? I mean, could she wear it in public?"

"Could she resist?"

The gown used Lily's slashed overskirt idea but went way further. The gores of the overskirt were slashed to the hip, not the knee, and were in panels of only six inches wide. Each panel was heavily beaded. Inserted between each were godets of silk chiffon which would see the overskirt, quite straight at rest, fan out in sunrays on movement. Several underskirts would usually conceal the wearer's legs; however, the illusion was daring indeed. Miss Laidlaw had designed a daring skirt but offset it with a modest bloused bodice with three-quarter sleeves caught at the elbow and waist with silk roses.

Lily said, "We could use that kingfisher blue silk for the panels with perhaps a paler chiffon for the godets." She paused, trying to visualise it, then slowly said, "No, Miss Laidlaw, I think we should make the whole dress white with pink or apricot roses. The modesty of the colours would be witty with the daring design."

She looked at Miss Laidlaw, and a smile spread between them. "I think you are right, Lily, how clever. All we must do now is sell the idea to Mrs Winchett."

Lily glowed with pleasure. "I can't wait to see this dress made up. I've never seen anything quite like it. The real dress will be magnificent."

Her face fell momentarily, she knew this was wrong thinking, but part of her wished they weren't making something quite this beautiful for Miss Marion. *But*, she thought, *it will be worth it if I get to London to see Aiden.*

That afternoon, Mrs Winchett, looked over the drawing, the swatches of the proposed fabrics, beads and two panels cut and sewn in miniature to demonstrate the flow.

She pursed her lips and then spoke as if to herself. "Hmm, ahead of its time and too daring for normal wear, but for the stage…." She looked up at Lily and Miss Laidlaw, and the ghost of a smile played about her mouth. "Ladies, I think you have done it. We have our design. You may make up a prototype, and I will write to ask Miss Marion when she wants to see it."

Miss Laidlaw cleared her throat. "We would be happy to attend Miss Marion for fittings in London."

Mrs Winchett looked at the excited girl and the poised young woman in front of her appraisingly. "Yes, that may work, or I may visit the metropolis myself with you, Miss Laidlaw. I will give the matter thought."

Lily was barely out of the office when she exploded. "Did you hear that? 'We have our design,' We indeed! She's going to take all the credit for our work. And she's going to steal my visit to London. It isn't fair!"

"Shhh." Miss Laidlaw shook her head and propelled Lily down the stairs. "Mrs Winchett will, of course, call it an original gown by Anastasia, it will be her who pays for the materials and our wages, but if we don't upset her, we may go to London at her expense."

Lily did not look convinced, and Miss Laidlaw added, "When you have your own workshop, the gowns will become your signature designs. Until then, we must be grateful."

"When I have my workshop, Miss Laidlaw, You will get full credit for your designs."

Miss Laidlaw laughed. "Anis and Lily — Costumiers. It has a ring."

"Is Anis a French name?" Lily asked shyly. "It's very pretty."

Miss Laidlaw blushed. "My father chose it from one of my mother's novels. He said it was distinguished, yet feminine."

Lily pulled a face. "At least no one can shorten it. The boy I sang my duet with on Saturday called me Lil'. I was furious."

"I hope you turned him to stone with a ferocious glare."

222

Lily giggled. "Wouldn't that be something wonderful?"

Back in the workroom, Miss Laidlaw took the measurements Greta had sent Mrs Winchett and adjusted her dressmaking mannequin to the correct size.

She and Lily showed their design to the pattern maker, who whistled through her teeth and said, "Just this side of the line, Miss Laidlaw." She jerked her thumb towards Mrs Winchett's office. "Her upstairs approved it?" Miss Laidlaw nodded, and the pattern maker continued, "If you leave Miss Matthews with me, I can show her how we make the pattern. She needs to learn some time."

Lily was delighted to accept the invitation. She spent the rest of the afternoon helping to deconstruct the dress and receiving instructions on how to size a pattern correctly.

She returned home, her head buzzing with all she had learnt and dreams of a visit to London. The latter was slightly tarnished by Mrs Winchett saying she may go in Lily's place. *She can't. She simply can't. Please, God, let me go to London if you're listening.* The prayer became a mantra repeated over and over in Lily's head.

She stopped short at the end of the road. Stephen Dent's car was parked outside her house.

Ma opened the door. "Ah, there you are, Lily. Mr Dent has this minute arrived with an invitation for you. I think you'll be excited."

Lily checked her appearance in the hall mirror and entered the front room, pausing by the door with her head held high. "To what do we owe this rare pleasure, Mr Dent?"

He pretended to be abject, a gesture quite belied by the amusement in his eyes. "You are justifiably angry, Lily. I have been to London to meet friends. But it is good to know you have missed my humble presence."

"No indeed, Stephen. I have no call on your time, and I am glad you have been enjoying a holiday. I have had little time to notice your absence as I'm gainfully employed."

Stephen laughed and said, "Delightful, touché Lily."

Ma stared at Lily and frowned, issuing a silent caution at her outspokenness which Lily pretended not to see.

"I trust you are well."

Her icily polite tone only made him smirk. "Very well, thank you. I am here to invite you to attend a private party my parents are holding for George and Grace's engagement and to request the pleasure of escorting you."

Lily flushed to the roots of her hair. He had wrongfooted her again and made her seem rude.

"With your parent's permission, of course." Ma acquiesced by inclining her head.

Lily dropped her gaze. "How very kind... of your parents. Please thank them for me."

Stephen coughed and said, "And the small matter of my request?"

She raised her eyes reluctantly to meet his dancing ones. "Thank you, that is most kind also."

"Well, that's settled, my mission is accomplished, and I must take my leave. I have left an invitation card with your mother."

Lily permitted Stephen to brush her hand lightly with his lips. He said, "Perhaps I may have the pleasure of seeing you at Mrs O'Shea's meetings beforehand?"

She nodded, and with that, he took his leave.

As Ma returned to the parlour, she raised her eyebrows. "Lily, I did not like to hear you speaking boldly to Mr Dent.

After all, he came to offer you a treat. One might infer you dislike him."

Lily looked at her mother. "I don't dislike him, Ma, but he thinks well of himself, which seems to bring out the worst in me. The way he assumed I was waiting on his next visit indeed."

"Mr Dent is older than the boys you are used to seeing. He naturally has more confidence and knows his mind. I was initially unsure of him too, but I have revised my opinion." She smiled at Lily. "He seems friendly and thoughtful towards you. It is quite common for a gentleman to lean towards a younger companion, and of course, you met through mutual friends. A little maturity is no bad thing, in my opinion. Someone with more steadiness."

"More steadiness than whom?" Lily flashed at her mother. "Than Aiden, I suppose?"

Ma looked at Lily sternly. "Lily, Aiden is hardly in question here. Mr Dent has kindly asked you to a party. He has scarcely proposed." She patted Lily's hand. "I'm sure it's normal that they should include you in the invitation as you know Grace and his mama is interested in the suffragists. You would hardly wish to attend Grace's engagement party without a partner and be a wallflower all evening."

All that her mother said was true, but somehow Lily felt Stephen was less altruistic than Ma supposed. With a sinking heart, she also realised that Ma and Pa had no thought a binding promise existed between her and Aiden. She wondered, did Aiden feel the same?

The next day at work, as she and Miss Laidlaw began to tack together the skirt of Miss Marion's dress, she included

Grace in their conversation by thanking her for the invitation and asking what would be appropriate to wear.

"George's mama has gifted me a dress for the occasion. She says I am too young for silk and suggested a muslin gown."

Miss Laidlaw interjected, "She is quite right, Miss Kirby. Silks are for when you are married or certainly older than you are now."

Grace sighed contentedly and appeared to drift into a small reverie before describing her dress. "It's beautiful, pale pink, with a square neckline and a short lace cape falling from the shoulders over the bust to the elbows on the sleeves." She smoothed her hands down her body. "The bodice is waisted, and the skirt has overstitched lace and self-coloured embroidery."

Lily teased, "It won't be as good as if we made it here." She sighed exaggeratedly. "Who is making it for you?"

Grace grimaced. "Mrs Dent's dressmaker is making it, she's frightening, and I think she feels I am an inferior person." Grace's usual cheeky grin peeked out again. "She's wrong, though. George and I will be successful, and then I'll come back and show her."

Looking serious again, Grace said, "You will make my wedding dress, won't you, Lily? I don't care if we must go to every jumble sale in town to afford the material. I can't bear that old gorgon to touch my dress."

Lily flushed red and glanced at Miss Laidlaw. She wasn't sure if Miss Winchett would approve of her making a dress outside the workroom.

Miss Laidlaw smiled calmly and said, "Do you know which style you'd like?"

Grace shook her head. Then her words poured out in a rush. "Not really, but I'd rather keep it simple. I don't think I can afford lace. It's expensive. Ma said she married in her best dress with a posy of flowers."

Miss Laidlaw looked thoughtful, then said, "Simple is pretty and often the best."

Lily gave Grace's shoulders a quick squeeze. "We'll make something beautiful, I promise."

Miss Laidlaw said, "I've seen some of the new styles from Paris. They have tulip skirts tapering at the bottom with a small 'v' at the hemline, allowing you to walk. I saw one fashion plate with a similar skirt. The designer showed it with a belted over-jacket with a high collar like a fan. Stylish and different to the usual lacy dresses."

Lily asked Miss Laidlaw, "Would you have time to sketch something similar to see if Grace likes it?"

She laughed. "I can do better than that. I have the fashion plate to show you. When I saw the design, I thought it would make a statement gown for someone, and you'd look well in it, Miss Kirby."

Grace grinned. "I'd like something out of the ordinary to show the family I'm my own woman."

Miss Laidlaw added casually, "As you're going away soon afterwards, with minimal alterations, you could wear it again as a smart day or evening outfit."

Grace looked grateful. "I won't have a lot of clothes to take with me, so that would be wonderful."

Chapter 24

Lily knocked eagerly at the Donnelly's door before the next meeting and could barely wait to set off before asking for news of Aiden.

"We had a letter yesterday, Lily. Aiden writes that Miss Marion is in a WSPU nursing home. She was imprisoned and force-fed after going on a hunger strike."

Lily's face blanched, and she looked at Mrs Donnelly. "Is Miss Marion alright? And is Aiden safe?"

Mrs Donnelly looked grave. "Aiden is safe, but he fears for Kitty's voice. They are brutal with the women, holding them down and forcing a tube into their stomachs whilst they are quite sentient. The vocal cords are delicate and can easily become scarred."

Lily felt queasy and asked quietly, "How did she get free?"

Mrs Donnelly smiled grimly. "The women's prisons are overcrowded, and the government fear the women on hunger strike will become martyrs. As soon as the women become too ill or weak, they are released, even temporarily. It's a ridiculous game. That's why it's called the Cat and Mouse Act."

"Has anyone died, Mrs Donnelly?"

Mary Donnelly looked at Lily. "Mary Clarke, Emmeline Pankhurst's sister, recently died after the brutal treatment meted out to her in prison. The women are serious, Lily. It is a spiritual calling for them. If the government think they will give up, they are wrong. For the WSPU, it's a war."

Lily was quiet, then said, "I don't think I could bear that to happen to me. Does that make me a coward?"

Mrs Donnelly put a reassuring arm around Lily. "We all have different roles to play, Lily. The work we do here with the NUWSS is equally important. Indeed, our leader Millicent Fawcett believes the suffragette's violent behaviour may be counter-productive because it hardens the government's hearts and turns public opinion by shocking them."

"Ma and Pa both say the democratic process is how real change happens, and I believe that too. But I wonder if I may not care enough to be a warrior because my life is too comfortable."

"You can only be yourself, Lily. We all fight in different ways. The NUWSS have had bills before parliament several times, and I'm sure if we persevere, we will prevail. I know you are always in Aiden's thoughts. He says you inspire him as he imagines the life you deserve to have when he fights for the cause."

Nora O'Shea's house was much quieter than when Miss Marion had come to talk. Only twenty women in their ordinary clothes were present, along with several husbands who supported women's suffrage. Shocked talk of the increasing violence, arson attacks and imprisonment dominated the conversation. There was no sign of Mrs

Dent and Stephen, and Lily wasn't sure whether to be relieved or disappointed.

Why do men promise things and then not deliver? Or was it her? First, Aiden pledged they'd go to London together and that he'd play for her at the concert – neither happened. It was all very well, being 'an inspiration', but she wanted to see him. This week, Stephen had looked longingly at her like she was something delicious to eat, saying he'd see her here, then had not turned up. She decided, on balance, she would rather they didn't promise anything.

She needed Mrs Winchett to let her go to London to see Aiden herself. She crossed her fingers as she thought of it in case that helped.

Mrs Donnelly was quickly drawn away into the other room for the committee meeting. Lily joined Jane and Rose in putting more leaflets in envelopes at a table. There was no Aiden to play while they were working, and the room appeared unnaturally large with so few of them in it. Everyone spoke in hushed voices, like in church.

"What news have you had from Aiden? He must be at the heart of the struggle working with Miss Marion." Jane's eyes shone eagerly, and she lent in, waiting for Lily's reply.

"He is her accompanist in the theatre, not her accomplice. He attends meetings and marches because he has a strong sense of justice, but that is all I assure you."

"I quite thought he would be part of an active cell. That would be marvellous. I'd feel like I was doing something." She looked at her sister, whose expression seemed to indicate less enthusiasm as she quickly shifted her eyes away and bit her lip nervously. "Rose and I have marched in London. They are more committed than here. No one will listen to us unless we do something more daring than this."

"Keep your voice down, Jane; you could get Aiden into trouble making suggestions like that in public. This isn't a joke. Pa read in the paper that the police have spies in these organisations."

Jane looked scornfully around the room. "Well, they'll be bored here. More likely to get a new recipe for cake than any juicy information." She leaned back in her chair and stretched. "I just wish something would happen!"

Lily's irritation at her romantic naivety boiled over. "You might think it's exciting to be in prison, but I don't believe it can be nice to starve and be force-fed or hit during demonstrations and flung to the floor by policemen."

Rose seemed to shrink into herself, and noticing her discomfort, Lily said, "Rose, you don't have to do any of those things if you don't want to. What you do here is important too. Don't let anyone make you do more."

Rose looked shyly at Lily. "I'm rather stupidly afraid of loud noises and crowds of people. I don't think I could go on a march again." She stammered and looked at Jane imploringly.

Movement in the doorway cut their conversation short, and Mrs Dent entered the room, accompanied by Stephen.

"Ladies, Gentlemen, I apologise for being late. My son was detained on business."

As Stephen made his bow to the room, he scanned the assembled company, caught Lily's eye, and flashed a dazzling smile.

"So gentlemanly," whispered Rose as she blushed red.

Stephen made a beeline for their table, and Lily thought Rose might faint; she looked so flustered.

He immediately dashed Rose's cherished hopes as he bowed low over Lily's hand. "Lily, my evening is now complete."

Embarrassed, Lily introduced Jane and Rose and watched as Stephen drew a chair up to the table and installed himself next to her without waiting to be asked. He flashed a winning smile at them and said, "May I be of assistance, ladies?"

Jane handed him a pile of leaflets and some envelopes. "The cavalry, no less. Please feel free to rescue us from this tedious slavery."

He laughed. "What a pleasure to find myself in the hero's role and in such beautiful company, too." He made an exaggerated fuss about folding a leaflet precisely, then shrugged as he slid it into the envelope. "It is indeed a dull task." He turned over the pamphlets and began to read one aloud but quickly stopped with a grimace. "It's very worthy, but not exactly Gilbert and Sullivan. I was in London a few days ago; the WSPU leaflets are much more dramatic."

"You see?" Jane pounced on his remark. "We are boring people with this dull stuff. Were you on the march to the House of Commons?"

"I?" He looked incredulous. "No, indeed, I was in London purely for selfish pleasure." He began to regale them with tales of theatres and fashion, completely ignoring Jane's disappointment and Rose's wistful smiles. "The Savoy Theatre attached to the hotel is a lively place. We ate well and enjoyed one of Mr D'Oyle–Carte's latest operettas HMS Pinafore. You would enjoy it hugely, Lily."

Pausing, Stephen claimed to be parched and offered his arm to Lily, suggesting they might help bring through the tea. Thus, he neatly removed her and left the others with the envelopes.

"You may thank me later," he commented to Lily as he steered her, not towards the kitchen but to Mrs O'Shea's small library. "For effecting your rescue. All that worthiness is quite exhausting."

He prowled around the room, then said, "Ah ha," and lifted a decanter of sherry. "I knew Nora would have something in here."

"But you can't help yourself without asking!"

Stephen laughed. "I've known Nora and her sister since I was in short coats. They won't mind."

"I don't feel comfortable doing this; I should return to the meeting."

Intent on pouring a glass, he offered her one and, when she shook her head, said, "Live a little, Lily, unless…" he glanced at his pocket watch. "Do you really turn into a pumpkin at nine o'clock?"

Lily stamped her foot in frustration at his taunting, but simultaneously, an involuntary giggle escaped her. He had a lively sense of the ridiculous.

He pointed at her and shook his head. "You see, I am more fun than the meeting. You and I would do well together, Lily."

He approached her, standing too close for comfort and, with his glass casually held in one hand, raised her chin with the other. Her heart began to hammer as she felt mesmerised by his dancing eyes, but then she caught the smell of alcohol on his breath and stepped back. For one moment, she thought he would kiss her.

Half running, she rushed to the door and glanced back to see him smiling. He blew her the kiss she was sure he would have placed on her lips if she had not moved.

Unsure how to proceed, she was aware that the committee could emerge from the study for tea at any minute. Lily couldn't bear for them to catch her and ask what she was doing there.

How could she face Mrs Donnelly ever again if she thought Lily was flirting? She adopted the original plan and headed for the kitchen to offer her services.

Carrying two plates of scones like a shield in front of her, she plucked up the courage to re-enter the meeting. There was, she decided, something safe and modest about scones.

Stephen was back in the room; he politely unburdened her, fetched a cup of tea in an unexceptional way and then strolled away to speak to Nora and her sister Margaret. He behaved as if nothing untoward had happened.

Lily was intrigued and confused in equal measure but thought *two could play that game* and deliberately ignored him until the meeting ended.

As she and Mrs Donnelly collected their coats, Lily struggled, one arm caught in the scarf she had forgotten she threaded through the sleeve. Stephen sauntered over. "Allow me." He lifted the weight of the coat and calmly extracted the scarf. "Chilly in here since tea," he laughed. "Or is it me?"

Lily narrowed her eyes. "They tell me alcohol only creates an illusion of warmth. Good evening, Mr Dent."

Mrs Donnelly looked confused as she glanced from one to the other. "Good evening, Mr Dent." She shepherded Lily through the door, then turned to her. "Lily, what a strange thing for you to say to Mr Dent. Are you feeling quite well?"

"Sometimes he is insufferable, Mrs Donnelly. Because my friend from work is getting married to his youngest brother, he seems to feel we must be best friends."

"I do hope he isn't going beyond the line of what is pleasing, Lily. You may tell me if he makes you uncomfortable."

She shook her head, revealing nothing of her torment. "I think he likes to tease by blowing hot and cold, nothing more."

Mrs Donnelly looked doubtful. "You are still very young, and he is a more sophisticated man, Lily. It is too bad of him to tease you."

Lily said, desperate to change the subject, "Let's not talk about him. Tell me do you miss Aiden most dreadfully?"

Mrs Donnelly looked wistful. "I miss the music in the house, Lily, and Aiden's company. Mr Donnelly doesn't admit it, but I think he pines for their conversations; they always discuss politics. However, we keep ourselves busy, and Mr Donnelly has accepted a steward's position with the trade union at the dockyard and is occupied with that now."

"I miss his company every morning on the tram and the fun we had. He seems such a long way away."

Mrs Donnelly nodded her understanding. "It's only miles, Lily. That's what I tell myself. I'm sure he misses us too."

Lily nodded but wondered whether Mrs Donnelly was correct. If you were someone's mother, she supposed the bond was unbreakable. But with Aiden surrounded by excitement and dashing new people, perhaps someone ordinary like her might be seen differently, even if he thought he was in love with her once.

The following week, no letter came from Aiden to reassure her, not even a postcard. *They'd spoken every day when he was at home and shared everything. Why didn't he write?*

"Before you ask, nothing today either," her Ma said briskly as Lily came in from work and scanned the hall table. "You can't expect Aiden to have time to write every week. He's working and travelling. You've had news from Mrs Donnelly, and fretting yourself to a fiddle string won't bring him back."

Lily looked at her Ma. "I'm worried he isn't getting my letters because they pass through the agent. They wouldn't deliberately withhold them, would they?"

Ma looked at her kindly. "I know it's difficult. He'll probably get a bundle all at once when he returns to London, and then he'll reply. In the meantime, you must keep going and make the best of every day. What will be, will be, Lily. Get on with your life. I'm sure Aiden is."

Fortunately, the next day brought exciting news to lift her spirits. Mrs Winchett had finally decided to let Lily travel to London with Miss Laidlaw to assist in fitting Miss Marion's new costume. She called them into the office and looked up at them from her desk with a smile.

"I have investigated your travel, and you will be pleased to know that there is an excellent train service from Portsmouth Harbour or Portsmouth Town to Waterloo station in London, which runs four times a day during the winter season. You should make the journey and return on the same day, and I expect you to return to work as normal the following day. I propose to write to Miss Marion and seek a suitable appointment. I will provide your tickets and an allowance for luncheon."

Miss Laidlaw said, "That is generous, Mrs Winchett, and I am sure I speak for us both in thanking you for this opportunity."

Lily dropped a slight curtsey, but her heart beat wildly. She was going to London after all.

"Now, I would like you to show me your progress on the design." Mrs Winchett stood, and Miss Laidlaw and Lily followed her downstairs to the workroom. Inside, Lily was cheering, and she wanted to dance a jig on the stairs behind Mrs Winchett.

Miss Marion's dress was almost complete and waited on a dressmaker's dummy, shrouded in a sheet. There remained just the beading on the skirt to be completed and any final fitting adjustments.

Mrs Winchett clapped. "Please gather around, Ladies, quickly now." She waved her hands impatiently as the staff around the room laid down their sewing. "Miss Laidlaw will guide you through her most innovative design for a theatrical costume to be worn in London by Miss Kitty Marion."

Miss Laidlaw removed the cover from the dress to exclamations. They had added the bodice to the skirt yesterday, and the effect of the simple pure-white gown, caught at the waist with roses and which hung beautifully, was stunning. However, when Miss Laidlaw demonstrated how the slashed skirt moved with its cleverly inserted chiffon panels, the workroom girls let out a ripple of applause. Lily was bursting with pride.

Miss Laidlaw explained, "We hope other performers, particularly dancers, will eventually use this new design with the split-panelled skirt. The panels will be weighted with beads to enhance the swing, but the design could be varied with the same illusion of movement created by feathers or fur around the hem. I want to thank Miss Matthews for introducing Miss Marion to Gowns by Anastasia and for her assistance with the design."

Lily noticed Grace, who beamed back and mimed applause. However, two girls who worked on the other table were muttering together and throwing her sour looks.

Grace's warning about jealousy rang in her mind, but she thought, *let them be jealous. I'm going to London, and I'll be seeing Aiden again, I hope.*

As Lily and Grace left the workroom that evening, Grace said, "I'm proud of you for your costume design. I can't believe I'll be leaving so soon. I don't know if I'll see the dress finished."

Lily looked at her friend sadly. "Oh, Gracie, I'm glad for you, but I'll miss you. Everyone I love is leaving."

"I'll write every week, Lily, I promise, and from what I hear, if you play your cards right, we could be sisters before long. With Stephen being the eldest, Lily, you could have a showroom in no time, and you deserve it. You're talented."

"Please don't say that. You know I love Aiden, Grace. I'm going to London to help with the dress fittings and see him. It will be wonderful." She turned her face to Grace, unable to hide her excitement.

Grace looked at Lily. "Sometimes things don't turn out the way they do in books. Aiden has a new life. Don't wait forever only to find out you're on the shelf like Miss Laidlaw."

A chill spread through Lily. Everyone seemed to be saying the same thing. She refused to believe them and held onto the hope in her heart. She would know when she saw Aiden if things had changed.

Chapter 25

Mrs Winchett set a date for the London fitting on the first of February, a week before Grace's engagement party. As soon as she knew, Lily wrote to Aiden to say she was coming.

Miss Laidlaw and Lily worked endless hours sewing tiny beads to the base and sides of each panel and crystals to catch the light and send rainbows across the white dress as it moved. In despair at the time it was taking, Lily told Miss Laidlaw they needed help.

Miss Laidlaw considered. "I can't spare anyone from my team, but I'll speak to Miss Gibbs, who leads the other team. She may see a benefit if they can cover their work."

The next day Miss Gibbs duly released two girls from their regular duties, and the four women sat around the dress, its skirt spread out on the table like sun rays.

Miss Laidlaw demonstrated the beading and watched to ensure the two newcomers to the project were proficient and then left them to continue.

As they left that evening, Grace said, "I'm glad you didn't nominate me for the beading. I can't think of anything worse, all those beads making you spotty-eyed."

Lily stretched her neck and groaned. "I'll be glad when we've finished but making such a wonderful dress is worth it. I do hope I'll see Aiden when we go for the fitting."

Grace looked at her and grinned. "Of course, you do. Have you heard back? Is he taking you somewhere special?"

Lily looked down. "I haven't heard back yet, but the letters go through his agent, and there's sometimes a delay."

Grace snorted. "He wants to make an effort, is all I can say."

In case her first letter hadn't arrived, Lily wrote another quick note that evening to advise him she was coming on a visit.

With more hands on the job, the girls finished the dress. After a week of being hung to let the panels drop and allow adjustments to the hem, it was finally steamed and laid in a long flat box wrapped in tissue paper.

Mrs Winchett handed money from the safe to Miss Laidlaw for their journey.

Although Lily had twice written to Aiden to tell him about their visit, no news had come in return. Despite this setback, her excitement bubbled over, and that evening, she flung her needlework aside and exclaimed, "I can't sit still."

Ma folded her knitting and looked at her daughter. "I don't doubt you're excited. I was myself the first time I went to London with the big house. They rented accommodation for two weeks, and I was lucky enough to go."

"Oh, Ma, what was it like?"

"Busy, my girl, busy, working in an old-fashioned kitchen, cramped, with a stove that smoked great gusts depending on the wind direction."

"No, Ma, I meant the sights. Were St Paul's and the big parks, Buckingham Palace, all the attractions, wonderful?"

Ma sniffed. "Noisy and dirty is what I remember, not but what St Paul's is a sight to behold. No, I prefer our sea air and a walk along the promenade."

Pa intervened, seeing the look of disappointment on Lily's face. "But you make up your own mind, Lily. Some wouldn't live anywhere else. That's the beauty of trips away; they give you learning that you don't get in books."

Retrieving her dreams from the bottom of her boots, Lily gave Pa a grateful smile, and he returned a wink. "Now, this is for you because I don't doubt you'll want more than your luncheon." He pressed a small purse into her hand. "I hope you enjoy your day."

Overcome, she hugged him and said thank you at least six times.

"Now, Lily, I've packed you and Miss Laidlaw some cake in case you get peckish waiting on Miss Marion. I don't doubt she'll keep you hanging around, don't be surprised."

Lily tossed and turned, unable to sleep. She got butterflies in her stomach when she thought of seeing Aiden again. She'd pictured the look in his eyes when he saw her and rehearsed what she'd say to him.

There was no help for it. Lily had to wear plain, neat clothes for the trip, as she was officially 'at work', but she'd asked to borrow Ma's paisley shawl in the event that Aiden had time to walk out anywhere. At least she could feel a little more elegant.

She had only just fallen asleep when she heard tapping at her door, and it was time to wake up again. She scrambled into her clothes, smoothed her navy skirt, and straightened the shoulders of her blouse. Lily decided that no one could object if she wore her Sunday hat and spent several minutes perfecting the chignon, which allowed it to perch at a becoming angle.

Ma had made porridge and handed Lily an apron to protect her clothes. She ate, although she didn't feel hungry. Ma wouldn't hear of her going out on an empty stomach, and she knew better than to try.

"Don't lose my scarf, please, Lily. Make sure you check you have everything each time you leave somewhere. Mind the traffic too, there are more motor cars in London, and they move at a pace."

Lily was sure the list of warnings would be much longer, but Pa saved her. He kissed his wife on the cheek and said, "She's not going to the moon, Maggie."

Ma pursed her lips. "She might as well be. It's a different world up there."

Lily also kissed Ma goodbye. "I'll be careful. Please don't spend all day worrying about me."

As they arrived at the station, Pa said, "Have a wonderful time, Lily, don't heed your Ma worrying; enjoy your adventure. I'll meet you off the evening train. Now, where's Miss Laidlaw?"

Lily saw her waiting by the London platform carrying the dress box and waved. She hurried over and introduced her pa.

"Well, ladies, if you have your tickets, why don't you find some seats."

"Yes, I have both tickets, shall we, Lily?"

Pa stood on the platform until the train pulled out, and the last Lily saw was him waving through the billowing steam.

Miss Laidlaw stowed the dress in the netting luggage rack and sighed. "It's several years since I've been to London. I'm rather excited; how about you, Lily?"

"I've never been before, and I can't wait." More diffidently, she added, "I am hoping perhaps to see Aiden when we're at the theatre. I wrote to tell him we're coming today, but he hasn't replied."

"I'm sure he'll try to be free if he knows you're coming. If the fitting goes well, there may be time for you to visit something together before we leave or at least have lunch."

Lily watched the city turn to fields as they drew into Havant station. More people boarded, and as the doors banged shut, whistles sounded on the platform, and the engine hissed steam as it engaged the weight of the train and began to build momentum.

"The old line used to finish here," Miss Laidlaw commented. "We had to get off and do the last leg into Portsmouth by coach. When they first ran the line through to Portsmouth, there were fights between the two rival train companies, each trying to block the other coming through."

Lily looked surprised. "Not real fights?"

Miss Laidlaw laughed. "Yes indeed, it's hard to believe, but workers from the two companies physically came to blows."

Lily looked solemn. "Jane, one of the girls at the suffragist meeting, said that the women fight with the police on the marches in London. They are thrown to the ground and punched or kicked. I can't imagine a policeman doing that to a lady."

Miss Laidlaw shook her head. "Fear, Lily, and insecurity. The women are challenging the old order and not doing as the government says. When people are afraid, they are capable of many dreadful things."

"But surely the government can't approve of how the police behave?"

"It doesn't suit the politicians to have women with an organised campaign. Mr Asquith is trying to push through other reforms, and he thinks that if women who own property get the vote, they will support the opposition, and he won't win the next election. Not all politicians have pure motives."

"Ma says men can only think of one thing at a time anyway."

Conversation dwindled, and both women watched the changing countryside as Hampshire turned to Surrey and Kent. The train slowed and lurched over several points as it approached Waterloo. The buildings close to the track were soot-blackened. Lily wondered how anyone who lived in them slept with the constant noise of the trains.

As they alighted and Miss Laidlaw carefully passed the dress box down, Lily's first impression of London was all noise. A dizzying number of people zig-zagged across the concourse, all appearing to know exactly where they were going. Lily looked at Miss Laidlaw wide-eyed and said, "Goodness!"

"You'll get used to it, Lily. Stay close."

They dived into the crowd and left the busy station to find a taxi.

"Mornin', Ladies." The cab driver looked smart in his peaked cap and greatcoat. He doffed his hat, opened the rear door for them to step in, and set the taximeter in motion. "Where can I take you?"

"The Savoy Theatre, please, stage entrance."

Outside the fast-moving cab, Lily didn't know where to look first. She overcame the desire to cover her eyes, and the driver wove successfully in and out of horse-drawn vehicles, bicycles, and pedestrians. He simultaneously pointed out tourist sites as soon as he had ascertained they were visitors, alarmingly taking his hands off the steering wheel several times to point out places of interest.

As they crossed Waterloo Bridge, the view downriver showed all the famous bridges she had seen in a newsreel at the cinema and even St Paul's in the background. It made her long to stop the cab and hang over the wall to feast her eyes. But first things first, they were here to see Miss Marion. And then, perhaps she could walk back to the river with Aiden later. Her heart began to flutter in anticipation. It would be romantic.

As Miss Laidlaw paid for the cab, the driver said, "'Ere, you know any actresses then? My Mrs, she collects autographs. I managed to get 'er the 'ome secretary the other day. Comin' out of 'is new club, 'e were, Mr Churchill. 'E stepped into me cab. They're here drinking all times of the day and night; the politicians. It's a wonder they find time to rule the country. Still, that's toffs for you."

Lily was about to claim acquaintance with Miss Marion when Mrs Laidlaw replied firmly in the negative. As the cab pulled away, she said, "Miss Marion may prefer not to be bothered, and it's not our place to ask. Discretion Lily is crucial in our line of work."

Lily looked down, embarrassed. "No, quite, I wasn't thinking."

The backstage area was quiet, except for a tired looking cleaner pushing a wide broom between the wicker trunks. The cleaner pointed out Miss Marion's dressing room, and on receiving no answer to their knock on her door, they drew up two hard chairs and prepared to wait.

After half an hour, Lily began to fidget and wonder if Mrs Winchett had told them the correct day. Suddenly there was a flurry of activity, and Greta appeared, followed by Miss Marion. Lily craned to see if Aiden was there too, but she was disappointed.

"Come in, come in." Miss Marion waved Lily and Miss Laidlaw into her dressing room. She was thinner than Lily remembered, and her face without makeup looked gaunt, her hair dry and brittle.

Miss Marion noticed Lily's stare and said brusquely, "The hunger strike, I am not yet fully recovered." She inclined her head towards Miss Laidlaw. "Please introduce me to your friend, Lily."

Flushing pink, Lily said, "This is Miss Anis Laidlaw. She's my teacher, and I hope you will think we have designed a beautiful dress."

"Good morning, Miss Marion. Are you ready to see the gown now?"

Miss Marion nodded and gestured to the empty mannequin in the corner. Miss Laidlaw slipped her dress over the dummy and shook out the folds of white chiffon. Miss Laidlaw talked through the design points of the gown and then waited, standing to one side as the other two women scrutinised the dress. Greta turned up the seams, checked the beading, stood back, and folded her arms.

Silence rang out in the room. To Lily, it seemed almost deafening. She became aware of blood rushing in her ears as she held her breath.

Miss Marion looked away from the dress. "Shall we try it on?"

Greta helped Miss Marion remove her outfit, and Miss Laidlaw slipped the white gown over her head. It was loose at the waist, Kitty had indeed lost weight, but a slow smile of delight spread across her face as she swayed and felt the skirt move. Kitty couldn't resist a full twirl feeling the skirt fly. "Wonderful," she said, looking at Lily and Miss Laidlaw. "Magical."

Greta folded her arms. "Bordering on the indecent, I'd say."

Kitty turned towards her. "But not quite," she laughed, "which is the whole point. It's perfect."

Greta and Miss Laidlaw were suddenly all business lifting and resetting the skirt. Lily watched their deftness with a keen eye. She was proud that she had helped to create this exciting gown.

Greta decided that final alterations could be made at the theatre, ensuring the dress could stay in London, and it appeared that their audience was rapidly ending.

Lily cleared her throat, feeling she had to be brave, "Miss Marion, I was hoping to see Aiden today. Will he be at the theatre? I wrote to him."

Miss Marion waved a hand. "He usually here around lunchtime. After the show, he haunts the jazz clubs, then can't get out of bed." She laughed. "Don't go making him homesick, Lily, he's the best —" she hesitated, "accompanist I've ever had." She was laughing, but Lily thought she heard a hint of steel behind the joke.

Greta offered to show Miss Laidlaw Miss Marion's costumes, and they soon had their heads together. Lily followed the sounds of musical instruments tuning up and stood patiently waiting by the pit.

A corpulent violinist with a black waistcoat stretched over his ample abdomen looked up from where he was tuning the strings. "You look like you lost half a crown and found sixpence, Love. Can I help?"

"I'm looking for Aiden Donnelly."

"What's he done now, then?" He looked over to his colleagues, who were all enjoying the joke.

Lily said, "Nothing. I wanted to meet with him before going home."

The men laughed again. "You and half the chorus, Love, he's quite a hit with the ladies around here."

Dismayed and not knowing what else to say, Lily stammered, "Thank you," and turned to go, tears misting.

"Lily, wait, Lily." A familiar voice was calling from the other side of the stage.

She turned and saw Aiden hurrying towards her. She barely recognised him. He was taller, she was sure and nattily attired in check trousers and a mustard jacket. As he approached, she saw blue circles under his eyes, and his hair flopped forwards. "Aiden, I thought perhaps you hadn't received my letters."

He shuffled awkwardly. "Yes, I'm sorry about not replying, it's hectic here, and I'm not such a dab hand at correspondence as I thought. Still, I'm here now. I don't have long before the run-through, but we could get something to eat."

Lily's dream of a romantic walk along the embankment or climbing to the dome of St Pauls vanished. "Oh, I had thought we might… but well, yes, lunch would be nice. I must check with Miss Laidlaw first."

They walked awkwardly towards the dressing room, then both started to speak together, "It's good to see…." They laughed, and Lily said, "How have you been? You look tired."

He grimaced. "Don't start sounding like my mother, Lily. I am tired, but I can't tell you how much I love it here. The music I've found is vibrant and exciting beyond anything I'd dreamed of. At a club that I go to, they play jazz. All sorts of people go to play together. Everyone is welcome. I've met black musicians from America, people from France." He turned to look at her, alight with a passion she realised was not for her. "Lily, you'd love to hear it. I want to show you how the music beats with a heart of its own."

Lily tried to understand; perhaps it was how she felt when beautiful silk ran through her fingers or saw her dress transform Miss Marion's simple dance steps into a fluid form. Lily did know that Aiden was describing a world that fulfilled rather than frustrated him. He saw a new horizon she couldn't be part of for a long time if they waited until she was of age like Pa wanted.

"And the WSPU, Lily, I feel like I'm part of something worthwhile, living with people who do things, whatever the cost, to make life fairer. It's different to the tea and talking at Mrs O'Shea's."

Lily hesitated. "I heard about Miss Marion. How terrible for her."

His brow clouded. "It's shocking the lengths the government will go to, turning a blind eye to prison treatment. She has recovered now, but the authorities brutalised Kitty. She could have lost her voice."

"What did she do, Aiden, to be put in prison?"

He gave a short mirthless laugh. "Kitty broke a window on a march after the police began pushing the women around. They won't stop her, though."

Lily was shocked at his casual acceptance of the vandalism and said quietly, "No? My goodness, she must be fearless."

Aiden stopped and smiled at her. "Not like my gentle Lily."

Lily stiffened. "Because I don't go breaking windows or setting fires doesn't mean I'm not serious about women's suffrage and trade unions, all those things. Miss Laidlaw says we can all contribute in our way, and I am. I believe in the democratic route, lobbying and getting signatures. Mrs Fawcett, who leads the NUWSS, her husband is an MP. He's helping us in parliament."

He laughed. "Of course, you are serious, Lily. I'm not getting at you. It was a compliment. But I prefer direct action." Lily was about to reply when he continued. "Go and see what Miss Laidlaw says. I'm starving."

Aiden exchanged greetings with numerous cast members as they drifted into the theatre. Show people kept different hours.

Deep in their discussion about theatrical costumes, Miss Laidlaw and Greta were on first-name terms. She smiled at Lily. "Of course, you may go for lunch if Aiden escorts you. Have an enjoyable time."

Lily scuttled out before Miss Laidlaw changed her mind and found Aiden laughing and joking with a group of girls from the chorus. They eyed her up and down, and Lily had never felt as prim or provincial in all her life.

Seeing the girls' gaze, he turned. "There you are; where would you like to go?" He crooked his arm, inviting her to take it, and they set off for the stage door.

"I'd like to walk along the river and see Big Ben if you have time."

"Tourist," he gently mocked, and for the first time today, Lily felt like she was with the Aiden she knew.

Away from the theatre, she was able to talk about home. Lily was happy to give news about his family and some of their friends.

They ate lunch in a café in a tiny back street near the grand Palace of Westminster with its tall clock tower. There was no choice. The waiter served enormous plates of savoury stew and thick chunks of dark bread.

"The owners are from Poland," he explained. "The chef is the uncle of one of the girls you saw earlier; we all come here."

As they strolled back to the theatre, Lily asked to walk onto Waterloo Bridge, and the two of them leaned on the side, watching the water flow by.

"Aiden," she began warily. "Aiden, I've been reading things in the paper, and I can't help noticing that some of the vandalism done by the suffragettes is in the same places you are performing. Please don't get led into taking any risks."

Aiden glanced over his shoulder. "Lily, be careful what you say in public, and it isn't vandalism; it's political protest," he hissed. "The government must be made to listen."

She swallowed. "You would tell me if you were in danger?"

He looked fierce for a moment. "Not if you're going to blurt out accusations in the street!"

She looked down.

Seeing her expression, Aiden took her hand. "I'm sorry, Lily, don't let's quarrel. I wish you could be here to share all this; I miss you." He leant towards her and kissed her cheek. "That's for my mother," he brushed her lips, "and that's for you. I don't know when I will get home again, but even if I don't write every week, I think of you."

Lily whispered, "I think of you too, Aiden." She brushed away a tear.

He said gently, "I must return to the theatre, Lily; I'm sorry. I wish you could have stayed longer and seen the show."

She took his arm and said, "I have to be back at work tomorrow, too, Aiden." Trying to keep the wobble out of her voice, she continued, "Perhaps Miss Marion will order another dress."

"Lord, yes," he replied cheerfully. "The girls always have new dresses. When I have enough money, I'll send for you for a visit, we can spend a day together, and you can see a matinee."

"Aiden, I've been thinking, if there's an opening for a seamstress at the theatre, I could come to London to work."

He looked uncomfortable and struggled to meet her eye. "That would be wonderful, but Lily, you haven't finished your training, and your pa would have me lynched."

Lily pleaded, "Surely there must be apprenticeships here? I could swap if Miss Marion put in a word for me."

"I don't know, Lily, there must be, but she keeps saying you need to get your qualifications, and pulling you away is unfair. Where could you live? I have a room in a house with some musicians, but I only earn enough to cover my rent and food. Until my songs are published, that is. Then things will be better. It's terrible to be apart, but I think we have to be patient."

Lily could feel tears of disappointment and frustration pricking behind her eyelids.

"Please don't be sad, Lily. Something will come up; you'll see." Aiden put his arm around her shoulder and hugged her to him, offering a suspiciously grubby handkerchief which she refused.

There was little chance of that, she thought despondently. *What's more, with his new life, did Aiden still really want her there? He said he was trying to protect her, encouraged by Miss Marion, but she wanted him to sweep her off her feet.*

It was only later that she realised Aiden hadn't answered her question about his involvement with dangerous activities either.

Chapter 26

O n the train, Lily became aware of Miss Laidlaw speaking. "What a wonderful day, Lily. Imagine, Greta has promised to stay in touch, and she likes the idea of my designs. Can you imagine rows of chorus girls wearing those short, beaded gowns I showed you?"

Lily nodded, but she couldn't agree. She'd pinned her hopes on this day for nothing. Scenery flashed past the window unseen. *How would she get through the days until she saw Aiden again? Without even the challenge of the costume to design? Seeing Aiden for a short time and always in public had been torture.*

"You seem rather quiet, Lily. Is everything alright?"

"It was stupid, but I hoped something dramatic might change today. How foolish. A day is just a day, after all. Aiden was busy and loves his new life. He's resigned to us simply carrying on as we are. I almost felt I didn't know him anymore."

Miss Laidlaw nodded sympathetically. "I must commend him for his restraint and for holding your best interests. Perhaps he didn't want to upset you by stirring up the pain of something which cannot yet be."

Lily looked mulish. "He's upset me by being so commonplace." She shook her head. "I thought he might be sad at the very least. Instead, he's having a marvellous time."

Miss Laidlaw rubbed one gloved hand along the other, appearing deep in thought. "Lily, not all gentlemen choose to display their emotions."

"He certainly isn't moping. He's been seeing all the sights we intended to see together and making new friends in some jazz club."

Miss Laidlaw hesitated and apparently decided on pragmatism. "Aiden is a young man in an exciting new life. I think it's commendable that he makes the most of this opportunity. Which doesn't necessarily mean he doesn't miss you."

Lily looked at her astounded, but Miss Laidlaw continued, "And I think you should do the same."

Lily snorted and said, "Because there is so much to do that's new and exciting in Portsmouth."

Miss Laidlaw leant forward and took Lily's hands. "We have Grace's wedding dress to design, and you have a party to attend related to the wedding. As I promised, we must look at my dresses. We will likely design more theatre costumes from what Greta said and may have carved a new niche for ourselves. I think that's exciting."

Lily looked at Miss Laidlaw blankly. "But I want to be in London with Aiden."

Miss Laidlaw said, "Lily, you did not previously find your career and your friends unsatisfactory. Aiden cannot offer you a life in London yet. Neither he nor Miss Marion has invited you. Moreover, you are underage, and your parents have not consented. I suggest, for now, you reflect on what is good in your life and enjoy it. Because we cannot have everything does not mean we have nothing."

Lily shrugged and looked petulant.

"Believe me. I understand how difficult it is to manage without someone we love. But in the end, happiness comes from within; we cannot expect someone else to create it."

Pa was waiting with Ma, looking anxiously along the platform as the train pulled in. Their faces lifted when they saw Lily alight, and they waved frantically.

After thanking Miss Laidlaw, they bore Lily away, pelting her with questions all the way home. There were more questions from Mrs Donnelly, who knocked barely after they had taken off their coats. No, they hadn't had time to see any of the show, but she had seen Big Ben. Yes, Aiden seemed happy, the theatre was spectacular, and he had made friends.

Glad to escape to the sanctuary of her room at bedtime, Lily wanted to cry, but no tears came. Instead, she thought about what Miss Laidlaw had said. If Aiden had a wonderful time, she would, too, even if it killed her.

She launched herself with determination into the alterations to her dress for the party and the design of Grace's wedding dress. Lily also began to accept Mr Dent's frequent invitations to take tea or drive into the country. She occasionally dropped hints to Aiden in her letters about outings she'd been on, but he didn't seem to notice, and she stilled her troubled conscience by thinking of the chorus girls and the jazz club. What was sauce for the goose....

Aiden's correspondence continued to be sparse and increasingly full of outrage at the government's position on women's suffrage. He spoke at length about people she didn't know, and there was no mention of returning home or sending for her to visit. It was all very well for him to champion her cause on votes for women, but that didn't ease her loneliness.

Before Stephen came to collect Lily on the night of the engagement party in March, Ma turned to her and said, "I'm pleased you're having fun with a new crowd, Lily."

Lily nodded, satisfied; *Ma hadn't noticed her forced gaiety.* "I'm enjoying all the outings and getting excited about Grace's wedding."

Pa nodded uncertainly and surprised her with his next remark.

"I think you've been trotting too hard since you returned from London. I think you've lost weight too."

Ma looked surprised. "Young women often slim down and lose their puppy fat. Lily is keen on fashion and design. It's to be expected."

Pa didn't look convinced but said, "I'm sure you know best."

The party was glittering. The Dents had opened the doors between their morning and sitting rooms to create a ballroom where couples could dance. A four-piece orchestra occupied one corner and was playing popular tunes. Crystal chandeliers winked in the bright electric lights. They acted as prisms that cast rainbows onto the walls.

Mrs Dent had ordered a sumptuous buffet for the dining room, and maids scurried to and from the kitchens, replacing dishes and clean plates. Champagne flowed, and Mr Kirby and his friends quaffed, frothing jugs of cask beer. Mrs Kirby watched proceedings from the sidelines, looking nervous and overwhelmed.

Lily was glad to be with Stephen, as Grace and George were busy greeting their guests. Apart from them, Lily only knew Stephen's patronising cousin Amelia from meeting her at the theatre.

Stephen moved from group to group introducing Lily, laughing with family friends, and whispering witty asides to her, making her giggle. Lily decided Champagne was giggly and began to take only tiny sips hoping Stephen would stop refilling her glass.

His eyes grew more sparkling and reckless as he drank, and she was surprised by his strength as he pulled her towards the dancefloor and placed an arm around her waist for the first waltz. He easily guided her amongst the crowd of couples, and she wasn't sure if the tiny brushes of his lips on her neck as he spoke into her ear were deliberate. As he led her around the dancefloor, she felt dispossessed of will in his arms as they whirled.

Lily felt sophisticated and intoxicated with the glamour of the evening. When Stephen suggested a stroll in the gardens and placed her wrap solicitously around her shoulders, she gave him her arm.

He kept the conversation light until they paused at a rustic bench to enjoy the spectacle of the moon shining across a small ornamental lake. He turned towards her and smoothly gathered her into his arms, kissing her gently at first, then with skilled passion, which left her breathless, heart pounding. Overcome, she realised what she had done. She had betrayed Aiden. It was more than she intended, and she pushed Stephen away. Undeterred, he traced the outline of her cheek with a light touch and said, "Lily, you are beautiful, and I am bewitched."

Lily dropped her gaze and tried to gather her racing thoughts. Stephen was assured. He always said the right thing to make her feel special. She had enjoyed the kiss, but that was wrong. Had she mistaken her feelings for Aiden, or was she what Ma called a loose woman?

"Lily," he whispered her name, then lifted her chin before placing the lightest of kisses on her waiting, wanting mouth.

Lily was sure he would propose, and a moment of panic overtook her along with a hint of relish. *Aiden Donnelly, it would be best if you took more care of me. If you truly loved me, you would.*

Stephen pinched her chin. "Where have you gone, my ethereal fae? The moonlight makes you shimmer. I could almost believe you might disappear."

Lily shivered. "I haven't gone anywhere. I'm still here with you; perhaps we should return to the party."

Stephen nodded. "As you wish." he offered her his hand, and as she rose, he pulled her against him, crushing a hungry kiss against her mouth and imprisoning her hand in his powerful grip. He tasted of Champagne and smelt of citrus cologne. Lily put her other hand up to his neck; she had the strangest sensation of losing all will to resist.

Later, in bed, Lily tried to conjure Aiden's face, feel the tenderness of his kisses, and blank out the temporary madness which overcame her when she was with Stephen. Both men looked uncannily alike, but Stephen haunted her tonight for the first time.

Guilt wracked her in the morning. How could she have let it happen? She wanted to make Aiden jealous and show him that he wasn't the only one with a life, but now Stephen must think she was a hussy, letting him kiss her like that.

She couldn't explain her impulsive behaviour and eventually put it down to Spring madness and Champagne. It must not happen again. If Aiden found out, he wouldn't be jealous; she was sure he would cast her aside.

Spring was early this year, and temperatures were uncommonly warm. Ladies dared to swap coats for wraps, and gentlemen began to don their linen suits.

Grace and George's wedding was upon them. Grace looked stylish in her avant-garde wedding suit, and Lily and Miss Laidlaw looked on with pride as well-to-do guests from the groom's side admired their creation, cut entirely from a second-hand ball gown. Grace threw her bouquet, intending it for Lily, who caught it neatly. As they embraced before Grace left for her wedding night at The Grand Hotel, before leaving for America, she whispered, "Marry Stephen, Lily, he's crazy about you."

Lily looked at the bouquet. Was this an omen?

Even Ma smiled in Stephen's direction.

Aiden said he was doing everything for them both. His ma spoke of his dedication to the cause. Lily wished that didn't mean they had to be apart.

She had been hoping for a letter from Aiden herself, but there was only a line in his mother's letter for her to say he was busy at work and with the WSPU protests and that he'd write to her soon.

The weeks passed, an eternity since they had travelled to work together, sharing all their hopes and dreams.

Temperatures soared to record levels at the start of May. The girls were mercifully cool in the basement workroom as they sewed, but Lily could not sleep at night. The sea breeze had died, and despite her windows pushed up as far as they would go, there was no air. She tossed and turned;

her body restless in the heat. Stephen's flirting ignited her senses, his ability to bestow the slightest touch and make her heart race. It was wrong but strangely alluring, and as she lay in the darkness, she was confused by her desire for him, different from the love she felt for Aiden.

Sometimes Lily felt torn beyond bearing. She had no one to talk to about such things with Grace gone away. At night by the light of a candle in her room, Lily wrote letter after passionate letter to Aiden, declaring her love for him and her need for them to be together.

She tore them up and put them on the fire in the morning, sending more restrained conventional letters. It wasn't her place to say those things, and she blushed at her night-time self.

If only Aiden would come home or send for her, but he didn't, and Stephen continued to be part of her life in many pleasurable ways.

Before the Coronation, there was to be an unveiling of a magnificent statue of the old Queen in London. The newsreels described it as 'A magnificent tribute to Queen Victoria.' The statue was supposed to serve as a reminder of her stalwart values and principles.

A business colleague had invited Mr and Mrs Dent to view the parade of royals from a balcony on Pall Mall. They were to spend the night at a hotel and enjoy the next day's sightseeing before coming home. Stephen invited Lily to accompany them.

He invited her on an outing with Ma and Pa. He drove them out of the city to Hambledon, where they enjoyed a picnic luncheon at a viewpoint on top of the South Downs. As they rested after lunch under a large umbrella that cast shade, Stephen had asked her parent's permission for Lily to accompany the family. His mother, he hastened to add, would act as Lily's chaperone.

"Lily would enjoy the outing, Mrs Matthews. We would see many of the royals at such a historic occasion."

Ma, a great follower of the royal family, was enchanted. "Lily, what a wonderful invitation, what a lucky girl you are. I am envious."

"Mrs Matthews, London will be busy preparing for the Coronation. I understand there is the spectacular Coronation Exhibition to visit, where one can wander and imagine oneself in all the corners of the empire."

Lily, who knew exactly how little Stephen cared for history or anything other than his amusement, took him to task when he invited her to stroll with him. "A historic occasion indeed, Stephen Dent; you don't fool me. This an excuse to 'take a bolt', as you call it, to London."

He glanced at her with a look of amazement on his face. Expecting a denial, Lily waited. "Well, yes! Goodness gracious, Lily, what else? There will be wonderful food and a party, plus I shall steal you away to show you my favourite places in London, and they won't be stuffy museums or cathedrals."

Shocked at his shameless confession, she laughed. "You have no remorse at all?"

"None," he replied promptly, "life is too short."

Looking more serious, she said, "What if I don't fit in with all your fancy London friends?"

Stephen shook his head. "Oh, nonsense, Lily, you already know the family, and you must simply be your adorable self. You will win everyone's hearts, I assure you. I'm sure you can persuade the old cat who owns your dress shop to lend you some town clothes, or I will buy you a new dress for the occasion myself."

Looking shocked, Lily said, "You will do no such thing. It would be most improper. You forget I am a designer and am well able to make myself a dress."

Stephen retracted his offer rapidly and apologised, much to Lily's relief. "I don't know when you thrill me most, Lily, when you look prim and Quakerish or fairly bristling with outrage, like now. Your eyes flash magnificently."

He made as if to observe her with a pretend quizzing glass, and she blushed. "Stop making fun of me and take me back to Ma and Pa. You thrill me least when you are in this mood."

"Ah, but you are intrigued to visit London with me, are you not?"

It was true. Lily thought of Aiden; would she tell him, she wondered? It might make him sit up and notice her. Guiltily, however, she thought not. She reasoned she would be unable to see him, and how long was it now since she'd received a letter? Three weeks and two days, she answered herself promptly. Not that she was counting.

She shrugged a pettish shoulder to Stephen, and he roared with victorious laughter.

Stephen's London would be different to Aiden's, she imagined. Stephen's London would glitter, full of amusements and parties. Aiden's was bohemian, based around music and politics. It was infused with righteous ardour and a sense of rebellion which Stephen lacked entirely. He seemed laconical, except on occasion when he had kissed her. She thought bitterly that Aiden's world was closed to her; Stephen's was open by invitation.

263

As the unveiling was on the sixteenth of May, a Tuesday, Lily applied to Mrs Winchett to take a holiday. She received a stern homily about reliability and that she shouldn't take her holidays piecemeal. However, Mrs Winchett grudgingly agreed to take three days from Lily's two-week allowance.

Miss Laidlaw once again came to her sartorial rescue. She pressed two other dresses on Lily as well as the dress Lily had worn to Grace's engagement.

"They are too young for me to wear myself now. I have only kept the dresses because they were my first designs. I'm sure they would love an outing to London."

Re-trimming and some alterations had brought them up to date, and Lily felt modish. The dresses had class and something out of the ordinary. Miss Laidlaw's flair was as noticeable in these early clothes she had made for herself as in her theatrical designs.

On the eve of her departure to London, Lily emptied her savings onto the bed, counted it, and then put the money in her purse. She bit her lip to stop herself from crying. They had intended to pay their train fare to London with their savings, but that seemed a lifetime ago. With Aiden distant, Lily felt she might never require them for that.

Chapter 27

L ily was astounded to see Mrs Dent's maid supervising the loading of a considerable number of valises onto the train.

Catching Lily's gaze, Mr Dent laughed. "That's my wife for you, Lily. She takes everything but the kitchen sink. I prefer to travel light with a slim portmanteau. You sensibly have opted for the latter, too, I see."

Lily flushed pink, knowing that inside was all she possessed, which was suitable. His smile was kindly, though, not mocking, and he added, "If you've forgotten anything, I'm sure we can procure it for you; London is full of shops. More's the pity."

Stephen sauntered over and said, "You look like you've seen a ghost, Lily. Is something wrong?"

"No, indeed, I'm quite well." Had Stephen been Aiden, she could have confessed her worries and perhaps laughed about it, but she didn't want to lose face before the outing began.

"You need a good breakfast inside you. The restaurant car will serve something on the train. When you travel with Ma and Pa, everything is on a grand scale and doesn't cost one a penny." He grinned at her and indicated the way to the first-class carriage his parents had reserved. "Relax and enjoy."

As the train pulled into Waterloo, the Dent's maid and manservant appeared as if by magic from the second-class carriages and organised all the luggage to be whisked away. Mr Dent led the party to where a car was waiting outside the station. "I think we'll go directly to Pall Mall. The streets are likely to be congested."

Lily marvelled at how the festivities had transformed London. Everywhere there was bunting, and workers were erecting vast stands of seats.

"For the coronation later on," Mr Dent told Lily.

As they drew closer to their destination, an impossible number of people thronged the pavements. Many carried flags, and small children hoisted on their father's shoulders waved them excitedly. Many lamp posts had floral baskets; pink carnations were the theme.

Mrs Dent pointed the baskets out to Lily. "Pink carnations are Queen Mary's chosen flower for the coronation year. The growers must be thrilled."

Lily nodded. "How pretty they are, delicate and frilled."

The driver negotiated the crowd and delivered them to a tall cream building on The Mall. Following Stephen's parents, Lily climbed the wide marble stairs and into a large, high-ceilinged room, where people were already gathering on a balcony overlooking the road.

A considerable buffet spread along the back wall of the room loaded with tiny pies, sandwiches and an array of delicate cakes and pastries. *Someone like Ma must have made all these,* Lily thought. She looked at the well-dressed ladies and satisfied men conversing together. *I bet no one here thinks how much hard work has gone into providing this.*

A footman showed Lily and Mrs Dent to a seat near the front of the balcony and invited her to help herself from a basket containing flags and small bags of rose petals. Mrs Dent waived enthusiastically to a lady on the far side of the room and beckoned to her. As she threaded her way through the guests, Lily saw with dismay that it was Amelia whom she'd met at the theatre and her mother.

"I thought you two girls would like to chat together. The men will be talking business forever, no doubt," Mrs Dent said with a kind smile. "Amelia, you remember Lily, Stephen's friend?"

Amelia gave Lily a saccharine smile. "Yes indeed, the dressmaker."

Mrs Dent frowned at her tone. "Dress *designer*, my dear. She has created a gown for Kitty Marion and, as you know, designed dear Grace's wedding ensemble. Wonderful for a modern woman to have a career."

Amelia flushed and looked down, but Lily caught a vitriolic side glance cast her way.

Feeling awkward, Lily tried to change the topic of conversation. "Have you any news of George and Grace?"

Mrs Dent shook her head. "It may take as long as three weeks for the post to come, and they will only just have arrived."

There was a sudden commotion in the room as one of the stewards announced the royal procession was approaching. The men crowded behind the ladies' chairs, and they heard cheers from further down The Mall.

Mrs Dent whispered to Lily, "Take no notice of Amelia, she's spoilt, and her mother fancied that she and Stephen might make a match." She patted Lily's hand and then turned to watch the approaching coaches.

Lily swallowed; the implication was obvious. Everyone here was drawing false conclusions. Lily felt sick. She ought not to have come. At that moment, Stephen approached with a glass of Champagne for her. Judging by the glitter in his eyes, not the first for himself.

"Enjoying yourself?" he asked, leaning down over her shoulder. "Look, here comes the parade."

Rows of soldiers marched by with immaculate dress uniforms. Followed by the Horse Guards, brightly shined spurs and buttons glinting in the sun, their huge horses snorting as cheers rose from the crowd. Finally, the state coaches rolled past. His Majesty King George sat poker-faced, nodding to acknowledge the support, while his wife, Queen Mary, waved graciously to the crowd.

Lily asked Stephen, "Who is that sitting beside the King with the large moustache?"

"It's Keiser Wilhelm and his wife from Germany."

Mrs Dent sniffed. "His wife could have made an effort. She has forgotten the period of mourning for poor Edward is over. Fancy coming to a celebration as a guest of honour in a shabby black outfit like that. At least Queen Mary looks the part."

Mrs Dent was right. The Queen looked handsomely dressed in a tan gown, heavily embroidered, with a lace bodice. Her hat was trimmed with roses and feathers, which danced in the breeze.

The statue was shrouded, and they could only see a small part from the balcony. The crowd fell silent as the massed choir sang with a band. The unnatural silence of such a large crowd brought goosebumps to Lily's arms.

They were not close enough to hear the King's address but could see the magnificent gold angel that appeared as the shrouding flowed away from the statue. Lily jumped as troops fired a deafening gun salute. Strains of the National Anthem drifted towards the balcony. Lily's throat tightened, her eyes smarted with unshed tears as the crowd sang and cheered. She wished Ma and Pa could see this and wondered where Aiden was. Perhaps he was in the multitude of people.

"Thank goodness that's over," Stephen's voice drawled, at odds with Lily's mood. "Let me get you some lunch, and then we can slope off."

Mrs Dent rapped him on the arm. "Shh, people will hear you."

Lily stared at him, amazed. "But I enjoyed it, so moving and to see the King right below us, close enough to touch. I can't thank you enough for inviting me."

"We shall walk up to see the statue when the crowds have dispersed."

Stephen rolled his eyes. "No, really, Mama, walking to see a larger-than-life edifice of Queen Vic, no doubt looking po-faced, is enough to give anyone a fit of the dismals. I shall take Lily somewhere more entertaining."

Lily looked uncertainly from Stephen to his mother, but Mrs Dent laughed indulgently. "Alright, but you must be back at the hotel in time for dinner at seven and leave Lily time to dress."

"Come on, said Stephen, grabbing Lily's hand. A quick bite at the buffet, then we'll make our escape."

As Lily followed Stephen, she asked, "I hope we haven't offended your parents?"

"Lord, no," he replied cheerfully. "My father will be talking business for hours, and Ma will probably have squeezed a fortune in promised donations for one of her causes when she's finished working the room. Redoubtable female, my mother."

"And will your father not want you beside him? It will be your business too."

Stephen looked incredulous. "Don't remind me! I've had it drummed into me enough over the years. There's time to be shackled to the factory when I must be."

Lily frowned but didn't comment. She knew her pa would disapprove strongly of such flippancy. But perhaps it was hard to have a career imposed if you had other ambitions.

After a light lunch, they left the building and strolled along The Mall towards St James' Park. Although the crowd was dispersing, the street was still bustling, and Lily was pleased to take Stephen's arm.

As they crossed the road, Lily caught her breath; Aiden was walking away from them, on the other side, with a dark-haired girl on his arm. Their heads were inclined together, and the girl nodded thoughtfully at something he said. Looking towards the park, Stephen had not seen them. Lily, horrified at the enormity of the situation, especially not wanting Aiden to see her with Stephen, hurried to turn away.

Her heart was in her throat as she surreptitiously glanced behind her, but Aiden had disappeared into the crowd.

A sense of indignation soon overtook her relief at not being seen. Aiden had time to jaunt about with other girls but couldn't find time to write to her. Grace had been right; Aiden was enjoying life fine without her. How could he have the cheek to keep her hanging on at home while he cavorted with other girls?

Amidst her sense of outrage, the small voice of her conscience nagged and said she was doing the same, but she argued back that she only saw Stephen to make Aiden jealous.

Trying to marshal her scattered thoughts and repressing an urge to keep glancing behind, she said, "Where are we going?"

He replied nonchalantly, "We're only a stone's throw from some good friends of mine. I thought we'd drop in."

Her heart sank. She hoped to have pleaded a headache and suggested they head back to the hotel, but she would have to sit through more conversation.

An elderly housekeeper opened the door and sniffed when she saw Stephen. "Mr and Mrs Knowles are out of town."

He grinned. "I know, Dawes, but Miss Felicity isn't, is she? I'll show myself up."

Dawes shook her head disapprovingly and muttered, "Goings on, I never did."

Stephen stepped past the reluctant woman and led Lily to the first-floor drawing room. He pushed open the doors and announced, "Stephen Dent for Miss Felicity," in a measured tone.

Lily saw that the three sofas arranged around an empty fireplace were occupied by a group of young women, two lounging aimlessly. The third lifted a weary arm to wave them in and said dreamily. "Darling, we are dying of boredom; you are just in time. Is this the child?"

Lily felt uncomfortable. She could see one of the young women appeared comatose and was staring into space in an unfocused way, her pupils huge.

Stephen introduced Lily and patted Felicity's leg. "Budge up, old bean, make space."

Felicity grumbled and swung her legs down. "What can I get you?"

Lily asked if she could have a cup of tea, which made Felicity laugh. "Dawes will be relieved." She cocked her head at Stephen. "Green Fairy?" she asked.

He grinned and nodded. "It's herbal," he explained to Lily, "Watch."

Stephen helped himself to a measure of a green drink and popped a small, slotted spoon over the glass. He balanced a sugar cube on the spoon, dripped more green liquid onto it, and then set it alight. A strong smell of caramelised sugar filled the room, followed by a hiss as Stephen plunged the spoon into his glass.

He sipped the drink with relish. "Your excellent health," he tipped his glass to Lily, Felicity, and Sarah. No one appeared the least put out by the odd girl on the other sofa, and Lily thought that despite her elegant clothes, she must be ill or out of her senses as she could see a small syringe on the table beside her and a vial of clear liquid.

The conversation veered to people Lily didn't know and in-jokes about them. As Lily sipped her tea, the imaginary headache became real. *Aiden with another girl.* The sight of their two heads together, deep in conversation, repeatedly replayed in her mind.

Stephen made two further Green Fairies for himself and the other girls. Their laughter became more raucous, and while Lily tried to smile along, all she wanted to do was leave.

Finally, Stephen glanced at the clock on the mantelpiece and said, "We must go. Duty calls."

Lily politely thanked Felicity, whose gait was now unsteady, and her response slurred. Felicity stumbled into Stephen as she kissed him goodbye, said, "Good luck with your inheritance project," and nodded toward Lily.

As they descended the steps into the street, Lily said, "Whatever did she mean?"

"Oh, that." He frowned, then his brow cleared. "It's the work project I'm involved with."

Lily desperately wanted to ask Stephen about the other girl, but she felt awkward, and he didn't mention it.

"They're good fun, the girls, aren't they?"

Lily didn't know what to say and settled for, "They're very jolly, except for the poor girl who's ill."

"Ill?" Stephen laughed, which he hastily turned into a cough. "Quite so, a sad case."

When Stephen's mother asked Lily where they had been, she seemed annoyed to hear that they had visited Stephen's friends. Stephen himself was brooding and distant at dinner. Lily was pleased when Mrs Dent suggested an early night.

The next day, Stephen and his father were engaged in business, and Lily spent what would have been a pleasant day shopping and sightseeing, despite the presence of Amelia and her mother.

Behind her smiles and apparent interest in the delights before her, Lily's thoughts veered from disbelief to anger at the duplicity of Aiden. Finally, they settled into a grim determination to show Aiden he had not broken her heart.

Despite being tired from the trip, Lily was up early the next day as she knew better than to be late for work. That evening, Lily sat down at the dining room table and penned a thank you note to Mr and Mrs Dent for a lovely treat.

Ma interrupted her several times, "Tell me again about the Queen's dress, Love." or "I never imagined a visiting royal would look dowdy like that."

"I wish you'd been there, Ma." Lily sighed. "You would have loved it."

"Hearing you talk about it is almost as good. You describe it so well. I'm sure your Pa will take us to see the coronation at the Electric Theatre unless the Dents invite you to that as well. Fancy, I shall soon be curtseying to my own daughter."

She laughed and patted Lily's shoulder.

"They may have money and a big house, Ma, but they aren't grand. You'd like Mrs Dent. Come with me to Mrs O'Shea's meetings. You could get to know her."

Ma shook her head. "No, Lily, political meetings are not my cup of tea, and by the time the evenings come, I feel like sitting down, not gadding off out. But, as a matter of fact, Mrs Dent has invited me to take tea with her one afternoon next week at The Grand, which I shall be pleased to do."

Lily was surprised and had the strangest feeling that a chain of events she had set in motion was turning into more than she ever intended. She shivered.

"Someone walked over your grave?" Ma joked.

Lily shivered again. "Don't say that, Ma. It's horrible."

She drew another sheet of paper, paused in indecision, and began, *Dear Aiden*…

Chapter 28

Dear Lily,

Your letter has affected me deeply. If I inadvertently caused you pain, please accept my apologies; I did not desire to do so. I do, however, feel you are unjust in what you say.

I have been a poor correspondent and will try to improve, but you are still my best and dearest friend and true love.

Working for Kitty means my life is busy beyond anything I have ever known, with travelling, rehearsals, and my work for the cause. I am inspired to work for social change by the events around me and the people I have met here. I am encouraged to think you understand how important this is. Indeed, I believe we will both benefit, as will the generations who come after us. The moment is now, and I cannot stand by and not participate. Dearest Lily, do not ask me to be someone I am not; by requesting I return to less active campaigning or return home, I cannot do either.

You want to share my life, and I want nothing less, but it has been represented strongly to us both that this cannot be for now. I left Portsmouth full of anger but have resolved to prove your father wrong and make something of myself.

What else do you want me to do? If you came to me, as you suggest, in defiance of their wishes, it would cause a rift between you and your family. My mother has implored me not to take this course, and I have promised her I will not. She rightly says it would forever be a shadow between us, and she speaks with some understanding. Lily, I love you too much to want any shame attached to us being together, and I, therefore, will not encourage any action which could cause this.

Regarding an apprenticeship in London, Kitty advises that you finish your dressmaking apprenticeship in Portsmouth, and then she can help you find work — she is wise in such matters.

With Kitty's unwavering support, my songwriting is progressing, and the music publishers have contracted me to write a further three songs. To have this many songs published is beyond my wildest dreams. Although the publisher's advance is modest, and I will not receive royalties until sales cover that, I am encouraged to think I shall soon be able to convince your father of my worth.

Please remain steadfast at home,
your loving Aiden.

Lily read with growing fury. She did not want reasonable platitudes and altruistic motives; she wanted passion and for Aiden to choose her over the suffragette cause and Kitty Marion. He had plenty of passion for them!

She flung the letter aside. Even after she had written to Aiden to plead, all she got back was Kitty, Kitty, Kitty! She would scream if she heard Kitty Marion's name one more time.

Flaming with righteous indignation, Lily tore the letter into tiny pieces, flounced downstairs and threw them on the fire.

She watched with great satisfaction as orange flames licked around the paper petals, flaring high momentarily, then dying back. She felt better for that, she told herself. Grace was right. She would no longer wait for the crumbs from Aiden's table.

She snatched up a sheet of paper and wrote hastily,

> *Dear Aiden,*
>
> *I had not imagined you to be so complacent about our situation when you are so passionate about other causes. I can only assume I am no longer a high priority.*
>
> *Perhaps we should end our correspondence until we both have fewer pressing agendas. I would not wish to burden your time or take you away from your obligations to Miss Marion.*
>
> *Lily*

She wouldn't tell anyone what she had written, well perhaps Grace, when she replied to her letters from America. It had felt good to vent her spleen, but when no reply came from Aiden, she believed herself, on the one hand, vindicated and yet was deeply saddened. Of this, she was determined; no one would know that Aiden had cast her aside for a political cause and a woman nearly old enough to be his mother.

Grace's letters were full of shared endeavour, the wonders of New York, and the excitement of being a married lady. She had, she told Lily, found her talent. George occupied himself with the manufacture of gloves, but she relished accounts and sales management. Lily was glad for her if wistful. Grace sounded genuinely contented, and if only things were different, she could have been married to Aiden and helped him build their dreams.

Pa had more shocking stories of suffragette violence to report from the papers each day until finally, Lily said, "Can't you read about something else, Pa? I am tired of hearing about fires and broken windows. I wish these women would help us convince politicians with rational arguments instead of acting like ruffians. Mrs Dent says it's too bad."

If Pa was surprised, he said nothing but raised his eyebrows to his wife over the top of the newspaper. "Well, Lily, how is this for you? 'Audiences were charmed by the dancing of Russian prima ballerina Anna Pavlova, the music hall programme star at The Palace Theatre for a second year. Her grace and beauty were not eclipsed, even by the huge basket of roses from which she enchantingly appeared'." He whistled through his teeth. "If she comes to Portsmouth, we should try to see a show."

"Oh yes, we must. Stephen has seen Nijinsky dance in London and says the Ballets Russes are all the rage. A little shocking, but quite breath-taking in their wildness — avant-garde," said Lily.

Ma frowned. "A nice dance that doesn't shock anyone will suit me," said Ma. "You youngsters never seem happy unless you are up to something risqué."

Pa laughed. "I'm sure our parents said the same about us, Maggie."

"I can't remember anyone cavorting about the stage in baskets of flowers in our day," said Ma.

"Well, we'd have been there watching if they had." He winked at Lily and received a stern look from his wife.

The prospect of the upcoming coronation produced a spate of orders for dresses in the workroom. Several brides had chosen that day for their wedding, and in Portsmouth, it was set to be a day of garden parties and celebrations.

Eastfield Road would stage a street party for the occasion, but the Dents had invited Lily and her parents to their home. Because of Granny and Gramps, Ma had regretfully declined but had allowed Lily to accept.

The households on the street were having such fun in preparation for the day. Messages passed from house to house, they held impromptu discussions on front porches, and promises for contributions came from all sides. As Lily hemmed one of her commissioned gowns in the workroom, she wondered if she wouldn't have preferred that jolly event.

The wedding dress that Lily and Miss Laidlaw had designed for Grace had found favour with Mrs Winchett and had been copied and modelled in the showroom.

Lily was still working officially under the tutelage of Miss Laidlaw. Still, in recognition of her design work and superior abilities, she had been given a pay raise and now designed some of her patterns for younger customers.

She was proud of her achievements at work and defiantly pursued her friendship with Stephen with a vigour which belied the persistent ache in her heart for Aiden.

Stephen was witty and beguiling, full of charm. When she was with him, he stirred feelings she couldn't explain, heady, a little dangerous and exciting, but for all that, Lily missed the easy rapport she had with Aiden. She and Aiden shared many memories, and he was sincere and comfortable. Lily firmly reminded herself her memory was the Aiden she knew before London, not the new activist Aiden who had left her behind.

During the preparations for the coronation, the weather was as hot as anyone could remember. For Lily, however, the illusion of the Summer idyl was shattered the week before the coronation was due when Mr Donnelly knocked on the door asking to speak to Pa.

"I've had word from Southampton that the men on board the Olympic have come out on strike. Several of the shipping lines are following suit." He looked grave, but the tension in his bearing was akin to excitement. "It's going to spread through the country. My men are serious about joining them; there's a ballot tonight. If you've got any goods in storage, get them out. Materials may be in short supply; buy anything you need fast."

Pa shook his hand and invited him in. "I appreciate you telling me, Donnelly." He shook his head and smoothed a hand across his moustache.

"We're expecting the National Sailors' and Firemans' unions to join us, and I'm travelling to Newcastle tomorrow to meet stewards from the northern docks to see if they'll come out in support."

Pa rubbed his chin thoughtfully, and his fingers scratched against the salt and pepper stubble. "Maybe striking so close to the coronation will make the government act quickly. They won't want a load of unrest to mar the celebrations."

"We've been trying to talk to Winston Churchill for months to address the men's concerns. Now all of a sudden, he's contacting us." Mr Donnelly chuckled, a wry look on his face.

Pa shook his head. "It's a bad business. I hope you bring it to some purpose."

"We're standing firm. Something has to change." He declined Ma's offer of a drink and stood up; he tapped his folded cap against the other hand. "If things get bad, we may need community backing, food, etc. I hope we can count on your support?"

Pa stood up, too, his thumbs hooked into the belt loops of his trousers. "I've always believed in a fair day's work for a fair day's pay, and if we've got food on the table, we are always happy to share with those less fortunate."

The two men locked their gaze and shook hands as if sealing a pact. Lily felt an awful sense of impending doom at odds with the gay preparations for the coronation. The same feeling, she had about Aiden's involvement with the suffragette's campaign of violence.

Stephen had arranged to meet Lily after work the next day and waited for her outside.

They drove to the seafront and strolled along the promenade, grateful for the breath of wind from the sea. Lily mentioned the strikes, expecting him to take the matter seriously, but he poo-pooed her alarms. "Lily, the sun is shining. We have all sorts of wonderful celebrations to enjoy. Let's leave the unions to sort out the men's problems, shall we? After all, what can we do?"

She felt he was patronising her and replied tartly, "For a start, Ma is organising to cook meals for the men and their families. Surely you could do something."

He gave her a measured look from under his straw boater, adjusted at a jaunty angle, which momentarily gave his face a mean expression but was gone as soon as it came. He laughed. "You think me a frippery fellow, don't you? I don't want you to be worried, is all, Lily. My father and mother will be busy on the striker's behalf, don't you worry. Pa is a great philanthropist, except towards his children; it's why his workforce is loyal. He brought us up to be gentlemen but now expects us to work our fingers to the bone and like it." There was no mistaking the bitterness in his tone.

Lily looked at him in surprise. He didn't seem to work hard to her. Stephen seemed to live a charmed life compared to the men she knew.

"I hear music. Come, dance with me, beautiful Lily. I will not hear of serious issues on such a beautiful evening."

He hurried Lily across the common and swept her, breathless, into the dancing couples around the bandstand. Stephen's arm was firm around her back, and he twirled her in circles until she was dizzy and said, "Can we stop, please?"

He found a seat in the shade of a tree and suggested procuring some lemonade.

Stephen passed her a cool glass but had chosen a punch that smelt strongly of rum behind the sweet smell of summer fruit for himself.

Stephen placed his glass on the grass, turning to face her as she pressed the glass of lemonade to the side of her neck in an unconscious gesture. "Lily, beautiful, sweet, Lily, it cannot have escaped your notice how strong my attachment has become, and I have dared to hope, these last weeks, that you return my regard." He traced the line of her jaw with one finger where the condensation from the cool glass had left a trail of moisture. His eyes followed his hand openly and rested on the pulse point now beating wildly at her throat before raising them to hers. "Marry me,

Lily, be mine, body and soul." He grazed the lightest kiss to her wrist, igniting a fire trail along her forearm. "You were made to be loved. Let me love you."

The way he said it made loving sound tantalising and dangerous, not safe, and homely.

A vision of Aiden with another girl on his arm whilst writing 'remain steadfast at home'. flashed into her head and momentarily blinded her. She recklessly returned Stephen's bold look, his face so like Aiden's, yet the man so very different, and said, "I will – that is, you must seek permission from Pa first."

Stephen laughed. "If he denies me, I shall abduct you like all romantic heroes, and we shall run for the border." He looked at her, his dark eyes blazing. "Lily, you don't know what this means to me."

He saluted her with his rum punch and chinked it against her glass of lemonade. "Mrs Stephen Dent, would you like to go to London to choose your ring."

Only weeks before, she had been plotting and scheming to get to London; now, she had no desire to go. "Could we perhaps use a local jeweller? My father supports local businesses, and I'm sure yours does too. There is a small jeweller that my grandfather knows; he has unusual antique pieces that I love."

For a moment, his brow darkened as if she had offended him, and she felt momentarily dismayed. But the frown became a smile, and although he pinched her chin a little harder than was comfortable, he replied warmly, "Whatever pleases you, Ma Chere, whatever pleases you."

"If Pa consents, will we announce our engagement at the coronation garden party? Only I should like my family to be there."

"As soon as possible, would please me, Lily. Perhaps we could move from one celebration to another if your parents can't attend the garden party. I shall tell my father this evening. Mother is taken with you already and will be delighted. I will call on your parents tomorrow. My father will have some paperwork to attend to regarding my income once I tell him."

Lily looked surprised. "Do you mean what you earn from the family business?"

He made an airy gesture with his hand. "Oh no, but it's nothing to worry your head over, Lily. I have an inheritance coming to me from my Godmother. She was a wealthy lady and left me an annual income to support me, I mean us, after my marriage."

Lily wrinkled her nose. "But surely, we will have plenty to live on with what you earn and my salary."

He looked at her strangely and raised an eyebrow. "But my dear, you will not continue to work after we are married. You will have the house to run and, in due course, perhaps a family."

Lily straightened her back, looked at him, and said earnestly, "But I wish to continue my design work with Miss Laidlaw. I could not consider giving it up."

"Such spirit, Lily. I see I shall have to beat you at least twice a day when we are married." He laughed and made a jokey slapping movement in the air. "Let's not quarrel about this now. I shall buy you ten dress shops should you wish for them. How's that?"

The slight tension between them lifted, and Lily laughed happily. "Just the one would be perfect as long as Miss Laidlaw continues to teach me."

He kissed her hand and said, "One more dance?"

Chapter 29

Laughter coming from the sitting room told her that her grandparents were visiting. Gramps had a hearty laugh that was unmistakable. Lily took a steadying breath and reflected that they would all know at once this way.

"Here she is," Pa beamed at her. "Have you had a lovely time?"

"Very nice, Pa. We went to the seafront and danced by the bandstand."

Pa turned to his parents as Lily went to kiss them and said in a teasing voice, "Lily has a new beau, a charming young man with an automobile, no less."

Granny exclaimed, and Gramps muttered, "I'll be bound he isn't good enough for our Lily. None of them young whippersnappers deserve her." He patted her cheek. "I'd marry you myself if I weren't your grandpa."

Lily laughed. "Well, I hope you'll think he is good enough when you meet him because he did me the honour of asking me to marry him this evening. He's coming to see you tomorrow, Pa."

Pa nodded. "There. I'm not surprised by the amount we've seen of him recently and inviting you away with his people as he did. I'd have to beat him off with a stick to get him to stay away."

Ma chipped in with a wry chuckle. "I don't suppose he took us out driving for the pleasure of our company either, turning us up sweet, no doubt."

Pa looked at Lily more seriously. "He seems a fine man with good prospects. I'll give you that. He's more mature, so he will know better what suits him and what to expect from married life than…."

Pa encountered a fierce look from Ma and changed tack after clearing his throat. "You share the same interests, what with your political meetings and love of the theatre and all, but it's you that has to be sure, Puss."

Granny said, "You'll have to live with the man, Lily, not all his fancy trappings. Look past those; the romantic gestures fade after a while. You be sure that he has stolen your heart. Men need some adjusting to, don't they, Maggie?"

Ma nodded. "They certainly do, what with their messy habits and forever being hungry."

Pa and Gramps looked offended. "Steady on. We are still in the room, you know," said Pa.

Lily loved these people and their cosy banter; if they seemed happy with her choice, she was perhaps right to have said 'yes' after all. As Grandma and Ma started to discuss embroidered bed linen and what should go into her trousseau, Lily felt as if all this was happening to someone else.

The next evening, Pa put on his best shirt and Ma her Sunday dress. She had made fresh biscuits and laid out tiny savoury snacks in the parlour. Pa ushered him into the front room after a firm handshake when Stephen knocked.

Both men emerged, wreathed in smiles to invite Lily and Ma for a glass of wine. Pa kissed Lily's cheek and offered congratulations. "I'm pleased to know you will be safely settled, Lily. Stephen is fortunate to have an excellent family business to join and his income. He has convinced me that he sincerely loves you, and I wish you both very happy."

Lily frowned slightly. Stephen had not told Pa of his hatred for the family business. However, Ma was joining in the toast, as was Stephen, who looked saintly and slightly smug as he smiled at her. She raised her glass and accepted a chaste kiss.

Stephen had arranged with Pa that they should all attend the start of the street party to celebrate their engagement with Lily's family and friends. He would then convey them to his parent's party to announce the news there.

In bed that evening, Lily wondered if Aiden would regret letting her slip through his fingers, probably not, with his new life. With a sinking feeling of dread in her stomach, she realised that she must speak to his mother without delay, certainly before the next suffragist meeting.

Aiden's ma and Mrs Dent were on the same committee. She didn't want Mrs Donnelly to know about her engagement through the grapevine. Try as Lily would, convincing words that exactly explained her sudden change of heart did not come to mind. She tossed and turned until half-phrases and words became hopelessly jumbled in her tired mind, and she fell into a fitful sleep.

On her way home from work the following evening, she knocked at the Donnelly's door.

"Lily, how lovely to see you. Come into the kitchen; it's warm in there."

Lily followed Mrs Donnelly and accepted a cup of tea before blurting out, "Mrs Donnelly, I've come to tell you that I'm going to marry Stephen Dent."

Mrs Donnelly quietly placed her cup on its saucer and looked at Lily. "Oh, Lily, are you sure?"

Lily couldn't bear her gentle distress. "Mrs Donnelly, it's for the best. Aiden has chosen a different path, and so have I."

Mrs Donnelly nodded resignedly. "I suppose there is nothing more to be said except I wish you happy, Lily. I hope you will find many blessings."

To Miss Laidlaw, Lily excitedly talked about the dress shop Stephen had promised and begged her to think about a wedding dress design.

"Stop, Lily, draw breath, do. I can't keep up. Firstly, many congratulations; if you are happy, I am too. You are sure you're happy?"

Lily nodded emphatically. "Very happy."

Miss Laidlaw said, "You know you have plenty of time, of course, and marriage isn't the only way to be successful and happy. Aiden is all in the past, is he?"

"Yes, yes," Lily replied airily. "Aiden has a new life, and so have I." She then switched the conversation to wedding dresses but was annoyed that designing her dress seemed less exciting than creating for others. Her imagination suddenly failed her. *What did one wear to become Mrs Stephen Dent?*

Once Stephen had an idea in his mind, Lily thought, he moved forward rapidly. He badgered her to think of a date, and they finally agreed on Saturday, the twelfth of August.

Delighted, Stephen had rushed away to put the announcement in the papers.

Lily wrote to America, lamenting that Grace and George could not attend.

When she expressed her disappointment to Stephen, he said, "Soon, Lily, we shall be able to fly to America. In Germany, a chap called Zeppelin has an airship for passengers, and single flights are getting longer and longer. When we are married, I shall learn to fly."

Lily had seen a newsreel about the Zeppelin, and it looked like one pinprick would deflate the whole thing. However, the dashing young pilot from Rolls Royce who had flown the airship to France and back had ignited her imagination. It must be wonderful to soar and have a bird's eye view. "I should love to learn to fly too."

Stephen laughed. "You say the strangest things sometimes, Lily."

"So do you," she retorted hotly. "If you can fly a plane, I'm sure I could. I saw a newsreel with Pa about an American aviatrice. She said any woman could learn to fly."

"I certainly wouldn't like to think of you behaving like an American," he said.

"Grace and George are in America!"

He gave a superior smile. "I rest my case."

Lily gasped. "What a hateful thing to say."

He laughed. "Joking, Lily. No one rises to the fly quicker than you, darling girl."

She laughed, too, relieved he had been joking. At least, she hoped he had been.

On the day of their engagement, Coronation Day, Ma kept lifting the nets to peer out and muttered without conviction, "Cloud seems to be lifting."

There was a street meeting at about eleven, and it was decided to leave the tables and food inside until twelve to be sure.

Lily, who had made her dress with the recent sweltering temperatures in mind, was trying on shawls and cardigans to see what might go. Nothing did, and she decided to bear the cold rather than spoil her outfit.

Ma, who had enough to do with the baking for the street party, lost patience with the endless parade of 'What do you think about this?' and sent Lily down the road to Granny to see if she had anything suitable or suggested tartly, that Lily could borrow her old coat.

Bunting fluttered in the breeze, strung between the lamp posts, and over-excited children ran everywhere.

"Granny, I've either got to freeze or look like a disaster. The weather is dreadful."

Her Grandmother took in the pinched face with blue smudges under the eyes and said, "Come in, come in, don't take on so, Lily. I bet you haven't eaten properly today. That's why you're cold and fidgety. Sit down there and try some of my shortbread."

Comforted by the flow of well-intentioned chiding, Lily took a mouthful of the crumbling, golden biscuit and let the buttery sweetness roll around her mouth.

"Granny, do you have anything to go over my dress to keep my shoulders warm?"

"I'll go and look in the chest."

She returned with a pale fur cape that sat over the shoulders and fell level with the elbows. The fur was soft and lined with silk. Lily's mouth fell open, "Granny, it's perfect."

"Take it with my love."

Lily stroked the fur. "It's beautiful, thank you."

"Now get back to your Ma. I don't doubt she's like a fly in a tarpot, what with the street party, then going out with you."

Lily laughed. "Ma is never like a fly in a tarpot Granny, but she is a bit sharp this morning."

Although rain threatened, none fell, so families carried their tables into the street and weighted tablecloths on the corners to stop them from blowing away. Cheerful women arranged dishes laden with party food in the centre of each. Scones, sponge cake, sandwiches, and biscuits decorated with crowns; the spread was mouth-watering. Every child received their coronation tin filled with crayons. The men looked on from around the beer station set up on a trestle, around which they coiffed foaming glasses.

Stephen, determined to please, gave the children rides up and down the road in his car. A big cheer went up when Pa stood on a chair to announce Stephen and Lily's engagement and called for a toast. Lily had chosen a gold Victorian snake ring with garnets and pearls set in the snakeheads. She loved it, and it sat on her finger well. The ladies crowded around to see her ring.

"It means for eternity," the jeweller had told her.

"Pearls for tears," Granny had warned, shaking her head, and had received a doubtful look in return.

It was a simple, uncomplicated party. Lily felt carefree and happy, laughing amongst the neighbours she had grown up with and accepting their congratulations. Only Aiden was absent. She wondered what he was doing today.

All too soon, and as the games and singing started, Stephen suggested they collect their things and drive to his parents. Ma asked Granny to find her plates at the end and return her table and chairs to the house.

"We can do all that," a quiet voice said beside them. Mrs Donnelly smiled, "Don't be late for your other party." Lily flushed scarlet as Mrs Donnelly asked to see the ring and felt an inexplicable desire to apologise.

Mrs Donnelly said, "Beautiful Lily, unusual." She observed Stephen standing beside Lily, beginning to look impatient, then turned to Lily, her gentle eyes tinged with a hint of sadness. She hugged Lily and whispered, "I bear you no ill will. You can come to me if you ever need to."

The Dent's garden party was an altogether more grand affair with an open marquee on one side of the garden, against the chance of rain, and small wrought iron tables and chairs painted white dotted about a perfectly manicured lawn.

They were greeted warmly by Stephen's parents without a hint of condescension, and having introduced Stephen's four brothers, George being in America, Mr Dent bore Pa off to find a drink. Mrs Dent introduced Lily and Ma to her sister and niece and instructed a passing maid to bring a pot of tea and one of the tiered stands with finger sandwiches and dainty cakes.

Full up and fit to pop from the copious feast at the street party, Lily and Ma picked at the food out of politeness but were relieved to agree to take a tour of the garden with Stephen's aunt.

Stephen, who carried a glass of Champagne, joined them. His voice slurred slightly as he said, "My beautiful Lily, Mrs Matthews, follow me." He waved his glass in the direction of the main lawn. "Pa is making a speech. He always makes a speech."

He shepherded the ladies to where people gathered around a small dais, and footmen handed out Champagne flutes from small round trays.

"Ah, there they are, the young couple." Stephen's father beamed at them and gestured them onto the dais. "We are delighted to welcome Lily and her parents to our family today and wish Lily and Stephen every congratulation on their engagement. Please raise your glasses for Lily and Stephen."

A polite murmur of 'Lily and Stephen' rippled through the guests. Stephen's father continued, "On this historic day, I am glad to be amongst good friends and neighbours, able to enjoy the fruits of our success in business and see the next generation of the family settled in their lives. We are indeed blessed.

I am sure I speak for everyone here when I hope our new King George's reign is blessed by continued prosperity and peace." He raised his glass and said, "Long live the King."

"Long live the King." A smattering of applause broke out, and the guests raised their glasses. Under the marquee, a four-piece ensemble began to play the national anthem. As the guests sang with the musicians, Stephen bent towards Lily and muttered, "Pompous old windbag."

Shocked at such disrespect, Lily frowned at Stephen. "Shh, people will hear you. What a dreadful thing to say about your father."

Stephen took a deep swig of his Champagne and laughed with little mirth. "You didn't grow up with him ramming his rotten factory and how to succeed in business down your throat every five minutes."

"Don't spoil our engagement day with bitterness," Lily pleaded with Stephen. "It's supposed to be a happy day."

He looked at her as if not seeing her for a moment, and then his face cleared. "Of course, happy day, you are right. Let's have more of Pa's excellent Champagne and enjoy ourselves."

Lily couldn't help thinking of the loving bond between Aiden and his father, between her and Pa, how they discussed matters together and laughed. She felt deeply sorry for Stephen and his father and resolved to try to mend matters if she could.

Chapter 30

"Lily, please concentrate and stand still." Miss Laidlaw looked at her disapprovingly. "Whatever has got into you? I am trying to make the last adjustments to this dress. By the sound of it, most of Portsmouth society will be at the wedding, and I will not have you walking down the aisle looking like you bought your dress off the peg at the Landport Drapery Bazaar!"

"Sorry, I'm nervous. I can't stand still."

Miss Laidlaw tutted. "The design is plain, it will only work if the fit is perfect, and I swear you've lost more weight since last week."

Sitting in the corner, Ma dabbed a tear as she watched her daughter transform into a sophisticated young woman — a vision in white silk.

Miss Laidlaw had taken the vintage theme of Lily's ring and produced a simple, unadorned white gown in a regency style. The dress was exquisite. High-waisted with a ruched bodice and wide-cut, square neck. Short, puffed sleeves and a plain round skirt. A soft, garnet-coloured belt highlighted Lily's waist and formed a large bow at the back with long ends which fell in a 'v' to the hem. Her lace-edged veil was held in place by a coronet of lily of the valley, echoed in her bouquet.

Lily had insisted they be married in her parish church, despite the Dent's connection with the cathedral, and her father was to walk her the short distance to St. Pat's. However, the reception had been taken over by Mrs Dent when she offered their garden as a venue.

Ma had made a stunning four-tier cake. Each tier appeared as an open basket of flowers, and the porcelain bride and groom stood on top under an arch made by the top basket's handle. She and Granny had taken weeks to make replica sugar flowers and pipe a woven effect on the sides.

"There, I think that's perfect." Miss Laidlaw stepped back and nodded.

Lily looked at her reflection in her bedroom mirror and swallowed hard. She was dressing in her childhood bedroom at the home she loved for the last time. She and Stephen would live in a three-storey townhouse in Southsea with a maid and Stephen's man. The house, originally owned by Mr Dent, was his wedding gift to Lily and Stephen.

Ma had been coaching her on running a home. Her head was nearly bursting with all that was involved.

Stephen laughed away her fears. "There's nothing to it. My mother does it with her eyes shut."

Lily thought it seemed easy because Mrs Dent was good at it, having run a home for years. Still, she comforted herself that Ma would not be far away and had taught her to cook and budget. She would have to get on with it.

Her goodbyes to Mrs Winchett and the girls had been heart-wrenching. She loved her work. She hoped some of them would come to the service to see her dress. She thought of the workroom and how much she loved dressmaking. She would ask Stephen again about her career as soon as they settled into their new life.

Lily already had a blue garter on under her dress, which was new. Ma handed her a dainty lace handkerchief. "Something borrowed," she said. Miss Laidlaw clasped a single pearl around her neck on a gold chain. "As promised, something old, Lily; the necklace belonged to my mother."

Stephen had presented her with delicate drop pearl earrings as a wedding gift which she was wearing.

Pa was already wiping a tear as Lily descended the stairs.

"Beautiful, my girl, I'm the proudest man alive."

Grampa stood behind him and said fiercely, "That Dent fellow better look after you, or he'll have me to answer to."

That made everyone laugh, and it was with smiles, not tears, that they left the house.

All down Eastfield Road, families stood on their fronts, calling good wishes. Some joined in the procession to the church. A shining laudelet, drawn by two stamping grey horses in gleaming tack, was outside, ready to take Lily and Stephen to the reception.

The guests who were attending the ceremony filed inside. Ma and Miss Laidlaw made final tweaks to the skirt of Lily's dress, then left Lily and Pa in the small entrance porch.

"I can't believe you're getting married, Lily-Lou. We brought you here in christening robes only five minutes ago. It's a big adventure, Love. Are you ready?"

Lily's stomach was rolling over and over, and her heart beat a tattoo in her chest, but she nodded. "Ready, Pa."

"I love you, Lily."

"I love you too."

He bent and kissed her on the cheek, then took her hand and placed it on his arm, giving it a gentle squeeze, maybe for her reassurance or his. Lily wasn't sure. As she walked down the aisle, a sea of faces turned towards her. The words shared naturally and true beyond doubt resonated in her head. She realised Stephen had never said 'I love you' to her nor she to him. With Aiden, it was different.

Stephen waited for her with James, the brother nearest in age to him, both in long black jackets with narrow grey trousers and the palest lilac ties. He gave her his dazzling smile and whispered, "Very elegant."

The service began. Lily wondered if Aiden would burst into the church and make an objection, but there was no disturbance. Lily repeated her vows and nearly giggled when the priest said, "I, Stephen, Algernon, Dent."

"Algernon!" If Grace had been here, she would not have dared catch her eye. They would both have been helpless with laughter. But Grace was far away, and Algernon was her reality now.

Seconds before they were pronounced Man and Wife, the latch of the church door clicked. Lily froze, and the hairs stood on the back of her neck. Aiden was in the church; she knew without looking. Her heart raced. *Why had he come now? It was all too late.*

"Lily?" Stephen's voice broke her paralysis. He was waiting to kiss his bride.

"Yes, yes, sorry." She looked at his handsome face — *Aiden was too late. Stephen is my husband,* she thought.

Stephen paused, looking down into her eyes. He wrapped her waist in one arm and tilted her chin with the other. When he touched her, she felt a shock of electricity.

These sensations must be what love feels like, she thought. *I do love him.*

They walked into the vestry with their parents to sign the register, and Lily cast a furtive glance into the church for Aiden. All she saw was the church door close and Mrs Donnelly rising quietly from her pew to leave.

As she walked back down the aisle, Granny handed her a silver horseshoe on a ribbon, and they were showered with rice and rose petals as they stepped into the waiting carriage. St Pat's only had one bell, but it rang furiously as the couple drove away.

The carriage drove into the gravel drive of Dent House with a scrunch of wheels and the muted crunch of hooves. Their reception guests had already arrived in a bus chartered especially for the occasion. They had gathered in front of the house. Someone shouted, "Three cheers." Stephen handed Lily down the steps to "hoorahs" from everyone. She faltered on the steps as she saw the crowd waiting to congratulate them.

All day she smiled until her jaw ached. She felt shown off like a prize cow. First, the photographer organised group after group, and then they greeted friends and business associates of the Dents. Of Stephen's London friends, there was no sign, and Lily couldn't help but be glad. They made her uncomfortable, and she knew her parents would disapprove.

The meal and speeches dragged on except for Pa's toast. In an uncomplicated and touching way, he told the world how much he loved his daughter and what a lucky man Stephen was. During the other speeches, she wondered who the girl they portrayed was, and she didn't find the Stephen she knew either.

After the luncheon, she and Stephen circulated again. Thankfully, Pa drew her away from a small group of the Dent's friends, who seemed intent on knowing every detail about her in a most probing way.

"Here, my girl, come and sit with us for a moment and catch your breath." He wiped his forehead with a handkerchief. "I'm sure they mean well, but I haven't spoken to one person yet who didn't want to climb a ladder of some kind, political or business." He winked at her. "Don't get me wrong, I may have done some good business here. If I get all the jobs promised, I shall need more men, but I've told them, 'It's my daughter's wedding, and business can wait until Monday.'"

"Oh, Pa, I'm exhausted. I never want to smile again, ever."

He laughed. "Your ma has managed to procure a nice pot of tea despite the fact no one seems to drink anything but Champagne here. You can relax for five minutes with us." He offered her his arm. "I'm not taking no for an answer."

He guided her to a shaded spot under an arbour of roses and clematis and delivered her to a garden chair where Ma, Granny, Grandpa, and Miss Laidlaw fanned themselves against the searing summer heat.

Granny told Pa, "Mind that chair is clean before she stains her dress."

Pa made a show of dusting the chair with a napkin and held it aloft to show no dirt.

"As if there'd be dust in this house," he joked.

Ma sniffed. "None where you could see it anyway."

Miss Laidlaw laughed. "One suspects Mrs Dent has an eagle eye. Are you having a wonderful day, Lily?"

"Yes indeed," Lily answered mechanically. "So many people have complimented your dress design. I fear the assembled ladies will inundate you with orders."

"I'm sure Mrs Winchett will be delighted. I'm glad that you feel special in your dress."

Lily glanced at Miss Laidlaw, worry etched on her face. "We will continue to design together sometimes, won't we? Even if I don't officially belong to the workroom now."

"Yes, we will, as soon as you feel ready. Don't forget our dream to start a showroom. I shall hold you to that promise."

"Ah, there you are, hiding in the shade." Stephen's voice broke into the conversation. "My dear, it is time for you to change. Pa's driver is ready to take us to our hotel."

Stephen's eyes glinted unnaturally bright, almost feverish, and Lily thought he may have drunk too much Champagne. "Thank you, Stephen. I will say goodbye to my parents and follow you into the house."

He strolled away, dropping a word or two at each group he passed.

"Enjoy your honeymoon, Lily. We'll be thinking of you every day." Ma kissed her cheek and patted her awkwardly on the shoulder. "Stephen will look after you, I'm sure. We'll be by the car to wave you off." Ma had the slightly wooden expression she wore when she fended off tears, and Grandpa patted her hand.

"How lovely to spend some days in Brighton in this glorious weather." Miss Laidlaw took Lily's hands. "You must visit me as soon as you're back."

Lily nodded, the lump in her throat making her swallow hard. "We shall stay outside Portsmouth tonight. It's a surprise, and then travel on tomorrow."

"Lily, I…."

"I know," Lily said softly and took his arm. "Walk me to the house, Pa."

Mrs Dent had allocated her the Blue Room to change in.

Inside the Blue Room, Lily leaned against the door and took a deep breath. She called out, "Betsy, I'm ready to change."

"I thought I would help you, my darling wife." Stephen's teasing voice made her start off the wall.

"But that is most improper, Stephen, and you won't know what to do. Go away and let Betsy help."

Stephen roared with laughter. "Little prude, do you think this is the first dress I've removed? I will show you I am quite skilled. Stand still."

Lily backed up, and he laughed again. "To have and to hold, Lily. You promised to love, honour, and obey, remember."

She felt her breath quicken as he spun her around, trailed his hand across the back of her neck, and then planted a kiss where his hands lifted away.

Stephen began to undo the tiny buttons at the back of the bodice, kissing each square of skin as he progressed down. Now kneeling behind her, Lily could feel his breath on her skin, bringing her up in goosebumps.

Lily gasped and clung to the front of her gown. No one had ever kissed her back like that. It was embarrassing and wicked and something else she couldn't identify.

"Let it go, Lily," he murmured, planting one last kiss at the base of her spine. Stephen pushed the dress off her shoulders and tugged lightly.

"No," she gasped, "stop teasing me and call Betsy."

"It would be a shame to tear your dress, and what would we say to Miss Laidlaw?" he took both sides of the back as if to rip the fabric, and she relented, allowing it to fall. She instinctively crossed her hands across her chest.

"Very nice," he whispered, running his thumb across the top of her garter. "Turn around."

Flaming red, she turned, and he smirked as he reached out his hand to pull hers away. "Very nice indeed, lovely Lily."

Just as she thought she would combust with shame and feverish excitement, he turned and picked up her going away skirt from the bed. He dropped it over her head and buttoned it expertly without touching her. Her blouse and jacket followed, fitted equally efficiently.

She watched him as he concentrated on the mother-of-pearl buttons, his long nimble fingers closing them quickly. She thought he had musician's hands, Aiden's hands, and blushed again as she wished it were Aiden's hands dressing her.

"Sit on the bed."

As she perched, Stephen drew one stockinged foot forwards and gently massaged the sole before sliding it into her boot, which he buttoned. The second, he kissed each toe before donning her boot.

Lily felt confused and elated at the tingling, sparking energy that fizzed at each touch. Then, in a sudden mood switch, he dropped her foot, taking her by surprise and saying, "Ready, Mrs Dent?"

Stephen handed her the parasol, which completed her outfit, as if nothing extraordinary had occurred and offered her his arm.

"Stephen, we can't just…." She smoothed her skirt to gather her scattered thoughts.

"What, Dear?" His voice was as innocent as any modest man's. His eyes belied the voice. "Remember, only you and I know. If you don't give us away, I won't."

She didn't know how to face the guests waiting to bid them farewell, and she clung to his arm, marvelling at his polite, smiling mask as he said goodbye with such apparent ease. *He was such a good actor; he should be on the stage.* Lily thought.

She stammered her goodbyes, and as she kissed her, Ma whispered, "Everything alright, Love?"

Lily nodded. How *could you tell your mother what just happened? Or ask if what happened was how it should be?*

Mr Dent's driver doffed his cap to Lily, offered congratulations, and closed the car door.

The gleaming car swept them away along the coast road. In a fever of nerves and anticipation, Lily refused to confess how she felt to her tormenting husband. She suspected he was enjoying her discomfiture.

The car turned into a long chase and stopped in front of a pretty stone cottage overlooking the sea at Littlehampton.

"It belongs to my parent's friends. They have kindly gifted it to us for tonight. We shall be cosy here." He raised an eyebrow as he said it, and his arm on her elbow as they alighted lingered too long and lightly brushed her inner arm.

The driver placed their bags in the hall along with a wicker hamper.

"Supper," Stephen said, "Ma thinks of everything."

He picked up both bags, pointed to the back of the house and laughed. "Into the kitchen, wench, feed your husband."

Lily laughed uncertainly but picked up the hamper and carried it to the kitchen.

Mrs Dent, or her cook, had indeed thought of everything. The hamper was full of cold meats, a pâté, salad, asparagus, and tiny knotted bread rolls shaped like hearts. More Champagne, *always Champagne*, Lily thought. Cheeses, port, and a small heart-shaped tin filled with petit fours finished the offering.

"I thought we'd eat on the terrace," Stephen said as he returned to the kitchen. He twisted the cork on the Champagne and watched as it rose slowly out of the bottle under pressure and popped with a muted whisper. He ran his thumb over Lily's bottom lip. "Fine wines, Lily, we open them slowly."

They ate overlooking the sea and talked until dusk began to spread shadows across the terrace.

Lily rose to clear the table, but Stephen toying with his second glass of port, said, "Leave it." He drained his glass and reached out his hand. "Come."

He scooped her into his arms as she approached, then carried her through the house and up the short flight of stairs. His strength always surprised her. He looked slender but lifted her as if she weighed nothing. He set her down inside the bedroom door and kicked it shut, advancing towards her.

Lily stood her ground, her heart thumping. Stephen didn't attempt to kiss her as she'd expected. He circled her slowly, "Hairpins out," he said sharply.

She turned to look at him. "Now!" he barked the order.

Lily jumped and let her hair down. "Good," he said, running his fingers through her hair. "Jacket and blouse."

"Stephen, stop it," she protested. "I don't have my things. I'm embarrassed."

"You won't need them, Lily – skirt!"

Standing in her underwear, Lily began to tremble as he circled her slowly, looking intently at every inch of her.

He stepped into her from behind, encircling her waist and kissing her neck, pulling her close. "You're mine, now, Lily. Say it."

"I am," she faltered, afraid to anger him.

She was alone with him, and he'd been drinking. He nuzzled against her neck, dangerous, fascinating, frightening. Her treacherous body responded to his practised touch, but in her head, a voice whispered, "I'm not yours. I'm Aiden's." That small act of hidden rebellion made her feel braver.

Tender and loving their first night was not. He made her feel exhilarated and wanton, he hurt her, and she cried as he slept. This was not what she had imagined intimacy to be. Stephen was not who she thought he was, nor was she any longer who she had believed herself to be.

Chapter 31

Lily woke before Stephen. He lay carelessly on his back, with one arm flung above his head. The sheet draped across his lower body, exposing a white chest smattered with dark hair. He still breathed heavily, and she slid out of bed, careful not to disturb him and collected her clothes from the floor. She couldn't see her case anywhere. She dressed in her crumpled clothes from the night before. She flushed hotly as she remembered last night and pushed down a feeling of shame. She wished, not for the first time, that Grace was nearby to talk to.

Dressing by guess in an adjacent bedroom still shrouded in dust covers, Lily smoothed her clothes as best she could and tiptoed down to the kitchen to make tea.

She was startled into a small scream as an unfamiliar man's voice said, "May I help you, Mrs Dent?"

"Who are you?" she managed to say.

"Forgive me for startling you, Madame. I'm Banks, Mr Stephen's man. He asked for his car to be delivered here this morning. I drove it up early."

"I was not aware. I wanted to make some tea."

He gave a half-bow. "Permit me to make it for you. If I may venture to suggest, the sun is on the lawn at the front of the house, which is sheltered. You may wish to take breakfast there?"

Feeling over-awed, Lily said, "I would prefer to wait for breakfast with Stephen, I mean Mr Dent."

A slightly pained look registered momentarily on Banks' face. "Mr Stephen most emphatically does not eat before noon." Banks relented, and a kindlier smile cracked his smooth face. "As you have risen early, you may have to wait sometime for him. Let me make you a small repast."

Lily thought of Ma in the kitchen at home making porridge and swallowed hard. Banks must despise this crumpled wreck with untidy hair, shuffling from foot to foot.

Banks continued as if he had read her thoughts, "Betsy will join us in Brighton. She is travelling on the train. In the meantime, if there is anything, I can assist you with…." His gaze flicked briefly to her creased skirt.

Lily began to feel cross at being caught out looking like this. "Yes, there is. Mr Dent took our cases upstairs yesterday, and I don't know where he set them down. I should like to find a clean dress."

"It's a quaint place, Madame. The dressing room does not adjoin the bedroom. After breakfast, I will show you. I have taken the liberty of hanging Mr Stephen's suit."

Lily nodded and, refusing to be intimidated, said, "I should like porridge for breakfast, Banks, with tea."

"Very good, Madame, an excellent choice."

Several hours later, Stephen appeared, by which time Lily had explored the garden and was reading a dull book on sailing from the bookcase in the cottage. He was unshaven in a dressing gown over trousers. He winced at the sunlight and said to Lily, "Have you ordered my coffee."

She looked surprised. "No, I didn't know you would want any, but I can ask Banks, or I'll make it myself."

"Fresh coffee, no food, every morning, Lily, that's how I like it. Number one rule, no conversation before lunch." He adjusted his chair to turn away from the sun.

When Lily did not respond, he said, "Did you hear me?"

She looked at him sweetly. "No conversation before lunch. I have taken note."

Fortunately, as Stephen did not look amused, Banks appeared with a pot of coffee and a folded newspaper. "Lovely morning, Sir."

"Mornings can go to hell, Banks. My head hurts."

Banks appeared unfazed and offered his patent pick-me-up, to which Stephen nodded assent. Banks poured the coffee and withdrew.

After draining the first cup and pouring a second, Stephen said, "That's better. I feel half-human again."

Lily noticed his hand had a fine tremor as he replaced the cup and saucer on the tray. He looked grey and drawn except for the dark stubble which shadowed his jawline. Was this the same charming man from yesterday's reception and the prowling predator from last night? Thoughts of last night brought a blush to her face.

"You, I have to say, look fresh as a daisy, Lily."

She looked at him. "I was up early." In her head, she thought, *I drank less Champagne than you did yesterday.*

She wondered how often he was like this in the morning but didn't dare ask. Pa would not have approved of a young man lying in bed until lunchtime nursing a hangover. He didn't believe in excessive drinking, but you got up and took the consequences if it happened. She wondered what Ma and Pa were doing today, their first day without her.

Banks reappeared discreetly and carried a glass of red liquid on a salver with a small dish of green powder beside it.

Stephen took the glass, sprinkled two pinches of the powder onto the thick drink and downed it in one. He shuddered. "That is truly disgusting, Banks, but it hits the spot."

A faint aroma of tomato assailed Lily's nostrils. "What was that?" she asked as soon as Banks had withdrawn.

Stephen laughed. "Banks' secret recipe — tomato juice, vodka, a raw egg yolk, and who knows what, he's never told me."

Lily wrinkled her nose. "Sounds dreadful. I'd be sick."

He wagged a finger in jest, his mood beginning to improve. "Well, my dear, abstain from drinking. Let this be a warning to you."

Lily, relieved that Stephen, less morose than earlier, said, "Has Banks been with you long?"

"Lord, yes, he's known me forever. He worked for m'parents and became my man when I graduated from university." He looked at Lily's thin summer dress. "I'd wear a coat and tie your hat down with a scarf. We're driving in my car to Brighton, and I shall fold the roof down." He slapped his thighs and surprised her with a kiss on the cheek. "Won't take me long to dress, then we'll be off."

Lily wondered how many different men were contained in the man she had married.

Stephen drove his car on the open road with reckless abandon. Lily clutched the side of the vehicle as the scenery rushed past. She feared she would be thrown out at any minute.

He laughed at her frightened face. "Look, no hands." He lifted both off the steering wheel and made her scream. "This is when I feel most alive, at the edge of life and death," he shouted over the rush of the wind.

"Be careful, Stephen. You'll kill us both," she pleaded.

He looked at her with haunted eyes and shrugged. "Maybe for the best."

She looked at him with wide eyes, was he mad, she wondered.

When they arrived in Brighton, they found the Dents had procured them the honeymoon suite looking over the sea with a darling balcony. Lily gasped in delight as the bellboy pushed open the French doors to show her the view.

Stephen watched her excited expression and said, "I envy your simplicity. Perhaps Ma is right, and you will save my soul." He then shrugged carelessly and ran his fingers down her cheek.

Lily froze. N*ot again*, she thought.

"Don't be afraid, Lily. I won't hurt you."

She stepped away from him. "You did last night. You hurt me — you deliberately hurt me. I was frightened."

He looked ashamed. "I promise I won't do so again." He pulled her to him and kissed her gently. "Come, Lily, let me make it up to you."

For the next two days, Stephen set out to win back Lily's trust. He was a charming companion, and Brighton was an exciting place to explore. They strolled on the promenade, visited the Royal Pavilion, and ate ice creams. In the evenings, they dined and danced. The memory of their wedding night began to recede.

Then a letter came, which Stephen opened at breakfast.

Lily looked up from her tea. "Darling Lily, you must excuse me, but I have to leave you for a day. I'm needed in London on business. You'll be alright without me, won't you? I'll leave you some money, and Banks will look after you."

She hesitated. The letter did not look like a business letter, written as it was on lilac notepaper. But seeing Stephen's eyes on her with eyebrows raised, issuing a challenge, she said, "Yes, I will. I want to write postcards home, and there is a dressmaker I should like to visit out of curiosity. It's just such a shop as I should like to run myself with the help of Miss Laidlaw."

He frowned. "We are barely married, Lily. It is far too early for you to be thinking of a shop."

"But not too early for you to be leaving on… business," Lily retorted and pointed to the letter.

He reached across the table and took her wrist in a painful grasp. Lily refused to admit he'd hurt her and raised her chin. All the while smiling, he said, "Do not question me, Lily; it does not become you." He left red finger marks on her skin as he let her go.

Stephen put his finger under her raised chin and said, "I won't forget your defiance." He left the table, folding the letter into his pocket.

Lily sat rigidly upright and thought, I *will not cry. I won't.*

Later that day, she carefully inscribed postcards to her family and Miss Laidlaw. "Brighton is wonderful. Having a lovely time. Your Lily."

312

She posted them, decided to visit the dressmakers regardless and read a book from the hotel library on the balcony.

As dinner time approached, she began to feel nervous. What had Stephen meant this morning? He'd had a mean look, and his grip on her wrist had been spiteful. Part of her wanted to jump on a train and flee back to Portsmouth, but she didn't have enough money. Could she ask Banks to take her? She thought not. He was, after all, Stephen's valet.

She declined dinner when Banks came to remind her of the time.

"Are you feeling unwell? Madame."

She sighed. "No, Banks, just not hungry. We have done nothing but eat for a week. It's hard to believe families are starving in Portsmouth because of the strikes."

Banks inclined his head. "Just so."

"Do you know what time Mr Dent will return?"

"He has not admitted me into his confidence, Madame, but he is sometimes gone for several days when he leaves for London. Regarding dinner, perhaps if I order you a sandwich or a small omelette?"

She thought he looked at her with a trace of pity and frowned. She would bet anything he knew precisely where Stephen was. Lilac notepaper meant a woman in her books, and as she admitted this to herself, she was shocked to the core. Lily was sure neither Pa nor Gramps had ever looked at another woman. She and Stephen had not been married even a week.

Lily sat on the balcony listening to the sea until the light faded, and moths began to flutter around the candles on her small table. The regular roll of the waves soothed her nervous anticipation, and she realised she was exhausted.

313

Her mind wandered to the night before Aiden left for London, how happy they had been watching the moonlight on the water and how delightful their stolen kiss was.

Feeling dejected, Lily called for Betsy to help her undress and fell into bed. Tomorrow was another day.

The following day, she was woken by Betsy pulling the curtains to let in the already bright sun and the promise of another hot day. Of Stephen, there was no sign. Fuming silently at this humiliation, Lily dressed in haste and called Banks. "Is Mr Dent's car still here, Banks?"

He nodded. "Yes, Ma'am, would you like me to drive you somewhere today?"

Spurred by a flash of inspiration and a strong desire not to wait for Stephen when he returned, she said, "I would indeed, Banks. You may take me back to Portsmouth. As Mr Dent is detained, I will settle into the new house. We were due to leave tomorrow anyway."

He looked surprised and seemed about to protest but said, "As you wish, Madame. And Mr Dent's belongings, Ma'am?"

"If he hasn't let you into his confidence about his trip, Banks, I suggest we leave them where they are. I'm sure the hotel will store them."

Banks seemed to struggle to compose his face, then added, "Miss, I mean Madame, if I may make so bold, it won't do to aggravate Mr Dent."

Lily sighed, some of her bravado leaving her. "We will, in that case, leave him a note of our whereabouts and ask the hotel to store his overnight things. Perhaps you know where you might send a note in London to inform him."

Banks nodded, but his face gave no other indication. "Very good, Madame."

314

Her first port of call after leaving instructions with Betsy to prepare a light dinner, in case Mr Dent should be joining them, was to surprise Ma with a visit.

Lily saw Ma baking from the flour on her apron as she opened the door. "Lily, love, I wasn't expecting to see you today. We got your postcard this morning." She looked past Lily. "Where is Stephen?"

Lily adopted an airy expression. "He had some work to attend to today, Ma." She hugged her mother, then stepped back, laughing at the flour on her dress. "It is good to be here. How are you and how is Pa? I've missed you both."

"It has done me good to see you, too. We've been thinking about you, Lily. I'm sure you've had a lovely time."

Lily nodded but said nothing more. "What are you baking? Smells good."

"Oh, I'm making pasties for the strike kitchen. Money is becoming scarce." She shook her head. "Hard times, the bosses aren't budging. Even some schoolchildren have come out of school on strike if you have ever heard of anything like. Imitating their fathers, no doubt."

Lily frowned. "I can make something as well, Ma. We have plenty of food."

"That would be welcome, Lily, but mind you check with Stephen first."

Lily looked mulish, but Ma said, "In the early days, it's best to discuss everything to avoid misunderstandings. After all, you are just getting to know one another."

She wanted to blurt out that she knew as much as she wanted to, and that Stephen was not what he appeared. But Lily couldn't find the words, and inside she felt ashamed to admit how things had been.

Ma looked at the kitchen clock. "Nice as it is to have you here, Love. Shouldn't you be getting back to see to Stephen's dinner and welcome him home if he's been working? Pa will be sad to have missed you."

Lily nodded resignedly and rose to go. Her Ma looked worried. "Everything is alright, isn't it, Love?"

Lily nodded. "Yes, Ma, of course; why wouldn't it be?"

Lily dined alone and considered retiring to bed when she heard voices in the hall, and the dining room door banged open. Stephen looked tired, ill even, and was in a towering rage. His dark eyes blazed, and his pupils had contracted to pinpricks. "What the devil do you mean by this? I return to the hotel to find you gone and an impertinent note left."

Lily jumped up and stood behind her chair, glad the table was between them.

"I didn't marry a girl from the workroom to have her defy me at every turn, Lily. You need to learn your place."

Her temper flaring to match his, she replied in an icy voice, "You didn't marry a girl from the workroom. You married Lily Matthews. I presume you are drunk again, Stephen. If you despise me, you should have married the woman you have been with in London."

He gave an ugly laugh. "Oh no, that would not have served, I had to marry someone Ma approved of, or I wouldn't have inherited the money." He snorted. "I can put up with your gauche innocence and tedious morals for the money, they even amuse me, but I won't have you question me. You'll pay for that."

He advanced around the table, and Lily took a firm grip of the knife on her plate, but quick as a flash, he wrenched it out of her hand and raised his hand to strike her. A cough

316

from the door stopped him, and he let her go as he spun around.

"Madame, the coffee you ordered."

Lily had ordered no coffee but looked gratefully towards Banks, her eyes wide with terror.

"Mr Stephen, may I pour you a cup as well," he continued as if he had seen and sensed nothing amiss. "I'll send Betsy in to make up the fire."

"Damn you, Banks, don't look at me like that," Stephen said. "I wasn't going to hurt her. Lost my temper, that's all."

Banks looked at him. "Perhaps if we are not feeling quite the thing, Sir, might I suggest you sleep at your club this evening?"

Lily held her breath. She had to get away; he was out of his senses.

"No, dammit, you might not!" Stephen looked at Lily. He reminded her of a cold-eyed snake. "I want to sleep with my lovely wife."

Banks cleared his throat again. "If I might have a word in private." He held open the door. Stephen narrowed his eyes and looked at Banks, who held his gaze blandly, then Stephen spun on his heel and flung himself from the room, his footsteps echoing in the hall.

Tiptoeing to the door, Lily listened to their hushed conversation.

"Mr Stephen be reasonable; you cannot answer for your actions in this state."

"Damn you, Banks, do not tell me what to do in my own home. You can pack your bags."

"Indeed, Sir. However, if the police became involved for a second time…."

After a pause during which Lily strained to hear, Stephen uttered an oath, hurried footsteps sounded, and the front door slammed. Lily heard Stephen's car engine.

Her knees buckled, and she sank into a chair, her head in her hands. '*A second time*', he had hurt someone else.

Banks re-entered the room. "Mr Dent wished me to inform you that he will stay at his club this evening."

Ignoring the discreet lie, Lily blurted out, "Thank you, Banks, thank you for saving me."

Banks acknowledged Lily with a half-bow. "I am afraid that Mr Stephen has been indulging in the use of certain substances again whilst in London. I shall inform Mr Dent Snr immediately. We had hoped this was behind us."

The full horror of the situation became apparent to Lily, and she stared wide-eyed at Banks. She stifled a sob. "Banks, will you take me home?"

Banks regarded her for a moment. "It is late. I assure you I shall bolt every door and will not retire tonight. You will be quite safe here until the morning."

Too tired to argue, Lily made her weary way to bed, locked the bedroom door, and placed a chair beneath the handle. She stared long into the night and berated herself. She had brought this on herself with her foolish pride and jealousy.

Chapter 32

L ily woke with a start. There were voices in the hall. She clutched the bedcovers, her heart racing and beads of sweat pricking her forehead.

A knock at the door made her start, and she looked around for a weapon to defend herself. Her mouth was dry as she croaked, "Who is it?"

"Madame, it's Banks. The police are here requesting to see you."

Lily jumped out of bed and wrapped a dressing gown around her. The night was sultry, but she still shivered. Lily removed the chair and unlocked the door. Banks looked unnaturally pale in the electric light. "What do they want?" she whispered.

"Prepare yourself, Madame. It is not good news." He turned and walked towards the stairs. Lily followed him blindly, her heart in her mouth.

Downstairs, two police constables stood legs apart, their helmets tucked under their arms. The older man stepped forwards. "Mrs Stephen Dent?"

Lily nodded.

"Perhaps you would like to sit down," he suggested. Lily swallowed. "Yes, yes, of course, follow me."

The dining room, the scene of the drama earlier that evening, appeared curiously normal, and Lily sat in a chair, offering seats to the men, who politely declined.

"Mrs Dent, we are sorry to inform you that your husband, Mr Stephen Dent, was involved in an automobile accident this evening. His car left the carriageway while driving on the London Road. The impact killed him as his car rolled down a bank. No other vehicles were involved. Our condolences to you and the family."

Lily stared at the two men, unable to understand what they were saying. "Dead? My husband is dead?" Her shoulders, still tense from the earlier altercation, sagged, and she wanted to laugh hysterically that this man was gone from her life. Shocked and ashamed to feel this way, Lily schooled her features into a blank stare.

The policemen both nodded solemnly. The older one cleared his throat. "Is there anyone we can notify to be with you, Mrs Dent?"

Lily desperately wanted Ma and Pa to come. She gave their names and address.

He nodded to the man beside him. "Right, Jenkins, get off there sharpish and accompany Mr and Mrs Matthews. Then get back to the station. I'll meet you there." He focused once more on Lily and said, "We'll be in touch, you know, formalities Mi.., I mean Madame. And once again, our deepest sympathy."

Banks showed them out, then returned to Lily. He tried to offer her a cup of tea, but she realised his voice had become suspended by tears, and his broad shoulders were heaving with suppressed sobs.

Lily looked for Betsy, who was hovering in the corner and said, "A tray of strong tea, Betsy, please." Then she went to Banks, guided him to one of the chairs, and put her arm across his shoulders. "You loved him despite everything, didn't you?"

Banks nodded. He produced a snowy handkerchief from his pocket and mopped his tears. "Beg pardon Madame. I was overcome. I'll be alright now." He looked into the distance as if seeing another time. "Stephen was such a happy boy, Ma'am, always laughing and full of play. Until his father insisted he go away to school. Mr Dent Snr sent him with the best intentions, 'to get a good education', he said."

Lily nodded with a half-smile and let the grief-stricken man continue.

"His brothers were still at home, him being that much older than the others, so he was at school all on his own. He wasn't happy, not ever; children can be cruel, and he missed his ma."

Banks paused and blew his nose, then dabbed at his eyes again. Lily said gently, "What happened to make him bitter?"

He sighed. "He got in with the wrong crowd, more money than sense and always up to tricks, but nasty with it. Stephen started drinking, eventually got expelled for it, and broke his ma's heart." He shook his head and looked up at Lily.

"Mr Dent Snr said he had to earn his living, come into the family firm, but he wasn't raised for it. That fancy school gave him fancy ideas." Banks sounded angry, and he glared at Lily. "Stephen had no feel for the business, he and his pa disagreed all the time, and anyway, his father wasn't interested in his ideas for modernising." He shook his head. "Don't get me wrong, his father's a good man, but he never understood Mr Stephen. They were so different."

Lily nodded. She remembered the bitterness in Stephen's voice whenever he spoke about his pa.

Banks stood up and paced across the room. "It's James who's interested in the machines and the business – well, I suppose the firm will be his now anyway." He dabbed with the handkerchief again. "Mr Stephen went from drinking to opium and the like. It turned him nasty, Madame. Paranoid, I think the doctor said. They spent a fortune getting him right, but it's all been to no avail."

Lily dropped her head. "How sad, Banks, and what a waste. He could have had the world at his feet." She couldn't help but remember their drive to Brighton. *"Maybe for the best,"* he had said when she accused him of risking to kill them both. Lily wondered, had he? Had he deliberately killed himself?

Banks looked at her, his red-rimmed eyes pleading. "Now that he's gone, Miss, please don't tell his parents or the police how he was at the end. It won't bring him back. They won't feel they failed him all their lives if they don't know."

Lily looked at Banks, who had stuck by the family through thick and thin, now looking exhausted and older than his years. She thought of her parents and wondered how they would feel if they found out what danger she had been in. If they found out she had never loved Stephen, nor he her. She was ashamed of their marriage of convenience and whispered. "I won't tell anyone, Banks."

Lily poured hot tea, which seemed to marshal Banks, and he stood with more purpose in his bearing. "If you don't need me, Madame, I should make preparations. The family will undoubtedly want to join you, and we should consider our mourning attire below stairs. There is also the question of clothes for Mr Stephen if you would permit me to choose something suitable."

About an hour later, in answer to a knock, Lily did not wait for Banks to come from downstairs. She flew to the front door, wrenched it open and hurled herself into her mother's arms. Finally, the tears that had stubbornly refused to come pricked at her eyelids and spilt down her cheeks.

"There, my girl, steady now." Ma patted her back and swayed with Lily, gently soothing her.

Pa closed the door behind him and acknowledged Banks, now waiting motionless in the hall. He cleared his throat. "I have served tea in the sitting room, Madame, if you'll allow me to show you."

Ma eyed Banks up and down with an appraising eye, then nodded and gently disentangled herself from Lily. "Let's dry your eyes, Love. Edward, your hanky, please." Ma held out her hand, took the proffered handkerchief then wiped Lily's eyes. She addressed the valet. "A nice cup of tea will do us all good after the shock, perhaps with a biscuit or a slice of bread and butter…" she paused, tilting her head enquiringly.

Banks' demeanour was once again schooled into a polite but neutral expression except for his red eyes. "It's Banks, Madame, and certainly, something to sustain you."

Ma guided Lily to the sofa and sat beside her when he had left the room. "This is a tragedy and no mistake. I'm sorry, Lily. I'm sure no one expected this, least of all you, and what's more, I don't think anything anyone can say or do will make things better. But we're here for you."

Lily looked from Ma's kind countenance to her father's solemn expression and said in a small voice, "I don't know what I've got to do now."

Pa said, "If the police need you, they'll let you know. I don't doubt they have spoken to the Dents. I expect his ma and pa will be here before long, or they'll send a car. Between us, we'll help you. There will be some legal things to attend to, and their solicitor will inform you about the terms of Stephen's will. Then you must decide what you wish to do or what circumstances dictate."

Lily looked at Pa; she hadn't thought about money or legal affairs. Her concern had been for the immediate arrangements. Ma said kindly, "Whatever happens, you know you always have a home with us."

Lily nodded, and for a moment, hope swelled inside her. She thought *I could return to my old life as if this never happened.* Thoughts swiftly followed by the realisation that she could never be the same innocent girl again. Lily pushed down a moment of panic. *Who am I now?*

Ma looked at Lily's summer dress. "As soon as the workroom opens, I'll get Pa to speak to Miss Laidlaw. You'll need to go into blacks, Lily, and I'm sure Mrs Winchett will be able to send something appropriate. You will undoubtedly need several things, as it would be respectful to be in black for several months, but they will know best. We wouldn't want the Dents thinking we had ignored any correct observation."

The Dents, when they arrived, were shell-shocked. Stephen's father looked smaller as if someone had deflated him, and his mother, wreathed in black, clasped Lily to her in a rustle of stiff silk crepe and a cloud of expensive perfume. "My poor girl, a widow barely after the wedding, and heartbroken for my son, as are we. I shall never get over it, never. He was my darling firstborn."

Guilt drained the colour from Lily's face. She was not, could not be heartbroken. She was sad about Stephen's unhappy life and the consequences of his choices, but for herself, she was relieved. Lily also felt ashamed of what she had done and carried the humiliation of their honeymoon branded in her mind,

Lily shook her head. Mrs Dent had conveniently forgotten or seemed blind to her son's dangerous faults now that he was dead. Lily had agreed never to tell her how he was that last night, and the burden of the promise sat heavily on her shoulders. She wanted to ask why, knowing Stephen as they did, the Dents had not been honest with her. Perhaps they felt his money was prize enough for a working girl like her. She shuddered.

She longed for Aiden, someone she could talk to openly, be herself, and be honest. He knew her, she trusted him, and he would understand. But Aiden was lost to her through her own wilfulness.

Mr Dent cleared his throat. "Stephen made a will before your marriage when he came into his inheritance. I insisted he do so. You can rest assured that you will be provided for by the will, Lily. You must not worry about the future when you are grieving."

Lily swallowed. "Oh, but I…."

Mr Dent broke in and raised a hand to silence her. "I know this is the last thing on your mind because you're a sweet girl, but it will be one worry less for you at this tragic time."

Mrs Dent nodded. "We consider you part of the family, which will never change. We want you to lean on us as you will your parents." She looked at the Matthews' and nodded to reinforce the sincerity of her words. Was she ever sincere? Lily wondered.

The following days went by in a blur, and there was much to think of. Miss Laidlaw brought skirts, blouses and two plain, high-necked dresses in black crepe. She hugged Lily close as she donned the first gown. Miss Laidlaw had felt genuine grief when she lost her family, and her gentle kindness made Lily feel even more like a wretched imposter.

Mrs Dent had a rope of jet beads with matching earrings sent from her jeweller and presented them to Lily. "You will not wish to wear gold, my dear. Please accept these in great sadness."

Once correctly attired, Lily spent much of her day at the Dent's home, as none of the family left the house. Even Mr Dent did not go to the factory. His foreman came to the house, and they remained closeted in the office for hours with Stephen's brother, James.

There were endless letters of condolence that needed replies, and Lily thought she would never come to the end of the black-edged cards announcing the funeral. Visitors came in a respectful but seemingly non-stop stream to extend their sympathy, most of whom Lily had never met. Of his so-called friends from London, there was no sign.

Mr Dent's secretary attended to the funeral arrangements on behalf of the family, and Lily allowed Mrs Dent to go over the fine details with him. She found the pomp and the hypocrisy unbearable. There seemed no time for genuine grief in planning the occasion. But then, no one was honest about Stephen.

Lily insisted on returning to her house, where she shucked off the cloak of pretence she wore all day.

Betsy walked everywhere solemnly and spoke in whispers until Lily said, "Really, Betsy, Mr Dent would not be offended, I'm sure, if we speak normally or even smile occasionally."

The funeral was a huge and public affair for the men. Stephen's coffin, born to the Cathedral by black horses, their harness decked with nodding black feathers, a dreadful parody of the recent white wedding carriage.

The Dents dealt with grief in the lavish way they did everything else. Neither Lily, her ma, nor Mrs Dent attended. They remained at home. Each read a chosen prayer and then reflected in the drawing room. Their conversation was desultory, and to Lily, it seemed that each lady felt the weight of their personal thoughts.

Later that week, Lily attended the will reading at Messrs Leyburn and Yarm, the Dent family solicitors.

Mr Leyburn regarded Lily solemnly over his glasses, pronouncing her the sole beneficiary of Stephen's estate. The estate included permission to use their house, currently held in trust by Stephen's father until Lily remarried. Also included were Stephen's inheritance and a small pension from the company.

He steepled his fingers, and a disapproving cast came over his countenance. "You will be aware that Mr Dent had substantial debts when he came into his inheritance, which you must now discharge from the estate."

Lily looked at Mr Leyburn, feeling him judge her harshly because of Stephen's debt. He continued to speak, but Lily was distracted by his jowls, which wobbled above his tight collar.

"It was fortunate that Mr Dent married when he did, as his obligations had become most pressing. I have prepared a list for your perusal and now need your permission to discharge them."

The sheet of cream vellum contained a list that made Lily gasp, clothes, expensive hotels, gambling IOUs, amongst other debts. The total was staggering. Lily felt someone had sucked all the air out of the office.

"Can I afford to pay all this?" She stammered.

He smiled a rusty attempt at reassurance, revealing tobacco-stained teeth. "It will reduce your annual income substantially, of course, but with sensible management, you should be able to remain in the house if you live quietly. You are young. You may wish to re-marry in the future."

Lily sat up straighter. "Then you must indeed discharge all the debts immediately, that I may sleep at night."

Mr Leyburn handed her a document to sign to that effect, and as she went to sign it, snatching up the proffered pen, he chastised her gently. "Mrs Dent, I must advise that you read any document thoroughly before you sign it."

She swallowed. "Yes, yes, of course." After perusing the document, she continued, "Mr Leyburn, eventually, after a suitable mourning period, I should like to pursue my work as a costume designer and develop a small workroom. Would this be possible in my new circumstances?"

He frowned as if about to dismiss the idea, but she pressed on, "It was a venture I had discussed with my husband. With the help of a former colleague of mine, we had intended to offer apprenticeships and training. Still, perhaps I could now offer hope to young widows like myself in less fortunate circumstances. Or the wives of the union men who sacrifice so much to uphold workers' rights. I would like some good to come of this dreadful tragedy."

Lily felt satisfied to see new-found respect creep reluctantly into his eyes. "We could certainly discuss those possibilities in the future. Of course, Mr Dent Snr could offer you sound advice in this area, and I am sure he would be happy to do so. As you know, he is of a philanthropic persuasion himself."

Lily nodded. She had no desire to be the Dent's pensioner and shuddered at the thought of being in the power of another man ever. She would prefer to live on money she earned herself. Lily felt she did not deserve to profit from Stephen's death, but if she used what remained of Stephen's estate to help others and it permitted her to get started, she was grateful for the opportunity.

"If that is all? I shall look forward to meeting you again in happier circumstances." She rose and shook his hand, suddenly eager to leave the paper-lined office.

Chapter 33

Throughout the expected six months of deep mourning, Lily sustained herself with the dream of her workroom. She rearranged the furniture in one of the spare bedrooms, which had good natural light and set up a large desk, which Granny helped her buy at auction. She also invested in a cutting table and a sewing machine.

Lily spent long hours there, sometimes accompanied by Miss Laidlaw in the evening or at weekends. The two women were interrupted only by Banks, who remonstrated with them about missing luncheon or straining their eyes. As they set neat stitches in gowns, Lily spoke of her discomfiture concerning her inheritance.

"Lily, if it is of any help, my father, who was a most moral man, believed that money was neither good nor bad of itself. It has the power to corrupt, but it can also benefit many others. Stephen would wish you to be comfortable in the circumstances."

The New Year celebrations of nineteen twelve came and went, barely noticed, and Lily looked forward to the end of this imposed period of deep mourning.

When the day of her release eventually came, she had designed and made a wardrobe of elegant dresses in restrained shades of grey and mauve to wear as she emerged into the world again. She saw no reason not to be stylish, even if restricted to half-mourning colours.

Lily's only outings had been to her parents and in-laws. She longed for the freedom to walk along the seafront or attend the suffragist meetings again.

Mrs O'Shea had taken pity on her plight, and with Mrs Donnelly, they brought small working parties to visit Lily at home. The ladies were delighted with their successes in aiding the striker's families and collecting signatures for their suffrage bill. The petition had sufficient signatures to be heard in Parliament.

Of Aiden, there was little news. Mrs Donnelly was vague about his activities. "Yes, he was well and still travelling with Miss Marion," was all she said. She suggested he was a poor correspondent as an excuse, but Lily felt she seemed ill at ease. She did say that Aiden had had three other songs published by Francis, Dean and Hunter with some success.

With this information, Lily had to be content.

"You did a terrible thing marrying Stephen," she told her neat reflection in the mirror. "Why would Aiden still love you? Be happy you have your work and a home. It's more than you deserve." Aiden was seldom far from her thoughts; it was a bitter pill to acknowledge she had driven him away forever.

Her conversation about the new workroom with Mr Dent provoked mixed reactions. He saw no reason for her to need to work beyond the charity work indulged in by his wife. "Lily, people will believe we are not supporting you adequately if they see you at work. As Mrs Stephen Dent, you have a place in society." He immediately offered to increase her pension if she was struggling financially. She assured him to the contrary and felt mortified.

However, she had found an unexpected ally in Mrs Dent, whose love of being identified with a philanthropic project and strong support for the women's movement perfectly saw the many advantages of Lily's ideas.

"I am envious of you, young women," she said, "You will not be shackled by social convention as my generation were. Stephen was unsteady as a young man, so I would like to see the memory of his reformed self upheld in this way. It would be a fitting legacy." She could not meet Lily's eye as she spoke, and Lily felt she and her mother-in-law were complicit in maintaining the same pretence about Stephen.

Mrs Dent was either unaware or chose not to acknowledge her son's continued excesses, but the whispered conversation Lily had heard between Stephen and Banks preyed on her mind. The law did not protect women against their husbands' violence but allowed them to retain the money they had earned. Lily decided it would be her mission within the women's rights movement to provide training and reasonably paid employment for such women to afford them a measure of independence.

Lily's idea was to have begun with the workroom based in her home, but the Dents would not hear of it.

"I do not think using your home that way is appropriate, Lily. Keep your home and business separate, my girl," Mr Dent insisted. "I shall look about for small premises that could be suitable. You may rent it from me, as I doubt, at your age, you would succeed in procuring a lease in your own right."

With no option but to accept if she was to advance her idea, Lily accepted Mr Dent's offer to rent premises on her behalf until she could procure the lease in her own right.

Later that evening, Lily sat with Miss Laidlaw, both employed in adding beads to one of Miss Laidlaw's stage designs. "Anis, I am excited by my project, and I cannot benefit from Stephen's money and simply be idle," she sighed. "I must swallow my pride and accept Mr Dent's help. I have the heart and know what I want to achieve, but am I too young to make it work?"

Miss Laidlaw set aside her sewing for a moment. "Lily, forgive me for being forward. Would you consider a partnership of sorts? Before, when it seemed likely, we spoke of it as a daydream, but I think we could complement each other well."

Lily momentarily held her breath and looked at Miss Laidlaw with widening eyes. "I would like nothing better, but I can't let you risk your position and savings."

"It is time I left Mrs Winchett to pursue my design creativity. I had thought perhaps with a fashion or theatrical house in London. You have my word that I would infinitely prefer to join your scheme, perhaps even have our own establishment in London one day. Who knows?"

"If you truly mean it, it would be wonderful indeed."

Anis Laidlaw smiled and toasted Lily with her teacup. "To us, Lily."

By the late Spring, 'Lily and Anis Couture' was steadily developing a loyal clientele.

Their early clients came from Mrs Dent, who influenced ladies from her charity boards and their friends to place orders for bespoke designs. Gradually the tiny cottage Mr

Dent had purchased, which they rented, with its comfortable sitting room and delicious pastries baked by Ma, became a fashionable venue to visit.

"We need more help." Lily put down the gown she had finished hemming and rubbed her eyes.

Anis nodded. She had not been home for three nights, snatching sleep at Lily's house as they worked into the night. Betsy, who was not needed full-time at the house and whom Lily could barely afford, had already begun to divide her time between the house and the cottage. Lily lived in constant fear of losing Banks, who was, after all, a gentleman's valet but had quietly become indispensable in his support of her.

Mr Dent continued to pay Bank's wages, saying he preferred to have a man at the premises with Lily. He also referred to his long service with the family.

Banks was close to retirement and reassured Lily he had no desire to seek a position outside the family at his age.

Despite her workload, Lily insisted on attending the Suffragist meetings regularly, it was her closest link to Aiden, and she was motivated by the independent women she met there. Through the sessions, she met Gladys Hallett, a gently spoken young widow who had trained as a dressmaker before her marriage. Lily talked to her privately as she knew Gladys struggled to keep her home and took in washing to make ends meet. "Gladys, please come and meet my partner, Miss Laidlaw. We are in desperate need of help."

Gladys blushed. "I could bring samples of my work, and I would not be offended if I didn't suit your needs."

In addition to Gladys, Lily also recruited her ma. Through her links with the church, Ma interviewed women who needed assistance. They would receive training and undertake homework when required, organising a network of homeworkers to support the main workshop.

It was during one of the training sessions for the homeworkers that Lily had another idea. All these women were interested in fashion but could never afford the bespoke gowns they made. However, what if the business were to introduce a line of simple, stylish clothes affordable for ordinary women who wished to take up work outside the home?

"We can't, Lily," Anis groaned. "The idea is wonderful, but we are already worked off our feet."

"We would design but could employ teams to make the clothes by machine to keep costs down. Maybe adding hand-finished details. Fashion for women by women."

Anis nodded. "I'm sure there would be a market if women could sell them directly to parties of friends for a percentage of sales. It would allow them to build small businesses while still looking after their home."

Both women were excited by the idea. It was a scheme for the future and may attract investment from the women's rights movements.

Mr Dent could see the possibility of franchising the model to allow entrepreneurial young women to make their own living, supported by a framework developed in Portsmouth. His workforce had machining skills they could consider a small pilot project he suggested. Persuaded not to let personal prejudice hinder their success, Lily agreed to ask Kitty Marion's patronage to introduce their ideas.

Miss Marion responded enthusiastically and invited Lily and Anis to address one of her London meetings.

Tired after a long day pouring over designs with Anis Laidlaw, Lily returned home and relaxed with a novel after dinner. Eyes heavy, she had been close to dozing when she was startled awake by a frantic tapping at the window. The pale face of Mrs Donnelly, head swathed in a shawl, appeared ghostly against the dark pane of glass.

Lily hurried to the front door and let her in. She began to say, "I don't know why Banks didn't hear you at the door. I am sorry…."

But Mrs Donnelly glanced over her shoulder, put a finger to her lips and said, "I didn't knock, don't tell anyone I'm here."

"It's Aiden, Lily. He's injured."

Flash memories of the night of Stephen's death made her face blanche, and she said, "Not, not seriously?"

"It's severe enough. Aiden has badly burned his hands."

Shocked by the implications for Aiden's playing, she wailed, "No, oh no." Images came of his beautiful slender hands moving over the keys and his long fingers entwined with hers. "Where is he?"

"He's here, but he needs a place to hide. The police may look for him and will come straight to us. You have a large house, Lily. Can you, will you help us?"

"Yes, of course, bring him to me, but I don't understand. Why might the police look for him?"

Mrs Donnelly looked down and said quietly, "They were attempting to set fire to the grandstand at Hurst Park Racecourse, but the police must have been watching Kitty because they arrested her."

Lily paced the room with a quick, agitated step. "I knew something like this would happen. I wish he had never become involved with the activists, never."

"A doctor who helps the WSPU has treated him, and members have driven him here, but he can't stay with us." Mary nodded and wrapped the shawl over her head again. "I will signal to the car to bring him. Thank you, Lily. I am eternally in your debt." She slipped away into the night, and Lily called for Banks.

"We will have an unexpected guest for some time. He is an old friend of mine, Banks. I can't explain, but he needs my help."

Banks barely blinked at the news and replied, "The Green Room, Madame? It has no front-facing windows."

Both hands bandaged to the elbow, Aiden arrived supported by his mother and another man but swayed perilously, sinking as if about to faint.

Banks rushed to his side, supporting him with the other man's help. He said, "Let's get you upstairs and into bed, Sir. Mrs Dent, if I may suggest, there are laudanum drops in the medicine chest for the pain."

Frozen to the spot at seeing Aiden again after so long, her love for him, so long suppressed, resurged, and their quarrel now seemed ridiculous.

By the time she had fled to the kitchen, found the drops, and mounted the stairs, Banks had undressed Aiden and put him in one of his nightshirts, which was at least two sizes too big. Aiden seemed to have drifted into a fitful sleep but stirred sufficiently to swallow when Lily offered him the red-brown tincture.

"Lily," he murmured and instinctively put a hand towards her, then winced in pain.

"Shh," she whispered. "Rest now. You're safe."

Aiden called out all through the night, delirious with pain. Lily and Banks sat beside him. They tried to keep him still and stop him from pulling at his bandages.

Banks had made a pitcher of lemonade, and when Aiden seemed lucid, they encouraged him to drink. Lily could only imagine his pain, and she watched and prayed through the night.

In the morning, Mrs Donnelly came in via the back door, her face pale. "How is he?"

Lily's pinched face told its tale. "He passed a restless night; I can't lie. The laudanum helps, but I think it makes him dream. He was confused and kept calling out about his hands on fire." Lily covered her face in her hands. "Poor Aiden."

Glancing behind her as if she feared police hiding in the shadows, Mrs Donnelly said, "I came by a circuitous route, and we have been meeting here, thank goodness, so I don't think my visits will arouse suspicion. I will sit with him now. Get some rest, Lily."

Lily nodded. "I think he needs a doctor. I can pay, but who should we send for? I don't want to give him away."

Mary reached out and squeezed her hand. "You're most generous, but the WSPU will pay his medical expenses. We are waiting for a doctor sympathetic to the cause to be in contact tomorrow."

The practicalities of keeping Aiden hidden had preyed on her mind during the watches of the night. "We must let Ma and Pa in on the secret and perhaps Miss Laidlaw. I cannot bar the doors to them. They are such frequent visitors. It would make them immediately suspicious."

When Ma and Pa arrived, they had more than a few words to say about the danger to herself and the propriety of having Aiden in the house. "What if the police come to the house? What will you do then, young lady? Your reputation and business would be in tatters, all you've worked for."

"I don't know what I'd do, Ma. Let's hope nothing of the sort happens, and if it does, Banks and I will think of something. We would conceal him, or the WSPU would move him. I'll not leave him to the care of strangers." Lily looked determined and every bit the young businesswoman she had become, not the child bride recently widowed.

Ma tutted and appealed to Pa, who watched his daughter closely. "Maggie, I think Lily knows her mind. Much as I don't like the situation, the best we can do is carry on as normal and not arouse suspicion."

Lily leapt from her chair and hugged her pa. "I knew you'd help; I knew it."

Pa scratched his face. "I can't promise to help, Lily. I have responsibilities to my men and their work. I can't be directly involved. What Aiden has done is wrong in my book, but it seems he already has his punishment, and I won't give him away."

Ma said, "You should be thinking of your ladies, Lily, not taking risks."

Lily rounded on Ma. "I won't let my ladies down. Work will carry on as normal. Anis and I have decided that I shall be ill for the next two weeks with a putrid sore throat. Only she and you will visit. I can continue with designs; I have everything here."

Upstairs, Mary Donnelly replaced the cool flannel on Aiden's forehead and smiled at Lily. "I've given him more laudanum." She pointed to the empty glass. "He's sleeping again, but he knew me and where he is. He begs pardon for all the trouble."

Lily raised a hand to push away the idea that Aiden was trouble. Mrs Donnelly continued, "He knew the risks but is at that immortal age. He didn't believe it could happen to him. Have you slept?"

Lily shook her head. "Banks sent Betsy to fetch Ma and Pa, and they're downstairs. Ma is making a bid to take over the kitchen, so heaven help Banks."

"I'm grateful for her help, even if Banks isn't. But Lily, please try to sleep."

The doctor arrived late in the day. He was a tall skinny man dressed in an old-fashioned tailcoat with a battered black bag. He removed the wound dressings, and Lily flinched to see the raised red skin, charred in places and blistered. She was relieved to see the care taken by the doctor and that he scrupulously washed his hands before working. Aiden cried out, biting his lip till it bled as the doctor removed the bandages.

The doctor looked to Lily, and Mrs Donnelly then addressed Aiden, whose face was pale with pain. "I see many of these injuries at the docks, Mr Donnelly. Your burns are deep in one or two places, but our enemy is infection. We must try to prevent gangrene."

The doctor continued, directing his remarks to the two women. "The new thinking from Europe is to keep the wounds moist and open to allow healing from the base. I have had some success with this method. I shall use iodine as an antiseptic and dress the wounds in honey gauze to keep them supple. Observe closely; You must re-dress the wounds every two days. If you suspect an infection, send for me immediately."

Chapter 34

The weeks passed in a routine of shifts; nursing Aiden, meals eaten in haste, fretful sleep, and the hideous dressing changes, which broke Lily's heart. She never showed Aiden anything but a smiling face, but alone in her study, she broke down and wept for his suffering.

The fear of visits from the police faded. With Kitty Marion in prison, they had ceased to search for accomplices.

Doctor Moffatt returned each week, nodding his approval at the progress, which seemed painfully slow to Lily. Finally, she could see that patches of the burns had closed with shiny red scars over them and bridges of raised white skin.

"Aiden must begin to move his hands now," Dr Moffatt advised. "We must help him gently stretch the scars, or they will pucker and retract. The scars can cause as many problems as the wounds themselves," he cautioned.

Aiden could now leave his room for periods of the day, and although he tired quickly, he spent time with Lily in the garden. She read to him from the newspaper, and they initially talked awkwardly, avoiding Lily's marriage and Aiden's life in London. They discussed the formation of Trade Unions and the success of the strikes. Aiden said his father's men at the docks were back at work, although grievances still simmered under the surface.

Reminiscing about people they knew, and childhood memories were safe subjects too, but the elephant in the room of their quarrel and Lily's subsequent marriage was present, nonetheless.

One fine Spring morning, after a long brooding silence, Aiden said, "Dammit, Lily, why did you marry Stephen Dent?"

She looked down and blushed a fiery red, then raised her head to look at him. "Because when I came to the theatre, I saw you flirting with the chorus girls, and you walked out with another girl. I saw you together when I came for a day trip. When you didn't write, I thought you had stopped loving me. You broke my heart."

Aiden looked astounded. "Saw me in London? When Lily? I never had another girl, ever. It was always you." He withdrew from his dressing gown pocket, the photograph she had given him the night he left, now battered from being carried. "It never leaves me."

Stumbling over her words, Lily described the girl and explained her pain at his lack of communication and their arguments.

Aiden looked down, shamefaced. "Lily, I should have written more often, been more careful, not taken you for granted. It's no excuse, but being in London — the shows, my songs, Kitty needing my help. It all went to my head." He looked at Lily beseechingly. "The girls, it was flirting, never more. I'm truly sorry for hurting you. Please say you'll forgive me."

Lily sat in silence, digesting what Aiden had said, and he continued, filling the silence stretching between them.

"The day you saw me, I must have been with Clara, one of the WSPU members. We posed as a couple sometimes to prepare for attacks on targets. No one suspects a couple. The crowds at the unveiling gave us cover to check out the coronation stands." Aiden looked at Lily, willing her to understand. "We were monitoring the placement of the police to decide if we could mount an attack the night before the coronation. Colleagues in the struggle for justice, nothing more. The central committee made a deal with the government not to disrupt the celebrations, and nothing came of the plan." He paused. "You have to believe me."

Her eyes flashed with anger. "The WSPU methods, Aiden, how could you be involved? Look what they have made you do. What you did when you burnt your hands was criminal, and you could have been killed. You could have killed someone else. They had no right to ask for such a sacrifice."

His eyes met hers, half-defiant, half-ashamed. "No one made me act, Lily. I wanted to." He leant forwards eagerly. "I want a change for our generation, for you, for us." Lily shook her head in despair, and he continued, "You deserve to vote and have the freedom to live your life without needing the permission of anyone."

Lily pleaded, "I want that too, but surely we can achieve those things in other ways without violence and vandalism?"

Aiden shrugged and muttered, his defiance turning sullen. "The government don't listen to arguments and petitions." Then came a more shocking truth. "Jane from Mrs O'Shea's couldn't wait to tell me about your new beau. News travels fast. I stopped caring about my safety when I realised how that man and his money had taken you away."

Lily tried to protest, but he continued. "I can see he was attractive. He could offer you the position and career you deserve. Even now, his father had to rent that property for you, controlling your destiny. It makes my blood boil."

Looking at his face, she dropped her gaze. "It wasn't about the money, or the cause, Aiden, nothing so noble." Lily stammered, "I was jealous of those other women and Kitty."

Aiden turned to face her, a picture of amazement. "Kitty?"

She nodded and continued, "I thought she had stolen you." Lily twisted and untwisted the corner of her handkerchief, then taking a deep breath, she confessed. "I wanted to make you jealous too, to take notice of me." She hesitated, then forged on. "The attention, the flattery, it was nice to be courted, not ignored. I convinced myself that perhaps I loved him, but I didn't. I knew before the wedding, but with all the arrangements in place, it seemed too late to turn back, impossible and…."

Aiden groaned and reached out to her, then withdrew his scarred hand. "I've been a fool, Lily, and what is worse, I can't offer you much of a future anymore," he said bitterly. "I may never play again." He glanced at his disfigured hands in disgust.

"Don't say that, Aiden! You, of all people, should believe you don't have to support me. We can live what we believe, and anyway, I'm sure you will play again with practise. I've arranged for Conrads to deliver a piano on loan as a treat. It might help your healing."

Aiden looked at her furiously. "You shouldn't have done that without asking me, Lily. I'm not a child. I can't play with my hands like this." He held the shiny mass of scars towards her. "A treat! Don't patronise me."

He stood up abruptly and walked away, shoulders hunched.

"Aiden," she called, horrified at this sudden attack. "Don't go, I didn't mean…" but the slamming of the garden door was his answer.

Banks looked out of the kitchen door. "Everything alright, Madame?"

Lily sighed. "No, Banks, everything is all wrong."

He ventured into the garden. "You know, Madame, perhaps it's time for you to return to work and let Mr Donnelly come to terms with things. He's angry, but not with you, not really. He's a proud young man who realises the injury may have snatched his future. It won't help, knowing he's brought it on himself."

Lily nodded thoughtfully. "You're right, Banks. I'll cancel the piano; I thought it would help."

Banks frowned. "I wouldn't do that. You may find he'll try to play when no one is about to hear."

When the piano arrived, Aiden stayed in his room and refused point-blank to touch it. However, taking Bank's advice, Lily began to go back to work and was heartened to see a manuscript book with some notes pencilled onto the staves beside the instrument one evening.

Wisely she did not comment and waited for Aiden to mention it, which he did over dinner. "I had an idea for a song today," he said casually. "These don't do what I want them to," he grimaced, looking at his fingers and wriggling them. "But I can tap out the tune."

Longing to hear it, Lily refrained from asking and merely said, "That's wonderful, Aiden."

The next day she heard music coming from the sitting room. She entered the room quietly and saw Mrs Donnelly playing for Aiden and him singing a new melody and adjusting notes in his manuscript book.

Mrs Donnelly said, "Come in, Lily, listen to this song. What do you think? Because Miss Marion is out of prison, thanks to the Cat and Mouse Act, Aiden's agent wrote to him. She's ready to perform and needs a new song. He says she won't take 'no' for an answer."

The elation Lily initially felt plummeted, and she replied sharply. "She never has."

In two strides, Aiden crossed the room and took Lily's hand. It was the first time she had felt the tight scarring from the burns, glassy and hard, like patent leather. His hand felt more like a claw, and she was shocked. Aiden waited for her reaction, his eyes fixed on her face. Gently, she closed her hand around his. "Don't be cross with Kitty, Lily. It's her way of trying to help, and it has. Despite all they do to her, she doesn't feel sorry for herself, and she doesn't feel pity for me. She expects me to carry on in any way I can."

Lily's eyes flew to Aiden's face. "You won't. She does not want you to continue your activism, surely not."

"The struggle must carry on, Lily, we have not succeeded in our aims, but I shall restrict myself to campaigning. I haven't Kitty's blatant disregard for my own safety." His face clouded.

Mollified, Lily allowed herself to be led to the piano to hear the new song, overjoyed that Aiden was composing again.

"Lily, I can't stay in hiding forever, I need to go out, build my strength, and you can't forever keep the Dents and your other friends away from the house with excuses."

"The Dents don't care as long as I visit them. They prefer it…."

He looked at her sad face and said softly, "I care, Lily. Neither of us has valued the other as we should. If you are willing, I would like to begin over and invite you to walk out with me."

His eyes shone with hope as he continued, "I must go back to London to see my publishers and see what chance there is for me to make a living. But mostly, I will not repay you by having a breath of scandal attached to your name."

"Aiden? What will you say to people about your hands?"

He shook his head and frowned. "The WSPU have suggested I say it was an accident with a kerosene lamp." He gritted his teeth. "I am to leave Kitty to take the whole blame, hardly heroic."

Lily looked at him and saw his wounded pride. "They are quite right, Aiden. The burns have been punishment enough."

He shrugged, drew her to the piano, and sat beside her on the stool. "Close your eyes, Lily." Checking she had shut them, he placed his hands on the keys and began to play. It was awkward and uneven, but to Lily, it sounded heavenly, the first step towards Aiden returning to his world of music.

He stopped playing and waited. Lily turned to him, breathless, as she saw the love on his face. He bent forward to kiss her for the first time since the men carried him into the house, and she melted into his arms.

As they drew apart, he said quietly, "Can we begin again, Lily, after all the mistakes?"

She nodded. "I would like that very much."

On the day of Aiden's departure, Lily made a decision. "Betsy, I would like one of my floral gowns and my pearl necklace, please."

Betsy looked at her in surprise, then broke into a wide grin. "Yes, Madame, straight away. It's been such a long time, you being so young and all."

Banks served their final breakfast. "It would appear that the sun has brought the flowers out, a welcome sight."

Her delight at wearing colours lasted for days, and it was as if she had shed ten years in one week. She skipped into work each day with a new-found zest for life.

As Summer drew into Autumn, Aiden spoke to Lily about marriage. "If you can bear to live with these scars and my terrible playing," he said, the joke barely hiding his frustration. "In London, people from all over the world live together despite their different backgrounds. There are good people from all creeds, Lily. Society needs to embrace tolerance. If that's painful for our community here, perhaps London is where our place is. It's what we dreamed of."

Lily felt a quiver of excitement as she felt his passion for change. Was it possible to convince Ma and Pa? They had been wrong about Aiden before, with the best intentions. Would they now see?

She smiled. "Yes, Aiden, I want us to be married above all things."

He bent to kiss her; their bodies entwined as if moulded to be together. He stood back. "Lily, could we? Would you agree to a modern, civil ceremony? Our different churches may still disapprove, so surely, we don't need to involve them. Would you mind?"

Lily remembered the pageant that had been her first wedding, a sham marriage, meaningless and cruel. She wondered at the prejudice that had deemed her relationship with Stephen more suitable than her love for Aiden, and she whispered, "I don't mind. The love at the heart of a marriage is important, not the ceremony."

Haltingly, one evening, she spoke to him of the abusive treatment and her shame, the words tumbling out faster and faster as she bared her soul and described the trauma.

Aiden remained immobile and unspeaking until she wavered. "You talked to me about living with your scars, Aiden, but can you live with mine?"

She feared from his silence that he could not, that she had shocked and lost him.

After an eternity, a growl of pain and anger emerged from him, a feral, primitive noise. "By God, Lily, if he were not dead, I would kill him myself. Never, never, I promise, will you be hurt like that again."

The following day, Lily hesitated outside her parent's house, pretending to fuss with her skirt, which was already precisely in place.

Aiden turned to her. "Lily, we are no longer children. Your father promised to give his blessing if we were still of the same mind when we had more life experience. We are only asking him to hold good on his promise. My parents, of all people, should understand, and we do not need their permission."

She sighed, fidgeting with her hair. "But Aiden, I would like their blessing."

349

He kissed her hand. "I know."

"I'll say this for you, Maggie, you lay a lovely tea." As ever, Granny sat ramrod straight in her chair and wiped a tiny smear of homemade strawberry jam from her mouth with a snowy napkin. "Now, if I'm not mistaken, these young people have an announcement, given that our Lily has been like a cat on a hot tin roof since she got here." Granny fixed Aiden with her direct gaze and said, "Well?"

Aiden cleared his throat and looked around the table. "Lily and I have decided to be married. We understand there may be opposition, but we have both suffered, and we are asking you, our families," he cast his gaze to each of them and took Lily's hand in his, "to support us without prejudice to find our true happiness."

Aiden looked directly at Lily's pa. "Mr Matthews, you once told us you would not oppose the marriage if we spoke to you when we were no longer children. Although Lily is not twenty-five, you must agree we have gained much life experience since then. We both have established careers and have tried and failed to live happily apart."

Granny sniffed. "Well, you have the right of it there, my boy." She folded her napkin and placed it on the table with a flick. "There will be talk. It's a difficult situation."

She made as if to go on when Grandpa raised a hand to silence her. "For my part, Lily, Aiden, you have my blessing. You deserve some happiness, and if you two can tolerate the censure you might meet, you will find no objection from me. If the almighty had intended things differently, I'm sure he would have arranged it."

Ma smoothed her skirt and watched warily as Pa rose slowly from his chair. He walked around the table to Aiden, who stiffened and stood, holding Mr Matthew's eyes. Pa looked at Aiden appraisingly and finally extended his hand. "Donnelly, you're a lucky man."

From the tension, suddenly, chatter erupted as the families exchanged handshakes and congratulations. Granny said, "I won't be coming to any new-fangled registry wedding because I don't hold with them, and I'm too old. My arthritis is getting worse by the day too. But I have some good sheets in the chest that I don't doubt you'll be glad of. I'll look them out."

Aiden put his arm around Lily's waist and drew her close. He smiled as she nestled against his shoulder. She felt safe and loved.

Without a doubt, there would be bridges to cross ahead, but Lily knew they would remain strong if they were together.

Epilogue

Aiden and Lily married in the Autumn of 1913 at the Bayswater Registry Office by dint of the London address of Lily and Anis Couture. A simple ceremony, their wedding was witnessed by Miss Anis Laidlaw and Mr Dan Kildaire, an American jazz musician of Jamaican descent, a great friend of Aiden's from the club.

The bride's dress was modish but avant-garde and daring, with its dropped waist and raised hemline disguised by zigzag fringes of heavy beading.

The Matthews and the Donnellys continued to be neighbours on Eastfield Road.

Grace and George Dent founded a successful glove factory in New York and became independently wealthy. Grace began to visit England regularly after the first world war, and she and Lily remained lifelong friends.

Kitty Marion continued campaigning for women's rights until she died in 1944. Born in Germany, she settled in the United States at the outbreak of the first world war to avoid deportation. It is estimated she suffered around two hundred and thirty-two episodes of force-feeding in British prisons.

In 1918 the Representation of the People Act was passed, allowing women over thirty with a property qualification to vote. This act increased the number of women eligible to vote to fifteen million. It was not until the Equal Franchise Act of 1928 that all women over twenty-one could vote, and women finally achieved the same voting rights as men.

The End

A Note to Readers

Although **A Song for Kitty** is a work of fiction, I have drawn on research and family archives to write an authentic account of the tumultuous years immediately before WW1. My grandmother, born in 1896 was a resident of the Milton area of Portsmouth for her entire 106 years and I spent many happy holidays there.

As with much historical fiction, I have selected factual material of the time but also creatively manipulated some facts and chronologies to suit the narrative. The story has particularly been inspired by the life of Kitty Marion, suffragette activist and music hall star.

If you'd like to read my contemporary novels set in the 1990's why not download Paradise, a prequel to the Ellie Rose Series, as a gift, by subscribing to my monthly newsletter, "The Windsinger."
https://angelacairnsauthor.co.uk/sign-up/

Each month, discover new books, meet authors, enjoy an exclusive short story and more.
Or get to know me better on my website and social media pages, links below.

Website: https://www.angelacairnsauthor.co.uk/
Facebook: @angelacairnsauthor
Instagram: @angelacairnsauthor

Please consider leaving a review on Amazon and Goodreads.

Perhaps talk about your favourite character, what you liked best about the story, and why you'd recommend someone to read it. Reviews are vital to authors, as they help other readers to find books they may enjoy.

I read and appreciate every review that is written.

Warm regards,
Angela Cairns

ALL BOOKS BY THE AUTHOR

Prequel to the Ellie Rose Series.
A summer love story

Touch – Volume One of the Ellie Rose Series.
A poignant story of lost love and second chances.

Dilemma – Volume Two of the Ellie Rose Series.
Will past trauma derail Ellie's new found peace?

Bloom — Volume Three of the Ellie Rose Series.
When longing brings heartache…and the waiting
seems endless.

A warm-hearted collection of the author's favourite short
stories. Here you will find life, love, laughter and tears. Oh, and
a few dogs, of course.

Seasonal Produce: An Anthology of Inspired Short Stories
about Seasons of Growth.

About the Author

Born in the U.K., director of two successful healthcare businesses and BBC guest broadcaster for over thirty years, Angela has been involved with fiction and non-fiction writing since 1986.

She writes books for readers who love people, and life in all its messy glory - the romantics who dream of love and happy endings. In her books, you will find resilient, relatable heroines with warm hearts who try to do the next right thing despite difficult circumstances.

Her first novel, Touch, became an Amazon best-seller. There are now four novels in the Ellie Rose Series, and a short story anthology titled Seasonal Produce.

Her short stories have been published in 'Yours' magazine and feature regularly on the radio.

A Song for Kitty is her first historical romance novel.

Angela is a writing coach and passionate about helping writers achieve their full creative potential while nurturing their personal well-being.

Married with two grown lads and three grandsons, Angela is owned by two Gordon Setter dogs.

BV - #0298 - 290923 - C0 - 203/127/27 - PB - 9781923020085 - Matt Lamination